NEVER FADE

ALEXANDRA BRACKEN

Quercus

In memory of my dad, whose love of life
and unflinching courage continue to inspire me every day

QUERCUS CHILDREN'S BOOKS

First published in 2013 by Hyperion
First published in Great Britain in 2016 by Hodder and Stoughton

9 10 8

A CIP catalogue record for this book is available from the British Library.

ISBN 978 1 78654 022 5

Typeset by Hewer Text UK Ltd, Edinburgh
Printed and bound in Great Britain by Clays Ltd, Elcograf S.p.A.

The paper and board used in this book are made from wood from responsible sources.

Quercus Children's Books
An imprint of
Hachette Children's Group
Part of Hodder and Stoughton
Carmelite House
50 Victoria Embankment
London EC4Y 0DZ

An Hachette UK Company
www.hachette.co.uk

www.hachettechildrens.co.uk

PROLOGUE

THE DREAM FIRST MADE AN APPEARANCE MY SECond week at Thurmond, and it came to visit at least twice a month. I guess it made sense that it was born there, behind the camp's humming electric fence. Everything about that place withered you down to your worst, and it didn't matter how many years passed—two, three, six. In that green uniform, locked in the same monotonous routine, time stopped and sputtered like a dying car. I knew I was getting older, caught glimpses of my changing face in the metallic surfaces of the Mess Hall tables, but it didn't feel that way. Who I was and who I had been disconnected, leaving me stranded somewhere in the middle. I used to wonder if I was even Ruby anymore. At camp, I didn't have a name outside of my cabin. I was a number: 3285. I was a file on a server or locked away in a gunmetal gray filing cabinet. The people who had known me before camp no longer did.

It always started with the same thunder, the same explosion of noise. I'd be old—twisted and hunched and aching—standing in the middle of a busy street. It might have been somewhere in Virginia, where I was from, but it had been so long since I'd been home I couldn't tell for sure.

Cars passed on either side, heading in opposite directions down a stretch of dark road. Sometimes I heard the thunder of an approaching storm, other times the blare of car horns louder, louder, louder as they approached. Sometimes I heard nothing at all.

But aside from that, the dream was always the same.

An identical set of black cars would screech to a stop as they reached me, and then, as soon as I looked up, they would reverse direction. Everything would. The rain would peel itself up from the gummy black asphalt, floating back up into the air in perfect sparkling drops. The sun would glide backward across the sky, chasing the moon. And as each cycle passed, I could feel my ancient, hunched back uncurl bone by bone until I was standing up straight again. When I held my hands up to my eyes, the wrinkles and blue-purple veins would smooth themselves out, like old age was melting clean off me.

And then those hands would get smaller, and smaller, and smaller. My view of the road changed; my clothes seemed to swallow me whole. Sounds were deafening and harsher and more confusing. Time would only race back harder, blowing me off my feet, crashing through my head.

I used to dream about turning back time, about reclaiming the things I'd lost and the person I used to be.

But not anymore.

ONE

THE CROOK OF MY ARM LOCKED OVER THE MAN'S throat, tightening as his boots' rubber soles batted against the ground. His fingernails bit into the black fabric of my shirt and gloves, clawing at them in desperation. The oxygen was being cut off from his brain, but it didn't keep the flashes of his thoughts at bay. I saw everything. His memories and thoughts burned white-hot behind my eyes, but I didn't let up, not even when the security guard's terrified mind brought an image of himself to the surface, staring open-eyed up at the dark hallway's ceiling. Dead, maybe?

I wasn't going to kill him, though. The soldier stood head and shoulders over me, and one of his arms was the size of one of my legs. The only reason I had gotten the jump on him at all was because he had been standing with his back to me.

Instructor Johnson called this move the Neck Lock, and he had taught me a whole collection of others. The

Can Opener, the Crucifix, the Neck Crank, the Nelson, the Twister, the Wristlock, and the Spine Crack, just to name a few. All ways that I, a five-foot-five girl, could get a good grip on someone who outmatched me physically. Enough for me to draw out the real weapon.

The man was half hallucinating now. Slipping into his mind was painless and easy; all of the memories and thoughts that rose to the surface of his consciousness were stained black. The color bled through them like a blot of ink on wet paper. And it was then, only after I had my hooks in him, that I released my grip from his neck.

This probably hadn't been what he had been expecting when he came out of the shop's hidden side entrance for a smoke break.

The bite in Pennsylvania's air had turned the man's cheeks bright red beneath his pale stubble. I let out a single hot breath from behind the ski mask and cleared my throat, fully aware of the ten sets of eyes trained on me. My fingers shook as they slipped across the man's skin; he smelled like stale smoke and the spearmint gum he used to try to cover his nasty habit. I leaned forward, pressing two fingers against his neck.

"Wake up," I whispered. The man forced his eyes open, wide and childlike. Something in my stomach clenched.

I glanced over my shoulder to the tactical team behind me, who were watching all of this silently, faces unseen behind their masks.

"Where is Prisoner 27?" I asked. We were out of the line of sight of the security cameras—the reason, I guess, this soldier felt safe enough to slip out for a few unscheduled breaks—but I was beyond anxious to have this part over.

"Hurry the hell up!" Vida said through gritted teeth, next to me.

My hands shook at the wave of heat at my back as the tact team leader stepped up behind me. Doing this didn't hurt the way it used to. It didn't wring me out, twisting my mind into knots of pain. But it did make me sensitive to the strong feelings of anyone near me—including the man's disgust. His black, black hatred.

Rob's dark hair was in the corner of my sight. The order to move forward without me was ready to spill out over his lips. Of the three Ops I'd gone on with him as Leader, I'd only ever been able to finish one.

"Where is Prisoner 27?" I repeated, giving the soldier's mind a nudge with my own.

"Prisoner 27." As he repeated the words, his heavy mustache twitched. The hint of gray there made him look a lot older than he actually was. The assignment file we'd been given at HQ had included blurbs on all of the soldiers assigned to this bunker, including this one—Max Brommel. Age forty-one, originally from Cody, Wyoming. Moved to Pittsburgh, Pennsylvania, for a programming job, lost it when the economy tanked. A nice wife, currently out of work. Two kids.

Both dead.

A storm of murky images flooded every dark corner and crevice of his mind. I saw a dozen more men, all wearing the same light camo uniforms jumping out of the back of a van, and several more from the Humvees that had bookended the bigger vehicle—full of criminals, suspected terrorists, and, if the intel the Children's League had received was correct, one of our top agents.

I watched, suddenly calm, as these same soldiers led one . . . two . . . no, three men off the back of the truck. They weren't Psi Special Forces officers, or FBI, or CIA, and definitely not a SWAT or SEAL team, all of which probably could have crushed our small force in one swift blow. No, they were National Guard servicemen, drawn back into active duty by the terrible times; our intel had been right about that, at least.

The soldiers had pulled hoods down tight over the prisoners' heads, then forced them down the stairs of the abandoned shop to the sliding silver door of the bunker hidden below.

After much of Washington, DC, had been destroyed by what President Gray claimed was a group of warped Psi kids, he had taken special care to build these so-called mini-fortresses across the east coast in case another emergency of that magnitude was to arise. Some were built beneath hotels, others into the sides of mountains, and some, like this one, were hidden in plain sight in small towns, under shops or government buildings. They were for Gray's protection, the protection of his cabinet and important military officials, and, it appeared, to imprison "high-risk threats to national security."

Including our own Prisoner 27, who seemed to be getting some special treatment.

His cell was at the end of a long hall, two stories down. It was a lonely room with a low, dark ceiling. The walls seemed to drip down around me, but the memory held steady. They kept his hood on but bound his feet to the metal chair in the center of the cell, in the halo of light from a single naked bulb.

I peeled away from the man's mind, releasing both my physical and mental grip on him. He slid down the graffiti on the wall of the abandoned Laundromat, still in the clutches of his own brain's fog. Removing the memory of my face and the men behind us in the alley was like plucking stones from the bottom of a clear, shallow pond.

"Two stories down, room Four B," I said, turning back to Rob. We had a sketchy outline of the layout of the bunker but none of the small directional details—we weren't blind, but we weren't exactly killing it in the accuracy department. The basic layout for these bunkers was always about the same, though. A staircase or elevator that ran down one end of the structure and one long hall on each level stemming out from it.

He held up a gloved hand, cutting off the rest of my instructions and signaling to the team behind him. I fed him the code from the soldier's memory: 6-8-9-9-9-9-* and stepped away, pulling Vida with me. She shoved me off into the nearest soldier, grunting.

I couldn't see Rob's eyes beneath his night-vision goggles as the green light flashed, but I didn't need to in order to read his intentions. He hadn't asked for us and certainly hadn't wanted us tagging along when he—a former Army

Ranger, as he loved to remind us—could easily have handled this with a few of his men. More than anything, I think he was furious he had to do this at all. It was League policy that if you were caught, you were disavowed. No one was coming for you.

If Alban wanted this agent back, he had a good reason for it.

The clock started the moment the door slid open. Fifteen minutes to get in, grab Prisoner 27, and get the hell out and away. Who knew if we even had that long, though? Rob was only estimating how long it would take for backup to arrive once the alarms were activated.

The doorway opened to the stairwell at the back of the bunker. It wound down, section by section, into the darkness, with only a few lights along the metal steps to guide us. I heard one of the men cut the wire of the security camera perched high above us, felt Vida's hand shove me forward, but it took time—too much time—for my eyes to adjust. Traces of the Laundromat's chemicals clung to the recycled dry air, burning my lungs.

Then, we were moving. Quickly, as silently as a group in heavy boots could be thundering down a flight of stairs.

My blood was thrumming in my ears as Vida and I reached the first landing. Six months of training wasn't a long time, but it was long enough to teach me how to pull the familiar armor of focus tighter around my core.

Something hard slammed into my back, then something harder—a shoulder, a gun, then another, and more, until it was a steady enough rhythm that I had to press myself against the landing's door into the bunker to avoid them. Vida let out a sharp noise as the last of the team blew past us. Only Rob stopped to acknowledge us. "Cover us until we're through, then monitor the entrance. Right there. Do *not* leave your position."

"We're supposed to—" Vida began. I stepped in front of her, cutting her off. No, this wasn't what the Op parameters had outlined, but it was better for us. There was no reason for either of us to follow them down into the bunker and potentially get ourselves killed. And she knew—it had been drilled into our skulls a million times—that tonight Rob was Leader. And the very first rule, the only one that mattered when you got to the moments between terrified heartbeats, was that you always, even in the face of fire or death or capture, *always* had to follow Leader.

Vida was at my back, close enough for me to feel her hot breath through the thick black knit of my ski mask. Close enough that the fury she was radiating cut through the freezing Philadelphia air. Vida always radiated a kind of bloodthirsty eagerness, even more so when Cate was Leader on an Op; the excitement of proving herself to our Minder always stripped away the better lessons of her training. This was a game to her, a challenge, to show off her perfect aim, her combat training, her sharply honed Blue abilities. To me, it was yet another perfect opportunity to get herself killed. At seventeen, Vida might have been the perfect trainee, the standard to which the League held the rest of their freak kids, but the one thing she had never been able to master was her own adrenaline.

"Don't you ever touch me again, bitch," Vida snarled, her voice low with fury. She started backing away to follow them down the stairs. "You are such a fucking coward that you're going to take this lying down? You don't care that he just disrespected us? You—"

The stairwell reared up under my feet, as if dragging in a deep breath only to let it explode back out. The shock of it seemed to slow time itself—I was up and off my feet, launched so hard into the door that I thought I felt it dent beneath my skull. Vida slammed onto the ground, covering her head, and it was only then that the roar of the concussion grenade reached us as it blew apart the entrance below.

The smoky heat was thick enough to get a stranglehold on me, but the disorientation was so much worse. My eyelids felt like they had been peeled and rubbed raw as I forced them open. A crimson light pulsed through the dark, pushing through the clouds of cement debris. The muffled throbbing in my ears—that wasn't my heartbeat. That was the alarm.

Why had they used the grenade when they knew the code for that door would be the same as the one outside? There hadn't been any gunfire—we were close enough that we would have heard the tact team engage them. Now everyone would know we were there—it didn't make sense for a team of professionals.

I ripped the mask away from my face, clawing at my right ear. There was a sharp, stabbing pain and the comm unit came away in pieces. I pressed a gloved hand against it as I stumbled up to my feet, blinking back one sickening wave of nausea after another. But when I turned to find

Vida, to drag her back up the stairs and into the freezing Pennsylvania night, she was gone.

I spent two terrified heartbeats searching for her body through the gaping hole in the stairwell's landing, watching as the tactical team streamed past. I leaned against the wall, trying to stay on my feet.

"Vida!" I felt the word leave my throat, but it vanished under the pulsing in my ears. "Vida!"

The door on my landing was mangled, dented, singed—but it still worked, apparently. It groaned and began to slide open, only to catch halfway with a horrible grating noise. I threw myself back against the wall, taking two steps up the fractured stairs. The darkness tucked me back under its cover just as the first soldier squeezed through the door, his handgun swinging around the cramped space. I took a deep breath and dropped into a crouch. It took three blinks to clear my vision, and by then, the soldiers were fighting through the doorway, jumping over the jagged hole in the platform and continuing down the stairs. I watched four go, then five, then six, swallowed by the smoke. A series of strange buzzing pops seemed to follow them, and it wasn't until I was standing, swiping my arm over my face, that I realized it was gunfire from below.

Vida was gone, the tact team was now deep into a hornet's nest of their own making, and Prisoner 27—

God dammit, I thought, moving back down onto the landing. There were upward of twenty or thirty soldiers staffing these bunkers at any given time. They were too small to house more than that, even temporarily. But just because the corridor was empty now, it didn't mean the firefight below had drawn all of the attention away. If I were caught, that would be it. I'd be finished, killed one way or another.

But there was that man I had seen, the one with the hood over his head.

I didn't feel any particular loyalty to the Children's League. There was a contract between us, a strange verbal agreement that was as businesslike as it was bloody. Outside of my own team, there weren't people to care about, and there certainly wasn't anyone who cared about me beyond the bare minimum of keeping me alive and available to inflict on their targets like a virus.

My feet weren't moving, not yet. There was something about that scene that kept replaying over and over again in my mind. It was the way they had bound his hands, how they had led Prisoner 27 down into the dark unknown of the bunker. It was the gleam of guns, the improbability of escape. I felt despair rising in me like a cloud of steam, spreading itself out through my body.

I knew what it felt like to be a prisoner. To feel time catch and stop because every day you lost a little bit more hope that your situation would change, that someone would come to help you. And I thought that if one of us could just get to him, to show him we were there before the Op failed, it would be worth the try.

But there was no safe way down, and the firefight below was raging in a way only automatic weapons could. Prisoner 27 would know people were there—and they weren't able to reach him. I had to shake that compassion. I had to stop thinking these adults deserved any kind of pity, especially League agents. Even the new recruits reeked of blood to me.

If I stayed here, right where Rob ordered me to, I might never find Vida. But if I left and disobeyed him, he'd be furious.

Maybe he wanted you to be standing there when the explosion went off, a small voice whispered at the back of my mind. *Maybe he was hoping . . .*

No. I wasn't going to think about that now. Vida was my responsibility. Not Rob, not Prisoner 27. Goddamn Vida the viper. When I was out of here, when I found Vida, when we were safely back to HQ, I'd play the situation out in my mind again. Not now.

My ears were still thrumming with their own pulse, too loud for me to hear the heavy steps coming from the lookout post in the Laundromat. We literally crashed into each other as my hand brushed the outside door.

This soldier was a young one. If I had been going on appearances alone, I would have thought he was only a few years older than me. Ryan Davidson, my brain filled in, coughing up all sorts of useless information from the mission file. Texas born and bred. National Guard since his college had closed. Art History major.

It was one thing, though, to have someone's life printed in crisp black letters and laid out in front of you. It was something else entirely to come face-to-face with the actual flesh and blood. To feel the hot stink of breath and see the pulse jump in his throat.

"H-Hey!" He reached for the gun at his side, but I launched a foot at his hand and sent the weapon clattering across the landing and down the stairs. We both dove for it.

My chin hit the silver metal, and the impact actually jarred my brain. For a single blinding second, I saw nothing but pristine white flash in front of my eyes. And then, everything returned in brilliant bright color. The pain filtered through next; when the soldier tackled me and I hit the floor, my teeth sank into my bottom lip and it burst open. Blood sprayed across the stairwell.

The guard pinned me to the ground with his entire weight. The instant I felt him shift, I knew he was going for his radio. I could hear chatter from a woman; I heard her say, *"Report status,"* and *"I'm coming up,"* and the knowledge of just how badly I would be screwed if either of those things actually happened sent me into what Instructor Johnson liked to call a controlled panic.

Panic, because the situation seemed to be escalating quickly.

Controlled, because I was the predator in the situation.

One of my hands was pinned under my chest, the other between my back and his stomach. That was the one I chose. I bunched up his uniform the best I could, searching for bare skin. My brain's wandering fingers reached out for his head and pried their way in, one at a time. They fought through the memory of my startled face behind the door, moody blue images of women dancing on dimly lit stages, a field, another man launching his fist at him—

Then, the weight was off, and air came flooding back into my lungs, cold and stale. I rolled over onto my hands and knees, gasping for more of it. The figure standing over me had tossed him down the stairs like a crumpled piece of paper.

"—up! We have to—" The words sounded like they were being carried along underwater. If it hadn't been for the strands of shocking violet hair sticking out from under her ski mask, I probably wouldn't have recognized Vida at all. Her dark shirt and pants were torn, and she seemed to be moving with some kind of limp, but she was alive, and there, and in mostly one piece. I heard her voice through the muffled ringing in my ears.

"Jesus, you're slow!" she was shouting to me. "Let's go!"

She started down the stairs, but I grabbed the scruff of her Kevlar vest and pulled her back. "We're going outside. We'll cover the entrance from there. Is your comm still working?"

"They're still fighting down there!" she shouted. "They can use us! He said not to leave our post—!"

"Then consider it an order from *me*!"

And she had to, because that was the way this worked. That was what she hated most about me, about all of this—that I had the deciding vote. That I got to make this call.

She spat at my feet, but I felt her following me back up the stairs, cursing beneath her breath. The thought occurred to me that she could easily take her knife and slash it through my spine.

The soldier I met outside clearly hadn't been expecting me. I raised a hand, reaching out for hers to command her away, but the sound of Vida's gun firing over my shoulder rocketed me back and away from the soldier so much faster than the splatter of blood from her neck did.

"None of that bullshit!" Vida said, lifting the gun still somehow strapped to my side and pushing it into my palm. *"Go!"*

My fingers curved around its familiar shape. It was the typical service weapon—a black SIG Sauer P229 DAK—that still, after months of learning to shoot them, and clean them, and assemble them, felt too big in my hands.

We burst into the night. I tried to grab Vida again to slow her down before she ran into a blind situation, but she shrugged me off hard. We started at a run up the narrow alley.

I hit the corner just in time to see three soldiers, singed and bleeding, hauling two hooded figures up out of what looked like nothing more than a large street drain. That access point *definitely* wasn't in the Op folders we were given.

Prisoner 27? I couldn't be sure. The prisoners they were loading into the van were men, about the same height, but there was a chance. And that chance was about to get into a van and drive away forever.

Vida pressed a hand to her ear, her lips compressing to white. "Rob's saying he wants us back inside. He needs backup."

She was already turning back when I grabbed her again. For the first time maybe ever, I was just that tiny bit faster.

"Our objective is Prisoner 27," I whispered, trying to phrase it in a way that would connect with her stupidly loyal sense of duty to the organization. "And I think that's him.

This is what Alban sent us for, and if he gets away, the whole Op is blown."

"He—" Vida protested, then sucked back whatever word was on her lips. Her jaw clenched, but she gave me the tiniest of nods. "I'm not going down with your ass if you sink us. Just FYI."

"It'll all be my fault," I said, "nothing against your record." No blemish on her pristine Op history, no scarring the trust Alban and Cate had in her. It was a win-win situation for her—either she'd get the "glory" of a successful Op, or she'd get to watch me be punished and humiliated.

I kept my eyes on the scene in front of us. There were three soldiers—manageable with weapons, but in order to be really useful, I'd need to get close enough to touch them. That was the single, frustrating limit to my abilities I still hadn't been able to break through, no matter how much practice the League forced on me.

The invisible fingers that lived inside my skull were tapping impatiently, as if disgusted they couldn't break out on their own anymore.

I stared at the nearest soldier, trying to imagine the long snaking fingers grasping out, stretching across the tile, reaching his unguarded mind. Clancy could do this, I thought. He didn't need to touch people to get a grip on their minds.

I swallowed a scream of frustration. We needed something else. A distraction, something that could—

Vida was built with a strong back and powerful limbs that made even her most dangerous acts seem graceful and easy. I watched her raise her gun, steady her aim.

"Abilities!" I hissed. "Vida, no guns; it'll alert the others!"

She looked at me like she was watching my scrambled brains run out of my nose. Shooting them was a quick fix, we both were well aware of that, but if she missed and hit one of the prisoners, or if they started firing back . . .

Vida lifted her hand, blowing out a single irritated breath. Then she shoved her hands out through the air. The three National Guardsmen were picked up with such accuracy and strength that they were tossed halfway down the block, against the cars parked there. Because it wasn't enough that Vida was physically the fastest or strongest or had the best aim out of all of us—she had to have the best control over her abilities, too.

I let the feeling part of my brain switch off. The most valuable skill the Children's League taught me was to purge fear and replace it with something that was infinitely colder. Call it calm, call it focus, call it numb nerves—it came, even with blood singing in my veins as I ran toward the prisoners.

They smelled like vomit, blood, and human filth. So different from the clean, neat lines of the bunker and its bleach stench. My stomach heaved.

The closest prisoner huddled near the gutter, bound arms up over his head. His shirt hung in pieces off his shoulders, framing welts and burns and bruises that made his back look more like a plate of raw meat than flesh.

The man turned toward the sound of my feet, lifting his face from the safety of his arms. I ripped the hood off his head. I had stepped up with words of reassurance on my tongue, but the sight of him had disconnected my mouth from my brain. Blue eyes squinted at me under a scraggly mop of blond hair, but I couldn't do anything, say anything, not when he leaned farther into the pale yellow streetlight.

"Move, dumbass!" Vida yelled. "What's the holdup?"

I felt every ounce of blood leave my body in a single blow, fast and clean, like I had been shot straight through the heart. And suddenly I knew—I understood why Cate had originally fought so hard to get me reassigned to a different mission, why I had been told not to enter the bunker, why I hadn't been given any information on the prisoner himself. Not a name, not a description, and certainly no warning.

Because the face I was looking at now was thinner, drawn, and battered, but it was one I knew—one that I—that I—

Not him, I thought, feeling the world shift sideways under my feet. *Not him.*

Seeing my reaction, he stood slowly, a rogue smile fighting past his grimace of pain. He struggled up to his feet and staggered toward me, looking torn, I thought, between relief and urgency. But the Southern lilt of his accent was as warm as ever, even if his voice was deeper, rougher, when he finally spoke.

"Do I . . . look as pretty as I feel?"

And I swear—I swear—I felt time slide out from under me.

TWO

HERE IS HOW YOU FIND THE CHILDREN'S LEAGUE: you don't.

You don't ask around, because no soul alive in Los Angeles would ever admit to the organization being there and give President Gray an itch to scratch. Having the Federal Coalition was already bad enough for business. The people who *could* tell you the way would only cough it up for a price that was too big for most to pay. There was no open door policy, no walk-ins. There were standing orders to dispose of anyone who so much as gave an agent a sidelong look.

The League found *you*. They brought you in, if you were valuable enough. If you'd fight. It was the first thing I learned sitting next to Cate on my way in—or at least the first real thought to solidify in my mind as our SUV zipped down the stretch of freeway, heading straight into the heart of the city.

Their primary base of operations—HQ, as everyone called it—was buried two stories beneath a functioning plastic bottle factory that kept limping along, doing its part to add to the congestion of the brown haze clinging to downtown Los Angeles's warehouse district. Many of the League agents and senior officials "worked" for P & C Bottling, Inc. on paper.

I kept my hands clenched in my lap. At least at Thurmond we'd been able to see the sky. I'd seen the trees through the electric fence. Now I didn't even get that—not until the League decided I was allowed to go aboveground and look.

"It's owned by Peter Hinderson. You'll probably meet him at some point. He's been a staunch supporter of the League's efforts from the beginning." Cate smoothed her hair back into a ponytail as the car turned into what looked like yet another parking garage. That was this city—fading paint in sunset colors and cement.

"They built HQ with his help. The structure is located directly under his factory, so if satellites were to try searching for us, the heat signatures they'd pick up from our ventilation system can easily be explained away."

She sounded so incredibly proud of this, and I honestly could not have cared less. The plane flight from Maryland had fought it out with the carsickness from the ride over from the airport and the city's unrelenting stench of gasoline for what was going to give me the biggest blinding headache. Every part of me was aching for the sweet, clean air of Virginia.

The other agents piled out of their car, their chatter and laughter dying off the second they spotted us. I had felt them staring the whole plane ride; they hadn't needed any other entertainment, apparently, than trying to figure out why I was important enough for Cate to have launched such a search for me. They were floating words over to me like little toy sailboats on a pond—*spy*, *runaway*, *Red*. All of them wrong.

We hung back while the other agents walked toward the silver elevator on the other end of the parking garage, their footsteps echoing on the painted cement. Cate made a big show of needing time to get our things from the trunk, each movement achingly slow, perfectly choreographed to give them a head start on us. I hugged Liam's leather coat to my chest until it was our turn.

Cate pressed some kind of ID card against the black access pad next to the elevator doors. It rumbled back up to us. I stepped through, keeping my eyes on its ceiling until the doors rushed open again and we were hit with a wall of heavy, damp air.

It must have been a sewer once—well, no, judging by the rats, and the acrid smell, and the weak ventilation, it almost definitely had been a storm drain or sewer. We set off some sort of motion detector as we stepped out and the dismal string of tiny lightbulbs they'd hung up along both walls flared to life, illuminating bright bursts of graffiti and the puddles of condensation collecting on the cement ground in long, loud drips.

I stared at Cate, waiting for the punch line of what was obviously a terrible joke. But she only shrugged. "I know it's not . . . beautiful, but you'll come to . . . well, no one loves it. You'll get used to it after a few trips in and out."

Great. What an awesome thing to look forward to.

Walking the length of one block, breathing in the Tube's damp, moldy air, was enough to turn a person's stomach; four blocks was pushing the limits of human endurance. It was just tall enough for most of us to walk upright, though a number of the taller agents—Rob included—had to duck below each of the metal support beams as they passed under them. The walls curved around us like laugh lines around a mouth, cupping us in darkness. The Tube had about zero luxury associated with it, but it was wide enough that two of us could walk side by side. There was breathing room.

Cate looked up and waved at one of the black cameras as we passed beneath it, heading toward the silver doors at the other end of the Tube.

I don't know what it was about that sight that made me rear back. The finality of it, maybe. The full realization of how hard I'd have to work, how careful and patient I'd need to be to give Liam time to get to a place where they couldn't touch him, until I could break myself out of here.

The access pad beeped three times before it flashed green. Cate clipped her ID back to her belt loop, the sound of her relieved sigh half lost to the *whoosh* of treated air that came billowing out of the doors.

I pulled away before she could take my arm, cringing at her kind smile. "Welcome to HQ, Ruby. Before you get the full tour, I'd like you to meet a few people."

"Fine," I mumbled. My eyes fixed on the long hallway wall, where hundreds of yellowing papers had been tacked up. There was nothing else to see; the tile was a gleaming black, the lights nothing more than long fluorescent tubes fixed over our heads.

"Those are all of the agents' draft notices," Cate said as we walked. Gray's mandatory conscription in the wake of the crisis meant that everyone forty and under would eventually be called upon to serve the country, whether it be as peacekeepers with the National Guard, border patrol, or babysitting freak kids in the camps as PSFs. The first wave of unwilling recruits had mostly been those in their twenties—too old to have been affected by IAAN and too young to have lost children.

"A lot of the agents here are ex-military, like Rob," she said as we walked. "Even more of us are civilians who joined because we believed in Alban's mission for truth, or to try to gain a little more information on what was happening to our kids or siblings. There are more than three hundred active agents, with a hundred or so in HQ monitoring Ops, training, or working on our tech."

"How many kids?"

"Twenty-six, if you include yourself and Martin. Six teams of four, each assigned to an agent—a Minder, Alban calls us. You'll train with the rest of my team and, eventually, be sent out on tactical operations."

"And the League pulled all of them out of camps?" I asked.

She had to flash her ID again at the next door. "Maybe four at the most in the five years the League has existed.

You'll find that these kids come from all over the country. Some, like Vida and Jude—you'll meet them in just a bit—were brought in when the Collections began. Some were lucky enough to be spotted during transports to camp or as the PSFs came to pick them up. Then we have a few oddballs like Nico, the other member of my team. He . . . has an interesting story."

I couldn't tell if that was supposed to be bait. "Interesting?"

"You remember what I told you about Leda Corp, right? About how the government gave them the research grant to study the origin of IAAN? Nico was . . ." She cleared her throat twice. "He was one of their subjects. He came in a few weeks ago, so the two of you will be able to learn the ropes together. I'd just warn you that he's still a little delicate."

Right away, I could see that the hallway hadn't been an accurate predictor of what the rest of the building's structure would look like. It was as though they had finished the entry and either ran out of funds or decided it was pointless to keep going. The general look of the place was what you'd expect walking through a half-finished construction site. The walls were exposed gray cement blocks, braced by metal supports. The floor was painted cement. Everything was cement, everywhere, all the time. I might as well have been back in Thurmond for how welcoming the place looked.

The ceilings hung low overhead, crowded with pipes and brightly wrapped electrical lines. And while HQ was nowhere near as dark as the Tube had been, without any kind of natural sunlight flooding in, the flickering fluorescent lights cast everything in a sickly, anemic glow.

The most interesting thing about HQ was its shape; the door from the entry opened up directly in front of a large, circular center room that was enclosed by curving glass walls. The hallway we stood in formed a ring around that room, though I could see at least four different hallways that branched out from it in straight lines.

"What is he?" My eyes kept darting to the right as we walked, watching the figures milling around the big room. Inside was a handful of TVs mounted to the walls; below them were what looked like round cafeteria tables and an assortment of League agents playing cards, eating, or reading at them.

The curving hall wasn't tight, but it wasn't enormous, either. Anytime more than one person tried to pass by us, heading in the opposite direction, one of us had to fall back to allow the other person room.

The first two agents we encountered, young women in army fatigues, confirmed another suspicion: my story had beaten me here. They were all friendly smiles as their eyes met Cate's, but when their eyes shifted down to me, they stepped around us and continued at a brisk pace.

"What is he?" I repeated. Seeing confusion cloud Cate's pale blue eyes, I clarified. "What color?"

"Oh. Nico's Green—incredible with tech. It's like he processes everything as a program. Vida's Blue. Jude is Yellow. This is the only team that has a mix of abilities. The others are strictly all one color each, and they serve different support functions on Ops." The overhead lights turned her blond hair a pearly white. "You're the only Orange here now."

Great. We were the goddamn Rainbow Connection. All we needed was a Red to complete the deck. "So you got stuck with all the leftovers when the other teams filled up?"

Cate smiled. "No. I just chose carefully."

We finally exited the outer ring, ducking down one of the straight hallways. She didn't say a thing, not even to the clusters of agents that squeezed by us as they passed. Their eyes followed us all the way to a door marked with Cate's name, and every single time it felt like jagged fingernails down my spine.

"Ready?" she asked. Like I had a choice.

There's something really personal about seeing someone's bedroom, and at the time—even now—it made me uncomfortable to see the little knickknacks she had smuggled in. The room was cramped but livable—compact but, surprisingly, not claustrophobic. A cot had been tucked into one corner, and behind it, Cate had tacked up a dirty patchwork quilt. The pattern of bright red and yellow daisies punched through even the worst of the fabric's stains. There was a computer on the card table serving as her desk, a purse, a lamp, and two books.

And everywhere, there were pictures.

Finger-paint drawings, shapes of people smeared into life by little fingers. Pencil portraits of faces I didn't recognize. Charcoal landscapes looking just as stark as life below ground. Photographs of warm faces and snowy mountains were taped up in neat rows, too far for me to see each beautiful, glossy detail. Not to mention the three bodies in the way.

A tall, whip-thin kid was somehow pacing the two feet of space between the desk and the cot, but he jerked to a stop at our entrance, swinging his head of reddish-brown curls our way. His whole face beamed as he threw himself at Cate, locking his pencil-thin arms around her shoulders.

"I'm so glad you're back!" His voice broke in relief.

"Me too," she said. "Jude, this is Ruby."

Jude was all bones and skin, and it looked like he had grown something like five inches in five days. He wasn't a bad-looking kid by any means; it was just readily apparent that he hadn't finished baking. There'd be time for him to grow into his long, straight nose, but the big brown eyes—those were like something out of a cartoon.

By the look of him, he was thirteen, maybe fourteen, but he moved like he was still mystified by how to control his newly long limbs.

"Nice to meet you!" he said. "Did you just get back? Were you in Virginia this whole time? Cate said that you guys got separated and she was so worried that something had—"

The kid didn't let one word finish before starting the next. I blinked, trying to twist away from his embrace.

"Judith, girlfriend looks fresh out of cuddles," came a low voice somewhere past his shoulder. "Unclench."

Jude backed off immediately, letting off a nervous laugh. "Sorry, sorry. It is nice to meet you, though. Cate told us a lot about you—that you were in the same camp as Martin?"

There was a weird twinge in his voice when he said the other Orange's name. His pitch went up, cracking on the word.

I nodded; he knew what I was, then. And he'd still touched me. What a brave, stupid kid.

"That's Vida on the bed over there," Cate said, nudging me toward the other girl.

I must have taken a step back; the force of her gaze made me feel like I had been shoved into the nearest corner. I don't know how I had missed her sitting on the cot, arms and legs crossed with total and complete indifference. But now that I was seeing her, I felt myself shrinking back just that tiny bit.

She was honest-to-God lovely, some perfect mix of ethnicities—her skin a glowing brown that reminded me of a warm autumn afternoon, almond-shaped eyes, hair dyed an electric blue. It was the kind of face you'd expect to see in a magazine: high, bold cheekbones and full lips that seemed always fixed in a small smirk.

"Hi. Nice of you to finally drag your ass in." Her voice was loud, rich, and every word felt like it was punctuated with a slap. When she stood up to hug Cate, I felt two inches tall and as solid as air.

Instead of reclaiming her seat, she stayed standing, inching in front of Cate so that she stood between us. I knew that stance. How many times had I taken that position in front of Zu, or Chubs, or Liam? How many times had they done it for me? With her back to the woman, Vida studied me closely. "You poor thing. Just follow me and you'll be fine."

It's like that, is it? I thought, bristling at her tone.

When she looked back at Cate, it was all sweetness again. Her dark skin had an unmistakably happy glow.

"That's Nico in the corner," Vida said, taking over the introductions. "Dude, can you unplug for two seconds?"

Nico was sitting on the floor, his back to Cate's tiny dresser. He looked small to me somehow, and I immediately saw what Cate meant when she had used the word *delicate*. It wasn't his stature or his build, both of which were slight, but the tense lines of his face. A stray strand of raven-black hair escaped from the clutches of the gel cementing his comb-back as he said, "Hi. Nice to meet you."

And then he dropped his eyes to the small black device in his hands, his fingers flying over the keys. The device cast his tan skin an unnaturally bright white, highlighting even his near-black eyes.

"So, what's your story?" Vida asked.

I tensed, one arm crossing over the other in a mimic of her stance. And I knew, without any doubt, that if this was going to work—if I was going to live with these kids and see them and train with them—then there needed to be distance. The one thing the past few weeks had driven into me over and over was the more you got to know someone, the more you inevitably came to care about him or her. The lines between you became blurred, and when the separation came, it was excruciating to untangle yourself from that life.

Even if I had wanted to tell them about Thurmond, there was no way to put that kind of pain into words. No way to make them understand, not when just the thought of the Garden, the Factory, the Infirmary was enough to choke me with anger. The burn stayed in my chest and lingered there for days after, the same way the bleach used to blister our hands in the Laundry.

I shrugged.

"What about Martin?" Jude asked. His fingers twisted around one another, wringing his hands pink. "Are we going to have five on our team?"

Cate didn't miss a beat. "Martin was transferred to Kansas. He'll be working with the agents there."

Vida swung back toward her. "Really?"

"Yes," Cate said. "Ruby will be taking his place as team leader."

It was over that quickly. Whatever fake pleasantries Vida had managed to summon up for Cate went out with a single, sharp breath, and in that second, I saw the flash of betrayal. I saw her physically swallow the words down and nod.

"Wait, what?" I choked out. I didn't want this—I didn't want any of this.

"Cool! Congrats!" Jude gave me a friendly punch to the shoulder, pushing me out of my daze.

"I know you'll all help Ruby feel welcome and show her the ropes," Cate said.

"Yeah," Vida said through her teeth. "Of course. Anything she wants."

"Let's go get dinner together," Jude said in a bright voice. Totally and blissfully ignorant of the way Vida's fists were clenching and unclenching at her sides. "It's pasta night!"

"I have to check in with Alban, but the four of you should go—then you can show Ruby where the bunks are and get her settled in," Cate said.

No sooner had I stepped out the door and shut it behind me than I felt someone grab my ponytail, wrench me around, and throw me up against the nearby wall. Black stars exploded in my vision.

"Vida!" Jude gasped. The outburst was enough to get even Nico to look up.

"If you think for one fucking second that I don't know what really happened, you're wrong," Vida hissed.

"Get out of my face," I snapped.

"I know that story about Cate losing you is bullshit. I know you ran," she said. "I will tear you to shreds before you hurt her again."

"You don't know anything about me," I said, feeding off her anger in a way I didn't expect.

"I know everything I need to," Vida spat out. "I know what you are. We all do."

"That's enough!" Jude said, taking my arm and pulling me back. "We're getting dinner, Vi. Come or don't come."

"Have a lovely fucking meal," she said in her sweetest voice, but the fury that radiated off Vida's form cut through the air between us and closed around my neck like a fist. Like a promise.

I'm not sure why the ring of empty tables around us bothered me as much as it did. Maybe it was the same reason Jude felt like he had to talk through the entire meal to make up for their silence.

We had only just sat down at one of the smaller circular tables when a number of agents and other kids got up from theirs. They either took their trays and left the atrium completely, or they squeezed themselves onto one of the already full tables farther away. I tried telling myself it wasn't because of me, but there are some thoughts that live in your mind like a chronic disease. You think you've finally crushed them, only to find them morphing into something newer, darker. *Of course they'd get up and leave,* a familiar voice whispered in my ear. *Why would they ever want to be around something like you?*

"—is where we eat and hang out if we have some downtime. After Mess hours they clean everything up so you can come in and play cards or, like, Ping-Pong, or even just watch TV," Jude said around a mouthful of lettuce. "Sometimes an agent brings back a new movie for us to watch, but I mostly stay downstairs in the computer lab—"

It was bizarre and sort of dizzying to be in the circular-shaped room, and the feeling was intensified by having ten televisions in eyeshot at all times. Each was tuned to the single surviving national news channel—it turns out when you're willing to jump into the president's pocket, you find quite a bit of money there—or giving us a riveting view of silent static. I didn't have the stomach for whatever horrors of the day the anchors were trotting out. It was a much more interesting game to see which new arrival to the atrium broke away to which table. The kids, after they picked up their food from the buffet tables, flocked toward the other kids. The beefier guys that were probably ex-military sat with all the other guys with the exact same look, with only a few female agents scattered in there for some variety.

I was so focused on counting the women off that I didn't notice Cate at all until she was standing directly behind Jude.

"Alban would like to see you," she said simply, reaching over to take my tray.

"What? Why?"

Jude must have mistaken my revolted look for one of fear, because he reached over and patted my shoulder. "Oh, no, don't be nervous! He's really nice. I'm sure . . . I'm sure he just wants to chat, since it's your first day. That's probably all it is. A one-and-done kind of thing."

"Yeah," I mumbled, ignoring the note of jealousy I detected in his voice. Apparently being summoned wasn't a typical thing. "Sure."

Cate led me out of the atrium and back into the hall, leaving my tray on a waiting cart beside the door. Instead of taking a right or left, she guided me toward a door on the opposite wall I hadn't noticed before, half dragging me down the stairwell behind it. We bypassed the second level, winding down and around to the third. I was happier from the second she shouldered the door open. It was warmer, dryer than the creeping dampness of the upper floors. I wasn't even bothered by the smell of static and hot plastic as we passed the large computer room that sat where the atrium did on that level.

"I'm sorry about this," Cate said. "I know you must be exhausted, but he's so eager to meet you."

I clasped my hands behind my back to hide the way they'd started to shake. On the flight over, Cate had tried to paint a noble portrait of Alban as a gentle man of true intelligence—a bona fide American patriot. Which was, you know, a little at odds with everything else I'd heard about him: that he was a terrorist who'd coordinated more than two hundred strikes against President Gray around the country and killed a good number of civilians in the process. The evidence was everywhere—agents had tacked up newspaper articles and newscast screen shots on the walls, like the death and destruction were something to be celebrated.

This was what I knew about John Alban from personal experience: he'd formed an organization called the Children's League but was only willing to break kids out of camps whom he saw as powerful. Useful. And that if the man was one to hold a grudge, there was a decent chance I'd be punished for making that plan as difficult as possible for him.

We walked to the other side of the loop. Cate tapped her ID against the black pad there, waiting for the beep. A part of me already knew to hope it wouldn't flash green.

There was no trace of heat left as we made our way down the cement stairs. The door slammed shut behind us on its own, sealing with a sucking noise. I turned back, startled, but Cate gently nudged me forward.

It was another hallway, but different than the ones I'd seen upstairs on the first level. The lights here weren't as powerful and seemed set on a flickering loop. One look was all I needed to rear back, my heart climbing into my throat. This was Thurmond—this was a piece of what it had been to me. Rusted metal doors, solid cinder-block walls only broken up by small observation windows. But this was a prison with twelve doors instead of dozens, with twelve people instead of thousands. The rancid smells tinged with a hint of bleach, the barren walls and floors—the only difference was that the PSFs would have punished us if we'd tried banging against the doors the way the prisoners currently were. Muffled voices were begging to be let out, and I wondered, for the first time, if any of the soldiers had felt the way I did now—sick, like my skin was tightening over the top of my skull. I knew exactly when their faces found the windows and their bloodshot eyes followed us to the end of the hall.

Cate tapped her ID against the lock on the last door to the left, turning her face down into the shadows. The door popped open and she pushed it in, motioning toward the bare table and set of chairs. The hanging bulb was already on, swaying. I dug my heels into the tile, pulling away from her.

"What the hell is this?" I demanded.

"It's all right," she said, her voice low and soothing. "We use this wing to hold assets or rogue agents we've brought in to question."

"You mean, interrogate them?" I said.

No, I thought, the realization blooming like black spots in my vision. *Martin interrogated them. I'm going to interrogate them.*

"I don't . . ." I began. I don't trust myself. I don't want to do this. I don't want any of this.

"I'll be here with you the whole time," Cate said. "Nothing will happen to you. Alban just wants to see what your skill level is, and this is one of the few ways we can show him."

I almost laughed. Alban wanted to make sure he had made a good deal.

Cate shut the door and drew me into a seat at the metal table. I heard footsteps and started to rise, only to be guided back down. "It'll just be a few minutes, Ruby, I promise."

Why are you so surprised? I asked myself. I knew what the League was, what they were about. Cate told me once it had been founded to expose the truth about the kids in camps; funny, then, how far off-message they'd traveled. I'd been here for less than a half a day, and even I could see that in five years, all they'd managed to accomplish was turn a few kids into soldiers, capture and interrogate people, and bring down a few key buildings.

With the size and shape of the door's window, I couldn't see much more than Alban's dark face when it appeared there, flanked by a half dozen other men. His voice filtered in through a crackling intercom. "Are we ready to proceed?"

Cate nodded, then stepped back, murmuring, "Just do as you're asked, Ruby."

That's all I've ever done.

The door opened and three figures appeared. Two male agents, beyond fit in their green fatigues, and a small woman between them, who had to be dragged in and bound to the other chair with plastic ties. There was some kind of burlap hood over her head, and judging by the grunts and moans of protest, her mouth was gagged beneath it.

A prick of dread started at the base of my neck and slowly zigzagged its way down my spine.

"Hello, my dear." Alban's voice filtered through again. "I hope you're well this evening."

John Alban had been an adviser in President Gray's cabinet until his own child, Alyssa, had been killed by IAAN. The way Cate explained it to me was that the guilt of it became too much for him; when he tried to take the truth—not the glossy, sugarcoated version of the camps—to the major newspapers, no one had been willing to run the story. Not when President Gray had wrangled an iron-fisted control over them. That was the legacy of the DC bombings: good men gone unheard and bad men taking every advantage.

His dark skin looked weathered by middle age, and the heavy bags beneath his wide eyes made his whole face sag. "It is a pleasure to have you here, of course. My advisers and I would very much like to see the extent of your abilities and how they might benefit our organization."

I nodded, my tongue fixed to the top of my mouth.

"We believe this woman has been passing information to Gray's men, sabotaging the operations we sent her out for his benefit. I would like you to explore her recent memories and tell me if this is true."

He thought it was that easy, did he? A peek inside, and there are the answers. I squared my shoulders and gazed at him through the glass. I wanted him to know that I knew—that I was well aware of the fact he was standing behind that door for protection not from this woman but from me.

All I had to do was earn his trust, gain a tiny bit of freedom. And when the time was right, he'd regret ever giving me someone to practice my abilities on; he'd wake up one morning to find me gone, every trace of me erased from this hole in the ground. This was a waiting game for me. Once I confirmed the others were safe, I'd get myself out. Break the deal.

"You'll have to give me a specific operation to look for," I said, wondering if he could even hear me. "Otherwise we might be here all night."

"I understand." His voice crackled through. "It should go without saying that what you hear and see when you are on this hall is privileged information your peers will never have access to. Should we find that any of this intel is being shared, there will be . . . repercussions."

I nodded.

"Excellent. This agent recently went to meet a contact to pick up a packet of information from him."

"Where?"

"Outside of San Francisco. That is as precise as I'm able to get."

"Did the contact have a name?"

There was a long pause. I didn't need to look up from the woman's hooded face to know the advisers were conferring with one another. Finally, his voice filtered back through. "Ambrose."

The two soldiers who brought the woman in retreated back outside. She heard the door lock, but it wasn't until I reached across the way to touch her bound wrist that she tried to jerk away from me.

"Ambrose," I said. "San Francisco. Ambrose. San Francisco . . ." Those words, over and over again, as I sank into her mind. The pressure that had been steadily building from the moment I boarded the plane in Maryland released with a soft sigh. I felt myself lean closer to her, a rushing stream of thoughts filtering through her mind. They were blindingly bright—there was a painfully intense sheen to them, as if each memory had been dipped in pure sunlight.

"Ambrose, San Francisco, the intel, Ambrose, San Francisco . . ."

It was a trick Clancy had taught me—that mentioning a specific word or phrase or name to someone was often enough to draw it straight into that person's forethoughts.

The woman relaxed under my fingers. Mine.

"Ambrose," I repeated quietly.

It was noon or near to; I was the agent and she was me, and we shot a quick glance up toward the sun directly above us. The scene shimmered as I ran through a deserted park, black tennis shoes gliding through the overgrown grass. There was a building up ahead—a public restroom.

It didn't surprise me, then, that a gun suddenly appeared in my right hand. The better I got at this, the more senses came to me with the images—a smell here, a sound there, a touch. I'd felt the cold metal tucked into the band of my running shorts from the moment I stepped into the memory.

The man waiting at the back of the building didn't even have time to turn before he was on the ground, a hole the size of a dollar coin in the back of his skull. I recoiled, dropping the woman's wrist. The last sight I had before I cut the connection was a blue folder and its contents scattering in the wind, drifting down into a nearby pond.

I opened my eyes, though the light from the hanging bulb made the throbbing behind my eyes that much worse. At least it wasn't a migraine—the pain might have been lessening every time I did this, but the disorientation was still just as bad. It took me two seconds to remember where I was, and another two to find my voice.

"She met a man in a park, behind the public restrooms. She shot him in the back of the head after approaching him from behind. The intel he carried was in a blue folder."

"Did you see what happened to it?" Alban's tone was tinged with excitement.

"It's at the bottom of the pond," I said. "Why did she shoot him? If he was her contact—"

"Enough, Ruby," Cate cut in. "Send them in, please."

The woman was limp, still half dazed with my influence over her. She didn't fight them off as they snapped her restraints and picked her up out of the chair. But I thought—I thought I heard her crying.

"What's going to happen to her?" I pressed, turning back toward Cate.

"Enough," she said again. I flinched at her tone. "May we have your permission to be excused? Are you satisfied with her results?"

This time Alban met us at the door, but he never crossed that last bit of space between us. Never even looked me once in the eye. "Oh yes," he said softly. "We are more than satisfied. This is a special thing you can do, my dear, and you have no idea the difference you can make for us."

But I did.

Liam hadn't told me a great deal about his time with the League; it had been short, and brutal, and so damaging that he had taken his chance and escaped at the first opportunity that presented itself. But without either of us realizing it, he had prepared me for the new reality of my life. Warning me once, twice, three times that the League would control every move I made, that they would expect me to take someone else's life, just because it suited their needs and was what they wanted. He had told me about his brother, Cole, and what he had become under the coaxing of the League's guiding hands.

Cole. I knew from League gossip that he was a hotshot—a deep-cover agent with terrifying efficiency. I knew from Liam that he thrived on the pulse of power that came from firing a gun.

But what no one, not even Liam, had thought to mention was how very, very much alike they looked.

THREE

FOR WHATEVER REASON, JUDE HAD NOMINATED himself to serve as the team's one-man welcoming committee. When I arrived back at HQ after my first Op with the League, it had been his lanky, pacing shape waiting for me at the end of the entry hall, torpedoing toward me, burying me under an avalanche of questions. Six months later, he was still the only one who waited there for us, rewarding our safe return with a smile that split his face.

I braced myself for impact as Vida tapped her ID against the door. Rob and the remaining members of the tact team had escorted Cole Stewart in a few minutes before, but I'd forced us to hang back, take our time going down the tunnel. It was important to make sure Rob got the full credit for this one, to let him roll around in the glory like a dog in the grass. We'd heard the cheers go up as they strolled through the entry, and watched them pump their fists as they strode into HQ, almost leaving Cole behind in his wheelchair.

Now there was no one left in the long white entry hall. The agents left a trail of celebratory noise behind them. It shrank with every step they took, until the only thing I could hear was my own breathing, and the only thing I could see was the empty space at the end of the hallway where Jude should have been.

"Oh, thank you, Jesus," Vida said, stretching her arms over her head. "One day I won't have to get my back realigned from his death grip. *Adios*, boo."

I think some people used the nickname "boo" as a term of endearment. Vida used it to make you feel like one of those little dogs that have brains the size of thumbs, and piddle all over themselves when they get too excited.

I let her go without a word, heading left toward Cate and the other senior agent quarters to check in. Five minutes of fruitless knocking later, I ducked my head into the atrium to see if she was there. She's probably with the others, I thought, scanning the near-empty space. And while I didn't glimpse her white-blond hair at one of the tables, I did recognize the mop of reddish-brown curls parked in front of one of the TVs.

I wasn't lucky enough to pull off a clean getaway—those two seconds of staring had been enough for him to register my gaze. Jude glanced down at his old plastic wristwatch and then back up at me again in horror.

"Roo!" he called, waving me over. "I'm so sorry! *So* sorry! I totally lost track of time. Did everything go okay? Did you just get back now? Where's Vida? Is she—?"

I wasn't a good enough person to say that no part of me wanted to turn and run out before he could come up and loop my arm through his, dragging me across the room with him.

It was only when I crossed the room that I noticed Nico was there, sitting at the opposite end of the table. One of the cement pillars had blocked the sight of him from the door, but it also didn't help that the kid didn't seem to be moving. At all. I followed his stony gaze down to the little device on the table. A Chatter.

It was the size of a phone and could easily have doubled for one if you weren't casting too careful of an eye on it. They'd salvaged an older generation of phones—the kind with an actual keypad, rather than a sleek touchscreen. The new shells they'd created for them were oval and thin enough to slide into a back pocket or up a sleeve during a lesson.

A couple of the Greens had developed this little gem with the idea that agents could relay digital messages, photos, and short videos back home without needing to ditch burner phone after burner phone. The tech behind them was mostly a mystery to me, but I understood they communicated on some un-hackable network the Greens had developed. They could only be used to contact other Chatters on the network, and only then if you had the other Chatter's secret PIN number. They were useless if you needed to send large images or video files longer than thirty seconds; Alban had rejected sending them out in the field for that reason, dismissing them as some bored kid's project. As far as I knew, the Greens usually just used them now to chat with one another in HQ when they were in different training sessions or at night after lights out.

"—really come back? Did you get to meet the agent? Was he as badass as everyone says? Can we—?"

"What's going on?" I asked, looking between Nico and the TV screen. They'd picked the one showing only local California weather and news.

It was like I'd sucked the words straight out of him. Jude tensed in that wide-eyed way of his before flashing the kind of smile that was trying too hard.

"What's going on?" I repeated.

Jude swallowed, glancing at Nico before leaning down to my ear. His eyes were scanning the atrium like they were looking for dark corners that didn't exist.

"They sent Blake Howard out on an Op," he said. "We're just . . ."

"Blake Howard? The Green kid from Team One?" The one who looked like you could take him out with one well-aimed sneeze?

Jude nodded, giving another nervous glance behind me. "I'm just . . . worried, you know? Nico is, too."

Shocker. Nico was never one to pass up a good conspiracy theory, especially when it came to the League. Every agent was a double agent. Alban was actually working with Gray to bring down the Federal Coalition. Someone was poisoning our water supply with lead. I don't know where he got it from or if it was just the way his brain was processing all of the information he was absorbing and he didn't know how to shut it off.

"They must be trading him for something," Nico said, gripping the Chatter. "For information? To get another agent back? That's not so crazy, right? There are so many Greens here already. They hate having so many of us. They hate us."

I tried not to roll my eyes. "Did the Op involve tech?" I asked.

"Well, yeah, but," Jude said, "when have they ever sent out a Team One kid? They're supposed to be for HQ use only."

He wasn't wrong. Vida called them the Squeakers, and the name had stuck with everyone. All Greens with supercharged logic and reasoning skills that the League put to use in deciphering codes and building computer viruses, creating these insane devices. They all had the same stumbling walk; Nico too. A weird half step where they dragged their feet against the tile, causing their sneakers to make these little squeaking noises. I'm sure they had picked it up from one another subconsciously; they were always moving in sync, just like the parts of a working machine should.

"He's of age and he has the right skill set to help them," I said. "I know for a fact the other Green teams are occupied this week. He might have been a last resort."

"No," Jude said. "We think they picked him on purpose. They wanted *him*."

It was a while before Jude built up the nerve to look at me again. When he did, his expression was so obviously ashamed and terrified that I felt myself soften just enough to ask, "Is there something you're not telling me? What am I missing here?"

Jude twisted the stretched-out hem of his shirt into a knot. Nico only stared straight ahead, eyes unblinking as they fixed on the Chatter.

"Me, Nico, and . . . Blake," Jude began, "the three of us were messing around a few days ago down here. We've been trying to build one of those remote-control cars from leftover computer parts."

"Okay . . ."

"Nico had to go up and talk to Cate, but me and Blake took the car on a test drive around this floor. It was around two in the afternoon, and no one was down here. So we thought it would be fine and that we wouldn't bother anyone. But . . . you know those rooms that we use to store things for Ops? Like, the vests, extra ammo, that stuff?"

I nodded.

"We heard voices coming from one of them. I thought maybe the guys were just playing a card game or something—sometimes they do it down here so they can bad-mouth Alban or one of the advisers," Jude said, visibly shaking now. "But when I heard them, what they were actually saying—they weren't playing a game, Roo, they were talking about us. It was Rob, and Jarvin, and a couple of their friends. They kept saying things like *Reducing the freak population* and *Getting Alban back on track* and how they were going to prove what a waste of time and—and resources we were."

It was a chill that sank straight to the bone. I pulled out the nearest chair and dragged it closer to Nico. Jude did the same, his hands twisting around each other.

"And they caught you listening?"

"I know it's stupid, but when I heard that, I freaked out—I didn't mean to, but I dropped the car. We ran before the door opened, but I'm positive they saw us. I heard Rob call my name."

"Then what?" I pressed. My mind was making connections now, dangerous ones.

"Then Blake got assigned to that Op even though he's on Team One. Jarvin said that they needed a Green to hack into the company's server room, and he didn't have a choice."

I leaned back slowly. Reduce the freak population. My ear, the one that had taken the brunt of the grenade's blast, seemed to have a pulse of its own.

That was an accident, I told myself. *Rob was just being reckless.* But the second lie sounded less convincing than the first. Reduce the freak population. How? By putting them in deadly situations on Ops that could be waved off as accidents? Rob had killed kids before—I only knew of those two I'd glimpsed in his memory, but what's to say there weren't more?

Jesus. A blinding wave of nausea blasted up from my stomach. Did he kill them to keep the number of kids here down?

No—no, I needed to stop. My thoughts were spiraling and getting out of hand. This was Nico and Jude—two boys with too much free time to sit around and trade nightmares. They were constantly poking at trouble, then acted all shocked when it turned around and bit them in their asses.

"It's just a coincidence," I said. I had another point to make, I'm sure, but it unhooked from my chain of thoughts when I heard someone call my name from across the room. One of Alban's advisers, good old Raccoon Face, stood in the atrium's doorway.

"He'd like to speak to you in his office an hour from now."

Then he turned on his heel and was gone, clearly angry he'd been tasked to play messenger.

"What does he want?" Jude asked, visibly confused.

You almost never saw the walking suits more than a few feet away from Alban; I wouldn't have been surprised if they broke into his quarters every night and took turns whispering plans and sweet nothings in his ear while he slept.

There were ten men total, all over the age of fifty, who had divided up the areas of Alban's focus and assumed control over each. They coordinated and approved Ops, brought in supplies and new contacts, recruited new trainers, managed the League's finances. All so Alban could focus on "big picture" goals and targets.

Jude claimed they were only there because Gray wanted them dead for one reason or another and they had no choice but to go underground. I still didn't know half of their names, since most made it a point to never directly engage with the Psi freaks. It was easier just to fixate on their features and nickname from there. Raccoon Face, Monkey Ears, Horse Teeth, and Frog Lips were the ones I saw most.

What the names lacked in creativity, they made up for in accuracy.

"A debrief? Already?" Jude asked, glancing to the TV again.

I reached over and manually flipped the machine off.

"Hey!"

"You're late," I said, pointing to the clock on the wall. "Another two minutes and Instructor Johnson will hit you with a demerit."

"So?" Jude shot back. "This is more important!"

"More important than eventually being activated?" I said. "Because the last time I checked, you were two demerits away from being stuck on HQ support forever."

It was a mean tactic to play; Nico's fuming look told me as much. But he knew, probably better than I did, that a future in which Jude never got to go out on an Op was a future Jude would have sold both arms to avoid.

I walked them out, tailing them all the way to the training room in case they got any ideas about slipping away. The teams we usually trained with—Two, Three, and Four—were already there, warming up, darkening the wall of mirrors. This was the one part in all of HQ that actually smelled fully human. The stench of sweat and warm bodies gave this hall a jolt of real, tangible life. It was better than the mildew, at least.

Instructor Johnson nodded in my direction as I held the door open, the fluorescent lights bleaching his already blond hair. Both Vida and I were excused from lessons and training for the day, but tomorrow they'd start all over again for us. I'd fall back into this place's pattern, grateful for the relief of not needing to think about anything other than moving from hour to hour, door to door. A life lesson on how to cope, courtesy of Thurmond.

Jude and Nico could both hate me for this; I didn't care. I just couldn't afford to feed on their fear and let it twist my own. I'd worked so hard to numb myself to this place, and they didn't get to blow that apart. They got my attention, my concern, my protection, but they didn't get that.

Showered, fed, clothing changed, and thoughts collected, I was ready to meet with John Alban. But he wasn't ready for me.

There was a lot you could say about the League's founder, and maybe two words of it were actually flattering. He was a smart man, no one was going to deny it. The League was what it was today because of him. It was just that some felt it was time for him to take the assaults against Gray to "a new level," and others were pressing for him to hold the course, since it was working.

I thought he had every right to want to think more about such a huge decision, but I understood their impatience. I knew they wanted to capitalize on the growing discontent and murmurs of protests we'd been tracking.

I heard voices beyond the door, soft at first, then enflamed enough to catch my attention. Every intention I had of knocking fell apart the longer I stood there, listening.

"No!" Alban was saying. "My God, no! *No!* How many times do I need to repeat the word for it to join your vocabulary? It was the answer the first time you presented it to the senior staff, when you convinced Jarvin to present it to the advisers, and, yes, now."

"You're not thinking this through—"

I rocked back on my heels instinctively, away from Rob's harsh voice.

"You think we can keep this up without making a big statement? How many of these things do you just have sitting around HQ, wasting our time and energy?"

Alban cut him off. "They are not *things*, as you, I'm sure, are well aware. This is nonnegotiable. The ends will never justify the means, no matter how you try to pitch this. Never. They are *children*."

In the back of my mind, a thought was beginning to knot itself with another, darker one, but I forced my attention to stay here. Now.

"You're the one who always says *anything to get Gray out*, aren't you? The distraction would be more than enough for us to go in and dismantle the camps, blast the news out to the rest of the damn country. This is the only way in now. They've wised up to our forged IDs—we can't even get in to extract the agents we still have embedded in the camps. They're waiting for us! We're all waiting for you to do *something*! Decide *something*!"

There was a long, bitter silence that followed. Whatever words Alban was looking for, he never found them. I couldn't keep my own mind in check. What kind of plan could get him this worked up?

"I'm just warning you," Rob continued, sounding calmer, "that even I've heard agents wondering about what kind of policy we're moving toward. A good number still think that you want to rekindle things with Gray in the end. That you miss your friend."

I closed my eyes. It was an unspoken rule that we didn't bring up Alban's former friendship with President Gray and the first lady for any reason. Cate told me once that Alban didn't even like to be reminded of the work he'd done as Secretary of Homeland Security—so I imagine he wasn't thrilled to be reminded he was once in a small circle of people who enjoyed private dinners in the executive residence of the White House.

A new voice chimed in. "John, let's not dismiss this entirely. This is a tactic that's been employed before, and it *is* effective. They wouldn't know. We have ways of hiding the mechanism—"

I was so focused on the conversation in front of me that I didn't hear the person who hobbled up behind me. Not until he was hovering at my back, tapping on my shoulder to get my attention.

"I'd keep this one to yourself, Keyhole Kate," Cole said. "Or do you need to hear the old one about that pesky cat and his curiosity?"

It was too late to jump back and pretend I hadn't been listening, and now I was too flustered to bother trying.

The medic on Rob's team had done a good job patching up the deeper cuts on Cole's face, cleaning away the filth from his skin. He was wearing a loose shirt and pants that were a number of sizes too big for him, but he was out of his old vomit-stained rags, at least. He looked like a different person, and I was grateful for it. It was easier to get a look at him.

And I finally was getting a good one.

When Liam had told me he had an older brother, I had imagined him to be *much* older—twenty-five or twenty-six, the same age as Cate. But I'd overheard some of Rob's tact team complaining about him on the flight back. About his punk-ass attitude, how he was only twenty-one, but Alban wasted all of the good Ops on him. *The little golden boy.*

Three years—that was all that separated him from Liam. From IAAN. Cole was a member of that narrow generation that had been just old enough to avoid the disease's grip.

"Didn't get much of a chance to talk on the plane, did we?" he said, bandaged fingers brushing the damp hair back over my shoulder.

He had a few inches on his brother, which I became well aware of as he leaned down to study my face, a pirate's smile working across his own. Cole might have been narrower through the shoulders and waist, but there was something familiar about his stance. . . .

I shook my head, trying to clear the flush from my cheeks as I knocked on the door. It brought the argument inside to an abrupt end. Alban rose from behind his dark wood desk as I came in, shutting his laptop and cutting off the low murmur of the radio scanners on the nearby table. Rob and the frog-lipped adviser were already standing, both of their faces flushed from the argument. Seeing us, Rob rolled his eyes up and away, leaning against one of Alban's many shelves of useless knickknacks from his old life.

"Sir," I said, "you wanted to see me?"

"Goodness, sit down, sit down," Alban said, waving a hand toward one of the folding chairs opposite him. "You both look dead on your feet."

"I'm fine," I said, then added, "thank you," as an afterthought. I hated how small my voice became around him. *Hated* it.

Alban settled back down into his seat, lips pulling back to reveal a smile of mostly yellow teeth. The man didn't make it out that much in public—not with a hefty bounty on his head. If they needed him to make a recorded video speech, they always cleaned up his pockmarked skin and brightened his complexion in post-production. They also liked to Photoshop him into pictures of American landscapes or cities to give the impression that he was a lot more fearless about going outside than he actually was.

"I'd like to have a casual debriefing about the operation to retrieve Agent Stewart last night, if the three of you are agreeable. I don't think it can wait."

He waited until Cole had eased himself down into the chair next to mine before reaching across the desk to clasp his hand. "I can't tell you how good it is to see your face again, my dear boy."

"Well, lucky you." Cole dragged the words out, with no short supply of bitterness. "It seems like you'll be seeing a lot of this beautiful boy from now on."

Cut it out, I told myself, before I could tense. Cole was not Liam, no matter how much alike they looked. No matter how similar their voices were. *Focus on the differences.*

Cole was more solidly built than Liam, and cleaner cut, too. He'd buzzed his hair down since I'd last seen him, making it look two shades darker than the blond I knew it was. The Liam I had known was scruffy around the edges, warm in every way imaginable. And here was his older brother, stiff and beaten within an inch of his life, looking like he had been carved from ice. Not looking all that different from the state I'd left Liam in. And it was so awful, so horrible how quickly my mind swapped in one brother for the other. How much it lifted my spirit and eased the tightness in my chest to imagine Liam was here next to me again.

Stop. It.

Frog Lips shut the office door and retreated to the corner of the small room, slipping into Alban's shadow.

"—would never normally interrupt your recuperation," Alban was saying, "but after hearing Agent Meadows's oral report, it sounds like there was some, shall we say, confusion. I'm interested to hear what happened from your perspective, Ruby."

I didn't register he had spoken to me at all until Rob pushed himself off the bookcase, the wide expanse of his shoulders spreading as he took a deep breath. Before leaving on the Op, he'd buzzed his dark hair short again; it made the bones in his face more pronounced. It changed the way the shadows fell against his skin.

God, why were we doing this? Where was Cate? I was never debriefed without her and never here, in Alban's office, behind a closed door. I was surprised by how anxious I was; I didn't trust her, but somewhere along the way, I guess I'd gotten used to her silent, steady presence waiting to catch me if I tripped up.

"Are . . . we waiting for anyone else?" I asked, careful to keep my voice steady.

Alban understood my question. "This is just a casual talk, Ruby. The level of secrecy surrounding this Op means that we can't hold the debriefing in front of the whole organization. You should feel free to speak your mind."

I pressed my hands down on my knees, trying to keep them from bouncing.

"Agent Meadows," I started, sounding too loud to my own ears, "ran through the mission parameters with us on the flight, laying out the objective and what we knew about this particular bunker's layout. He also reminded us of the fallback plans we had discussed prior to leaving."

Alban's mouth was wide and fairly unskilled at hiding his feelings. One corner twitched up. "And did any of these fallback plans include you and Vida leaving the bunker?"

"No, sir," I said. "Agent Meadows ordered us to hold our position in the stairwell to cover them from there."

Alban placed his elbows on the table and leaning his chin against his fingers. "Can you explain, then, why you left?"

I didn't turn to look at Rob, but I knew he was looking at me. Everyone was, and from the weight of their stares, I got the impression that "Meadows" had already answered this question himself.

If I get Rob in trouble, I thought, *how much trouble will I be in?* He had a hot temper. I had known he'd be angry even when I made the choice to stay outside with Vida, but it would be nothing compared to his fury if I sold him out and told the others about what happened on the stairs. I couldn't let them see the creeping suspicions on my face; I couldn't ask the questions I wanted to. *Why didn't you warn us?* My comm had been working then; I would have heard him.

"The stairwell was . . . compromised. I gave Vida the order to leave so we could monitor the situation from outside."

"And you didn't tell me this because . . . ?" Rob asked, his anger already betraying him.

"My comm was broken," I said. "As you saw when we regrouped."

He grunted.

"All right," Alban said after a moment. "The stairway was compromised? How so?"

There was a grenade. Rob set off a grenade. Nine words. One perfect way to ensure Rob would be forced to swallow every ounce of bitter reprimanding he deserved. Alban would believe me. He had never, not once, doubted my word—had defended it, even, to his advisers after I'd pulled some unwanted news out of an unfortunate mind. Nine words to tell him the truth: that Rob had jacked his own Op, by sheer stupidity or intentionally, and came within a hair's width of killing both Vida and me.

I don't know how I knew, or even why I felt so sure of it; it was as certain as the blood thundering in my ears. If I nailed him on this, embarrassed him, next time he had me in his sights, he wouldn't miss.

"It wasn't . . . well built, and it collapsed," I explained. "It couldn't handle the weight of all of us at once. Crappy construction."

"All right," Alban said, drawing the words out. "Agent Stewart reported that it was you and Vida who actually retrieved him. How did that come to pass?"

"She and the other one completely ignored my order to return to the bunker, that's how!" Rob said. "I know for a fact she heard it. I know that *you* were the one who refused to double back."

All four men had turned toward me. My vision narrowed, black seeping in again at the edges. I pressed a hand to my throat, pulling at the tight collar, trying to free the breath that was caught there.

I wanted Liam. All I wanted was Liam right there, standing close enough for me to breathe in the leather, the smoke, the sweet grass.

"Ruby," Alban said, his voice as calm, and deep, and patient as the sea, "will you please answer my question?"

I just wanted this to be over. I wanted to go back to the sleeping room, crawl into my bunk in the cold darkness, and drift into nothing.

"He's right. I told Vida to disregard the orders. Once we went aboveground, we saw that the National Guardsmen were moving the prisoners out of an entrance we didn't know about. I didn't ask for permission to proceed. I know I should have."

"Because you goddamn know the only thing you're supposed to do is follow your Leader's orders!" Rob barked. "You think we would have lost so many men if you'd been there to cover our escape?"

The TVs behind Alban were off, but I swear I could hear their static breath growing louder and louder the longer the man stayed silent. He pressed a hand to the top of his head but didn't once tear his gaze away from me.

And then came Cole's voice, Southern as sweet tea: "Well, thank God you *disobeyed*; otherwise I'd be halfway to hell by now."

It was clear that I had underestimated just how much influence Cole actually carried in the organization. *Influence* wasn't the right word for it. A sway, maybe, that was mostly charm backed up by deadly results. Alban's eyebrows rose, but he only nodded, allowing Cole to continue.

"I mean, let's call a spade a spade here," Cole said, leaning back to make himself more comfortable. "She's the one who got me out. Why would she be in trouble?"

"She disobeyed my direct orders!"

Cole dismissed Rob with a bored wave. "I mean, Christ, look at the poor girl! She got the shit beat out of her on my behalf. If you think I'm gonna stay quiet and let her take the blame for a mission that wasn't, by the way, a failure, you have another think coming."

No one spoke; I stared openly at Cole's smug expression, then at Rob's murderous one. The sliver of space between them was filled with more than just distrust and annoyance—there were years of history resting there, colored with a hatred I didn't understand.

The tension in Alban's face bled off like running rain until he, too, was smiling.

"I'm inclined to agree with Agent Stewart here, Ruby—thank you for thinking so fast on your feet." Alban shuffled a few papers around on his desk. "Agent Meadows,

I'll review your full report this evening. For now, you're dismissed."

When the senior agent stood, so did I, swinging toward the door for a quick escape. Instead, Alban's voice caught me. "Just one more thing, Ruby, if you don't mind. I'd like to discuss something with you and Cole."

Let me go, let me go, let me go. . . .

Rob did not like this, that much was clear, but he also had no choice. The door shut so hard behind him, it actually rattled the old glass Coke bottles lining the shelf over it.

"Now, on a different note . . ." Alban looked my way. "I should begin by saying that you're being trusted here, my dear, well above your security clearance. If I hear a word of this conversation being breathed outside of these office walls, there will be consequences. The same rules apply here as downstairs."

No, please not this. Please don't let it be this. "Yes, sir."

Satisfied, he turned toward Cole. "I meant what I said before. I'm sorry to have to do this before you've fully recovered. *But*, as you're well aware, we need to retrieve the intel that was taken from you."

"I *am* well aware," Cole said, "but I told you, I don't know who has it. They knocked me out, and I saw someone take it, but truthfully, sir, I don't remember much beyond what happened after they got me to the bunker. I'm not sure it was my contact who picked it up."

I watched him drag a bandaged hand over his close-cropped blond hair, wondering if it was as obvious to Alban as it was to me that he wasn't telling the truth.

"And that's understandable considering the circumstances," Alban said, leaning back in his chair. He threaded his fingers together and rested them over the bulge of his stomach. "This is where Ruby comes in. She's been instrumental in helping . . . to jog the memories of assets. She's helped us track down more than one piece of information that's gone astray."

Please, please, please, not him. I didn't want to see inside his mind; I didn't want to see flashes of Liam or their life. I just wanted to get away from him before my shrinking rib cage shredded my heart.

Cole went pale under his tan, from the creases between his brows down to the fingers clenching the armrests of the plastic chair.

"Oh, come on now." Alban laughed. "I've been told it's completely painless—and if it's not, we'll have her stop immediately."

That, I didn't doubt. Even if I went rogue and didn't release Cole's mind, all of the advisers and senior agents carried these hand-held speakers that functioned like miniature White Noise machines.

"You're the first to volunteer to jump off bridges and infiltrate the PSFs, and you can't let a girl take a quick peek inside your memories for the good of your family here—for the good of your country?" Alban's smile never wavered, despite all of his needling.

Clever, I thought. The Do It for Your Glorious Country speech was one step above a direct order, and Cole was smart enough to realize how much better it would look if he agreed by his own "free will."

"All right," Cole said, finally turning to look at me. "What do you need me to do?"

It was several moments before I found my voice, but I was proud of how strong it sounded. "Give me your hand."

"Be gentle with me, sweetheart," Cole said, his fingers giving a slight twitch as they touched mine. Alban laughed outright at this, but Cole blew out an uneven breath and closed his eyes.

His hand was ice cold and slick to the touch. I tried to ignore the insistent press of his thumb against mine. I'd always felt like Liam's hand swallowed mine when he held it, but this one was somehow bigger, the palms rough with the kind of calluses that only came with years of being shredded by weights and weapons and fights. The way the fingers on his left hand kept twitching every few minutes.

I didn't want to think about any of it. I kept my eyes on his left hand, the two fingers that twitched now and then as he quietly fought through the pain of his injuries.

"Try to relax," I said. "Can you tell me what it is that I'm looking for? What it is, what size, what color—as detailed as you can possibly get."

Cole's eyes were still closed. "A standard-size flash drive. A little black stick about the length of my thumb."

I had done this so many times over the last six months that I no longer felt any kind of pain, but I braced myself anyway. His hand was shaking slightly—or maybe it was mine? I tightened my fingers around his, trying to steady the both of us. "Think back to the last moment you remember having it. Try to bring it to mind, if you can."

The breath went out of Cole in two short bursts.

It felt like slipping beneath the still surface of a sun-warmed river. For all the effort it took to get through his natural defenses, there was nothing cold or still about the smears of colors and shapes streaming past me. But they were moving too fast. Here and there, I saw faces or objects—a green apple, a lonesome swing, a small stuffed bear burning in dying grass, a door with a messy KEEP OUT! sign scribbled in crayon—almost like he was trying to think of everything *but* the thing I had specifically asked for.

Cole was practically limp in his chair, his head slowly falling toward my shoulder. I thought I felt him shake it, his hair brushing against my neck.

"Show me when you lost the memory card," I said quietly. "The black flash drive."

The memory floated up as quickly as if I had plucked it from the water. A little boy wearing overalls, no more than two or three, sitting in the middle of a sea of taupe carpet, bawling at the top of his lungs.

"The flash drive," I said again. The scene smeared down and away, replaced by a nighttime sky and a crackling bonfire that cast a warm glow over the nearby tent and the dark silhouettes moving inside of it.

"Philadelphia!" I heard Alban say behind me. "Philadelphia, Cole. The lab!"

Cole must have registered the man's voice because I felt him flinch against me. I pressed harder, plunging my hands into the stream, suddenly worried about what would happen to me if I couldn't produce the kind of results that Alban was after. *The flash drive,* I thought. *Philadelphia.*

The memory wavered, hovering black and still like a drop of loose ink at the tip of a pen. And with one last shudder, it finally slid free.

The scene shifted around me, throwing me out into a rainy night. A flash of light cut across the brick wall to my left, then another—car headlights. I couldn't hear the squeal of brakes or the accelerator revving, but I was Cole, seeing things as he was seeing them then—and Cole was running.

Dirty water and stray garbage flew up around my ankles; I kept one hand against the brick wall, feeling through the dark. The concrete flashed as if something sharp had sparked against it, then again and again, until I knew exactly what was happening. I was being shot at, and their aim was getting better.

I took one flying leap up, catching the black ladder of a fire escape and dragging it back down to the ground. My hands were stiff and frozen, to the point that I could barely curl them around the bars as I climbed. And still the shooting didn't stop, not until I was rolling onto the rough finish of the roof, catching dust and loose plaster in my hair. Then I was up and off like a shot, jumping from that building's roof onto the next. I saw the ground in the second it took for me to soar over it. The flashing red and blue lights of the police car tracked my progress across the building tops like a mocking shadow. Overhead, the wind stirred, plucking at the loose button-down shirt I wore.

I dropped over the edge of the next building, gagging slightly at the overpowering smell of rotting garbage. My feet hit the rubber lid of the Dumpster, and the shock of the impact buckled my knees and hurtled me headfirst into the ground.

There was a heartbeat, maybe two, but I was too stunned by the pain to actually move. I had just gotten my hands under me when the alleyway flooded with pure white light.

You can't move very fast with a limp, and you can't go very far with a dead end at your back. But I scrambled up anyway, bolting for the battered door to my left, letting the soldiers and police holler what they would after me. My steps were slow but sure—I knew where I was going, and I made sure the door locked in place behind me.

It took two precious seconds for my eyes to adjust to the dim hallway. I stumbled up the stairs to 2A, a pale blue door, and shouldered it open.

The apartment was lit—coffee was still brewing on the counter, but there was no one inside. I checked every room, under the bed, in the closets, before making my way back out into the hall, reaching for the black jacket hanging there.

The building seemed to shake with the force of boots on the narrow stairwell. My hands shook as they grabbed the jacket, feeling the inside lining, running over the bottom seam in disbelief over and over again.

The door exploded open beside me, and there was no opportunity to move, to fight, to run. I was tackled onto the ground, my arms wrenched behind my head and locked there. I saw their boots step over me, heading toward other rooms, their guns up and ready to fire as they cleared each one. And it was only then, after they reappeared, that I was dragged downstairs. Past the shocked faces of my neighbors, through the battered outside door, back into the rain where a black van waited to carry me off.

There were PSFs, National Guardsmen, police. There was no way out; I didn't struggle as they lifted me up into the rear of the van and locked my handcuffs into place. There were other people in there, but none of them were familiar. None of them were him.

I don't know why I looked up then—instinct, maybe, or desperation. The door was slamming shut on my life, and still, the most important thing was that half-second image of Liam's terrified face beneath the nearby flickering streetlight, disappearing into the dark.

FOUR

"HOW COULD YOU?" CATE'S SHRILL VOICE RANG OUT. "She hasn't slept for the past two days, and you put her through *this*?"

I kept my eyes fixed on a small garden statue of a prancing boy, half hidden by the American flag hanging from Alban's desk. I was on the floor, flat on my back, but I had no memory of getting there.

"She is not a trained puppy who will perform tricks for you at the drop of a hat!" Cate had a way of yelling without ever raising her voice. "She is a *child*. Please do not solicit her *services*, as you so eloquently put it, without checking with me first!"

"I think," came Alban's thin reply, "that's about all the lecturing I can stand to take from you today, Agent Conner. This *child* is of an age now to make her own decisions, and while she may report to you, you report to me and I do not—*ever*—need to 'check' with you or vet my decisions with you, and I will ask you now, very kindly, to leave this office before you say something that you will regret."

I forced myself off the ground and back into the chair. Cate lunged forward to help me, but I was already there, brushing her off. It looked like she hadn't sleep, either—her hair was matted and stringy, her face as ashen as I'd ever seen it. She had burst in here like a tornado five minutes ago and hadn't stopped to even take a breath. I don't know who tipped her off—Rob, maybe—but the only thing she had accomplished in that time was making me feel like a humiliated five-year-old.

"I'm fine," I told her, but she didn't look convinced.

"I'll wait outside," she said.

"Then you'll be waiting for some time. We have a guest downstairs that I'd like Ruby to meet."

Of course. Why would I get a day off from "entertaining" the guests?

"Oh?" Cole's gaze shifted among the three of us. "Am I invited to this party?"

Alban stood, finally, and came around to the front of his desk, standing between Cole's and my chairs. He lowered himself back down on the edge of the desk with care, and it was the first time I had ever been close enough to him to realize he smelled like the mildew that we could never fully scrub from the showers.

"I'll see you at senior staff meeting, Agent Conner." Then, in a lower voice, "Come prepared. Agent Meadows is bringing his proposal to vote again."

Cate whirled on her heel, her hands half raised, like she

could shove the thought of it back at him. She was still shaking when Frog Lips escorted her out.

Alban didn't so much as flinch when she slammed the door shut behind her. "So, you found our little missing treasure, did you?"

Cate's interruption had broken into my haze of fury, but just like that, I was free-falling back into it, twisting my hands under the desk to keep from wrapping them around Cole's neck.

In the end, it hadn't mattered a single bit that I had managed to get the League to cut Liam loose. His brother, apparently, had found some way to drag him back into the thick of things. I didn't really understand what I had seen, which was not, as Alban believed, the flash drive itself, but it was clear enough to me that Liam had somehow been involved.

"Well, don't keep us in suspense," Alban said. "We need to get protection to the informant as soon as possible."

Or you need to send someone to kill him for it.

"I just think—" Cole began.

The one thing, the single, solitary gift that Thurmond had given me was the ability to lie, and with a straight, unflinching face.

"I didn't recognize them," I said, "so I can't give you a name. Maybe if I described them, Agent Stewart will be able to give you one?"

"Maybe," Cole managed to croak. Then, after clearing his throat, he added, "I worked with a lot of people in Philly, though. . . ."

Alban gave me an impatient wave, his dark muddy eyes on mine.

"It was a woman," I explained. "I could see her standing near the PSFs' van. She looked nervous and kept glancing around, until she saw something on the sidewalk—then she must have found it. Late into her forties, a bit heavyset. She had long, dark hair and glasses with green frames. Her nose was slightly crooked at the end."

And she was also my first-grade teacher, Mrs. Rosen.

Alban nodded with each and every small bit of description, then turned to Cole. "That ring any bells?"

"Yeah," Cole said, his fingers drumming on the armrest. "I can work with that. I'll write up the full report for you."

Alban nodded. "Have it on my desk by eight tonight."

"Yes, sir," Cole said, struggling back up to his feet. I was afraid if I looked at him, I'd give myself away. He lingered for a second by the door until Frog Lips ushered him out, too.

Alban stood, making his way over to the row of dull, mismatched filing cabinets behind his desk. He slid a ring of keys out of his shirt's front pocket, giving me a small wink. I almost couldn't believe it—every single time I'd come to his office, I'd stared at those ugly things, wondering what was inside, and now, he was actually opening one?

He tapped his finger against the nearest drawer. "The advisers think it's archaic and backward for me to keep these, considering we're in the height of our digital game. Isn't that right, Peters?"

The adviser gave a tight-lipped smile.

Whatever they really thought, to me, it was Alban's one

"old school" trick that actually did what it was supposed to. The records or files or whatever he kept in there were only ever going to be seen by one person: him. There was no chance someone would hack into them or install some kind of backdoor program and download their contents. He'd insisted on installing both a retinal scanner and digital key-pad lock on his office door—the two most expensive pieces of tech at all of HQ. If someone wanted in those files, they needed his permission or to be *very* creative.

He slid a red folder out of the dented black cabinet at the far right, pushing the drawer shut with his hip as he turned back toward me. "I just had a thought, Ruby—I haven't had a chance to thank you for the excellent work you did pulling this information together about the camps. I know you gave it to me a few months ago, but I've only had a few minutes to glance through. I can tell that a lot of effort and thought went into it, which I admire."

I don't know that he'd ever actually surprised me before that moment. I'd given up weeks ago on that folder ever catching his attention, when I'd seen only the smallest sliver of a corner sticking out beneath a stack of papers on his desk that was as tall as I was. That was my last hope, I remembered thinking, and it is being crushed.

Why name an organization the Children's League if you were only going to pretend to help kids? The question stayed with me every day, through every class, through every Op. I felt its teeth tighten around the back of my neck each time I was dismissed without a second look; it had locked its jaws and wouldn't let me or my conscience go. Most of the agents, especially the ex-military guys, couldn't have cared less about the camps. They hated Gray, hated the draft, hated having their service orders change, and this was the only organization that was visible and actually trying to accomplish something aside from sending out vaguely threatening messages every few months. Trying to get them to do *anything* to help other kids was like shouting in a room where everyone was already screaming. No one wanted to listen because they had their own plans, their own priorities.

From the first night at HQ, I knew that the only way I'd be able to face myself in the future was if I tried, as hard as I could, to redirect the League's resources into freeing the kids still in camps. Over the past months, I planned, sketched, and wrote down everything I remembered about Thurmond, from the way the PSFs patrolled, to when they rotated, to two camera blind spots we'd discovered.

It became an addiction in a way; every time I sat down, it was like being around the fire pit at East River, listening to Liam talk passionately about how we needed to be the ones to help ourselves and one another, that no organization would ever get past its own needs or image to help us. He was right, of course—that had become more than apparent to me over the last six months.

I believed him. Believed *in* him. But I had also thrown him off this path when we separated, and now I needed to be the one to continue down it.

"I understand, sir."

"I've had copies made," he said. "We'll discuss it later at our senior staff meeting. I can't make any promises, but after all of the hard work you've done for us these past few months, you—"

I had no idea where that sentence was headed, and I never would. Without bothering to knock, another one of the advisers, Horse Teeth, stuck his head of silver hair in and opened his mouth—only to close it again when he saw me sitting there. Frog Lips pushed himself off the wall he'd been leaning against and said simply, "Snowfall?"

Horse Teeth shook his head. "It's what we were afraid of."

"Damn," Alban swore, standing again. "Is Professor alive?"

"Yes, but her work—"

All three sets of eyes were suddenly turned toward me, and I realized I should have left thirty seconds ago.

"I'll be in the atrium," I murmured, "if you still need me."

Alban was the one to wave me off, but it was Frog Lips's voice that followed me out of the office, carrying through the door as it shut behind me. "I *never* thought this was a good idea. We warned her!"

Curiosity kept me standing there, waiting for some kind of hint as to what they were talking about. The man was practically spitting with anger, the words pouring over his oversize lips in a torrent. I tried to remember the last time I had seen one of them so worked up, and couldn't—Jude always joked they were part robot, programmed to do their tasks with the least amount of heart possible.

"She took precautions; it's not all lost," Alban said calmly. "Let it never be said that woman lets herself be blinded by love. Walk with me—Jarvin will be back and I need to loop him in. He might have to take a team to Georgia to salvage the mess there—"

I only needed to hear the footsteps approaching from the other side of the door to know I'd gotten what little information they'd be giving. I turned as a cluster of kids passed by me on their way to the atrium, letting myself be drawn toward the back of the crowd.

When I glanced back, Alban stood outside his office door, letting the advisers work their whispers into a buzz around his ears. He didn't acknowledge me, but I felt his eyes follow me the whole way, like he couldn't quite let me out of his sight.

A few hours later, I was still in the atrium. Still waiting for a convenient slot in Alban's schedule for me to scramble someone's brain. Nico had shown up a few minutes before and brought a sandwich over to me, but between the two of us, I'm not sure who was less interested in their dinner.

Snowfall. The League was careful to give code names to every agent and every Op. At this point, I knew HQ's roster well enough to know that we didn't have a "Professor" working out of Los Angeles. But *Snowfall* . . . My brain was turning the phrase over the way it would sound out a foreign word. Slowly. Methodically. I'd had access to names of classified missions and projects well above my security clearance in the League just by virtue of the dirty work I was doing for them downstairs, but that wasn't one of them.

"Hey," I said, glancing over to where Nico was staring at his laptop screen. "If I were to give you an Op name, would you be able to search the servers for it?"

"The classified servers?" he asked. Anything less secure was a waste of the Greens' time and talents. "Sure. What's the name?"

"Snowfall. I think the agent in charge is called Professor—it sounds like a woman who might have been working out of the Georgia headquarters."

Nico looked like I had picked up my plastic tray and slammed it into his face.

"What?" I asked. "Have *you* heard of it?"

The agents sitting nearby had gotten up and left when I sat down, giving me my own private section of the round hall. I had glared at the loud table of Blues nearby until they left, too. So it was quiet enough for me to actually hear him swallow as he looked back down at his keyboard and then back up at me.

It also meant it was quiet enough to hear Jude's panting as he came bursting through the atrium's doors.

He bypassed the other tables of agents and kids and came straight toward us. Ignoring him wasn't going to make him disappear—he was the rash that kept coming back, even after six different kinds of silent treatment.

"Hey," Nico said, "what are you—"

I kept my eyes on my untouched sandwich, only looking up when he grabbed both of our arms and started to pull us out of our seats.

"Come with me," he said in a tight voice. *"Now."*

"I'm busy," I muttered. "Go find Vida."

"You have to come—" His voice was hard, low. I barely recognized it. "Right. Now."

"Why?" I asked, refusing to look up.

"Blake Howard came back from his Op."

"And I care because . . . ?"

His fingers seemed to burn my skin. "He came back in a body bag."

By the time we arrived at the entrance hall, the small crowd of spectators, senior agents, Alban, and his advisers were flocking down one level to the infirmary in a long line of drawn faces and furious whispered questions.

"You're sure?" I asked Jude as we tailed the crowd. "Positive that's what you saw?"

He gulped back a deep breath. This close, I saw the red rimming his eyelids, and I wondered if he had cried himself raw before coming to get me.

Jude's hand floated up to grip the small, nearly flat silver compass that he wore around his neck with a string. Alban had given it to him out of his personal collection of junk, along with the personal prophecy that Jude would turn into "a great explorer" and "a traveler of the first order." The kid never took it off, even though his abilities rendered the small device mostly useless. As a Yellow, Jude's touch always carried a faint electrical charge that messed with the magnet inside. It meant the colored arm always pointed toward Jude and not to the actual direction he was headed.

"I saw them come in, then Cate made me leave. But I heard Alban asking Agent Jarvin how it could have happened, and Rob said it had been an accident." Jude glanced around us, peering over my head to make sure no one was close enough to hear. "Roo, I don't think it was an accident."

When we reached the second-level landing, Nico blew right past us, heading down to the third, lowest level.

"Hey!" Jude called. "Nico—"

"Let him go," I said, half wishing I could follow him and avoid this mess altogether.

The infirmary was directly beneath the atrium, occupying the large circular space on the second level, with the computer lab directly beneath it on the third. Despite its size, it was almost always clogged with machines, beds, and the few nurses and doctors the League kept on staff for emergencies and training accidents. I'd had to go in more than once to get patched up and hadn't missed the fact that they wore special, thicker rubber gloves to touch me.

Now they wore the usual clear ones as they moved Jarvin and his other teammates in to be examined. Jude tried to go inside, his breath hitching as he reached for the door handle. I dragged him away to the observation window, where a few other agents were crowded, watching as a gurney was navigated through the beds and medical carts toward the screen at the back of the room. On top of it was a black body bag, occupied.

I squeezed up to the front of the window with Jude in time to see them unzip the bag and lift Blake Howard onto a flat metal table. A white sneaker dangled from his right foot, and the blood soaking his clothes was visible from where we were—and then nothing. Alban stepped through with Jarvin and Cate and Rob, and the screen was drawn back in place, leaving us with only shaded silhouettes.

"Oh my God, oh my God, oh my *God*," Jude was whispering, his hands fisting in his reddish-brown curls. "It was him; it was really him—"

I reached out to steady his elbow as he swayed. I hadn't really known Blake at all. I didn't know any of the kids who weren't on my team aside from their names, and my winning personality guaranteed they would never know me. But Jude and Blake had been as thick as thieves; the two of them and Nico spent most of their downtime together goofing off in the computer lab or playing some kind of game. The only time I had ever seen a smile crack Nico's face was when Blake had been with him, green eyes flashing, hands waving, telling some story that had Jude practically sobbing with laughter.

"We should go find . . . We should go find Nico, I think. I think he went to check on something," Jude finally managed to get out. I guided him away from the door and down the hall toward the stairs. We had to squeeze past the agents jogging down the hall to confirm the rumors that I'm sure were blazing through HQ.

"I have to tell you something," he whispered as we reached the stairs. "You have to see that . . . that I don't think it was an accident. I think—I think I did this."

"This had nothing to do with you." I sounded so much calmer than I felt. "Accidents happen all the time. The only one to blame is Jarvin. He's the one who picked someone who didn't have the full field training."

Jude didn't give me a chance to bail. He seized my wrist and dragged me after him all the way down the stairs to the third level. I watched the sharp angles of his shoulders move beneath his ratty old Bruce Springsteen shirt, and I noticed for the first time that he'd worn a hole through the collar. He knew exactly where Nico had gone.

It was several hours past our allotted training time in the computer room, but I was still surprised to find it so empty. Usually there was any number of Greens haunting the room, typing away at whatever computer program or virus they were perfecting. If it hadn't been a dinner hour, Nico's expression alone probably could have cleared the joint out.

"I found it," he said.

"And?" The word trembled as it left Jude's mouth.

"It wasn't an accident."

Nico was prone to ugly feelings that he chose to deal with inwardly, in what I'm sure were ugly ways. But he never inflicted those bitter, venomous thoughts on the rest of us. Not until now.

"Found what?" I asked. "One of you needs to explain what's going on *right now*."

"You said it was nothing," Nico said. "You thought it was a coincidence. You should have believed us."

His voice was acid on my already exposed nerves. I kept my eyes on the screen as he clicked on a video file. The player popped up, expanding to fit the black-and-white footage. Tiny human-shaped figures milled around a room full of long machines. I had seen enough of them to be able to identify it with a single look—a server room.

"What am I looking at?" I asked. "Please tell me you weren't stupid enough to download the security footage from the company Blake and Jarvin's team broke into. . . ."

"And give Jarvin or one of his friends the chance to remotely delete the evidence?" Nico fired back.

It was a thirty-second clip; that was all he needed. I wanted to tell him that he had taken a horrible risk in downloading it—that the computer corporation could trace it back to us—but Nico wasn't careless.

Thirty seconds. But it happened in less than fifteen.

Blake had gone into the server room, dressed in the usual black Op attire, and located the machine straight off. The sudden appearance of the guard made me jump; a nightly patrol that whoever planned the mission had been too careless to look into. Blake dodged behind the server tower, ducking around that aisle and into the next one to avoid being seen. The guard might not have noticed anything was wrong at all if Jarvin and another member of the tact team hadn't burst into the room, guns blazing.

I leaned forward toward the screen, marveling at how sharp the footage was. How we could see the two agents take cover, the careful way Jarvin moved his gun from the security guard to Blake's exposed back. The burst of light as he aimed at the kid and fired.

Jude spun away, pressing his face into his hands to avoid seeing.

Shit, I thought, *shit, shit, shit.*

Nico had clearly watched it before we arrived, but he pressed play again, and again, and again, until I had to be the one to click out of the window. He said nothing; there was no expression on his face at all. His eyelids were hooded, and I could almost feel the way he was slipping back, away, into that place that was his alone.

"This . . . I can't . . ." Jude cut in, his voice rising with every word, his palm pressed flat against his compass. "It's just these guys—they're the bad ones. The other people here care about us, and once they find out what happened, they'll punish them. They'll stand up for us. This isn't the League; this isn't—this isn't—"

"Do *not*," I said, "tell *anyone* about this. Do you hear me? No one."

"But, Roo." Jude looked horrified. "We can't just let him get away with this! We have to tell Cate, or Alban, or—or someone! They can fix this!"

"Cate won't be able to do anything if you're already dead," I said. "I mean it. Not a single damn word. And you never go anywhere alone—you stay with me, or Vida, or Nico, or Cate. Promise me that. If you see one of them coming, you have to turn back and head the other way. Promise."

Jude was still shaking his head, his fingers fussing with his compass. I tried to think of something comforting to say to him. And it was so strange how torn I felt between wanting to protect them from the truth of what the League really was and the kind of vicious cruelty it took to be an active agent, and the small satisfaction that came with knowing I had been right about them all along. This was not a safe place. Maybe it had once been for kids like us—but now the foundations were cracking, and a misstep could bring all of HQ crumbling down on top of us.

Rob and Jarvin weren't patient souls. They always finished their Ops on schedule. This would be no different, I was sure of it. Cate and a few other agents might be sympathetic toward us kids, but for how long? If we became liabilities, if it looked like we were nothing more than messes to be cleaned up, would they still stand with us?

Again and again, my mind kept turning back to the grenade, the way it had exploded directly under our feet. The way Rob had ordered us to stand exactly there.

I had the power to fix this; I knew I did. It was just a matter of getting close enough to Rob and all of his friends to do it. And, unfortunately, that was going to be the hardest part.

"Not a word," I said, turning to go. "I'll take care of this."

And I would. I was Leader. Any thought I had been entertaining about escaping once I had word on Liam and the others fled like a dream in the morning.

Jude was alive, and Nico was alive, and I was alive—and, for now, I needed to focus every ounce of my energy on keeping it that way.

FIVE

INSTEAD OF HEADING BACK TO THE ATRIUM, I HIT the stairs and went up a level, following the second floor's curve to the locker room to shower and change. HQ was cold and dingy as always, but every inch of me felt sticky and hot, like I was on the edge of a fever. A few minutes under freezing cold water would help me clear my head. I could use the rare quiet to try to put together some kind of plan to make sure one of us was with Jude at all times.

The lights were already on when I stepped inside. They had automatic motion sensors, meaning someone had either just come in or just left. I stayed completely still, my back flush against the door, listening to the steady drip of a faucet somewhere across the room. No one was in the showers; all of the yellow curtains had been thrown open, and I didn't hear the squeak of faucets or the usual explosion of pressurized water.

What I did hear was quiet—almost undetectable under the drip. A steady tapping, like a boot against cement, and a rustling, like a page turning . . .

I took the long way around the lockers, crossing one foot over the other as I ducked around the corner and stepped into the other long row of gleaming silver metal.

Cole didn't look up from where he was sitting on the bench, a folder in his hands. I caught a glimpse of the familiar sketch of Thurmond's electric fence as he turned the page.

". . . was Caledonia a lot like this, do you think?"

Every muscle in my back tensed, forcing me to stand up straight when the sight of him was enough to make me want to sink into the ground. I flexed my hands into fists at my sides and took a deep breath.

"No," I said. "Caledonia was smaller. They remodeled an old elementary school. But some of the details are the same."

He nodded absently.

"Thurmond, man," he said, dropping a finger on it. "I saw some rudimentary sketches of it a few years back, but nothing this detailed. The agents we had there didn't get to see half of this stuff—not even Conner."

I stayed exactly where I was by the lockers, waiting for him to leave.

"Alban passed these handy copies out at our senior staff meeting tonight," Cole said. "Cate got up to excuse herself halfway through. Any idea why?"

I said nothing. In truth, I did have an idea. Cate had been trying to drive me off this track for months. I had to slip the folder to Alban when she wasn't around.

"And here I thought you were a mind reader," he said with a faint laugh.

Cole's muscles were still stiff, and it was obvious he was in a great deal of pain as he stood. He tilted his head toward the showers.

I followed him into one of the shower stalls. The curtain rings screamed as he pulled the cheap plastic shut behind us, making me jump and press my back against the cement wall. It was tight quarters, and I was already feeling uncomfortable when he leaned around me, bruised face a few inches away from mine, to turn the shower on at full blast.

"What are you doing?" I demanded, trying to push my way past him. He grabbed my shoulder and held me next to him under the stream. We were drenched before Cole began to speak.

"The showers are the only place in HQ that aren't recorded. I don't want to take a chance that the other cameras in the room can pick up our little chat."

"I have absolutely nothing to say to you," I said, pulling myself free.

"And yet I have so much to say to *you*." Cole put both arms out to block me and nearly lost his balance. Unsteady on his feet, not performing up to maximum strength, tired—an easy target. I rammed my shoulder into him, but I must have telegraphed my plan. He caught one of my arms and twisted until my muscles screamed and my joints felt like they would pop. His skin was hot, like he was trying to spread the fire burning in his blood to mine.

He's one of them, he's one of them, he's one of them—

"Calm down!" he barked, giving me a hard shake. "Get a grip! I'm not gonna hurt you! I want to talk about Liam!"

Cole released his iron grip on my arm, then took a step back, holding up his hands. I was still breathing hard as I turned. The water served as a nice barrier that neither of us was willing to cross. Steam curled up around my soaking sneakers, then my knees, and then I was breathing the hot damp air into my tight chest.

"Liam who?" I said, when I got a grip on myself.

Cole gave me an exasperated look, and I knew the game was up.

"You brought him back in," I said, an edge to my voice. "I did *everything* to make sure he'd be safe."

"Safe?" Cole laughed without a hint of humor. "You think sending the idiot out into the world to be captured or killed was a kindness? He's lucky I still check for our contact procedure, otherwise the skip tracer on his ass would have happily delivered him to camp."

I couldn't help it; my fists clenched. "How did you force him to help you?"

"Why do you assume I forced him to do anything, darlin'?"

"Don't," I gritted out, "call me that."

Cole's light brows rose. "I guess that answers my question about why you lied to Alban. Care to explain how you even know my brother?"

Now it was my turn to be surprised. "Cate didn't tell you?"

"I have my suspicions, but there wasn't any mention of him in your file." Cole cocked his head to the side, a gesture that was Liam to a *T*. The second and third fingers on his left hand tapped against his leg—a nervous tic, maybe. "Alban seems to have some idea, but the others don't."

He leaned out of the stream, resting against the stall for support. Still suffering, but coasting on a wave of pride that kept him from showing it. Classic Stewart move. "Look, he wasn't working with me at all. That night—the one you saw—was the first time I had seen him since he split from the League years ago. We set up a contact procedure for emergencies, and he used it. I thought it was a life-or-death situation, otherwise I *never* would have told him how to find me."

"Because you were on a deep cover Op?" I asked. "What the hell is on that flash drive? I've never seen Alban so worked up."

Cole kept a steady gaze on my face, and, I think—because I was so furious—I was finally able to match it. "Tell me."

He blew out a long sigh, rubbing the top of his head with bandaged fingers. They'd broken every single one on his left hand to try to get information out of him. Alban had told me as much, with no small amount of satisfaction.

"I'm guessing your Op, whatever it was, ended up being compromised and that's why they stormed your apartment?"

Cole looked insulted at the suggestion. "Hell, no. My cover was impeccable. I could have stayed there forever and they wouldn't have suspected a damn thing. I only got hauled in because the skip tracer trailing Lee saw him go into my apartment and called me in for aiding a fugitive Psi kid. None of this would have happened if he hadn't shown up—I was *three hours* away from being extracted!"

"Fine, but you still haven't told me what the hell you were doing in Philadelphia. I want to know what was on that flash drive and why you couldn't find it at the end. That's what you were looking for, right?"

"Yeah," he said finally. "That's what I was looking for. The dumbass took it without even realizing it."

I balked at that. "What?"

"I was deep cover at Leda Corp, working as a lab tech on their Psi research that Gray commissioned. You heard about that program, right?" He waited until I nodded before continuing. "My original objective was just to keep an eye on how things were going. Alban wanted to know what kinds of tests they were running and if they had figured anything out, but I was also supposed to report back if I thought it was possible to extract any kids from the program."

"You did," I said, making the link so suddenly it surprised even me. "Nico—that was the testing program he was in."

Cole hunched his shoulders against the stream of water. "He was the only subject that was . . . strong enough to be taken out. The others were just . . . I can't describe it to you without it sounding like a horror show."

"How did you get him out?"

"Simulated cardiac arrest and death," he said. "The 'disposal service' the lab used was called, but the League picked him up first."

My brain was firing at a rapid pace, drumming up one horrible possibility after another. "So the intel on that flash drive—it was research that you stole?"

"Yeah, something like that."

"Something like that?" I repeated in disbelief. "I don't even get to know what's on the stupid thing?"

He hesitated long enough that I was sure he wouldn't actually tell me. "Think about it—what's the one thing every parent of a dead kid wants to know? The one thing scientists have been after for years?"

The cause of the Psi disease.

"Are you—" No. He wasn't kidding. Not about this.

"I can't give you details. I didn't have time to look through the research before I downloaded everything, but I heard the talk in the lab that afternoon when they concluded their experiments. They had proof the government is responsible for all of this." Cole clenched his hands into tight fists. "Though the fact that they shuttered the lab and permanently silenced all of the scientists the day after I got picked up by PSFs should be proof enough for most people."

"Did you tell Alban?" I asked. No wonder he was so desperate.

"Not until I got back and I had to think up some excuse for why my cover was blown. I told him I downloaded it, but it set off some silent security system. I'm sure my pride will recover from that in about a thousand years." Cole sighed. "I was afraid if I told him what I had, the agents here would already have figured out how to use it before I even got back with it."

Cole's fingers tapped at his side. "I couldn't tell him before and risk the news getting ahead of me. As disconnected from HQ as I was, I saw things were changing here. People I knew and trusted were being shuffled out to the other bases, and people I didn't like all of a sudden had Alban's ear. It was enough to make a guy a little uncomfortable, you know?"

I nodded.

"I knew if I had something real to offer Alban," Cole continued, "there'd be a good chance we could outmaneuver the agents trying to change the League. But if word got around here what it was, they'd be able to start planning ways to use it. That intel is the currency we need to buy this joint back from the bad seeds, to convince Alban to stick with us. It's the only way to outgun them at the staff table when their plan starts looking like the only real option we have."

Random bursts of Rob and Alban's argument were blasting in my ears. *Big statement. Children. Camps.*

"If this intel is so important, how did you get it out of Leda in the first place?"

"Sewed the damn flash drive into the lining of my jacket. I walked right out of the building with it, because I was on the security team, and my buddies there didn't feel the need to frisk me. I knew someone would be alerted I downloaded the files, but I used one of the scientists' network IDs," he said. "Easiest damn thing I'd ever done. By the time they figured out she was innocent, I was going to be long gone. Until my *precious* little brother saw the PSFs coming toward my apartment while I was out getting us food. He bailed and grabbed my jacket instead of his by mistake."

If Cole hadn't looked so angry about it, I'm not sure I would have believed him. I was torn between laughing and beating his head into the concrete wall behind us.

"How could you have been so stupid?" I asked. "How could you make such a dumb mistake? You've put his life in danger—"

"The important thing is that we can still get the intel back."

"The most important—" I was almost too outraged to string a sentence together. "Liam's life is more important than that stupid flash drive!"

"My, my." A feral grin spread across Cole's face. "Little brother must be a good kisser."

The rage flared up in me so fast, so strong, that I actually forgot to slap him.

"Go to hell," I said, and tried to charge past him. Cole caught me again and pushed me back, chuckling. My hand twitched at my side. Let's see who'd be laughing when I fried every single thought out of his brain.

The same idea must have crossed his mind, because Cole released me and took a step back.

"Have you at least been able to establish contact with him since you got back?" I asked.

"He's dropped off the radar," Cole said, crossing his arms over his wide chest. The fingers on his left hand tapped against his right arm. "Funny thing about him not realizing the payload he's carrying: I can't predict where he might take it or try going. It means it's next to impossible to track the little jerkass, other than to assume he's still trying to find our mom and stepdad. Chaos theory at its finest."

"Why are you telling me this?"

"Because you're the only one who can do something about it." The steam overtook his shape and he disappeared into it. "No, listen to me. I've been made. The League won't let me out of HQ. I won't even be able to run Ops, never mind search the eastern seaboard for a fugitive. Once they realize our little fictional informant isn't real, they're going to start going through the other options. They're going to ask themselves, Who's the only person these two strangers both know? They're going to ask, Who would this girl do anything to protect?"

I bristled, crossing my arms. Cole's eyes flicked down from my face to where my shirt clung to my chest, and I raised my arms that much higher. He let out a thoughtful hum, an absentminded smile stealing back over his face. "Have to say, you're not really his type. Mine, on the other hand . . ."

"You know what I think?" I said, taking a step closer.

"Not really, darlin', but I have a feeling I'm going to hear it anyway."

"You're actually a lot more worried about Liam than you are about this intel. You want me to find him to make sure he's okay. That's the real reason you're asking me instead of someone else."

Cole scoffed. His shirt had wilted against his skin with the steam, and it was impossible not to look at the strong lines of his shoulders as he set them. "Sure, fine. Run with that theory, but can you stop thinking about my brother's dreamy eyes for two damn seconds and put your head on straight? This isn't about him or me—it's a matter of making sure that *we* control the intel so *we* can bring it to Alban and shut the door on Meadows and all of his little buddies. You have no idea what kind of shit they want the organization to start pulling—what they'd do to you kids if they got their way. And they *will* if we don't figure out a way to outplay them."

You think we can keep this up without making a big statement? Rob's words echoed back to me. "What are they planning? Something to do with us and the camps?"

The water sputtered between us; the timer they'd installed to limit the use of hot water clicked off. The water was still flowing, but it was cooling off to its usual frigid temperature. And neither of us moved.

"His big idea," Cole began, his voice brittle, "is to use some of the 'nonessential' kids here and the information you provided about the camps. You know, the ones too young to be activated, some of the Greens."

"To do what?" I demanded.

"You said in your report that they don't search or pat down the kids who are supposedly pre-sorted as Green, right?" He waited until I nodded before continuing. "That was backed up by one of the other kids we pulled from a smaller camp. Meadows thinks that their intake security procedures have become lax over the past year—since there are so few kids left outside of the camps, they're usually only bringing a few in at a time. That, and the PSFs are stretched too thin at the bigger camps."

"That's true," I said. I'd noticed the number of soldiers decrease over the years at Thurmond as the camp reached maximum capacity and they closed it off to new arrivals. But decreasing the bodies present only translated to them increasing the weapons present and the willingness to hit us with White Noise anytime anyone so much as looked on the verge of acting out.

"He thinks—" Cole cleared his throat, pressing his good hand against it. "Meadows wants to strap explosives to the kids. Turn them over to the PSFs, then set the bombs off as they're being driven into camps. He thinks it'll stir enough fear and discontent among the PSFs to get them to ditch their required service."

I didn't hear the last part, not fully. There was a static in my ears that burned and burned and burned away every thought, every sound, everything outside of my racing thoughts.

"If you think you're going to faint, sit your ass down," Cole ordered. "I told you this because you're a big girl and I need your help. I know you didn't mean for this to happen, but you're in it. Knee deep. You're as responsible for righting this as the rest of us."

I didn't sit, but the dark blotches in my vision were growing, expanding, swallowing his face. "The other agents . . . they want to do this?"

"Not everyone," he said, "but enough that if Alban weren't here, it wouldn't even be a question. Read between the lines there."

Oh my God. "Cate knows about this, but. . . . she's still with him? Why would she stay with someone who could even *think* about something like that?"

"Conner is a smart woman. If she's with him, it's for a reason, and probably not the one you think. We've both seen how Meadows handles things."

"Then you know that Jarvin 'handled' Blake Howard?" I asked. "The kid he shot in the back on the Op last night?"

"You know that for sure?" he demanded. "You have some kind of proof?"

"Security camera footage," I said. "It was downloaded before anyone could wipe it remotely from here."

"Keep it to yourself for now. When you bring the intel back, we'll take that to Alban, too. Nail Meadows and the others into their coffins."

"I haven't agreed to anything yet."

"You're killin' me, kid," he said, rolling his eyes again. "You'll go and find Liam. You'll bring the intel back. There's never been any doubt in my mind about it. Because, Gem," Cole said, smiling when I rolled my eyes at the new nickname, "I know that you don't want Alban to figure out what really happened and that Liam's involved, and I know you don't want to give him any reason to invest in Meadows's plan. And I'll make sure Alban does turn his attention to freeing the camps—the *right* way, the one you suggested in your report. That's what you've been after all this time, right? The reason you put together that whole packet of info for him? I know it wasn't to give Meadows a way to turn it against you."

You can find him. Want was overpowering the cooler, quieter, rational part of my brain. *You can see him again. You can make sure he gets home this time. And you can help all of those kids. All of them.*

"If I agree to this," I started, "you have to guarantee I won't be reprimanded when I get back for taking this little joyride. And you have to swear on the terms, because if you go back on your word, I will tear every thought out of your head until you're nothing but a drooling puddle of snot. Got it?"

"Atta girl," Cole said. "That's my Gem. I'll see if I can't get you on the next Op back east. You'll have to get creative in how you ditch the Minder they send with you, but I think you're up for the challenge. Address is 1222 West Bucket Road, Wilmington, North Carolina. Can you remember that? Start there. Lee's a creature of habit; he'll try heading home to see if our stepdad left a clue about where they were headed."

I took a deep breath. My body was completely still, but everything inside me seemed to be galloping—my heart, my thoughts, my nerves.

"You can do this," Cole said quietly. "I know you can. I'll have your back the whole way."

"I don't need your protection," I said, "but Jude does."

"The beanpole? Sure. I'll keep an eye on him."

"And Vida and Nico."

"Your wish is my command." Cole gave a small little bow as he backed out of the curtain. I closed my eyes, trying to block out the familiar tilt of his smile and the way it made my chest feel like it would explode. "Pleasure doing business with you."

"Hey," I said suddenly. If anyone might know, it would be another deep cover agent. "Have you heard of an Op they're calling Snowfall? An agent called Professor?"

"I think I've heard of Snowfall, but only that it was a

project they were running in Georgia. Why? Want me to look into it for you?"

I shrugged. "If you have time."

"I have all the time in the world for you, Gem. Trust me on that."

I was still standing there when the locker room door slammed shut and the last of the water drained at my feet.

Two long, torturous weeks passed before I found the red folder in my locker. I felt each day tick by, went through the carefully structured routine of training, food, training, food, bed. I kept my head down but my thoughts moving. I was too afraid to look anyone in the face on the off chance that he or she would see the guilt or what I was planning. I almost cried, half in relief, half in panic, when I saw the Op folder balanced on my small stack of books.

The locker room was roaring with speculation around me, one voice bleeding into another. Someone had been brave—or stupid—enough during our lesson for the day to ask Instructor Johnson what they had done with Blake's body and whether we'd have any kind of service for him. Nico had gone green around the gills, but Johnson had only waved the question off.

Team Two's Leader, a Blue named Erica, was loudly airing her opinion that he was still down in the infirmary being studied, but another, a Green named Jillian, insisted she had seen them take a body bag out through the Tube a few days before.

"They obviously buried him," she was saying.

I stood by my locker, reading the folder behind the cover of the door. I could hear Vida a few feet away, laughing loudly at something another Blue had suggested. When I turned, I craned my neck around, trying to look into her locker. Good. Nothing but the messy heap of shirts she had shoved in there. She would be here. I could tell Jude and Nico to stay close to her—no one would try anything with her there, not even Jarvin. There was too much sting in that honeybee.

I opened the folder again, letting my eyes skim down each line. Please be East Coast, I thought, please be back east. . . . I could get to North Carolina so much easier from Connecticut than I could from Texas or northern California.

OP ID: 349022-A
TOD: 15 Dec 13:00
Location: Boston, MA

Massachusetts. I could work with that. Some of the train lines were still running.

Objective: Pull Dr. P.T. Fishburn, Director of Administration Department of Genetics and Complex Diseases Harvard School of Public Health; disable lab.

I felt my stomach clench—"Pull," meaning I would interrogate him there in Boston at a League safe house, or, if he proved to be uncooperative, we would bring him back to the nearest base. My job. "Disable," meaning fry, destroy, demolish. The tactical team's job.

Tact Team: Beta Group
Psi: Tangerine, Sunshine
Minder: TBD

"Oh," I whispered, feeling leaving my hands completely. "Hell no."

I left the folder in my locker and slammed it shut, twisted my wet hair back into a loose bun. I was out before anyone could notice I was gone. It was three in the afternoon—if Cate wasn't in a meeting, she would be in her room, most likely, or in the atrium.

A drip of water fell from my hair onto my cheek and I swiped angrily at it, plowing through the hanging strips of plastic that were, in theory, supposed to help insulate what little warmth we had in HQ. I glanced up at the low ceilings to avoid making eye contact with yet another cluster of agents, stepping off to the side to allow them to pass.

The hair on the back of my neck rose with each step that echoed behind me, keeping pace with my own.

There was someone behind me. There had been since I stepped out of the locker room.

The heavy steps and the throaty gulps of air made me think it was a man. I glanced up as I passed one of the steel beams overhead, but whoever was following me was doing it at the exact right pace. I couldn't see his reflection, but I could feel him behind me. Feel every ounce of his disgust for me cutting through the hallway's damp chill, gripping the column of my spine.

Don't look, I thought, clenching my jaw, *just keep going.* It was nothing; my mind was playing tricks, like it loved to do. *It's nothing. It's no one.*

But I could feel him hovering behind me, like his fingers were trying to smooth down the goose bumps on my skin. There was no stopping the sudden upswing of my heartbeat. I knew what I could do and that I had enough training to fight someone off, but all I could think about was Blake Howard's shoe dangling off his pale, stiff toes in the infirmary.

I found the double doors I'd been looking for and burst into the atrium, half out of breath.

They were in the middle of setting the round tables and folding chairs again, returning the space to its usual use as a rec room. Here and there, I saw agents dressed in their finest League sweats, dolling out playing cards, watching the news on the TV screens, or even playing with a mismatched chess set.

Cate came in through the opposite set of doors, cutting a sharp image in her unusually polished navy skirt suit. Her blond hair was twisted back into a tight bun. She absently bumped into an agent sitting at a nearby table, murmuring a faint apology. I didn't realize she was looking for someone until her eyes landed on my face.

"There you are," she said, jogging over the best she could in her heels. I opened my mouth, but she held up a hand to quiet me. "I know. I'm sorry. I did everything I could to change Alban's mind, but he insisted."

"He's not sixteen yet!" I said. "He isn't ready—you *know* that; we all do! Are you trying to turn him into the next Blake Howard?"

I might as well have socked her in the face. Cate reared back, a look of horror filtering through her usual mask of calm. "I fought to get him off this, Ruby. I assigned Vida to go with you, but someone convinced Alban that Jude should be activated early. They need a Yellow for the security system, and Alban said it didn't make sense to bring in two different teams on a simple Op."

We were attracting a few stray glances. Cate took my arm and steered me over to an empty table, forcing me to sit down.

"You have to try harder," I insisted.

Our little Sunshine didn't perform well in high-pressure situations, and he had the tendency to wander off to explore shiny things when he needed to be conducting surveillance. The only thing he knew about using a firearm was that the end with the hole needed to be pointed away from his face.

"He'll be fifteen in a few weeks." Cate kept one hand on mine. "I'm sure—I'm sure it'll be fine. This is a good, straightforward Op to let him dip his toes in the water."

"I could do it by myself. If this involves sabotaging some kind of electrical equipment, I can—"

"My hands are tied, Ruby. I can't keep pushing back against Alban, or he'll start seeing me as a problem. And—" She took a deep breath, absently smoothing first her hair, then her skirt. Her voice sounded stronger when she spoke again, but she wasn't looking at me now. "The only comfort I have in all of this is knowing that he'll be with you and that you'll look after him. Can you do that?"

Her skin was hollow beneath her high cheekbones, like she had just recovered from a long illness. I leaned forward, noticing now the way her makeup had collected in the new, fine lines around her eyes—how dark the circles were that rimmed her eyes. She was only twenty-eight and was already starting to look older than my mother had when I left her.

Sometimes it felt like this was where I found the real Cate—in the pauses. I wouldn't describe our relationship as "good," because it was built on a lie, and a pretty cruel one at that. She could say one thing and mean something else entirely. But right then, surrendered to the quiet, her face told me everything. I saw the struggle in the lines of her face and knew whatever words came next were more for the agents around us than they were for me.

"I have to go up north," she said in an even voice, "for an assignment."

"Up north," meaning the surface streets of Los Angeles. Meaning it probably had something to do with the Federal Coalition. Cate was a senior agent now. She'd earned her wings. If they were sending her up there, it was to do something important for Alban.

"So you won't be coming with us?" I asked.

Cate glanced behind me and waved at whomever she saw standing there. I felt something cold drip down the back of my neck, though my hair was nearly dry.

"There you are," Cate said. "I was just about to tell Ruby that she'll be in good hands on the Op. You'll keep a careful eye on my girl, won't you?"

Rob had never, not since the first day I met him, willingly touched me. He, like the others, knew better. Still, I watched his hands where they hung at his sides, dark hair curling on the backs of his knuckles. My throat tightened.

"Don't I always?" Rob said with a faint chuckle.

Cate stood, her moon-pale face glowing in the artificial light. "See you later, gator."

It was her stupid, childish send-off, the same one she always gave us when she left. The others wouldn't have hesitated to finish her little rhyme; Jude had thought up the little good-bye as a play off her call sign. Now, I could barely choke the words out.

"In an hour, sunflower."

As soon as they walked away, I saw Cole sitting at the other end of the room, an open book on the table in front of him. By the dark look on his face, it was more than clear he'd heard the entire conversation.

You said you would protect him. Was there really no one in the entire League I could trust? These people couldn't be counted on for anything. All of their promises bled into lies.

Cole shook his head, turning his palms face up on the table. It was a weak, silent apology, but at least he understood. Shifting this one single piece on the board was enough to change the whole game.

SIX

THEY SMUGGLED JUDE AND ME INTO BOSTON IN broad daylight, riding in the jump seats of a fat-bellied cargo plane. It was an older model than the one we'd used to fly back from Philadelphia, and its smell lent some possibility to Jude's theory it had once been used to move dead meat.

I watched the enormous crates in front of us, trying to ignore the way they creaked under the strain of the straps holding them in place. All of them were marked with Leda Corporation's elegant golden swan, which felt like some kind of horrible wink from the universe. The rational part of me knew it didn't mean anything—that it wasn't some bad omen. We flew on Leda Corp's planes all the time. They'd realized the benefit of playing nice with both Gray and the Federal Coalition, which meant they had special "privileges" to travel to and from California to move their product. As uncooperative as always, Gray had the brilliant idea to try to starve the Federal Coalition out of California by forbidding imports into the state and exports out of it—unfortunately for the rest of the country, California was where most of the fresh produce was, and they had easy access to the oil they were drilling in Alaska.

The Federal Coalition was our matchmaker, though. We got to piggyback on flights like this in exchange for serving as their knife in the dark. Alban saw it as a "fair trade" for the intelligence we'd gathered and countless Ops we'd run on their behalf over the years, though I knew he wanted more. Specifically: respect, money, and the promise that he'd be given a place in their new government once Gray was out.

On the other side of the plastic-wrapped heap of crates was Beta Team, laughing, laughing, laughing at some joke that had been lost to the steady snarl of the engines.

I pressed the backs of my freezing hands against my eyes, trying to ease the throbbing there. What little heat was still circulating in the cargo space must have been clinging to the ceiling, because I felt exactly none of it. I sank down lower in my seat, wrapping the black puffer coat as tightly around my center as I could with the seat belt in the way.

"Deep breath in," Jude was chanting, "deep breath out. Deep breath in, deep breath out. You are not in an airplane; you are floating through the sky. Deep breath in . . ."

"I think you actually have to be taking deep breaths for that to work," I told him.

The plane dipped, only to bob up a second later.

"Is that—" His voice cracked. "Was that normal?"

"It's just a little turbulence," I told him, trying to pull away from his grip. "It happens on every flight."

Jude had strapped a tact team member's helmet to his head and a pair of goggles over his eyes. I didn't have the heart to tell him that if the plane went down, a head wound would be the least of his worries.

God. He couldn't handle the stress of a *plane flight*.

This was a mistake—I should have fought harder, argued, swayed someone to get Jude off this Op. Back at HQ, the thought of having to bring him along to search for Liam had been frustrating, an annoying dose of reality to swallow, but now . . . now I was just scared. How was he going to handle the pressure of escaping Rob and Beta Team if he couldn't sit still for five minutes? If his imagination had already stolen his courage and had made a run for it?

Maybe I can find a way to leave him with Barton, I thought, rubbing my forehead. The problem was . . . how did I know that Barton wasn't one of the agents who sided with Rob in arguing for attacking the camps? How did I know that any of his teammates wouldn't gladly put a bullet in Jude's skull, neat and easy?

"This is going to be great. It's going to be so cool." Jude's Op folder was stained with specks of whatever he had eaten for dinner the night before, and he was looking a little soft around the edges.

I wanted to scream. *Scream*. It was another mouth to feed and another back to protect. Jude was the living embodiment of a distraction. But what was the alternative here? Sending him back to that hellhole, hoping he'd still be there, alive, when I got back and Cole put his plan in action?

No. Jude was dead weight, one I was going to have to

carry on my shoulders the whole way, but I was stronger now. I could do it. I'd find Liam, and I'd keep both of them safe—because that was the only option. That was the only one I was willing to accept.

"Bartlett. What do you think he does?" Jude asked. The pages fanned under his fingers. "I recognize the other names. Frances is nice—she gave me a candy bar once. I like Lebrowsky and Gold and Fillman, too. Cool guys. They taught me how to play solitaire. And I like Leader, too. I'm glad Barton got promoted. But who the heck is Bartlett?"

"Don't know, don't care," I said, focused squarely on the medical crates in front of me. Actually I did know who Bartlett was—some new guy who transferred in from the Georgia base of operations. I had overhead some of the Green girls in the locker room talking about what a "fine specimen" he was, but they had spotted me and split before I could find out anything useful.

Jude was humming now, one foot tapping out a frantic rhythm against the mats underfoot. The compass hanging around his neck had slipped out from under his jacket and was swinging in time with him. I don't think he had stopped moving the entire five hours we were in the air.

"Bartlett got his training at West Point—do you think that means he's good?"

"If you have the personnel files in your folder memorized, why are you asking me?"

"Because people are more than what a piece of paper or computer file says about them. I don't really care that Bartlett's specialty is knife fighting—I mean, don't get me wrong, *holy crap*, but I'd rather know why he joined the League, what he thinks about that decision now. Favorite food—"

At that, I turned to look at him, half amazed, half horrified. "You think his favorite food is more important than knowing his preferred method of killing you in a fight?"

"Well, yeah, it kind of is—"

I couldn't stop myself, and I couldn't explain why anger flashed so fast and hot through me. "You want to know about Beta Team?" I could hear my heart hammering in my ears. "For the next twelve hours, they are the only six people who won't be trying to kill you. But they don't have to protect you, especially if it interferes with the Op. So follow Leader's orders and keep your damn head down. *That* is all you need to know."

"Jeez," Jude said, blinking. "Not every adult in the world is trying to bury us."

My tongue was trapped behind my clenched teeth. *You think killing you is the worst thing they could do to you?*

"I just want to know people," he explained. "What's wrong with that?"

"Well, sorry," I said. "Most of them won't want to know you."

"No, I mean . . ." He waved his hands through the air, like that was going to unravel the mystery of whatever he was trying to say. "It's just that nowadays people are so quick to boil you down to bare bones of info and upload you into a system, you know? And I think no one can ever really know another person unless you really pay attention." He stopped, stretching his long neck out to glance around, but our minder for the Op was busy playing a game of cards with Frances.

"Like, look at Rob. His file is perfect. He went to Harvard, was an Army Ranger, then an FBI agent for a while. He's six feet tall exactly and weighs two hundred and three pounds. He knows how to use firearms and speaks decent Spanish. But that . . . Nowhere in there is anything that hints at the fact that he . . ." Jude trailed off. "I don't want to just see someone's face; I want to know his shadow, too."

I don't think Jude had ever lost anyone before Blake. He had heard about agents killed on this mission, or on that raid, or in that explosion—but once you fully settle into the special brand of pain that comes with being separated from someone you know down to the marrow of his bones, you learn not to try.

"Yeah?" I asked. "And do you know my shadow?"

Jude looked away, down to where the heels of his comically large boots were bouncing against the mat. "No," he said, so quiet it was almost lost to the thousands of miles of crystal blue air beneath us. "Sometimes I don't think I've even really seen your face."

It didn't bother me. Feeling left my hands, but it was only because of the cold, not the ice that had somehow manifested between us in the span of a few seconds. My jaw only clenched to keep my teeth from chattering, not to bite back an ugly, frustrated noise. I didn't need to be liked, or wanted, or cared for—I didn't need friends, and I certainly didn't need the kid who once brought down the League's entire computer network tripping over his own huge feet, trying to guilt me into being something I wasn't. I was fine. Just a little cold.

I burrowed down just a little farther into my coat, watching him fidget out of the corner of my eye. He was wringing his hands red.

"Beta Team is a good group," I said finally. "They'll treat you right as long as you follow their orders. Alpha doesn't give a damn, so try to make sure you're paired with another kid who can watch your back. Delta's run by Farbringer, and he likes kids."

"Yeah?" Jude said, but the life had gone out of his voice. He was studying the stretch of black fabric clinging to his knees. "Ruby," he said, so softly I almost didn't hear him over the roar of the plane. "Did Rob pick me for this Op so he could kill me?"

I met Rob for the first time right after Cate had gotten me out of Thurmond. The two League agents had planned to rendezvous at an abandoned gas station, both bringing with them any kids they'd managed to free. He had claimed he couldn't get his batch of kids out and had to escape alone to avoid being detected by the camp controllers. Cate, who was so tangled up in him, had believed it instantly. But one slip, one careless touch, and his mind had opened to mine. I had seen the truth of it.

On the nights I didn't stay awake terrorized by thoughts of what had happened to Liam and Chubs and Zu and the girls I had left behind at Thurmond, Rob's memories came slithering in. I would see the hooded boy in the ground, his entire body convulsing as the agent shot him at point-blank range. I saw the girl's face, saw her lips move to beg for mercy, and the way the Dumpster had rattled when Rob had thrown her body into it. And by the end, I would wake up feeling sick, not just for the loss of life, but because it had felt like I had killed them myself. Talk about knowing someone's shadow—try *being* his shadow.

"I can't stop thinking about Blake. I think about him every day, all the time. We should have told someone," he said. "Jarvin and the others would be kicked out—the League would go back to the way it was before . . . before all this happened. They're the bad ones. If you get rid of them . . ."

That wasn't always how infections worked. Sometimes the rot spread too far to be removed with one single cut. Rob and Jarvin and the others might only be a few of many. I was so tempted to tell him the truth then, everything Cole had told me, but panicking him just to make a point was by far the stupidest course. If this was going to work, he couldn't know what the plan was in advance. I couldn't give him any chance to slip up and give us away to Rob and the others.

"You'll be fine," I told him. "I'll be there the entire time."

He was shaking; I don't think he heard a single word that left my mouth. "How could they do this? What did we ever do to hurt them—why do they hate us that much?"

I closed my eyes at the sound of Rob's booming laugh cutting through the air.

"Why don't you try to sleep?" I said. "We're going to be flying for a few more hours. There's no reason we both have to be tired."

"Okay," he said. "I just wish . . ."

"You wish what?" I asked.

"Can we keep talking instead?" He confessed it to his knees, awkwardly drawing his feet onto his seat.

"You really can't stand sitting in silence, can you?" I asked. "It actually kills you a little bit, doesn't it?"

It was a long time before he replied, as if he were trying to prove me wrong. "No," he said. "It's just that I don't like the quiet. I don't like the things I hear there."

Don't ask. Don't ask. Don't ask. "Like . . . what?"

"I hear them fighting, mostly," he whispered. "I hear him screaming at her and the way she used to cry. But it's . . . I hear it through closed doors. My mom, she used to put me in her closet, you know, because his temper was better when I was out of sight. I don't remember what she sounded like normally, just the way she sounded then."

I nodded. "That happens to me sometimes."

"Isn't that so weird? It's been, like, eight years, and I hear them, and I think of how dark and tight it was, and it feels like I can't breathe. I hear them all the time, like they're chasing me, and I can't escape them, not ever. They won't let me go."

I knew he was exhausted, and I knew firsthand what exhaustion did to your mind. The tricks it played on you, just as your defenses were dropping one by one. Ghosts don't haunt people—their memories do.

"Will you talk until I fall asleep? Just—I mean, just until I fall asleep. And can you maybe never tell anyone about it, like, ever?"

"Sure." I leaned my head back against the seat, wondering what on earth I could say to calm him down.

"There's this story I used to really like as a kid," I began quietly, just loud enough that he could hear it over the roar of the plane's engines. "About these rabbits. Maybe you've heard it before."

I started at the beginning, the escape. Fleeing through the forest, meeting a new danger at every turn, the desperation that came with trying to protect everyone when you could barely take care of yourself. The boy with the bottomless dark eyes, the betrayal, the fire, the smoke. And by the time I realized I had told him my own story, Jude was fast asleep, tucked firmly into dreams.

Here's the thing about places like Boston: no matter what they were before, no matter the look of the population, no matter what businesses had flourished once, no matter what great person was born there, the city that people knew was gone. It was the loved one you saw in a rearview mirror, growing smaller and smaller the more time and distance you put between you, until even its shape became unrecognizable.

Red brick buildings remained firmly rooted in the ground, but their windows had been bashed in. The grass on the Common was dead in patches, overgrown in others, and scorched to ruin where there had once been trees. Grand townhouses were locked and shuttered, ice and old snow clinging to their dark stones. There was a crowded lane open on each road for cars and bikes to inch their way down, but many of the old, overlapping streets were filled with makeshift tents and the people huddled inside of them.

It was bizarre to see the bright, colorful bursts of old umbrellas and children's bedsheets propped up as makeshift shelters. Some of the worse-off folks were exposed to the freezing air with nothing more than a sleeping bag or a wall to lean against.

"I don't get it," Jude said, staring through the tinted windows. None of the streetlights were on, but there were enough fires burning that we could see the scene—and the first flurries of snow—from the back of the ambulance a hospital had oh-so-helpfully exchanged for the Leda Corp supplies we had dropped off.

"A lot of people lost their homes and housing when the markets crashed," I said, trying to be patient with him. "The government couldn't pay off its debt, and because of it, these people lost their jobs and couldn't afford to keep what they owned."

"But if everyone everywhere is like this, why didn't the banks just let everyone stay where they were until things got better? Isn't there something we should do to help?"

"Because that's not the way the world works," Rob called from the driver's seat. "Get used to it." He was wearing a dark blue EMT uniform, and he seemed to relish his ability to flash the lights and sirens when people in the streets didn't move out of his way fast enough. Sitting up front with him was the one member of Beta Team who had been assigned to serve as support on our half of the Op—his name was Reynolds, and I only had to take one look at Jude's face as Reynolds and Rob slapped each other's backs to know he had been one of the agents Jude had overheard plotting against us.

The rest of Beta Team were three blocks ahead of us, all seven crammed into the back of an old pickup truck. They were dressed as protesters of some kind—street clothes, ragged hair, Red Sox caps, jackets thick enough to hide the weapons tucked underneath.

This professor we were looking for lived in Cambridge, just over the Charles River. Harvard's medical school, where he was conducting his research, was happily situated in the middle of Boston proper. Rob had decided, in his questionable wisdom, to divide the Op into a two-prong simultaneous assault. Beta Team would handle "disabling" the lab, and Jude and I would break into the target's house and "pull" him in for questioning.

At least, that's what Rob thought.

We backtracked to the Longfellow Bridge, crossing the river to the sound of Jude's eager questions about baseball, the river, what the sticky substance was on the floor of the ambulance, how we were getting home, until Barton finally buzzed the comms in our ears.

"This is Leader in position, ready to commence Op at twenty-two thirty. What is your status, Minder?"

"Five minutes out from the Goose's nest," Rob answered, and I felt the ambulance accelerate under me. My anxiety took that exact moment to wake up. I sat a little straighter, bringing my knees to my chest and wrapping my arms around them.

"Are we connected to Home Front?"

"Home Front here. Line is secure, tracking both units now. Okay to proceed at twenty-two thirty. Satellite feed shows

minimum interference at Target Two. Minder, we're showing considerable activity in your sector."

I'm not sure who was more disgusted to hear him referred to as "Minder," Rob or me. He didn't have a team of kids like Cate, but anyone who supervised a freak kid on an Op was slapped with that title.

"There's a protest in the Old Man's Yard," Rob said. I looked up, scrambling on all fours to get to the back window. He was right. We were passing by the university's tree-lined park, with its crisscrossing paths. Hundreds, maybe even thousands, of bodies clustered around a large bonfire, ignoring the sleet falling around them. Signs and drums littered the nearby patches of snow, the only thing between the protesters and the small ring of disgruntled police officers that had them surrounded. People seemed to be hovering at the edge of the small park, as if looking for a way to break through the line of uniforms and guns.

"What are they protesting?" Jude whispered, his breath fogging up the glass. I didn't answer, just motioned for him to get down. I began counting the blocks we passed—one, two, three, four, five.

The ambulance came to a shuddering stop a short distance away from the professor's pleasant little white house with a slanted gray slate roof. Rob unhooked his seat belt and stood, stretching slightly as he climbed into the back.

"We're in position," he said, pressing a hand to his ear. I felt his eyes slide over to me, but I kept mine fixed firmly on Jude, who had started shaking again.

This kid is going to get himself killed, I thought, pinching the bridge of my nose.

"*You have the all clear,"* said the agent monitoring the Op at HQ. *"Goose Egg is a go."*

"Roger," Barton said, and Rob echoed him.

He was looking a little ragged, a dark beard coming in along the edge of his square jaw, but Rob's eyes were alert. He tossed the boy the other EMT jacket and a cap—like that could hide the fact that Jude looked about two years younger than he actually was.

"Don't say a word, don't fidget, and follow my lead exactly, then get your ass back here," he told the boy. Then, turning to me, he added, "You know what to do?"

I met his dark eyes straight on. "I do."

Rob needed Jude to disable the house's alarm system and man the gurney to get the professor out on the chance that any neighbors got nosy and opened their curtains at the wrong moment. We were supposed to take him around the city in a long fifteen-minute lap so I could work him into a state of cooperation, then dump him back on a sidewalk, his memory erased of the encounter. If he proved to be too hard to crack, Rob had a safe house we could bring him to for more . . . painful methods of persuasion, I guess.

Rob opened the back door, letting in a freezing draft of air. He and Reynolds pulled the gurney down, along with a duffel bag. Jude was wringing his hands again.

I grabbed his arm just before he jumped down after Rob. "Be careful."

Jude gave me a little salute and clenched his teeth in a way that made me think he was trying for a reassuring smile or trying not to puke all over himself. "Later, gator."

The door slammed shut behind them. *In an hour, sunflower.*

In all of the wild daydreams I'd had about the day I'd finally pack it up and leave, none of them had come close to resembling this moment. I didn't expect to feel as calm as I did. The first time I had escaped from Cate and Rob, the fear had flamed up fast and true, moving my feet before my brain could catch up. I hadn't known where I was going or how I was going to get there. I had just run. It was only dumb luck that I had found Zu and the others.

I couldn't rely on luck this time. I didn't have time to feel afraid of what would happen if I were caught. The steady composure I felt made me feel so much stronger than any of the wild, raw emotions I had surrendered to in the gas station. I had something to accomplish and people to protect, and no one—especially not Rob Meadows—was going to keep me from it so long as there was breath in my body.

The porch light flipped on as the three of them passed under it. Jude threw one quick glance back over his shoulder at me, then disappeared around the side of the porch to the little power box that controlled the house's electricity.

When the porch light switched off and Rob bent over the gold door lock, I shrugged out of the League's heavy black coat, pulling out a lighter and the Swiss Army knife I had stashed in one of the pockets and tucking them in my boots. Liam's old leather jacket wouldn't keep the cold out for long, but it didn't have a tracking device in it.

I climbed up to the driver's seat and popped the door open. My boots had just landed in the snow when Jude came around the back of the ambulance.

"What are you—?"

I bolted forward, clapping a hand over his mouth. His eyes went wide in panic until I pressed a finger to my lips. Jude was too confused to process what was happening. I had to take his wrist and drag him behind me, letting the ambulance's bulk block us from view.

"We're inside," came Rob's rough voice in my ear. *"Status, Leader?"*

"On schedule, Minder."

I glanced up at the street sign—Garfield Street—and tried to get my bearings. I had to put as much distance between Rob and us before he realized we were gone; I could outrun him on foot, but I couldn't outrun a car . . . especially not with Jude. If we could make it back to the protest, we might be able to lose him and Reynolds in the crowd. Rob wouldn't think to look for us in the one place we had a decent chance of being caught. He was a brute, and a vicious one at that, but he wasn't very imaginative.

Jude panted beside me, looking slightly frazzled but otherwise all right. The wind was knocking around his hat and tugging at mine. I pulled the black knit cap down snug over my ears, trapping my loose long hair and muffling sounds from both prongs of the Op.

The cold was like nothing I had ever felt in Virginia. It was sharp, a persistent clawing at every bare inch of skin. I tried picking up my pace into a faster run, blinking back the tears and snow flurries, but Jude was struggling to keep up as it was. Patches of ice snapped underfoot, branches hidden beneath the old snow crushed as I trampled through the trees separating the houses and buildings. South, south, south—I just needed to keep heading south, and I'd find Harvard Yard, and the protesters, and escape.

"Target acquired. Tangerine, is the perimeter clear?"

Jude jerked toward me in wild fear, but I shook my head in warning.

Rob's voice went down my spine like a match against a matchbook. The fire it lit was small, but it was burning through the tight control I had over my voice. "Oh yeah," I said after I pressed a finger to my comm. "The coast is all clear."

I knew the moment Rob opened the ambulance door, the very second he found us gone. His end of the line went silent, even as HQ and Barton were requesting status updates from him. I could see his face in my mind, white, rapidly turning purple with the effort to hold back his fury. A small smile curved the corners of my mouth. He couldn't call out for me without revealing that he had lost me in the first place. A Minder's job, above anything else, was to mind the freaks under his care.

"Tang—" Reynolds began to say, only to be sharply cut off.

"Hey, Rob," I said in a low, even voice. I saw the light from the bonfire in the yard, the new orange hue of the sky. Jude caught the back of my jacket, his long fingers twisting in the leather as he struggled to keep up with me. Snow was falling harder now. I pulled the hood of the fleece I was wearing under my jacket up over my head, stuffed my hands into my pockets, and crossed the last street. "I got a question for you."

"Roo," Jude whispered. "What are we doing? Where are we going?"

"Tangerine, keep all non-Op transmissions off the line," came Barton's voice.

Good. I wanted him to hear. I wanted all of them to hear this.

The ring of police and National Guardsmen had been busted open, and the protesters gathered there were streaming past them, signs clutched in their hands, drums beating. A midnight march, I guess, though I had no idea for what. And judging by the variety of signs I saw, they weren't really sure what they were protesting, either. The draft that forced them into PSF service? President Gray's unwillingness to negotiate with the West Coast government? The general state of awfulness spreading like poison over the entire country, as the pollution had over Los Angeles?

Most of the faces around us were young but not teenagers. A good portion of the country's universities and colleges had been temporarily shut down due to lack of funding, but if a few still had money left, I guess Harvard would have been one of them.

WE ARE YOUR TIRED, YOUR POOR, YOUR HUDDLED MASSES . . . read the sign next to me.

I let them get ahead of us, trailing far enough behind that the others had less of a chance of hearing the chanting over the comm. I waited until they had cleared out of the square before touching the comm again to activate the microphone.

"I just want to know—what were their names?"

"Tangerine." Rob's voice was tight, and he sounded slightly breathless. *"I have no idea—"*

"Tangerine, cease—" The woman at HQ didn't sound particularly happy with me, either.

"What the hell is going on, Minder?" Barton was still listening, too.

"Those two kids you took out of that camp, the night before we met," I said, keeping my eyes straight ahead on a young guy with dreadlocks waving us all forward. "The boy and the girl. I'm sure you remember them—it must have taken a lot of effort to get them out, never mind to tie their hands and feet that way."

Jude stared at me, his dark brows drawn together in confusion.

"It doesn't make any sense to me. You got them out, and then you killed them in that alley and left them there—why? What was the point? What did they say or do to make you so angry? That girl was begging you. She didn't want to die, but you took her out of that camp, and you executed her. You didn't even take that boy's mask off."

I clenched my fists to get them to stop shaking. And in that brief second, suddenly it was Alban's voice crackling in my ear.

"What's all this?" He took a deep breath. *"I need you both to meet Leader. If you don't want to return to HQ with Minder—"*

"We're not coming back to HQ," I said, "until he's gone forever."

It was a dangerous play; if Alban took the bait and booted Rob, there was still a good chance that others in his bloodthirsty pack would retaliate against the kids at HQ. But—*but*—now that Alban knew Rob was hostile, he and the agents we could trust would be on the lookout for more of that attitude, at least for the next few weeks. Jarvin and the other conspirators would feel safer knowing that Jude was away and couldn't rat them out. And I didn't need forever—a few weeks and I would be back with all we needed to force them out.

"Rob, listen, I just want to know their names. I want to know if you even bothered to ask before you killed them."

"Do you think this is a game? Stop lying, goddammit! When I find you—"

"You better hope you never find me," I said, ice edging each word. I didn't even have to close my eyes to see that girl's face. I felt her walking beside me, her eyes open, forever fixed on the barrel of the gun and the hand that held it steady. "Because what I'll do to you will be so much worse than a bullet in the skull."

I didn't wait to hear the response to that. I yanked the comm out and dropped it, letting the feet behind me smash it and scatter the pieces. I motioned for Jude to follow me as I jogged to catch up to the protesters. We were swept into the flood of people pouring down Massachusetts Avenue's wide berth. I was being jostled from all sides—arms were being thrust around, people were yelling and screaming, and it was the safest I had been in months. I threw a glance behind me as I surged forward, looking for Jude's pale face—there he was, eyes wide, cheeks and nose pink with the blistering cold. I was coasting on a wave of simmering power and control. I had gotten us away, and now no one was even looking at us.

I felt Jude grab the back of my jacket again and guide us forward, flowing with the crowd. The drums up ahead rattled to life with a frantic rhythm, and for the first time, I felt a twinge of panic. I thought I heard someone calling my name behind me, but even the chanting was drowned out by the fury gripping my mind.

The crowd around me was still growing, and the farther they moved down the street, the more they seemed to work themselves into a frenzy of excitement. The same chant was singing through their blood, *More, more, more, more*. That was the only thing they had in common. The only thing they all wanted—more food, more freedom, more money, more.

I realized where we were headed almost immediately: back into the heart of Boston. The Massachusetts Avenue bridge was up ahead—and so were the familiar blue and red flashing lights of the police cars that were blockading it.

The protesters didn't stop.

There were dozens of policemen in riot gear, National Guardsmen taking aim, and not a single one of the protesters stopped marching forward. I felt my feet slow and was shoved forward by the momentum of the crushing wave behind me.

The policeman in the center of all this, a grizzly old man staring the rest of us down, held up a megaphone. "This is

Sergeant Bowers of the Boston Police Department. You are trespassing in violation of Mass General law, chapter two sixty-six, section one twenty, and are subject to arrest. You are unlawfully assembled. I demand you immediately and peacefully disperse. If you do not immediately and peacefully disperse, you will be arrested. This is your only warning."

I didn't see the first stone that was thrown. I didn't even see the second or the third. But I heard the clatter of their impact against the clear shields of the riot police.

"Fire, then!" someone was yelling. "Fire! Fire! *Fire!*"

The girls around me picked up the word and began screaming it. "Shoot, shoot, shoot!" was the only rival to the chant.

I took a step back, elbowing my way through the crowd's throbbing crush. They wanted the police to open fire on them? To make a point, or—

To capture it on video. I saw the handheld devices clutched in their stiff, frozen fingers. The snowflakes clung to the cameras' glassy eyes, following the path of every rock, snowball, and brick that was launched toward the men and women in uniforms. I ducked, holding my arms over my head as I fought my way to the back of the herd. A stray elbow nailed the back of my head, and it was enough to knock me out of my haze.

I reached behind me, grabbing Jude's arm as I turned—but the person holding my jacket was a short Asian girl with thick black glasses, who seemed just as startled to see me as I was to see her.

"Sorry!" she shouted. "I thought you were my friend—"

Dammit. I whirled around, scanning the nearby crowd. *Where is he?*

The gunshot was the only thing sharp enough to cut through the chanting, the only thing strong enough to silence them. The girl and I both jumped back but were roughly shoved aside by the people still marching forward behind us. Maybe the officer or soldier thought the threat of it would break up the crowd, but they had seriously misjudged the anger powering these people.

The protesters at the head of the pack were clearly used to this kind of bullying. I glanced back over my shoulder; they were struggling against the clear shields blocking their paths, clamoring over the hoods of the police cars. The unlucky ones were yanked back and beaten into the ground by batons.

"Jude!" I called, my guilt nearly cutting me down at the knees. *"Jude!"*

The first can of tear gas released with a sinister hiss, but it wasn't enough to shift the crowd. They only launched themselves toward the officers at a run. I felt someone try to grab my arm and haul me back around to face it with him, but I yanked myself free.

Bad plan, I thought, choking on the poisoned air. *Bad, bad, bad plan, Ruby.*

It was dumb luck I even saw him then; I had started turning the other way, only to catch a glimpse of a curly head of hair out of the very corner of my eye.

The blue EMT jacket was flapping in the wind, one sleeve torn with a ragged edge. Jude was standing on his toes, one hand on the nearest streetlight to keep himself upright, the other curled around his mouth as he shouted, *"Ruby! Roo!"* over and over again.

I saw now the way that fear fed anxiety and turned it into chaos. Jude's shape went out of sight, tucked into a cloud of tear gas, hidden behind the sudden stampede of bodies trying to get away from the guns, from the smoke, from the bridge. People were screaming and the gunfire hadn't stopped. There were new noises, too—a helicopter hovering above us, casting a light down over us. The whirring of its blades drove some of the smoke away, clearing the way for the National Guardsmen to rush toward us. For the first time, I noticed more than one black uniform in the mix.

If it had been a clear night, if my eyes weren't streaming with tears, if I could have heard anything other than the thrumming thunder of my own heart, I would have noticed it sooner. The air seemed to vibrate against my skin, and I caught the whiff of ozone a second too late to do something about it.

"Jude, don't!"

The line of streetlights along the stretch of road began to buzz, their orange lights bleaching to a molten white a second before they blew out together, sending a shower of glass and sparks down on the already terrified protesters.

I'm not sure anyone recognized what Jude was, not until the lights from the nearby buildings switched on after months or years of darkness.

I reached him half a second before the National Guardsman and his gun did, throwing my shoulder into his chest and driving us both to the ground. The impact blew the air from my lungs, but I scrambled up, shielding him from the butt of the soldier's rifle. With one blow, it cracked against my skull and sent me spinning into darkness.

SEVEN

THE GROUND GRUMBLED BENEATH MY CHEEK, A LOW clattering that underscored the dull pain in my brain. Feeling was slow to come back to my limbs. I took a deep breath, trying to swallow the taste of iron and salt from my dry tongue. Matted hair stuck to my neck in clumps. I tried to reach up and brush it away only to realize that my hands were trapped behind me, something sharp digging into the skin there.

My shoulders ached as I twisted to readjust myself on the van's grimy floor. It was dark in the back, but every now and then a flash of light would come through the metal grating separating the front seats from the rest of the vehicle. Just enough for me to see that the uniformed driver and the man sitting in the passenger seat were dressed in black.

Damn. My heartbeat was in my ears, but I didn't feel afraid, not until I saw Jude sitting pin-straight on one of the benches, his hands bound and his mouth gagged.

While the PSFs had bound my hands, for whatever reason—probably because I was already unconscious—they hadn't used a gag on me, and I was grateful. Bile rose, burning the back of my throat, and the only way to make the whole thing worse would have been to choke on my own vomit. I could feel the anxiety in me building to a slow and steady beat of *Not again, not again, I can't go back there, not again.*

Calm down, I ordered myself. *You're no good like this. Get a grip.*

I couldn't get my jaw to move, to say something to get Jude's attention. It took several precious moments for him to notice that I was even awake, and when he did, his body gave a huge jerk of surprise. He tried in vain to rub the cloth out of his mouth with his shoulder. I shook my head. If we were going to do something, it would have to be quietly.

Jude's fear was an actual, living thing. It hovered over his shoulders, black, thunderous. He began to shake violently. He tossed his head, trying to draw desperate gulps of air into his lungs.

He's having a panic attack. The thought was a quiet, sure one, and I was surprised by how much resolve it flooded into my veins.

"It's okay," I whispered, hoping the guys in front wouldn't hear me over the chatter of their radios. "Jude, look at me. You have to calm down."

He was shaking his head, and I could read his thoughts clear as if I had actually been inside it. *I can't, not here, not now, oh God, oh God.*

"I'm here with you," I said, bringing my knees up close to my chest. It was painful, but I managed to drag my arms up around my legs, so my bound hands were in front of me.

"Take a breath through your nose, a deep one," I said. "Let it out. You're all right. We'll be fine. You just need to calm down."

And he needed to do it sooner rather than later. My mind was going in circles trying to think of where the nearest camp was—upstate New York? Wasn't there one in Delaware, out near a whole town of abandoned farmland? Where were we now?

I held Jude's gaze with mine. "Calm down," I said. "I need you to focus. You have to stop the car. Do you remember Saratoga?"

If there was only one good thing I could say about the League's methods of training, it was that the instructors were creative. They tended to have a supernatural sense of what kinds of situations we would find ourselves in, including a practice run-through of almost this exact scenario. In that simulation, Vida, Jude, and I had been on a make-believe Op in Saratoga and had been taken hostage. Vida and I had fought our way out of the van and both ended up "dead," shot in our escape. Instructor Fiore pointed out everything we should have done, which included Jude doing something other than cowering in the back of the car.

I saw him take a deep breath and nod.

When I had traveled with Zu, the biggest hurdle she had to overcome was controlling her Yellow abilities. She had worn rubber gloves for the better part of our time together to avoid zapping machinery or the car, but we'd seen her lose control twice without them to block her charged touch. Jude, though—he'd been trained. He'd had the benefit of being around other Yellows who were willing to help him learn. Although he ran at a speed that was ten times faster than everyone around him, he kept his abilities in check. The scene out by the protest had been the first time I'd ever seen him slip, and in such a huge, horrible way.

He closed his eyes, and I rolled over onto my knees, trying to brace myself.

I felt the huge swell of electricity, felt it ripple along the hairs of my arms. It crackled in my ears, heated the air until it burned white.

It was too much for the car's battery to take. The car didn't even shudder as it died; it was like it had slammed into an invisible wall. I went sliding toward the front grate with the force of it. The two PSFs cried out in confusion.

But I didn't think it through. Cars on the East Coast were rare, with the sky-high prices of gas and the cost of upkeep. I had just assumed that there would be no one else out driving, that the van would stop, and I would find a way to take the PSFs out one at a time.

I saw the flood of white headlights at the same moment the PSFs did. The force of the impact as the semi truck clipped the front of our van sent us spinning fast and wild. The airbags exploded with a scent like burning. I slammed into the bench opposite of Jude, who went tumbling to the floor.

The van went onto its right tires, and for a split second I was sure we'd start rolling and that'd be the end of the story.

Instead, the van slammed back down onto all fours. Over the hiss of the smoking engine and the cusses one of the PSFs was hollering, I heard the semi truck's tires squeal as it slid to a stop.

"—Flowers, Flowers!"

I shook my head, trying to clear my double vision as my hands felt along the ground for Jude. They didn't stop until they met with his boney, warm ankle and I felt him twitch in response. Alive. It was too dark to see if he was in one piece.

"Flowers! God*dammit*!"

If it had been anyone else beside the PSFs, I might have felt sorry for the trouble we'd caused them. One of the men in uniform—Flowers, I guess—was slumped forward in his seat, his deflating airbag smeared with blood.

"Shit!" The driver was pounding on the steering wheel. He felt around the crumpled dashboard until his fingers latched onto the radio. Jude had done his job, though. Anything electronic within fifty feet had been fried. The man kept trying to click it on, kept saying, "This is Moreno; do you read?"

The PSF must have remembered protocol, because he reached over and forced the door open, jumping out into the snow. He'd have to secure us, make sure we were all right.

I was ready for him.

My legs were shaking like a foal's as I dove over Jude's prone form, beating the soldier to the door. He had his gun in one hand but needed the other one free to unlatch the back door. I had my handcuffs looped over his neck and his face between my hands before he could let out a gasp of surprise.

The soldier, Moreno, was rattled enough that his brain didn't put up much of a fight. Taking control was smooth, easy, without the slightest whimper of pain in my mind.

"Take . . . our handcuffs off," I ordered. I waited for him to reach up and do it before ripping the gun out of his hand. Jude let out a blissful moan as their metal grip released.

"Turn around and start walking back toward Boston. Don't stop until you reach the Charles. Understand?" My finger curled around the trigger of the gun.

"Walk back toward Boston," he repeated. "Don't stop until you hit the Charles."

I felt Jude at my back, swaying, but kept the black handgun trained on the PSF's head as he walked away, disappearing into the swirling clouds of snow, deep into the night. My arms began to shake, both from the frigid cold and the stress of keeping myself upright.

The truck driver took his time, but he appeared at the driver's side window, pounding against it. "Is everyone all right? I've called for help!"

I signaled for Jude to stay back. The PSF was still visible as he made his way down the highway despite his dark uniform and the pitch-black road. The truck driver spotted him immediately. I counted off his steps as he ran after him, calling, "Hey! Where you going? *Hey!*"

At the sight of him, Jude slipped the cuffs from his shaking hands, and they clattered as they hit the floor. When the truck driver spun on his heel, I was already waiting for him, gun up, hands steady.

The truck driver's face went stark white under his beard. For a moment, we did nothing but stare at each other, the snow collecting in his wiry hairs. His jacket was a vivid red plaid and matched the knit cap he had pulled down low over his ears. Slowly, he raised his hands in the air.

"Kids," he began, his voice shaking, "oh my God—are you guys—"

Jude's hand tightened around my shoulder. "Roo . . ." he began uncertainly.

"Get lost," I said, nodding toward the gun in my hands.

"But . . . the nearest town is miles away." I saw the driver relax, his hands dropping back down to his sides now that the shock had worn off. Clearly he thought I wasn't capable or willing to shoot him if it came down to it. I didn't know whether to be furious or grateful about it. "Where are you going to go? Do you need a ride? I don't have much food, but . . . but it'll be warm, and—"

Maybe the driver thought he was being kind. Jude obviously thought so. I barely caught the back of his jacket to keep him from jumping out of the van and throwing his arms around the man in weepy gratitude.

Or maybe the driver just wanted the $10,000 per head he'd get for turning us over.

"I need you to *get lost*," I said, switching off the gun's safety. "Go."

I could tell that he wanted to say something else, but the words caught and stuck in his throat. The driver shook his head once, twice, and gave me a weak nod. Jude let out a strangled protest, lifting a hand in his direction, like he could compel him to stop. The driver was slow to turn and slower to walk away.

"What did you do that for?" Jude cried. "He was just trying to help!"

The thin layer of ice on the road cracked as I jumped down, snapping me back to full alertness. I didn't have time for explanations, not when the need to run was singing through my veins. The night was long and the piles of snow in the heavy woods around us unmarred. We would have to move fast and cover our tracks.

"We help ourselves," I said, and led him into the dark.

The distant specks of headlights down the highway did nothing to ease up on the chill that had dug its fingers into my chest as we ran. I kept hoping to come across a car we could use, but every single one that had been abandoned on this stretch of road had a dead battery or no gas. Five minutes of charging through the knee-deep snow of the nearby woods, following the edge of what I assumed was the Massachusetts turnpike, finally turned up an exit sign for Newton, Massachusetts, and another one telling me it was forty-five miles to Providence, Rhode Island.

This was what I knew about the state of Rhode Island: it was south of Massachusetts. Therefore, we were going to Providence. And then I was going to look for a sign for Hartford, the only city I knew in Connecticut, and then one for New Jersey. And that was how my fourth grade education was going to get me down the eastern seaboard, at least until I found myself a goddamn map and a goddamn car.

"Wait . . ." Jude sputtered, gasping for breath. "Wait, wait, wait . . ."

"We need to move faster," I warned. I'd been dragging him along behind me, but I'd carry him if I had to.

"Hey!" He let his body go limp, dropping to his knees. I jerked back with the suddenness of it, almost losing my balance.

"Come *on*!" I snapped. "Get up!"

"No!" he cried. "Not until you tell me where the heck we're going! Barton's probably been searching for us all night!"

The highway was lined on either side by hills and pockets of dense trees, but we were still far too exposed. Every time a passing freight truck bathed us in white headlights, I had to steel myself all over again.

I took a deep breath.

"Do you have your panic button?" I asked. "Jude—look at me. Do you still have it?"

"Why?" he asked, patting around his pants pockets. "I think so. But—"

"Toss it."

His thick brows were drawn together, the tip of his long nose red and running with cold. He used his free arm to swipe it against his coat. "Ruby, what's going on? Please, just talk to me!"

"Toss it," I said. "We aren't going back to LA. At least not yet."

"What?" Jude sounded small, far away. "Are you serious? We're . . . ditching?"

"We *are* going back—eventually," I said, "but we have another, special Op first. We need to keep going before someone comes looking for us."

"Who assigned it?" Jude demanded. "Cate?"

"Agent Stewart."

Jude didn't look convinced, but I had him on his feet now.

"I have to recover information from one of his sources," I explained, trying to make it sound as mysterious and dangerous as I could. And it worked. The nervous look he'd been wearing changed to one of interest. And a small, fizzing excitement.

"It's vital to the mission of the League, but I couldn't let Barton know the real reason for leaving. I had to figure out a way to make sure that Rob was gone by the time we get back."

"You should have told me!" Jude said. "From the beginning—I could have handled it."

"It's classified. A need-to-know Op," I said, adding, "a dangerous one."

"Then why the heck are you taking me?" he asked.

"Because if you go back now, they'll kill you just like they killed Blake."

I felt ashamed—the feeling snuck up on me, gripping me by the throat. I'd taken him without giving him any kind of choice, and then simplified the truth to make this reality go down that much easier. Hadn't I hated Cate for doing the exact same things to me? Had she felt as desperate to get me to agree as I did with Jude now?

Jude slowed again, looking at me like he'd never seen me before. "I was right," he whispered. "That is why he picked me. I was *right*."

"Yeah," I admitted. "You were."

Jude nodded, working his jaw back and forth, trying to get the words out. Finally, he reached into his EMT jacket and pulled out the familiar black button, tossing it aside.

"It was dead anyway," he muttered, pulling back out of my grip. "I fried that car and everything in it, remember?"

Right. Of course. The trackers in his clothes would be dead, too.

"All right," he said, his voice sounding stronger. This was the Jude I had been counting on—the one who thought all Ops would be as cool as the video games he played with Blake and Nico.

I reached over and brushed the snow powder from his hair and shoulders. "You have to follow what I say exactly, understand? We're going completely off the grid, and no one can know where we are. Not Cate, not Vida, not even Nico. If they find us and bring us in, we ruin every shot we have at this Op—at making sure the League is a safe place."

As quickly and simply as I could, I laid the Op out for him. Everything, from where we were headed first to what Rob and the others had been planning. I gave him a sliver of the truth: that I had been traveling with Liam for a while, but we'd split up before Cate brought me in and I'd lost track of him.

Would it really be so awful to just tell him the whole truth? I was surprised there was a part of me that was even tempted to talk about those last few precious moments in the safe house. It just . . . didn't make sense to complicate everything by letting him into that moment of good-bye. I was the only one I wanted living in it, thinking about it, dreaming of it. And, to be honest, I needed him to trust me absolutely now, more than he ever had, if this was going to work. If I told him what I had done to Liam, every look Jude would give me from that moment on would be tainted by the fear I could do it to him, too. If he could even bring himself to look at me at all.

This was the kid who had sat with me for every meal, when half of the League was too afraid to look me in the eye. He didn't flinch when I touched him; he waited for me to get back from Ops to make sure I was safe. As annoying as it had seemed to me then, I had never thought about what it would be like to lose it. Him.

Jude listened to it all, strangely calm for him. He didn't react at all when I told him what was on the flash drive Liam was carrying. At first I thought he had stopped paying attention, but at the end of it all, he nodded and simply said, "Okay."

"What's wrong?" I asked. I was fully aware of how stupid that question was. What *wasn't* wrong? "Are you feeling okay? Nothing bumped, bent, or broken, right?"

"Oh, uh, no, I'm fine, all in one piece, at least." He knocked on the top of his head. "It's just I was wondering . . ."

"About?" I prompted.

"About before. *Before*-before, I mean." He turned to look at me. "Did you have to deal with the PSFs a lot at your camp?

It's just—you were so calm. Don't get me wrong, when you were all, *Get lost!* it was pretty epic, but you didn't seem, you know, scared."

My brows rose. "You think I wasn't scared?"

"I wasn't scared, either!" Jude added quickly. "It just made me wonder about before you came to HQ. . . ."

"Are you trying to ask me what I was doing before Cate brought me in?"

"Well, yeah!" Jude said. "We all wondered—there were rumors, but they seemed really hard to believe."

"Really."

"Really." Seeing that his line of questioning was a one-way road into Silenceville, USA, he changed the subject as awkwardly as he could manage.

"Do you really think the scientists discovered what caused it?" Jude asked. "Idiopathic Ado-blah-blah-blah?"

"Idiopathic Adolescent Acute Neurodegeneration," I supplied. Otherwise known as the reason most of us died and the rest of us turned into freaks. How could he ever forget what those letters stood for?

"Right, whatever," Jude said. "Oh man, can you imagine what the League could *do* with that?"

I could hear the hope underlying his voice and felt my heart break, just that little bit. How could I tell him it would be a miracle if we actually found Liam, let alone found him still in possession of the flash drive?

"I think about it a lot," he said, "don't you? There's a lot I don't understand, and Cate and the others don't really give me anything to work with, but it's sort of cool to think our brains somehow mutated. I mean, it would be slightly cooler to know how and why that happened, but still cool."

I used to think about it, when I was at Thurmond and there was very little else to focus on outside of my own misery. I spent countless days staring up at the bottom of Sam's bunk, wondering how and why any of this had happened to us. Why some of us were Green and others Orange and others dead. But almost from the exact moment Cate got me out, I forced myself not to dwell on it. There were more important things to focus on—like surviving. Not being recaptured. Liam, and Chubs, and Zu.

"I know it's dumb, but I've been trying to puzzle it all out. Sometimes I really do think it's a virus, and then other times . . . I mean, how could it be a virus or disease if it barely spread outside of the US?" Jude was saying. "What was different about us from those other kids, the ones who died?"

All fair points. All distracting points. "Let's not get ahead of ourselves here. We have to find Cole's brother first."

Jude nodded. "Man, that's going to be so . . . weird. Meeting him, I mean. I remember when he ditched. No one even noticed he was gone until they did the headcount at the end of the simulation."

I glanced over. "You knew Liam?"

Jude glanced up, his amber eyes widening slightly. "Oh, no, not, like, personally. Knew *of* him. He was training at Georgia HQ, and Vida and me have always been in LA. Liam's the reason they moved all of the Psi training to California, though. Less chance for people to go missing when everyone is underground, I guess."

Right. Of course. Liam wouldn't have been in California. I was surprised at how much better the thought made me feel, knowing that he hadn't been forced to live in that dank hole in the ground.

"Is Liam one of the people you search for on the PSF network every week?" Jude asked. "Nico mentioned it once. Are we going to look for them, too?"

I felt my patience snap like the icy layer over the snow we were crunching through. I don't think it ever stood a chance against tonight.

"Because it's none of your business!" I hissed. "You wouldn't even be here if you hadn't waded into such deep shit!"

"I know, okay? I *know*!" Jude said, throwing his hands up. "You don't like us, you don't like the League, you don't want to be Leader, you don't want to talk about yourself or Cate or training or your favorite food or your family and friends. Fine. *Fine!* Wait—what are you doing?"

I thought I had imagined them as we were walking; they'd been little more than distant, unidentifiable shapes. But as I guided us down the crest of the next hill, the woods suddenly pulled back, revealing a small, cramped neighborhood street.

I heard Jude slide to a stop at the edge of the icy street when he saw that these houses had lights on. That there were cars in the driveways and people moving behind the window curtains, ready to mark another Wednesday as finished.

A man with a beat-up truck was trying to plow the street, struggling through the thick blanket of snow. I nudged Jude back behind me again, eyes on the house directly across the street, an idea worming its way up through my haze of exhaustion. There was a small silver sedan parked in the driveway, but, more importantly, I had seen a blurry shape through the little window of the house's front door.

Sure enough, as soon as the plow passed, a woman stepped out and turned to lock the door behind her. Her hair was an ashy blond, shot through with strands of silver. It peeked out between the emerald knit cap and black coat she was wearing. I saw a flash of her dress as she buttoned her coat up over it. The cut and design made it look like something a waitress in a diner would wear.

She swung her keys around her fingers as she walked, glancing up at the night sky and the snow falling in soft breaths around her. I waited for the *beep beep* of the doors unlocking before I moved.

"Come on," I said, grabbing Jude's arm.

The woman heard us coming. Her back went rigid with panic when she saw my face reflected behind hers in the car's dark window. I saw fear chase confusion in her eyes and took the opportunity to slip one of my cold hands up the sleeve of her coat to her warm, bare flesh. She smelled like pineapples and sunshine, and her mind was just as bright. It was a quick touch; it had to be—so fast I didn't even experience the usual flood of memories. I wasn't even sure I had her until she blinked slowly at me, her eyes going glassy.

"Get in the car," I said to Jude, looking over my shoulder to where he stood, mouth agape. "We have a driver."

The benefits of coercing someone to drive us were twofold: she couldn't report the car stolen and phone in the plates, and, even better, she could pay tolls and get us waved through security stations set up at town borders by the National Guard or police. After taking two seconds to really think it through, I compelled her to take us to whatever was the nearest transportation hub. In a perfect world, Amtrak and all of its many lines would still have been around, but the economic crash did such a bang-up job exposing its many flaws, it lasted only a year before collapsing. Now the government ran two electric trains up and down to the major cities on the eastern seaboard each day, mostly to shuttle National Guardsmen, PSFs, and senators around. The Elite Express, they called it, and tickets were priced to match its name.

Train jumping would be *a lot* riskier than driving a car, but I couldn't shake the nightmarish image of us having to stop and siphon gas every ten miles. It would eat away every valuable hour we needed. We could luck out and get a nearly empty train, at least for a few cities. If it looked too dangerous, or the train started to feel too crowded with unwanted eyes, we could always bail early. I had a way of making us disappear.

"Turn on the radio, please," I said. "One of the news stations."

Jude and I were crouched behind the two front seats, nestled in the hollow of space between them and the backseat. It was awkward to sit that way and still be reaching around to touch her to maintain the connection. I took a deep breath, slowly pulling my hand away, but focusing on that shimmering line of connection between our minds.

Maybe this was how Clancy worked his way up to not needing a physical touch to establish a mental connection with a person—by letting go for a little longer each time.

The woman obeyed, and the speakers behind my head burst to life with the sound of a catchy commercial jingle. Amazing—they were still advertising pool supplies, even though a good portion of Americans had lost their homes.

She flipped through the channels, skipping over music and static until she reached a man's droning voice.

"—the Unity Summit, as it is being called, will be held on neutral ground in Austin, Texas. The state's governor, who recently denied allegations of aligning with the Federal Coalition in California, will moderate the talks between several key members of President Gray's staff and the Coalition to see if common ground between the rival governments can be reached in time for the completion of the construction on the new Capitol building in Washington, DC, on Christmas day.

"President Gray had this to say about the possibly historic event." The voice changed abruptly from the grave tone of the reporter to the silky, easy tone of a president. *"After nearly a decade of tragedy and suffering, it is my sincerest hope that we can come together now and start making strides toward reunification. My advisers will be presenting economic stimulus plans over the course of the summit, including programs to jump-start the construction industry and return Americans to the homes they may have lost in economic calamity of recent years."*

Calamity. Right.

"Do you think Gray will finally give up the presidency if they agree to the terms?" Jude asked.

I shook my head. I didn't know Gray personally, but I knew his son, Clancy. And if the son was anything like the father, Gray definitely had another motive for wanting this summit to happen. The last thing he would want is to lose control.

Clancy. I pinched the bridge of my nose, forcing the thought out.

The nearest Amtrak station ended up being the one in Providence, Rhode Island—an enormous concrete building that might have once been beautiful before the times and graffiti artists found it. I glanced at the clock that had been built into its lone tower's face, but it either wasn't working or it had been 11:32 for the past four minutes by the dashboard clock's estimate. There were a few cars in the nearby parking lot, but at least three dozen people piled off a city bus that rumbled up to the drop-off lane.

I touched the woman's shoulder, surprised to feel her jump. Her mind was very quiet now, as milky white as the sky outside. "We need you to buy us train tickets that'll get us to North Carolina—as close to Wilmington as possible. Do you understand?"

The loose flesh on the woman's cheeks quivered slightly as she nodded and unbuckled her seat belt. Jude and I watched her stagger her way through the new snow, heading for the automatic sliding doors. If this worked . . .

"Why are we trying to take the train?" Jude asked. "Isn't that going to be dangerous?"

"It'll be worth it," I said. "It'll take us twice as long to drive if we have to keep stopping for gas."

"What if someone sees us or there are PSFs on the train?" he continued.

I pulled the knit cap off my head and threw it to him, along with the thick white scarf I had wrapped around my neck. When we were seated on the train, I'd be able to cover him up with my jacket, but until then . . . we would just have to find a dark corner.

The woman came back faster than I expected, her eyes on the ground, something white clutched in her hands. She opened the driver's door and slid into the seat, letting in a breath of freezing air.

"Thank you," I said when she handed me the tickets. Then, as Jude stepped outside, I added, "I'm really sorry about this."

I only looked back at the car once as we headed into the station. I had told her to wait two minutes, then drive back to her house. The woman—maybe it was my tired eyes playing tricks on me or the whorls of snow between us—but when the headlights of a passing car flashed through her windshield, I swear I saw the gleam of tears on her cheeks.

She had been able to get us tickets to Fayetteville, North Carolina, which could have been clear on the other side of the state from Wilmington as far as I knew. Worse, the boarding time was listed as 7:45 A.M., a good ten hours away. It was too much time to kill, too much of an opportunity to be caught.

The inside of the station wasn't nearly as ornate as the outside of it was. There was too much concrete for it to be truly beautiful. I found us a bench in a corner, facing a wall of unplugged arcade games, and we planted ourselves there and didn't move, not for anything. The overnight trains came and went, feet shuffled behind us, the arrivals-and-departures board clicked and spun and beeped.

I was tired and hungry. There was a coffee cart still open by the ticket windows, the only thing standing between the clerks and sleep, but I didn't have any money, and I wasn't desperate enough to use my abilities on the poor guy stuck manning the cart.

Jude dozed against my shoulder. Every now and then, the automated announcer would come over the speakers with an update on the time or delayed trains. But the silent gaps between them seemed to grow longer with every hour that we waited, and I was beginning to regret the decision more and more. Somewhere around four o'clock, right when I was teetering at the edge of exhaustion, the doubts came storming in. By the time we got down there, I wondered, would Liam still be in North Carolina? He was resourceful when he needed to be. He could cover a huge amount of distance in the time we sat here—in the time it took us to get down there.

There had been cars in the parking lot. Maybe the smart thing to do was boost one of those and try avoiding the tollbooths and National Guard check stations set up around the bigger cities? No, because that would also mean being spotted by the thousands of highway cameras the government had installed for the exact purpose of looking for kids like us.

It wasn't the *whoosh* of the sliding doors opening that snagged my attention but the heavy steps. Now and then a few people would drift in and out of the station, and a good number of homeless had been allowed to sleep in the heated space for the night, provided they took up a corner and not a bench. But this sounded like a good number of feet; the rubber soles of their shoes squeaked as they struck the tile. Out of the corner of my eye, I saw the window clerk sit up straighter.

I just needed one glance over my shoulder to confirm it. Black uniforms.

I grabbed Jude and pulled him down off the bench with me, putting it between us and the dozen or so uniformed PSFs pooling in the center of the station.

"Holy crap," Jude was whispering, "holy, holy crap."

I put a hand on his shoulder, keeping him firmly planted next to me. I knew what he was thinking—the same questions were flashing through my mind. *How did they find us? How did they know we would be here? How do we get out?*

Well, the answer to the last question wasn't to freak out and panic; in one of those rare, fleeting moments when I was grateful for the lessons the League had taught me, I took a deep, steadying breath and began to reassess the situation.

There were eleven uniformed PSFs taking their seats on the benches near one of the bus gates. Two were women, and both got up to check the monitors. Their hair was neatly braided or combed back, but the men's looked freshly buzzed. More importantly, at their feet were eleven camo duffel bags, not guns.

A guy at the center of the group stood, laughing loudly as he made his way over to the vending machines. The others called after him with their orders of Doritos or gum or Pop-Tarts. They weren't scanning the premises; they weren't questioning the guy in the ticket booth. They were in uniform, but they weren't on duty.

"They're new recruits," I told Jude. "Hey, look at me, not them. They're taking one of the buses to go report for duty somewhere. They're not looking for us—we just need to find a quiet place to sit until our train comes. Okay?"

I turned my back toward the soldiers, scanning our section of the open room for a door that might be unlocked or a hallway I hadn't noticed before. I barely felt Jude stiffen again beside me, but I *did* feel him yank on my braid, turning my head back toward the sliding doors just as Vida led Barton and the rest of Beta Team into the building. All of them were in street clothes, eyeing the PSFs who hadn't seemed to notice them at all.

What's she doing here? What are any of them doing here? There was no way . . . no way they could have tracked us. . . .

"Holy crap, holy crap, holy crap," Jude whispered, clutching at me. At least he understood the danger of being brought back to HQ. I didn't have to explain again that Vida wasn't here to help us. I looked around frantically from the arcade games, to the Amtrak kiosks, to the nearby women's restroom. This was so much worse than even *I* could have imagined. Half of me just wanted to sit down and give in to the overwhelming urge to burst into full-on tears.

I didn't stop to break down the plan to Jude, who looked near tears himself at whatever he had just seen. There really was no plan. I dragged him after me—literally dragged him—into the small family restroom.

The door squeaked as I pushed it open with my shoulder. There were no windows in the restroom, no vents big enough for us to climb out. There was one toilet, one sink, and no way out aside from the way we came in. I reached up and switched off the lights before flipping the lock over. No more than a second later, the door rattled as someone yanked on it.

I sat down on the floor and I drew my legs up against my chest, trying to steady my breathing. Jude collapsed down next to me. I pressed a single finger to my lips.

We couldn't hide in there forever—someone, eventually, would realize the restroom shouldn't be locked and come with a key. So I counted. I counted out four minutes in my head, stopping and restarting every time I heard someone's boots clobbering by.

"Come on," I whispered, forcing Jude up onto his feet. "We're going to have to run."

We didn't even get two feet.

Vida pushed herself up from where she leaned against the wall directly across from us, her brows rising along with the gun in her hand.

"Hi, *friends*," she said sweetly. "Miss me?"

EIGHT

EVERY SINGLE WORD THAT FILTERED THROUGH MY mind was of the four-letter variety. "What are you doing here?"

The triumphant smile I expected to see there never made an appearance. Instead, she gave me a once-over and snorted. "Wow, your danger instincts are set on high-fucking-alert, aren't they? And they said it would be hard to find you."

I pulled the gun out of my waistband slowly and took careful aim. I let the invisible hands inside my mind unfurl, imagining them launching toward her, driving into her thoughts. But . . . nothing. Nothing at all.

"How cute," she said. "I have one of those, too!"

For one long beat, neither of us moved; her dark eyes flicked down over me, the same way they did when we sparred in training. Sizing me up. Wondering if I'd really do it.

Neither of us saw him move; one minute Jude was cowering behind me and the next, he had sidled up to Vida, one hand on her shoulder. "I'm really sorry about this."

A tiny arc of blue electricity leaped up from the walkie-talkie clipped to her belt, stroking Vida's skin softly, like a snake's exploring tongue. Vida must have realized what he was about to do at the same moment I did, but she couldn't move away fast enough. Her eyes rolled back as she crumpled to the ground.

"Oh my God," I said, dropping down beside her to feel for a pulse in her neck.

"I just gave her a little love zap," Jude said, every hair on his head standing on end. "She'll—she'll come around in a minute, but, Roo, tell me I just did the right thing. I don't want to leave her here. I don't think we should go without her, but she wasn't going to help, and we have to find Liam, and she would have told, and he's important—"

"You did the right thing," I said. "Jude, thank you. *Thank you.*"

"What are we gonna do now?" Jude whispered, following me down the hallway to a room marked EMPLOYEES ONLY.

A quick look around told me that the tact team had divided—half were upstairs, visible in the glass offices above us, and half were heading out onto the train platform. What PSFs weren't sprawled out and still on the floor were bound together in an unwilling huddle of black.

We followed the long hallway to its end, narrowly missing a station worker going into the employee break room. I kept my eyes focused on the double doors at the very end of the stretch of concrete, too scared of what I would see if I tore my gaze away.

I opened the right door as quietly as possible, motioning for Jude to follow. It shut with a faint *click*. It took me two precious seconds to figure out we were even looking at the bus terminal, and another two to see the old man in a navy uniform come hustling around the corner, a huge, wet coffee stain all down his front.

Every bone in my body went hollow as I grabbed Jude's arm and hauled him closer. The man came up short of us, his already wide, panicked eyes going just that bit wider as he gave us the once-over. For one long, terrible moment no one said anything at all. There was only the sound of gunfire from inside the station and the screech of car tires from the parking lot on the other side of the building.

I raised a hand out toward him on instinct, but Jude caught it and pushed it down.

"Are they . . . ?" The man—Andy, his nametag said—was having a hard time choking the words up. "Are they soldiers?"

"They want to take us in," Jude said. "Please, can you help us?"

And then Andy did the absolutely last thing I expected him to.

He nodded.

We rode under the bus in the luggage compartment for the first twenty minutes of the trip, until the train station and the PSFs and Vida were too distant to be caught in his rearview mirror. It was freezing and uncomfortable to be tossed around under there; we'd slide across the cold metal with every single turn, hunched over our knees and disoriented. I let Jude loop his arm through mine, adding my little bit of body heat to his.

He was muttering something under his breath. I felt him shaking his head, his curls brushing my shoulder. Finally, when the road quieted, I heard what he was saying. "She's never going to forgive us."

"Who?" I asked, my hand squeezing his arm. "Cate?"

"No. Vida."

"Jude . . ." I began. The guilt had clocked in at record time.

"We did the same thing her sister did to her," Jude explained, cutting me off. "We just left her. She's going to hate us forever."

"What are you talking about?"

Jude turned back toward me, rubbing his eyes with the back of his hand. "Well, you know about Cate, right? How she was our CPS case worker?"

Something heavy and slick rose in my stomach.

"You know," he said quickly, "Child Protective Services? Okay, maybe not."

"You and Vida both?"

"Yeah," he said. "You seriously had no idea about that? Cate never told you what she used to do?"

No, but then again, it wasn't like I had ever asked. "So she, what, pulled you out of foster homes and brought you into the League?"

"Sort of." He leaned back against the door, sliding against me with the next big turn. I had to strain to hear him now. "When IAAN happened, a lot of kids got turned out of their foster homes—the ones who, you know, didn't die. It was just a bad situation all around, because there was no one to even claim them for burial or anything like that. Cate said a lot of the case workers had a hard time trying to find out what had happened to their kids. She found me before someone turned me in for the reward or I got picked up in the Collections."

The Collections had been a series of mass roundups of the survivors of IAAN who hadn't already been sent to camps. Any parents who felt like they could no longer care for their freak kids or wanted them to enter the "rehabilitation" programs of the camps just had to send them to school, and the PSFs stopped by to round them up. It was the first big organized intake of kids. The next step was forcing them into the camps, whether the parents wanted them gone or not. Involuntary Collection.

"That must have been a really scary time."

I felt him shrug, but he struggled to get the next words out. "It's . . . Well, it's over. It was better than being at home, anyway. Dad was a real winner."

I forced my eyes on the road. The way he said it, with such forced brightness . . .

"And Vida . . . ?"

It was like I had turned a key inside of him, or he was too exhausted to try to keep it all buried. "I don't know what the deal is with her family. She has an older sister, Nadia, who was taking care of her for a while. Cate lost track of her—I guess they were squatting in some building? Vida woke up one morning to find her sister gone and the PSFs there. She thinks that her sister called her in to get the reward money."

"How did Cate get to her, then?" I asked.

"The PSFs had packed about ten kids into this bus to ship them east to the camp in Wyoming, but the League got there first. You know this story, right?"

I did, actually. The League had found themselves in possession of five kids they had no idea what to do with, so they started the training program. I knew Vida had been with the League for a long time, but I had no idea she was one of the Wyoming Five.

"Wow."

"I know."

I didn't know what to say, what I could say, so I settled on, "I'm sorry."

Jude made a face. "What are you sorry for? You didn't do anything. And besides, we were the lucky ones. Cate's the one who has the hardest time. I don't think she ever got over the kids she lost. Especially the ones who died in the fire."

"What?" I breathed out.

"It was this group home she was in charge of keeping an eye on," Jude explained. "A few of the kids started showing signs of Psi abilities and the person in charge just freaked out. Cate doesn't know if one of the kids accidentally started it or if the woman did it herself—I guess she was really, really, *really* religious, but, like, crazy religious. When the police found her, she kept saying how she had done God's work."

"That's . . ." There was no word for how horrible that was, so I didn't try.

"Anyway, that's the whole story." Jude shrugged. "The beginning, at least."

I held my breath as the bus stopped at what I assumed was a checkpoint and someone, probably a PSF, boarded. We couldn't hear their conversation, only the heavy steps as they walked up and down the length of the bus aisle over our heads. A more thorough soldier would have forced him to open the luggage compartment, too, but we were waved on and soon the only sound was the growl of the road beneath us.

Still, he apologized repeatedly when he pulled over to retrieve us. I had every intention of wiping his memory and booking it, but there were no cars—there was *nothing* on that stretch of highway aside from trees and snow. It was either Andy or another fun day or two wandering around with Jude in a winter wonderland, looking for civilization.

"Are you sure this is okay?" Jude and I had taken one of the front seats to have a better look at the road while he was driving. "Can we repay you somehow?"

"Don't get me wrong," Andy said. "This is a *spectacular* waste of gasoline, but I don't mind sticking it to my fine employer every now and then. They cut my benefits the hot second things got bad, so I'm not feeling too generous toward them myself. Besides, the drive down is usually pretty empty, and I have to bring the bus to Richmond whether I have passengers or not. The return trip is usually pretty full.

Some folks seem to have the notion that there's more work up north than there is in the south, and hardly anyone can afford those stupid trains."

Jude had proven to me about six times over in the past day just how naive he was, so it was a wonder he could still surprise me with his carelessness. After a few minutes he dropped off into an easy, trusting sleep. Like there was no danger of this bus driver using his radio to call us in or driving us to the first functioning police station he happened across.

"You look like you're about to roll right off that seat and hit the floor, young lady," Andy said, glancing up at me in the large mirror over his head. "Maybe you'd consider taking a cue from your friend and getting a little rest?"

I knew I was being rude and irrational and all sorts of sour, but I kept my eyes fixed on the bus's radio and frowned. Andy glanced down, following my gaze, then started to chuckle.

"You're smart," he said. "I guess you'd have to be in this day and age to be out wandering around. Oh—tollbooth coming up; better get down."

I slipped down between the metal guard and the seat, adjusting the blanket over Jude's sleeping form. Andy waved back to whomever had let him through.

Finally, I couldn't stand it anymore. "Why are you helping us?" I asked.

Andy chuckled again. "Why do you think?"

"Honestly?" I said, leaning forward. "Because I think you want to turn us in for the reward money."

The bus driver let out a low whistle at that. "That is a nice chunk of change, I will admit. Funny that the government can dig up the cash for that but can't afford any sort of assistance for food." He shook his head. "No, sweetheart, I have a job. I make do. I don't need the guilty conscience or the blood money."

"Then why?" I demanded.

Andy reached over with his left hand, plucking something off his dashboard. The tape around it peeled off without protest, like it was used to being lifted and then stuck back on. He held it out, waiting for me to take it.

A little boy smiled back at me from the glossy surface of the photo, dark hair gleaming. He looked ten, maybe twelve if even that. I recognized the muted colors of the backdrop behind him—a school portrait.

"That's my grandson," Andy explained. "His name is Michael. They took him from his school about four years ago. When I tried to contact the police about it, the government, the school, they wouldn't tell me anything. Same for everyone. Couldn't post about it online without my access being shut off. Couldn't go on TV or write in to the papers because Gray was all over them, too. But some of the parents at his school, they said they overheard some PSFs talking about a place called Black Rock."

I wiped the smudged fingerprints from the photo's surface and handed it back to him.

"You're right," he said, "I'm not entirely selfless. I guess what I'm hoping is that maybe you can give me some information. Maybe you know what or where this Black Rock is and we can call it even?"

It was the pleading quality to his voice that did me in. I couldn't detach it from the thought of my own grandmother, left wondering what had happened to me. My skin felt tight around my chest.

"I do. Black Rock is a camp in South Dakota."

"South Dakota!" Andy sounded astonished. "All the way out there? You're sure?"

I was more than sure. The League had a list of all fifteen camps the surviving Psi kids were divided among. Some were itty bitty—a couple dozen kids. Some were converted schools that could hold a few hundred. Then, you had camps like Black Rock and Thurmond that, because of their remote location, could hold thousands.

The South Dakota camp was of special interest to the League because of the rumors surrounding it. All new births from the time IAAN was officially recognized had to be registered in a special database. Those children were supposed to be brought into local doctors or scientists every month for tests, so they could chart any "abnormalities." Any child that developed Psi abilities before the age of ten was put into a special study program run out of Black Rock. The other kids, if they survived IAAN and developed their abilities on the normal schedule, were forcibly picked up and brought to the "normal" rehab camps.

"They might have transferred him at some point," I said. "Do you know what he is?"

"What do you mean, what he is?" Andy said, turning slightly. "He's my grandson, that's what he is!"

I only meant to find out if he was one of the dangerous ones—a Red or Orange like me. To see if there was a chance he had already been erased, permanently.

"These camps . . ." Andy began, shielding his eyes from the headlights of a passing truck. "You know what they do there? Have you seen one yourself?"

I glanced sideways at Jude. "Yeah."

"And they let you out because they fixed you?" he asked, and the hope in his voice broke my heart. "You're better now?"

"They can't fix us," I said. "All those kids they took aren't doing anything other than working and waiting. I only got out because someone helped me escape."

Andy nodded, like he had already suspected as much.

"These are terrible times," he said after a long while. "And you're right not to trust any of us. What we've done . . . what we allowed them to do to you, it's a shameful thing. A shameful, shameful thing, and we'll go to our graves knowing it. But I want you to know that for every person who would turn in a kid out of fear or for funds, there are hundreds and thousands more who fought tooth and nail to keep their families together."

"I know."

"It's just . . . they were such bad times then, and the government kept saying—they kept going on about how if parents didn't send the kids to go through the programs they would die like all of the others. Then it wasn't a choice at all. They knew we couldn't do anything to get them back, and it kills me. It *kills* me."

"Did people really think the rehabilitation programs were going to work?" I asked. Jude shifted in his seat, trying to get more comfortable.

"I don't know, sweetheart," Andy said, "but I think they hoped like hell they would. You get down to nothing—no money, no work, no house—and hope is all you tend to have left, and even then, it's a rare commodity. I doubt anyone believes the lies these days, but . . . what can we do about it? We have no information to work with, only rumors."

It hit me then, how equally important it was for me to find Cole's flash drive as it was to find Liam. All along, I had been thinking of it as this little plastic device, not sparing much thought to the value of what was locked inside of it. Finding Liam mattered to *me*, meant everything to *me*, but finding Cole's data . . . that would help everyone. That had the potential to reunite families, loved ones.

"I'm going to get every kid out of every camp," I said. "I'm not going to stop until they all get home."

Andy nodded, keeping his eyes on the road ahead. "Then we're more than even."

The conversation died out, and the radio came on. I watched the sunrise, the colors lighting the horizon a mellow pink, feeling sick to my stomach with exhaustion. But still, I couldn't fall asleep.

I pulled Liam's leather jacket up over me like a blanket and felt something slip past my hand, out of one of the pockets. The two train tickets the woman had bought floated lazily to the ground, one facing up, the other down.

STAY

The word had been scribbled several times over by pen on the back of one of the tickets, the letters wild and jagged, and with each stroke, darker and deeper.

I picked them up, checking the other ticket.

SAFE

STAY SAFE

Apparently I hadn't had as firm of a grip on that woman as I thought. It was stupid of me to feel so frightened and anxious when she was hundreds of miles away, but I couldn't stop myself from picturing the worst. How she could have warned everyone about the terrors in her backseat. She could have gone into that train station and run or called us in to every nearby skip tracer. She could have had the reward, the satisfaction of knowing we were off the street and out of her hair.

But instead, she had done *this*. Andy had done *this*.

I ripped up the tickets before Jude could wake up and see them. I didn't want to give him the false hope that these people were anything other than lone candle flames in a sea of never-ending black.

Jude was still singing—literally singing—the praises of his new hero, Andy, when we saw the first signs for Wilmington. Just after he'd dropped us off near Richmond, he'd given us detailed instructions on the right highways to avoid on the way down. I'd been too flustered and annoyed with the delay to thank him at the time. Now, every clear road our little stolen car flew down filled me with a sharp pang of regret.

Wilmington kissed the Atlantic on one side and a river on the other. It surprised me to see how similar it was to the parts of Virginia that I knew—the style of the houses, the way the neighborhoods were laid out. Even the way the sky grayed out over the roofs, darkening until the clouds finally burst and it began to rain.

The address Cole gave me, 1222 West Bucket Road, Wilmington, North Carolina, was in a little neighborhood called Dogwood Landing, not too far from what I assumed was a university campus. It was a quiet part of the city, surrounded by frosty woods and filled with a good number of empty lots and crooked, weathered FOR SALE signs. I picked one and parked the green Volkswagen we'd stolen after parting with Andy in front of it.

"Is that it?" Jude asked, peering closer at the nearest house.

"No, it's a ways down, I think." I took a deep breath, wondering how it was possible to feel excitement and dread in the same breath. "I want to approach from the back in case anyone is watching the front."

That had been the reason why Liam and the others hadn't gone straight home after escaping Caledonia, right? I was torn about it. Alban's advisers were always reminding us how overstretched the PSF forces were, but Liam was a priority catch. What were the chances that the government would still have someone posted here, watching Liam's parents a good nine months later?

God. Liam's parents. What the hell was I going to say to them?

I signaled for Jude to follow me around the side of one of the houses. Most were on the smaller side, just one story, with gray slanted roofs, brick faces, and white trim. I pulled

Jude closer behind me as we made our way through the trees, following a small dirt access road that ran alongside the houses' backyards.

Liam's house was nestled deep into a pocket of trees set a ways off from the other houses on the block. It was a similar creature to the other homes around it, with sweet blue shutters and a long driveway leading up to the garage. What I really needed was a view of the front.

I held Jude back and forced him to crouch down beside me, and we watched. We looked for surveillance cameras, for footprints and tire tracks, for the undercover PSFs to come strolling around on patrol.

"It looks . . ." Jude began, hesitating.

Empty, my mind finished. It looked like no one was home, and the way the gutters were clogged with fall leaves and grime made me think they hadn't been back in some time.

"Maybe they just ran out to do some errands?" he offered.

"At four in the afternoon on a Thursday? Seems sketchy," came a new voice behind us.

The girl was a snake. It was the only explanation for how silently she slithered up through the leaves.

"Leader," Vida said, nodding as she crouched down behind us. "Judith."

Jude actually fell over.

"What are you—" I began. "How did you—" She couldn't have just guessed where we'd be. She was good, but she wasn't *that* good. I must have missed a tracker, *something* . . .

"The collar of the undershirt," Vida said, nodding toward Jude. "Next time you decide to cut it and run, make sure you get *all* the damn trackers."

"Trackers?" Jude repeated, looking between us.

"Jude fried the car," I said, "and everything electric inside of it." Including, I had assumed, the trackers in his clothes.

"That would be why they coat all of the Yellows' trackers in rubber," she said, shaking her head. "God, you didn't *know* that?"

She was clearly proud of herself despite looking like she had just been ridden hard and put away wet. Her blue hair was twisting into its natural curly texture.

I hauled Jude closer, unzipping his coat to feel around his undershirt's stitching. Sure enough, I felt the small bump, no more than the size of a grain, sewn into the collar. I cut it out with my Swiss Army knife and held it for him to see. Before he could grab it, I crushed it with the hilt of the knife.

"They . . . put trackers in our clothes?" Jude looked between us in disbelief, though it was clear he was talking to himself. "Why would they do that? That can't be . . ."

Vida looked like she was about to burst into her particular brand of cruel laughter, but her expression changed—narrowed somehow. Her full focus shifted behind us, and she rose back onto her feet, swinging her gun up out of its holster in one smooth motion. I turned, my hair tumbling down around my face as I scrambled back onto my knees for a better look.

The world dropped.

I actually felt it cave under me, felt every bone and muscle in my chest fall with it. I don't know how I managed to pull myself back up or how I came to be standing, but I was too numbed by shock to care that I was in full sight of whoever might have been watching.

Then, I was running. I heard Vida and Jude call after me, but the wind and rain carried their voices up and away, and I wasn't hearing anything over the thrum of blood in my ears. I shoved my way down the slight roll of the hill, through the tangle of tree branches, through the collapsing fence, through to him.

He slipped out of the window, climbing through the torn dark screen one leg at a time until, finally, his shoes sank into the mud below. His hair was longer than I remembered it, the bones in the profile of his face sharper. He had gotten larger, or I had become smaller, or memory really was a lie—it didn't matter. He heard me coming and spun around, one hand going for something inside of his heavy camo jacket, the other for something in the waistband of his jeans. I knew when he spotted me—every part of him froze.

But then his full lips began to work, silently, until they finally settled on the tiniest of smiles. My feet slowed but didn't stop.

I was breathing hard. My whole chest heaved with the effort to keep the air moving. I pressed a hand hard against my heart. Exhaustion and relief and the same bitter terror I had felt the afternoon I'd lost him came flooding in. I just didn't have the strength to fight them back anymore.

I burst into tears.

“Oh, for the love of . . .” Chubs shook his head and sighed, but I heard the affection in his voice all the same. “It’s just me, you dumbass.”

And without another word, he crossed those last two steps between us and wrapped me up tight in his arms.

NINE

THE PROBLEM WAS, ONCE I STARTED, I COULDN'T stop. I felt every bit of me sag against him, needing the reassurance that he was solid and that the heart beating next to my ear was his. Chubs patted my back awkwardly as I buried my face in his jacket and went to pieces.

"How?" I choked out. "Why are you here?"

The rustling in the trees behind us barely registered in my mind, but Chubs looked up, calling, "Oh, come on, Lee—I know you want a hug, too—"

It happened too fast for me to warn him—to stop any of it. Chubs released me only to spin me behind him, throwing me more off-kilter than I had been before. I thought, for sure, that my mind was playing tricks on me, because it looked like he had pulled a long hunting knife up out of the waistband of his pants. It looked like Vida was pointing her gun straight at him, switching off the safety.

"It's—" I began, feeling his arm strain under my grip. "Chubs—"

"Who the hell are you?" he demanded.

"Not the person who brought a knife to a gunfight," Vida said, waving her weapon for emphasis.

"Wait, wait, wait!" Jude said, popping out from behind the tree to her right. He slid partway down the muddy hill, throwing himself between them. "Not Liam," he said, pointing at himself, then at Vida. "Not Liam, either." Jude turned back toward Chubs, his thick eyebrows drawing together as he moved his finger our way. "Also not Liam . . . ?"

At that, Vida turned to stare at him. "In what universe does this tool look *anything* like Cole Stewart?"

Jude's voice went high when he got defensive. "I don't know! Brother from a different mother? There *is* such a thing as adoption—"

Chubs lowered his knife. I could see his mind working behind his eyes, jumping from one horrible possibility to another as he took account of the strangers, my tears, and the absence of Liam.

"Oh my God," he said, going gray in the face. He pressed a fist against his stomach, like he was about to be sick. "Oh my God."

"No, *no*," I said quickly. "He's not dead!"

That you know of, my mind whispered.

"Why aren't you together?" Now he looked close to tears himself. Chubs's hair had grown out past its usual neat crop, and the silver-rimmed glasses that actually fit his face made him look so much more mature than I remembered.

He didn't really look like himself, not until I saw the fear come crashing over him—this was the Chubs I remembered, always between one panic and the next. "He never would have left you, never!"

I looked away. Not toward Vida and Jude, who had gone silent watching this, but to soft mud cupping rain puddles at our feet.

"Ruby," Chubs began, his voice strained. "What happened?"

I shook my head, pressing my freezing hands to my face.

"You left him?" he guessed. "You had a fight? You split up for a few days?"

By whispering it, I was hoping I could take some of the sting out of the truth, but that wasn't the case at all. Chubs took a stunned step back, his eyes flashing with horror.

"No, you didn't!" he said, gripping my shoulders. "That was the only reason I thought it would be okay! I thought you two would stay together!"

"What was I supposed to do?" I demanded, not caring that my voice was rising. "You were—you were dead, and they had taken us in, and I made a deal, and I knew, I *knew* he wouldn't go otherwise. What the hell was I supposed to do?"

Chubs shook his head. "And these kids, they're League? You're with them?"

"They're—" I started to say.

"—still standing here, waiting for an explanation as to who the hell this is," Vida cut in, every trace of amusement gone from her face.

My brain was finally starting to reassemble itself into working order, and with it came fresh, sharp fear.

Vida was here. Vida, who had been chasing us down to bring us back in to the League. Vida, who had now seen Chubs and could identify him to the League, if it came to that. Who might even try to bring him in.

I pushed him back, trying to keep him behind me. "He's no one," I said. "He's not any concern of yours."

"Uh, yeah he freaking is if he's coming with us to find Stewart," Vida said.

"What did you say?"

"Plug your empty-ass brain in," she said. "I'm not here to take you back; I'm here to help you." She turned on Jude. "Nice of you to repay me by electrocuting me, you little shit."

"If you weren't there with Beta Team and Barton to take us in to HQ, then why?"

Vida rolled her eyes but did answer eventually—with the smuggest look possible. "I was looped in on your little romantic quest. The only way to get me out without it looking suspicious was to suggest that I come after you dumb asses, since I supposedly know your crappy personalities so well."

"What about Beta Team?" Jude asked.

"Recalled to HQ. Orders to bring Rob back in or something—you two lace panties about caused a fucking riot back home with your little stunt." She tossed her hair back. "Alban gave me two weeks to find you. So let's get this horror show on the road."

I stared at her, shaking my head. "You are *so* full of it. You think we're just going to skip away with you into the sunset?"

"No," Vida said, "I expect you to fucking *prance*, and you're going to do it with a smile and the least amount of bitching possible, or Cole isn't going to honor your stupid deal to have the League free the camps."

It was true, then—she was telling the truth about being here to help us. Cole wouldn't have looped her in otherwise. The objective was too valuable. It surprised me how much it stung my pride to know he didn't think I could handle this Op on my own. That I needed backup.

Jude turned to look at me, totally lost.

"Okay, *vámonos*!" Vida said, clapping her hands. "If you're going to check out the house, then do it fast."

"I'm not going anywhere with you," Chubs cut in. I recognized the expression on his face—how many times had I seen it after the others took me in, before he came to accept the fact I was staying with them? Chubs had never been one to hide his feelings, whether it was anger or fear or suspicion. He and Liam were alike in that way, only it came to Liam by nature and Chubs by choice. I'm not sure he saw a point in pretending to be anything he wasn't.

"Yes," I said, taking Chubs's arm again. I felt the muscle there strain under my fingers. "Come on, we need to talk. I'll explain everything."

Chubs cast his unhappy expression down at me. "Just us, then. I don't—"

All four of us heard it at once. Car doors slamming. One, two, three.

I pulled Chubs back so we were flush against the house, motioning for Jude to come toward us and quickly. Vida circled around the nearby trees, her boots silent in the soft mulch. Her head of bright hair was the last trace of her to vanish into the rain.

I glanced up at the window Chubs had wiggled out of, my hand stretching up to touch the loose screen, then back toward the woods. We could maybe make a run for it, maybe. Try to disappear into the wildlife and lose them that way.

"Is it Barton?" Jude was whispering.

Chubs and I both shushed him. The back of Liam's house was lined with five white-trimmed windows and one perfectly sweet little screen door, which had been nailed into place with sturdy plywood boards. A square of bricks had been lovingly placed to serve as a patio at the back entrance to the home. Now, green grass, glowing in the misty rain, had crawled up through the cracks.

I dropped to the damp bricks on hands and knees, slowly working my way along the length of the house until the voices became louder. My nails dug into the fabric of my pants, ears straining. Two men. One woman.

When I finally turned back around to tell the boys this, Vida was already there, crouched between Chubs and Jude. When she felt my eyes on her, she glanced up and gave an impatient jerk of her chin.

"There are four altogether," she whispered. "One woman, three men. They look like they're PSFs."

I covered Jude's mouth with my hand. "Are they armed?"

She nodded. "The usual. What's with this house? Why is it important enough that they installed motion sensors?"

"Sensors?" Chubs said.

"They stuck them under the roof overhang at all four corners of the house," she said, clearly annoyed he didn't immediately take her word for the gospel truth.

I shared a glance with Chubs, letting Jude pry my hand away from his face. Of course they would have installed *something* to monitor the house. If not for Liam, then for Cole. Interesting that Cole hadn't bothered to feed her any of his brother's back story. Maybe there just hadn't been time.

The voices had quieted down, but I heard their heavy tread through the overgrown garden at the right end of the house. They'd be too close now for us to try to run out into the trees. There was no way they wouldn't spot us.

With a sigh that shook his entire tall frame, Chubs stood and pushed the dangling flaps of the window screen aside. Resignation made his shoulders slump.

"Do you trust me?" he asked, seeing my expression.

"Of course."

Jude made a small noise behind me, but I ignored it.

"Then tell your friends to get inside"—he nodded to the now open window—"and stand up. I'm going to have to handcuff you."

Here was the nice thing about being shocked senseless: I didn't have to pretend to be terrified. I stood there, feeling the sharp edges of the clear plastic ties cutting off my blood supply at the wrist. I let them disconnect every single thought in my head.

Who is this person? I thought, studying him closer now. He was wearing the hooded camo hunting jacket I had vaguely noticed before, a gray wool turtleneck, and a pair of faded jeans, battered by dust and long wear. Strapped to his hip was what looked like a small cell phone and a leather pouch. When we had traveled together before, he had kept all of his possessions in a battered leather briefcase he had found. That had suited him so much better than this weird . . . imitation of what he thought a hunter should look like.

It should have been reassuring to see him so prepared and well supplied, but, somehow, it only frightened me more.

Chubs's hand was steady as he took my chin in his hand, turning it to and fro, inspecting the cuts and bruises from the night before with a disapproving look. The others watched from behind the closed window, Jude's face so close it was almost pressed up against the glass.

"It might be better if you pretend to pass out," he said.

The suggestion came just in time. As I hit the ground, I saw the flash of black as the PSFs rounded the corner.

Four. Vida had been right. The brown-haired woman was the tallest of the group, standing several inches above the men. One was an older guy, his hair puffing out in an ashy blond ring around his head. The other two were younger and looked enough alike to be brothers. All armed with standard-issue rifles, handcuffs, the works.

"Can I help you?" Chubs's face was set in stone.

The soldiers didn't know what to make of us, but they also didn't lower their weapons. I was starting to put it together, though, long before Chubs began to speak again.

"What, so you're here to swipe my score out from under my nose? Trying to weasel out of having to pay me?"

The older soldier cocked a beetled brow. "You're a skip tracer?"

My thoughts exactly. If that was the ruse we were running with, we were in more trouble than I thought. On a good day, Chubs was about as threatening as a potted cactus.

"Here!" He reached into the leather pouch on his belt and thrust something at the PSF. It looked like a small booklet, about the size of a passport.

The old man stepped forward but turned to look back at the woman. "Take a walk around the perimeter. Make sure she was traveling alone."

Chubs waved the booklet again as the three others took their walk. The old man sighed, glancing back and forth between Chubs's face and whatever was written there.

"All right, Mr. Lister," he said, passing it back to him. "Have you run this one through the database?"

"She's not in it," Chubs said. "She's probably been coasting for quite some time. There aren't any records of her."

"Did you test her?" he asked. "If she's Blue or Yellow, you'll need—"

"She's a Green," Chubs interrupted. "Why? Want a demonstration?"

"We can take her," the man offered. "Save you the trouble of transporting."

"I told you, she's not in the system," Chubs said, the nasty edge to his voice more pronounced. "I know how this works. You can't line up my payment if she isn't registered. I have to go into the nearest station and do the paperwork if I want the bounty."

The man snorted but didn't try to deny it. "Was that car on the road yours?"

"No," Chubs said, rolling his eyes. "I flew in on a cloud and came blitzing down from the Heavens like a bolt of lightning on this kid."

"Hey, now," came the PSF's gruff reply. "I can take her, and there's not a damn thing you'd be able to do about it. So watch your attitude, boy."

That attitude was what was throwing me off, too. Chubs wasn't brave by nature; courage tended to rear up when he felt that his friends were threatened, true, but this wasn't so much bravery as it was recklessness. And that was the last—the very last—thing I associated with him.

I don't know how much time passed between then and the moment the PSF's radio buzzed. A minute. Ten years. Forever. *"This is Jacobson, do you read?"*

The man unclipped his black walkie-talkie from his belt. "I read. Did you find anything?"

"No, nothing out of the ordinary. It's hard to tell much with the rain coming down. Any footprints would be washed out, over."

"She's alone, I'm sure of it," Chubs was saying. "I followed her."

"All right," the man said. I saw his boots sink that much deeper into the dead, muddy grass as he took two steps toward me. My eyes squeezed shut again, and it was near impossible to force my body to go limp with him so close. I didn't want him touching me. Panic flared up bright as morning light as his boot nudged my ribs.

The cold, wet leather of his glove closed around my upper arm and he yanked me off the ground. My arm twisted, sending sharp, shooting pains into my shoulder.

"Don't!" Chubs snarled. "Don't touch—!"

The PSF's grip didn't ease up.

"I mean," Chubs began again, this time his voice neutral, "they take out the cost of medical care from the reward money if the kids are injured. I can handle it from here . . . sir."

"That's better," the man said, dropping me facedown into the dirt. "Get her and clear the hell out of here. You're trespassing, and if I find you back here, I'll arrest you myself."

The rainwater was collecting in my ear, running free down the curve of my cheek, and soaking Liam's old jacket. I waited for it to carry my fear away, too, down into the earth where it couldn't touch me again. I took in one deep, wet gulp of air and held it.

A car engine started in the distance. I opened my eyes again, watching Chubs come toward me. He knelt, one hand smoothing the tangled cloud of hair off my face. We listened to the wheels churn up the loose gravel of the driveway, both of us still and silent.

"I'm sorry," Chubs said finally. "Are you okay? Did he dislocate your shoulder, because if he did—"

"I'm all right," I said, "but—but could you please cut the zip ties off now?" I was horrified by the way my voice shook, but in addition to the discomfort, my brain was starting to spark up old memories that were better left buried deep. The bus ride into Thurmond. The sorting. Sam.

The minute I heard the plastic snap under his knife, I was pushing myself up onto my knees, ignoring the ache in my right shoulder. Chubs began to reach over to check on it, but I leaned back, just out of his reach.

We sat there, staring at each other, letting the space between us fill with rain and silence. Finally, I held out my hand, and without a word, he pressed the black booklet into it.

The cover was a tough faux leather, and I hadn't necessarily been wrong in thinking that it was a passport. At first glance, it looked exactly the same—from the faint blue paper and the iridescent United States of America seal overlaying it.

FUGITIVE PSI RECOVERY AGENT. God, there was an official title for it?

"Joseph Lister," I read. "Age twenty-four, six feet, a hundred and seventy pounds, from Penn Hills, Pennsylvania." I glanced over at him. He was wearing an identical scowl to the one in his official photograph. "You know, it's funny. The least believable thing about all that is your weight."

"Oh, hilarious," he groused, snatching it back from me before I could skim through the other pages. It was so Chubs—so the Chubs I knew—that I smiled. He struggled to keep his lips pressed in a stern line, but I saw the beginnings of a curve.

"I really thought you were dead," I said quietly. "I shouldn't have let them take you."

He brought a hand up to his shoulder, pressing it there, as if his mind was cycling back to that moment, too. "You pushed the panic button, right?"

I nodded.

"I would have done the same thing," he said. "The exact same thing. Well—" He stopped, actually considering this. "I probably would have been a little steadier in applying pressure to the wound, but other than that, yes. Well . . ."

"You'll want to stop now," I told him dryly. "Before you ruin our touching moment."

The window above us suddenly opened and Jude's curling mass of hair appeared there. "Roo—are you okay? Oh my God, Vida wouldn't let me watch, but I tried to go around front, but the doors are all boarded up and there's nothing in here so I just—"

Chubs helped me up, giving me a look that clearly asked, *What fresh hell is this?*

"I'll tell you everything later, and you're going to do the exact same. But for now, we have to see if we can find some kind of clue about what direction Lee might have headed—"

Chubs's brows drew together as he lowered his voice. "Didn't Lee tell you the procedure he and Harry set up to make contact?"

"I knew he had one, just not what it was," I said. "But he told you?"

He nodded, shifting so his back was facing the window. And, I realized, the people inside. "We need to go. Now."

"Wait," I began, but he already had his arm looped through mine.

"They're watching the house; we *have* to go," he said. "And I'm sorry, I'd much rather not have the League riding with us."

I detangled my arm from his, taking a step back. "I can't leave them."

"You are *not* League," he insisted. "You are not one of them. You're one of *us*."

"Don't think about it as *us* and *them*," I pleaded. "We can all work together on this for now. You don't have to come back with us to California after we find Liam; you just have to stay with us now."

Out of the corner of my eye, I caught Vida's electric blue hair through the window screen. "Back then, you didn't want me to stay, either, remember?"

"Yeah but that was . . . different," he said, his voice low. "And you know it."

"But at the time, *you* didn't know that."

I had read him right. I saw it in his face, in the rigid lines of his tight shoulders.

"You asked me if I trusted you," I whispered. "Do you trust me?"

He blew out a long breath, his hands resting on his hips. "God help me," he said finally, "I do. But I trust *you*, not them. I don't even know who they are."

I only held out my hand and waited for him to take it. I needed his long fingers to close around mine, wanted that final proof that his better sense and reasoning had given way to the belief he used to have in me. I waited for him to come with me, to accept that we were now in this together again, that time and distance and uncertainty hadn't been enough to shake *us*.

And he did.

TEN

THE TAN SUV REEKED OF FAKE EVERGREENS. THE smell of the air freshener was so overpowering, I had to roll down my windows to get fresh air circulating.

"You wouldn't be complaining if you were there to smell the guy I bought it off of," Chubs said, handing me a pair of sunglasses to wear. "Now. Put your seat belt on, please."

Vida and Jude were already buckled into the backseat, though they hadn't gone quietly. My favorite team member got one look at the metal grating that separated the front seats from the back and just about ripped my hair out at the roots trying to yank me out of the front seat.

"Are we driving this slowly because you have no idea where we're going," Vida asked, "or because you're hoping we jump out of the car and put ourselves out of our misery?"

Jude sat straight up, alarmed. We both recognized that tone. Vida picked fights when she was bored, and battles when she was stressed. If it were the latter, only one of them was going to make it out of this car ride alive. We'd be washing the blood off the windows for weeks.

"That'd be doing the psychos holding your leashes a favor."

For the first time, I was grateful for the metal grating between us. "They are *not* psychos, you condescending dick!" she snarled.

"I'm condescending?" Chubs asked. "Do you even know what that word means?"

"You piece of flaming—"

"So," Jude said, his voice high. "Roo, how do you and Chubs know each other?"

"Charles," he gritted out. "My name is Charles."

"That's supposed to be better?" Vida scoffed. Chubs let the car roll to a stop at a red light and turned to look at me, fire burning behind the lenses of his glasses.

"Yup," I said. "She's always like this."

The tension that welled up in the car hovered among us, strung tight. One word or wrong move would snap it. Jude drummed his fingers against the armrest.

"Cut that shit out, nimrod, before I cut them off," Vida said.

"Nimrod?" he shot back, his voice jumping an octave with outrage. "You don't have to be so mean, you know."

I pressed a hand to my forehead. "*That* gets you upset? That dumb name? She's been calling you Judith for months."

Chubs laughed but turned it into a cough when he saw my look.

"Yeah, well," Jude huffed, drawing his boney knees up to his chest. "I guess I just don't see what's so insulting about being called a girl. The two of you seem to do okay when you're not biting my head off or acting like I'm five years old."

"As opposed to what?" Chubs said, flicking on the turn signal to merge onto a highway. "The ten-year-old you actually are?"

"Hey," I warned. "None of that. He's almost fifteen."

"Roo," Jude began, his eyes shining, "thank you."

"You were that gawky when I first met you," I continued, poking Chubs in the shoulder, "and you were eighteen."

"Never mind," Jude grumbled.

"You were the gawky one," he corrected, "Lee was the reckless one, Zu was the cute one, and I was the wise one."

There was a knock on the grate behind us. Jude's face was floating there, his dark brown eyes peering between the two of us from behind the metal screen. "It would be nice," he said, "if we had any idea what you guys are talking about. Like who this Zu person is?"

Chubs's eyes slid over to meet mine. "Exactly how much did you tell them?"

"Exactly nothing," Vida said. "And if it stays that way, I will make you regret it."

This time I rolled my eyes. "Sure. Whatever you say."

I felt the familiar warm tingling at the center of my chest and had just enough time to gasp as some invisible hand yanked me forward, smacking my forehead against the dashboard with enough force to stun me dumb.

Chubs slammed on the brakes, forcing my seat belt to do its job and lock against my chest. I was thrown back into my seat, an explosion of colors bursting in my vision.

"Oh, *hell* no!" Chubs roared, slamming a hand against the steering wheel. "That's it! We do *not* use our abilities on one another, goddammit! *Behave yourself!*"

"Chill the fuck out, Grannie," Vida said. "You're going to give yourself a stroke."

"You cannot give yourself—" Chubs began in a growl but caught himself.

Jude let out a nervous laugh behind us, but I only pressed a hand to my stinging forehead. She had made her point.

"Zu was a friend of ours," I said. "We traveled together for a while."

"I thought Cate got you out, though," Jude said. "Did you guys get separated or something? It seems like it would be dangerous just to be out wandering around."

"It wasn't like that," Chubs said. "After the three of us broke out of camp—"

He might as well have told the others that he was a wizard. Even Vida leaned forward, suddenly so much more interested. "You?" she began. "You broke out of a camp?"

"Liam planned it," Chubs gritted out. "But yes. I did."

"Does that kid think he's some kind of expert in getaways?" Vida muttered. "Goddamn."

Jude's eyes were bright with interest. "What was that like? Did you have your own room, like a little prison cell? Did they make you do hard labor? I heard that—"

The kids in the League knew about the camps—vaguely. There were only a few of us who had actually lived in one and experienced the life firsthand, but there was an unspoken rule we didn't talk about it. Everyone knew the truth, but the truth didn't live inside them the same way it did for us. They'd heard about the sorting machines, the cabins, the testing, but most of their stories were gossip, completely wrong. These kids had never stood for hours on end in an assembly line. They didn't know fear came in the shape of a small black camera lens, an eye that followed you everywhere, at all times.

My chest tightened with the effort of keeping silent. One by one, my fingers closed around the seat belt's silver fabric until I was all but choking it.

"Do you not remember it or something?" Jude asked. "Were you only there for a little while—is that why you can't talk about it, because there's nothing to say?"

"I would shut your mouth," Chubs advised.

"Come *on*," Jude whined. "If she'd just *talk* to us—"

"What?" The word exploded out of me. "*What* do you want me to tell you? You want to hear about how they tied us up like animals to bring us into the camp—or, hey! How about that time a PSF once beat in a girl's skull so badly she actually lost an eye? You want to know what it was like to drink rotten water for an entire summer until new pipes finally came? How I woke up afraid and went to bed in terror every single day for six years? For God's sake, leave me *alone*! Why do you always have to dig and dig when you *know* I don't want to talk about it?"

I regretted the outburst halfway through, but the speech tumbled out, one vile, traitorous word after another. Chubs only glanced at the glowing blue clock, then back up at the soggy road. In the backseat, Jude was as silent as snow falling on asphalt, his mouth opening and closing, like he was trying to taste the burn of his words after they left his lips.

"I don't know about the rest of you, but I'd be up for hearing about the one-eyed chick," Vida said with a shrug.

"You are actually the worst person I have ever met," Chubs said.

"And people like you are the reason we have middle fingers."

"Guys . . ." I started.

Cate had told me once, a long time ago, that the only way to survive your past was to find a way to close it off behind you, to shut one door before passing into another, brighter room. I was afraid. *That* was the truth. I was terrified of the guilt and shame that would come flooding in when I retraced my steps, turned the lock, and found the girl I had abandoned. I didn't want to know what the darkness there had done to her, if she would even recognize herself in my face.

I didn't want to know what Chubs would think of me after he found out what I'd done for the League.

I didn't want to know what Liam would think of me or of the smell of smoke in my hair that never went away, no matter how many times I washed it.

"At least tell us about how you ended up splitting with Liam," Jude said. "If you guys were traveling together, why did you . . . um, stop? Cate came to get you when you pushed the panic button, I know, but was Liam gone by then? What about him?" He pointed at Chubs.

Those memories weren't any less painful, but they were important.

"All right," I said. "You know that we traveled together—Liam, Chubs, Zu, and me. But what you don't know is that we were looking for a place, a safe haven called East River. To understand why I did it and how he ended up on his own, I have to start there."

"Fine," Vida answered, leaning back away from the grating, her eyes drifting over to the window at her right. The first traces of snow drifted into our roaring path.

I told them about East River, how it had felt like a dream until we woke up and realized we were trapped in a nightmare. About Clancy, which was so much harder than even I expected. How we escaped, how Chubs was shot, and how it was just the two of us in the safe house. Jude started to interrupt, his eyes wide with either anxiety or confusion, I couldn't tell. I felt my own heart drift up and up and up until I had to swallow it down to get through what came next. *My decision and Cate's deal.* What I had seen in Cole's memory and his own explanation of it.

In the strangest way, it made me feel closer to Liam. He was alive and vivid in my thoughts. Solid, warm Liam with his sunglasses on, the sunlight in his hair, and the words of a favorite song on his lips. I half expected to look up and see him in the driver's seat.

No one spoke. I couldn't bring myself to look behind me; I felt both Jude's and Vida's conflicted feelings cling to my skin the way condensation was gathering on the windows.

I felt a light touch on my shoulder. I turned, slowly, to see Jude retract his finger back through the metal grate. His bottom lip was white where it was caught between his teeth. But he was looking at me—not with fear or any of its ugly cousins. Just a deep, sincere sadness.

He could still stand to look at me.

"Roo," Jude whispered. "I'm so sorry."

"Can I just ask one thing?" Chubs said, his voice sounding tight in his throat after I finished. "What are you doing with the flash drive?"

"I was going to bring it back to Cole," I said. "He and I have a deal—if I get the intel back to him, it'll be enough to shift the priorities of the League back to freeing kids from camps and exposing the government's lies."

Chubs rubbed his forehead. "And you believe him? The only thing Liam ever said about him was that he used to set his toys on fire when he didn't get his way."

"I believe him," I said. "He won't hurt us. He's one of the few who doesn't want us gone, apparently."

"Gone?" Chubs asked, alarmed.

I let Jude explain; his stumbling, rambling explanation was coated by rough grief, and it made the story that much more horrible to hear.

"No, no, no, no, *no*," Chubs said. "You're just going back, hoping that they manage to pick out all of the bad seeds?"

"Don't say it like that," Jude cried. "It'll get better. Rob's gone, right? Cate will let us know when we can come back."

"You and Liam will be safe—at least from the League,"

I told Chubs. "They won't come after you. You get it, right? You understand why I told Cole I'd do this?"

"Sure. I get it," he said, his voice cold enough to drive a chill through even my veins. And again, I read the question he was really asking in the silence he left to fill the space between us. I knew what he wanted to ask, because it was the same thought that had been circling in on me for days.

If the intel is that important, why would you ever give it to the League?

Of all the training, and Ops, and the League-sponsored explosions I'd been unfortunate enough to witness, none seemed half as dramatic as Chubs's thrilling tale of escape.

We pulled into an old camping ground for the night, just outside of a city called Asheville in western North Carolina. I'd managed to fill most of the five-hour drive with explanations, and the whole thing had left me drained. I didn't put up any kind of struggle when Chubs and Jude argued for stopping.

We did a quick walk-through of the area to make sure it was clear of other visitors before returning to pull supplies from the SUV. I popped the latch, stepping back from the door as it opened.

"Oh my God," I managed.

The whole thing was just so . . . impressive. A wall of small, stacked plastic tubs and drawers, all labeled with handy reminders like: FIRST AID and ROPE and VITAMINS and FISHING HOOKS. The care and forethought it had taken to put this all together was impressive, if not completely terrifying in how ruthlessly thorough it was.

Jude gave Chubs a long look of appraisal. "You had day-of-the-week underwear growing up, didn't you?"

Chubs merely pushed the glasses up the bridge of his nose. "I don't see how that's any of your business."

He laid out the entire story for me as we set up the tent that had been folded neatly under the backseat. Vida, at least, was able to get a small fire going with a lighter.

"I don't actually remember most of this stuff happening," Chubs said, struggling with the tent's frame. "The League brought me to the nearest hospital, which happened to be the one in Alexandria."

"Not Fairfax?" I asked, smoothing the damp hair away from my face. Jude and Vida were doing their best to listen to all of this while pretending they weren't.

Chubs shrugged. "I have a vague memory of seeing some faces but—I told you that I look like my dad, right?"

I nodded.

"Well, one of the doctors recognized me. She used to work with Dad, but transferred— Anyway, it's not important. They managed to stabilize me, but this doctor and her staff knew I needed to be in a better-equipped hospital. So she got on the phone and tracked Dad down. He was going to meet us at my aunt's restaurant, remember?"

"I remember."

"He was able to meet the ambulance when it arrived at Fairfax Hospital; they already had a fake ID prepared for me, so that's what they registered me under. They kept an oxygen mask on my face the entire time. I got walked through two sets of security guards, and no one looked twice."

"And they didn't tell the agents who brought you in," I finished. "The League has no idea what happened to you. You're still listed as MIA in all of the related Op files."

Chubs snorted. "They tried telling the agents I coded out and died, but they didn't bite. One day my dad had six different people come to him fishing for information, but they didn't get a word out of him."

The real trick hadn't been admitting him at the new hospital under a false name. The hospital had become well versed in a don't-ask-we-won't-tell policy when it came to dealing with the government and their requests for information, so much so that they were nearly shut down a good half dozen times. Dr. Meriwether's stroke of genius was to hide his son, "Marcus Bell," in an isolated room in the maternity ward for treatment. When he was strong enough, he was zipped up in a body bag and taken out of the hospital in a rented hearse. The League agents found the transfer paperwork and tried to connect the dots, but Chubs became a ghost the moment he had been wheeled into Fairfax Hospital.

From there, it had been a matter of finding a place for Chubs to recuperate and build his strength back up again.

"I will leave it to you to imagine what it was like to live in a ramshackle barn in upstate New York for four months," he said, grimacing as he rolled his shoulder back. "I will go to my grave smelling hay and manure every time I close my eyes."

The old barn belonged to a close family friend in the Adirondacks—and it had been isolated, cold, and lonely, by the sound of it. His parents could only come up twice to see him without sparking suspicion, but the elderly woman who owned the farm was there twice a day to help with his physical therapy and provide food. Mostly, though, he was bored to tears.

"I like to think I get along pretty well with the elderly, but this woman looked like she dragged herself up from the crypt every morning."

"Yeah, to feed and nurse *you*," I reminded him.

"The only books she had were about a crime-solving spinster bothering people in her small village," he said. "I'm allowed to be a little bitter about the experience."

"No," I said, "actually, I'm pretty sure you're not."

"How did you end up doing all of . . . *this*, though?" Jude asked.

Chubs sighed. "I actually have to give Mrs. Berkshire credit. It was something she said after I told her about how I got out of Virginia—that the last place people tend to look for the hunted is among the hunters. She fell asleep midsentence, of course. I had to wait four hours to be blessed with the second half of her old-lady mysticism."

I pressed a hand over my eyes.

"I'll have you know I haven't been suspected *once*," he said, a bit too pleased with himself. "My parents got the doctored birth papers, which was the hardest part. It's actually not that difficult to be registered as an official skip tracer. You just have to provide the right paperwork and establish yourself."

The fire popped loudly, collapsing the small pile of wood we'd gathered. It seemed to be the right place to take a break in the story. I stood and pulled Chubs up off the ground to come with me. Jude started to rise, but I waved him back.

"We're just going to get some food," I said. "We'll be right back."

"Don't worry," Vida said in her sugary sweet voice. She wrapped an arm around Jude's shoulders. "We have been known to survive two whole minutes without you."

I tried very hard not to stomp over to the car.

"I really do not trust that girl," Chubs said, glancing back over his shoulder to where Vida was still sitting, her legs stretched out in front of her. "Youths who dye their hair are always battling inferiority complexes. Or hiding secrets."

I raised an eyebrow. "Youths?"

He was so focused on her that he almost whacked himself in the face with the rear door of the SUV. Chubs's hand flew to his left shoulder, as if to protect it.

"Let me see it," I said, stopping him before he could reach for the tub labeled PROTEIN BARS. He sighed and slipped that arm from its jacket sleeve. There was enough stretch in his shirt's fabric for him to pull the collar down across his left shoulder where a quarter-sized patch of pink, puckered skin stood out stark against his otherwise dark skin.

"Did they . . ." My throat suddenly felt dry. "Did they get it out? The bullet?"

He adjusted his shirt, smoothing it back down again. "It was a clean shot. It went straight through. As far as bullet wounds go, it wasn't anything awful."

It wasn't anything awful. I swallowed, a weak attempt to keep from crying.

"Oh jeez, not again," he said. "I'm *fine*. I'm alive, right?"

"Why did you come back?" I whispered, hearing my own voice break. "Why didn't you stay up there, where it was safe?"

Chubs, food cradled against his chest, reached one long arm up to close the door. "And leave you two idiots out on the run?"

I watched him heave in two deep breaths, then send them sailing out in a long white cloud.

"I'm so angry with you," he said finally, his voice low. "I'm *furious*. I know why you erased yourself, I understand, but all I want to do is shake some sense back into you."

"I know," I said. "I know, okay?"

"Do you, though?" he asked. "You won't leave these two, even though they could report me—and Lee—back to the League. You put yourself in the line of fire, with the *worst* people, and you did it without someone there to watch your back. How do you think Lee's going to react when he finds out what you did?"

The knot in my stomach tightened to the point of pain. He *was* furious; the strength of the anger powering him was like a beacon to my mind. It made him vulnerable, exposed.

"He won't find out," I said. "I told you, all I was going to do was get the flash drive and make sure he was all right. I wasn't going to . . . I'm not going to interfere."

"That is the most bullshit, cowardly thing I have ever heard come out of your mouth," he shot back. "You lied to us before about what you are, and I got it. I understand why you did it, but now . . . you're out, and we can all be together again, and you're choosing the only option that ends with us apart? Maybe Liam could forgive you for what you did, but if you go back to them, to California, *I* will never forgive you."

He started to turn back to the fire and dark-green tent, only to pivot back to me. "Do you remember what it felt like when East River was attacked and we hid in that lake? All that night, I kept thinking, Well, this is the worst thing that will ever happen to me. I thought the same thing when we escaped Caledonia and we had to leave the other guys in our cabin behind, bleeding to death in the snow. And again, when I was shot—but the thing is, I was wrong. Ruby, the worst thing—the worst feeling—was being safe up in that barn and not knowing, for six months, what happened to you and Liam and Suzume. It was seeing your names pop up on the skip-tracer networks with upped rewards and potential sightings, and not being able to find *any* of you for months."

Sometimes . . . most of the time with Chubs, really, it was impossible to tell his anger from his fear. They fed into each other.

"Then, all of a sudden, you were showing up everywhere. In Boston, in a train station in Rhode Island—you were being really careless there, you know." He shot me a disapproving look. "Liam's even worse. For months, nothing, then a tip about him being sighted in Philadelphia. I had to doctor evidence that the tip was bad to get it deleted off the network."

The League had backdoor access to both the PSF and skip-tracer databases of kids, but neither of Liam's profiles looked like they had been updated in ages. I knew—I checked twice a week. No wonder it looked like it hadn't been updated the last time I looked.

"How did you know to go to his house?" I asked. The timing couldn't have been a coincidence.

"I figured it had to be something to do with the protocol Harry set up to help them find each other—based on the sightings, I thought maybe the two of you were coming down to his old house to check to see if his stepdad set up the procedure."

"Which was what?"

"When Cole and Liam left to join the League, Harry told them that if he and their mom felt like they needed to get out, he'd leave coordinates under the windowsill of Liam's old bedroom."

"And you have the coordinates?" I asked.

"No," he said, "there was nothing there."

"That must be why he went to find Cole in Philadelphia—to see if he knew anything."

Chubs rubbed a knuckle over his lips, nodding. "That's what I'm thinking, too. It doesn't help us, though, if Cole had no idea, either."

"I know," I said. "Running blind, just like old times."

Chubs sighed, and I swayed toward him, resting my forehead against his upper arm.

"We'll watch the skip-tracer network, see if there are any other sightings." Chubs shifted, hiking the cans up against his chest. "He's screwed up a few times in the past. Chances are, he'll do it again."

It was a terrifying thought. We might pick up hints of him here and there, but chances were, we'd be too far away to swoop in and help if he were captured. He had a big enough head start on us that he could put some real distance behind him. And it was overwhelming to know that; suddenly, everything seemed so much harder and more impossible than only a few minutes before. It all felt so pointless.

"I'm so tired of this," I told him. "I know I don't have any right to be; I know I did this to us, to myself, but I don't want to fight anymore. I'm so tired of everything, of all of this, and knowing it's never going to get any better—that nothing I do will ever make anything better. I'm so sick of it all."

Chubs shifted the cans in his arms, ducking down to get a closer look at my face. I wasn't crying, but my throat ached and my head was pounding.

"No, what you are is exhausted," he said. "Depression, anxiety, difficulty focusing—you're a classic case. Come on, you'll feel better after you get food and some sleep."

"That won't solve anything, either."

"I know," he said, "but it's a start."

I learned a long time ago that it was possible to be so far past the point of exhaustion that sleep no longer felt like an option. My stomach ached with the need for it, and my head felt heavy, but I could feel myself waiting for something, muscles tense and brain unable to settle. It was like no matter how hard I fought to focus on the point of the tent's roof, to count off sheep, my mind kept drifting back to the night we had spent in the abandoned Walmart. To the kids we had been so convinced were going to screw us over in the worst way.

I must have nodded off at some point, because the next thing I knew, I was startled awake by a cold blast of air. Vida was at the opening of the tent, unzipping it slowly and as quietly as she could and stepping through. My head was slow to come up out of the fog of sleep, but I was alert enough to be suspicious, no matter how much I wanted to drift back into dreamland.

I counted to thirty, to sixty. I listened as her footsteps grew softer. Watched, waiting for her to come back.

She didn't.

What are you up to? I thought, crawling over Chubs's long legs to the tent's opening. If she had needed to get a breath of fresh air or relieve herself, she would have been back by now.

Despite the crippling dark, I spotted her right away. She was shivering, rubbing her arms to try to shake off the night's icy grip. I saw her glance back toward the tent once, and pulled back, hoping the moon wasn't bright enough for her to make out my shape behind the tent's thin waterproof covering.

Vida slinked her way around Chubs's tan Ford Explorer, circling it twice before coming to stop by the driver's side.

Sucks to be you, I thought, feeling a little smugger than was probably necessary. I had reminded Chubs to lock it, and with the gun inside the glove box, she'd have to find a rock or something heavy enough to break the glass if she wanted in—something that would be difficult to manage quietly.

If it hadn't been for her bright hair, I would have lost her in the darkness as she headed off the trail into the forest.

I stood and slipped out, tracing her steps around the car, trying to see how far she'd go. My toes were frozen stiff, sticking to the frost of the clumps of wild grass and mud. Vida kept walking, and I kept inching forward, more and more, until she was far enough for her hair to disappear into the night-cloaked trees completely—but not far enough to hide the blue-white glow of the device in her hands that cut through the darkness.

ELEVEN

WAIT FOR HER TO COME BACK, MY MIND REASONED. *Surprise her here.*

But I was running, even before the thought had fully formed in my mind. All of the training the League had tried to drill into me, all of my better judgment, all logic was ripped away with the first flash of that strange light. If she were contacting Cole, why would she have to hide it from us? Why would she need to send a message to him in private?

Because she's not contacting Cole.

I slid around the car. The coming winter had stripped the nearby trees bare; the naked branches snapped against my face and arms. The fine patches of ice and frost coating the clumps of grass stung my feet like hell, but it was nothing compared to fighting my way through the thickets of dead brush.

It didn't matter how much noise I was making. I wasn't aiming for surprise; it was impossible to get the jump on

Vida. I just wanted as much momentum as humanly possible when I tackled her to the ground.

She was still clutching the device when I lowered my head and rammed my shoulder into her. Vida had enough time to try to swing a knee up, square into my chest. With my full weight on her, and only one foot planted on the uneven hill, we slammed into the ground.

I hooked my leg around hers, and she reached up to get a good grip on my neck, and neither of us was willing to let go, even as we rolled down the slope, smashing through underbrush and nailing what was very likely every single rock on the damn mountain. We didn't stop, we couldn't, not until we crashed into a tree and sent a shower of dead brown leaves down over us.

My vision swam both from the spinning and the blows, but I was on top—I had the advantage, and I took it. A warm burst of Vida's breath clouded the air. I had my legs locked around her center, trying to keep her in place as I started to reach for the black device lying beside her neck.

Never in my life had I seen terror like that in Vida's eyes.

She reared up under me, freeing her arm from where it was pinned beneath her, and slapped me hard enough that, for a second, my vision blanked white. With a grunt, she swung her open palm again, clubbing me in the ear and effectively knocking me off her.

Vida jumped to her feet and I staggered up after her. My sight split in two, and I wasn't sure which one of her feet was actually flying toward my stomach until it made contact. I threw my arms up in front of my face to block the next one.

"How could you—?" I gasped out.

My fingers caught her wrist, but she ripped it free. I swung my fist toward her again and watched, stunned, as she went flying back through the air a good two dozen feet before I could even touch her.

"—op! *Stop!*"

I panted hard and was only able to keep on my feet for one more second. I sagged sideways into the rough embrace of a tree and slid all the way down onto my knees. The words were faint under the roar of blood pulsing in my ears. I turned, watching as Jude stumbled down the slope, tripping through the dense cluster of branches and soggy leaves until he dropped to his knees at Vida's side.

Chubs stood a short distance away, his arms still outstretched in the direction he had thrown her. "What," he called, "the hell is going on?"

"S-She—" I sputtered, bringing a shaking hand to swipe at my mouth. He marched toward me, flicking his flashlight in my direction. "She had—device—calling—DC—"

When he finally reached me, he grabbed my arm. I squirmed away from the intense light he was trying to shine directly into my face. I lurched away from him, the ground rising up to meet me. "Do you see it?" I heard myself asking. "Do you see it? Give me—give me the light."

"—ask *her*!" Vida was shouting. "She attacked *me*!"

Chubs dutifully aimed the flashlight where I pointed. "You need to sit down. Hey! Are you even listening to me?"

I patted around the dirt, fingers groping through the mulch, rocks, and roots. I knew the moment I had found it;

the black shell was unnaturally smooth and still warm to the touch. During the fight, the screen had flipped down to the ground, stifling the glow.

"What is that?" Chubs crouched down next to me. "A phone?"

Close, but not quite.

"A Chatter?" came Jude's startled voice. "Where did you get that?"

He was standing behind us, supporting a swaying Vida. No—he wasn't supporting her. He had one arm across her chest to keep her from going at my throat.

Dumb, brave kid, I thought for the thousandth time. I turned my eyes back down on the screen and flicked it on.

I had interrupted her in the middle of typing a message. Good. I brought the screen up close to my eyes, squinting at the series of nonsense numbers and letters. The little black line was still blinking, waiting for her to finish up.

I HAVE THEM // PHASE TWO INSTRLWJERL:KS SLKJDFJ

"You *bitch,*" I said, looking up. "You really thought you could play us? Turn us back over to the League? What did Alban promise you—that you could take over as team leader?"

I was half blind with rage, too angry to let her answer. I stood, throwing the device on the ground. Vida and Jude both took generous steps back. My brain was humming with need, with nothing more than the desire to pry into hers and leave it mangled and ruined. My anger added a boost to their strength and I thought, I really did, if I let them loose, the invisible hands would take her this time without me needing to grab her. I turned, ready to let them fly.

Instead, I felt a hand close over my wrist and pull me back. Chubs was on his feet now, too, his eyes fixed on the screen. I heard him click a button, and then the Chatter was hovering in front of my face, and I was reading an old, received message.

HEAD SOUTH ON 40 // ADDRESS AS DISCUSSED // EXPLAIN UPDATED OP IMMEDIATELY UPON CONTACT // TELL HER I AM SORRY

"Tell her I'm sorry?" I turned back toward Vida, who had turned away, her face a stone mask. "Who is this? Cole?"

Vida's swollen lip slurred her speech, and when she spoke, it was so quiet I had to strain to hear her. Her reluctance proved the blossoming theory in my mind—after all, there was only one person she protected like this.

"No," she said, "it's Cate."

I was ready to have it all out there, but Chubs insisted that we return to the camp and rebuild the fire with a sharp "I prefer to not take my bad news in the freezing dead of night, thank you very much."

He steered me toward one end of the smothered fire and headed for his car. I was distantly aware of the beep of the car unlocking and the door slamming shut. When he sat back down next to me, Chubs started in on cleaning the cuts on my face and arms with a total lack of sympathy.

"Someone better start talking now," he said, "because, trust me, you don't want to hear what I have to say about all this. Especially at one o'clock in the morning."

Vida sniffed, drawing her knees up to her chest. The right half of her face was cast entirely in darkness. Or covered in an enormous bruise.

I held up the Chatter to the dim firelight, turning it back and forth. "Who gave you this? Nico?"

She waited so long to answer I thought for sure she wouldn't. All I got was a shrug. Her nails were clawing into the dirt, dragging clumps of it up into her clenched fists.

"So he and Cate are in on this, too?" I demanded. "Who else?"

Vida crossed her arms over her chest and stared out into the dark distance.

"Why keep this from us?" Jude asked. "Did she ask you to? It doesn't make any sense, and it *really* doesn't make sense that you still won't talk about it. You got caught, and now the Op has been compromised. And what are you supposed to do when that happens?"

Accept, adapt, and act. Quickly. The words had been scrawled onto one of the walls in the training room. They might as well have been tattooed directly onto our brains.

"Fine," she said, circling her shoulders back as if to ease the tension there. *She's angry,* I realized. Vida was furious—with herself. The perfect little soldier had blown her own Op, the special one Cate had entrusted her with. She was breathing hard, sucking air up between her clenched teeth. Cate was the single most important person in her life, maybe the only one who really mattered to her. I had an idea of why she had withheld that information, but I wanted to hear her admit it.

"Cate and Cole planned this whole thing, pretty much from the second we brought his ass back to HQ," Vida said. "They go back. She took him under her wing when he first joined, helped train him. He told her the truth about your dumbass Prince Charming and the flash drive, and you were the solution they came up with. For whatever reason, Cate stupidly trusts you to handle shit."

"Why have Cole give me the story, then?"

"They're watching her. Rob and the others. She knew what he was like, or at least figured it out a few months ago, but she was trying to stay close to his creepy ass to make sure he didn't come after us. She couldn't go to Alban or any of the advisers, because she was afraid she'd be reassigned from us if they saw her as being 'difficult.' Nico showed Cole, Cate, and me the video of Blake being offed and she just about went ballistic."

"When was this?"

"Just after you left HQ." Vida tucked a strand of hair behind her ear, glancing over at me. "Nico said you told him not to, but something you said to Cole made him push the issue. They're sitting on the video until we bring the intel back."

Of course—because keeping the Children's League together was the top priority here. Not protecting kids. Not cutting off the psychopaths.

"Let me see if I understand this," Chubs began. "Cate was in on everything from the beginning, but she kept silent on it? Was that to act as some kind of fail-safe?"

"Not bad, Grannie," Vida said. "Cole said Cate's role had to stay a secret, even from you. If you dipshits got caught and were brought in for questioning, he didn't want you to be able to implicate her—if he took the fall, at least Cate would still be around to be on our side. She hated it, but I told her she had to agree, otherwise I wasn't going to help you. She didn't say yes until she realized there was no way to get Jude removed from the mission without it making people suspicious. Rob requested him personally."

Jude looked like he was a breath away from throwing up all over himself. The firelight drew out the flush of panic in his cheeks.

Vida threw a truly pitying look his way. "Cate said he ran after you called him out. Went totally off the fucking grid before Barton could bring him in for questioning."

"So he won't be there when we get back," Jude said, sighing in relief.

No, but it meant that I had released a furious monster out into the world to rip it apart and remake to his own liking.

"That's everything I know," Vida said. "The end. But I'm telling you now, if either of you breathe a word—one goddamn word—about Cate, I will come down on you so hard, they'll be naming hurricanes after me for a fucking century."

I opened my mouth to fire back at her but thought better of it in the end. For as long as I'd known Vida, I'd felt a sharp sense of pity over her obvious worship of Cate. I thought I'd been given a glimpse of the real Cate that lived below the pristine exterior. But now it was becoming harder and harder to believe that either one of us was completely right about who she was. To me, her belief in the League had always seemed naive—I really thought she blinded herself to everything going on around her to stay in that happy world that existed only in her mind. Maybe Jude really was right, and the League of today didn't remotely resemble the one she had willingly joined years ago.

Then why did she only give herself up to me in pieces? And why had it taken me so long to put them together into a somewhat complete picture?

"You've been communicating directly with Cate, I suppose?" Chubs took the Chatter out of my limp hand and turned it over. "She's been guiding you along?"

"Yeah," Vida said. "She sent me the routes to get down here. Too bad she couldn't just load his ass into Google Maps. Not even Nico has been able to track him."

The screen between Chubs's fingers flashed to life and let out a low, vibrating growl. The light it emitted was bright enough that we could all watch as his eyebrows rose steadily up past his glasses' frames to his hairline.

"Well, maybe she can't send exact coordinates," he said, flipping it around, "but she has an idea of where we could start."

TWELVE

TARGET SIGHTED OUTSIDE NASHVILLE //
HOSTILE BLUE TRIBE IN NEARBY AREA //
APPROACH WITH CAUTION

"The sighting isn't listed in the skip-tracer network," Chubs said. His finger flicked against the screen of the small tablet I had fished out of the glove box for him, scrolling down. "That's not surprising, though. I haven't been able to pick up an Internet signal in a few days to download an update."

"What is that thing?" I asked. At the top of the color screen was Liam's bruised, scowling face—the picture that had been taken, I guess, when he was brought into Caledonia. Next to the photo was a list of the same information I had been able to access in the PSF network—the only update being that his reward had gone up to $200,000 and his last reported sighting was outside of Richmond, Virginia.

"It has direct access to the skip-tracer network," Chubs said. "You get one after you register and are approved by the government. The information on there is closely guarded—the PSFs don't have access to it, so they can't swoop in and steal a score."

It was a touch screen, easy enough to flick through the various listings beneath it. A skip tracer named P. Everton had been the one to sight him in Richmond—he had posted the following on Liam's listing: *Stewart driving red Chevy truck, stolen plates. Target in jeans and black hooded sweatshirt. Lost sight of car during pursuit.*

"Why would they be sharing information with one another like this?" I asked. "If only one of them gets the reward?"

"Because if a tip turns out to be good, you're upped in the standings. Each kid, especially the big bounties, are assigned points in addition to dollar amounts—but you can also earn points by adding tips or supporting the PSFs when they are trying to locate a kid." Chubs shrugged. "The top twenty or so skip tracers get more supplies from the government, not to mention better equipment—and easy access to the Internet. That alone makes a huge difference. I can't even tell you how many stupid kids have been found because of the pictures and postings their families had online. I think that's probably how the PSFs found me the first time. Mom forgot she had an album of our cabin up on some website."

I nodded, continuing to scroll through the list. There were only about a thousand or so active listings of kids, many of them without pictures. These, I assumed, were the lucky ones who had been added to the online IAAN registry by their unsuspecting parents for updates and instructions from the government, but who had avoided being collected and brought into a camp. They had either found a great place to hide or had mastered the art of living off the grid. I kept scrolling.

Dale, Andrea. Dale, George Ryan. Daley, Jacob Marcus.

Daly, Ruby.

The picture was of a ten-year-old me, eyes wide under a ratty mess of wet, dark hair. *That's right,* I thought. *It had been raining the day they brought us in.*

"What the hell?" I held it up for him to see. "Four hundred thousand dollars for a reward?"

"What— Oh, that." Chubs plucked the tablet from my hands and said grimly, "Congratulations, you're officially a big score."

"That's— I just— *Why?*"

"Do you really need me to break it down for you?" he said, sighing. "You escaped from *Thurmond* with the help of the *League*, and are, oh, by the way, an *Orange*."

"What are all of the listings?" I asked. "I've never been in Maine or Georgia."

He held the screen up for me to see. "Look closer."

Sighted outside of Marietta, Georgia, moving east. J. Lister.

At least five of them were from J. Lister, otherwise known as the teenager in the driver's seat next to me.

"I would have done more, but you get penalized for spamming the network with false tips. I try to do that for you and Lee whenever I can, to throw off the other skip tracers."

"What about Zu?"

"Same," he said. "But not nearly as much. It looks bad when you're only updating for the same kids and not thinking about distances and all that. I can't post that I saw you in Maine and, two minutes later, post I saw her in California. I have a story for her figured out, though. As far as the skip tracers know, she's somewhere in Florida."

"Do you think she and the others actually made it to California?" I asked. "There haven't been any updates in the PSF network the League had access to. I checked last week again, and still nothing."

"I . . ." Chubs cleared his throat. "I'd like to think she did. Once we find Lee, we'll just have to go see for ourselves."

The others were in our line of sight out of the front windshield. Vida was attempting to take down the tent by beating it into submission. Jude was simply stretched out on his back in a grassy patch of earth, staring up at the sky, the compass resting on his chest. It was cold, but the sunlight was out for the first time in days. He was regarding the sky with a kind of amazed wonderment.

"What do you think he's looking at?" Chubs asked, craning his neck forward over the wheel to follow Jude's gaze up. "Is that kid mentally . . . sound?"

"I would guess his brain is about ten thousand miles away from here, crafting the tale of this heroic adventure," I said. "But yeah. He's a sweet kid. Hyperactive, totally unwilling to accept reality, but sweet."

"If you say so," Chubs muttered.

Vida let out a strangled scream, uprooting one of the pikes holding the tent in place. She reached down and flipped the whole structure over onto its side and smashed her foot into it for good measure. "Why am I the only one working?" she yelled. *"Helloooo?!"*

Chubs was already bursting out of his door before I had a hand on mine. "Could you *not* destroy *my* tent, you incompetent, ungrateful wretch?" he bellowed.

"*I'm* incompetent?" Vida's voice went hoarse. "Who's the stupid asshole who threw away the instructions?"

With one quick glance to make sure Vida wasn't going to impale Chubs with the pike she held in her hand, I reached for the tablet and switched it back on.

For two, three, four agonizing seconds, all I saw was the slow spin of a gray circle as the device loaded itself. It snapped to the home screen with a small beep; a tiny menu that ranged from EMERGENCY to DATABASE to UPDATES. Above that was a digital map of the United States, one that looked like it could be used for actual navigation.

That wasn't what I needed it for.

My stomach was clenched into a tight fist of anxiety, but my fingers were steady as I typed in the name.

Gray, Clancy.

And then, the pain released with a single long breath.

No records found.

It was another four hours to Nashville, with Chubs and me splitting the driving duties. Seeing him behind the wheel instead of the seat behind me was strange enough, but his relaxed, confident posture there made him look like a different person. I was forcing myself to adapt, trying to come to terms with the fact that this Chubs was not the one who had been taken from me. How could he be, after everything?

Aside from his reaction to Vida's baiting and insults, he was calmer—outwardly. Every now and then I would look over and see a shadow flit across the sharp lines of his face. *Tell me,* I would think, but the thick clouds would pass overhead, peeling back to submerge the road in brilliant sunlight, and he'd look like himself again. At least until it came time to eat.

In the past, Chubs had complained and railed against just the *idea* of stopping to have one of us go in and buy food from a store or restaurant. It had always been Liam who went out to buy it, with Chubs's loud protests trailing behind him like a nagging shadow.

"Oh, come on. It'll be fine," he said when he insisted on parking at a rest stop with a handful of people already milling around it.

It was becoming readily apparent that he used his skip-tracer identification like it was a bulletproof shield, flashing it to anyone who gave him a second look. A part of me wondered if he was too used to playing this part or if something inside him had really shifted.

The rest of us waited, scooted as far down in our seats as possible, while Chubs took his time using the restroom, mining the vending machines, and breathing in the fresh wintry air.

"I thought you said this kid was smart," Vida hissed.

"He is." I watched him over the curve of the dashboard.

"Then he's just freaking rude," she shot back. "Or he's trying to get us caught."

No—it wasn't that. Chubs was a lot of things, but he wasn't malicious enough to try to push someone out who needed his help.

Oh really? came the small voice at the back of my mind. *Isn't that exactly what he tried to do with you?*

I shook my head as he climbed back into the SUV, tossing his haul of chips and candy onto my lap. Chubs glanced at me, then looked again. "What are you doing?"

My lips parted in surprise. "What do you think? Any of these people could have reported us!"

Chubs's brows drew together, the realization finally coming to him. He looked at the others, still crouched down in the back. Jude had his arms wrapped around his knees, burrowed down into the gully of space between the metal grate and his seat.

"Yup," Vida said to no one in particular, "just a fucking idiot."

"It's okay," Jude said with forced brightness. "They wouldn't have called us in. They didn't look like PSFs or skip tracers anyway."

Skip tracers didn't have a *look*—Chubs was evidence of that. He had maybe dressed the part, but he wasn't one of them. He didn't have that detached coldness that seemed to permeate from the others. His reaction now, the way he jammed his key into the ignition, made me wonder if he had ever noticed how irresponsible he was being until this very moment.

It didn't become a real problem until we reached the outskirts of Nashville and the blockade the National Guard had set up and staffed with a few dozen of their finest.

"City closed," Jude said, reading the spray-painted sign we flew past. It was a series of signs, one after another. "Flood zone. Slow. City closed. Turn back. National Guard entry only. City closed." Jude's voice dropped just a little bit more with each one he read, but the SUV only picked up speed. The makeshift station began as a dark, blurry line at the horizon of the snow-slick road and took shape, one barbed tangle of wires and fence at a time.

"Slow down," I told Chubs. "Stop for a second." He ignored both requests.

Vida glanced up from where she had been typing out another message to Cate on the Chatter. "Oh. Yeah. Cate said the city's been blocked off since the summer. Something about how a river flooded the city and some people started rioting when they didn't get any aid."

I sighed, pressing my face into my hands. "That information would have been useful to know twenty minutes ago." Back when we were, you know, in the middle of a discussion about the best way into the city.

Vida shrugged.

"Uhhhh," Jude began, a distinct note of panic in his voice. "There's a guy coming toward us. He is coming toward us really freaking fast."

Sure enough, a National Guardsman had pulled away from the chain-link fence and dirty yellow barrels they were using to block our path down the road. He was jogging, his gun and supplies jostling with each step. A spike of cold panic shot straight up my spine.

The National Guardsman stopped, his hand drifting to the firearm at his side.

Then Chubs asked, "Does everyone have their seat belt on?"

"You're joking," I began. There was no way. He would never.

Vida finally looked up from the Chatter.

Jude yelped as the car lurched forward. Chubs had floored the pedal.

I reached over and jerked the wheel, forcing the car to veer sharply to the left. Chubs tried to shove me off, but I guided the car around, narrowly missing the soldier who had come out to meet us. He eased up immediately on the gas, but we were already headed back in the right direction—away from the fence, the soldiers, and danger. Vida slammed her palm against the grate and the pedal floored under her influence, locked hard against the SUV's dirty carpet. Chubs tried pumping the brakes, and the car seemed to shriek in protest.

When the blockade was finally a small blip in the rearview mirror, Vida lifted her hand and Chubs's foot came down on the brake. The seat belts snapped over our chests.

"I . . ." I started when I'd finally caught my breath. "Why . . . You . . ."

"Dammit!" Chubs began, slapping his hand against the steering wheel. He didn't sound like himself; he had yelled at me before, countless times, but this was . . . I actually felt myself shrink. "How *dare* you do that! How dare you!"

"If you're going to fight, can you do it outside?" Vida said. "I already have a big enough headache without hearing Mommy and Daddy at each other's throats."

Fine by me. I unbuckled my seat belt, ignoring Chubs's growl as he did the same.

"What?" he demanded, coming around to meet me at the front of the SUV. His boots slid through the snow clinging to the dark surface of the road. His breath was hot with anger. It fanned out white and sticky against my stinging cheeks.

"What was that?" I asked. "Were you really going to force your way through?"

It was how he shrugged, like it didn't matter, like it was nothing, that made me crazy.

"I can't believe it," I said. "Wake up! *Wake up!* This isn't like you at all!"

"I wouldn't have had to do it if you didn't stick me with those stupid kids—I could have flashed some papers and we would have been in!" He dragged a hand through his tuft of dark hair. "And you know what? Even if I *had* gone through with it, it's not like they would have caught up to us. Honestly, weren't you and Lee the ones who always said we had to take risks if we were going to get by?"

"Are you . . ." I could barely choke the word out. "Are you *serious*? Risks? Where is your head? You are so much smarter than this!"

Did it matter that I was yelling or that he was doing his best to try to tower over me with his height? Did it matter that the other two were watching us through the windshield?

"Sure, we would have gotten through the blockade, maybe even miles away, but what if they got your license plate number and reported that? What if up the road there was another blockade, and they were waiting for us there? What would you have done? You're the only one with papers; you would have been fine—but if they had taken me? Or Jude or Vida? Could you have lived with that?"

"What about *Liam*?" he shouted. "You know, the one whose brain you decided to fry? The one who's lost, or dead, or near to it because you decided to screw with him? Remember *him*?"

Every inch of my skin felt like the branches of the trees overhead, stripped bare and coated with frost. "You do blame me."

"Who else would I blame?" he shouted. "It's your fault, dammit! And now you're acting like this? Like those kids are more important to you than us? Yeah, I've had to make a few changes. So what? I've been getting on just fine making my own decisions. You keep acting like I'm still bleeding out in your hands, but I'm *fine*! I am better than *fine*! You're the one who's wrong! You're—"

I hadn't even heard the door open, but Vida was suddenly standing beside me, her shoulder pressed against mine.

"Back. Off." I felt her hand close around my wrist. "You don't want us here, ass-clown? Fine. We're out."

Jude was white-faced as he scurried around the back, clutching our few possessions in his hands. "I'm ready," he said, his voice betraying none of the fear I saw in his eyes. "Let's go."

I took the leather jacket that Jude passed to me, my mind trying to catch up with what was happening. Chubs's fingers caught the pocket and held tight. "What are you doing?"

"I think . . ." My whole face felt numb. "I think this was a bad idea."

No, my brain was screaming, *no, no, no!*

"Ruby!" he said, shocked. "Tell me you're not . . . *Ruby!*"

"You think we're worthless? You want to prove that you're so damn brave?" Vida shouted back. "Go ahead and get your stupid ass killed. We'll see who finds Stewart first!"

Vida hooked her arm through mine and began to haul me down the slight curve of the highway's shoulder, down into the snow-splattered forest ahead. It was deep, and dark, and lovely. I couldn't see the beginning or end of it.

"Asshole," she was muttering. "God damn him, I hate his stupid-ass face and his stupid-ass driving—acting like we're as dumb as dirt. *Asshole!*"

Jude jogged to keep pace with us. Branches snapped around my face, clawing at my hair. The flashes of sunlight through the treetops were disorienting, blinding red one moment and orange the next, and all I could think was *fire*. All I could see was Chubs's face close to mine as we clung to each other under the dock at East River while the world burned above us.

I felt a hand touch the small of my back, and I just couldn't do it anymore. My legs buckled, and I barely managed to catch myself on a tree before I collapsed completely.

What are you doing? I thought. *This is Chubs. This is still Chubs.*

For several agonizing minutes, I couldn't hear anything beyond my own harsh breathing. I felt physically ill, like I was about to heave up everything in the pit of my stomach.

This is Chubs. Who says things he constantly regrets, even if they're the truth. Who lets his anger get the best of him—especially when he's afraid. And you left him. You walked away. That was Chubs, and you left him.

I felt a hand tugging on mine. Jude stood beside me, his EMT jacket crinkling.

"I think you were both wrong," he said quietly. "He doesn't blame you for what ended up happening with Liam. He blames himself. He's only acting like this because he's gotten to the point where he's willing to do anything to set it right."

"Why would he think any of this is his fault, though?" I asked.

"He's a loose cannon," Vida said, glancing back over her shoulder. "He survived being shot. Some part of him thinks he's invincible and that he can make stupid mistakes and get away with it. There are other ways he could have traveled, but he chose to run with the fucking wolves. If he's not desperate, if he doesn't hate himself, then he really is just a goddamn idiot."

"You guys don't know him," I started.

"No," Jude said carefully, "but we know you."

"And if you think you haven't been acting the same exact way he has for the past six months, then you're a goddamn idiot, too." Vida turned me back in the direction of the road and gave me a hard shove. "Go get him, then. If you're not back in five minutes, we'll head out on our own to find Stewart. You said you didn't have a choice in joining the League? Well, congrat-u-freaking-lations. Now you do. Come back with us or don't, but I'm more than capable of doing this Op without all of your boo-hoo issues holding me down."

I read her meaning loud and clear. "I'll be back," I told them. "Right back, I swear."

I took a lurching step forward, keeping my eyes on our staggered footprints in the snow. Keeping them focused down and ahead, because I couldn't stand to think of the others watching me go.

I can't leave them. Any of them. Not Vida, who was too headstrong for her own good. Not Jude, who couldn't stand the silence or the dark. Not Chubs, not after everything.

The SUV was still there, parked crookedly on the shoulder. He was in the driver's seat, leaning against the steering wheel. I walked around the back of the car, glancing both ways down the road to make sure there were no other eyes on us, then pulled Liam's jacket around me tighter for support.

He didn't see me. His shoulders were shaking, but I wasn't sure if he was only breathing hard or actually crying. I knocked on the window. And Chubs—my Chubs—about leaped into the passenger seat in terror.

I'm sorry, I mouthed through the glass.

He had been crying. Something inside me twisted, sharp and firm as Chubs opened the door. "You scared the *hell* out of me!" he shouted. "Do you know how easy it is to fall and break an ankle when you're walking without directions? Or into a frozen river? Do you know what happens when you get hypothermia?"

I leaned in and wrapped my arms around his shoulders.

"I'm— I mean . . ." he began. I felt his hands bunch up the back of Liam's jacket with the effort to keep me there. "I'm not the same person. I'm not, and I know that. I'm not okay with who I am or what I had to do, but I'm also *not okay* with us separating again! Don't *do* that! Don't just disappear! If you're mad at me, then hit me or something—just don't think that I don't want to stay with you. I'll *always* want to stay with you!"

I tightened my grip on him, pressing my face against his shoulder.

"You're different, too," he said. "It's all different now. I just want it to go back to the way it was, when we were in that stupid minivan— Jesus, will you say something?"

"Don't," I said, "call Black Betty stupid."

I don't know if he was laughing or just crying again, but both of us shook with the force of it. "I miss him," he was saying. "I miss him so much—I know it's stupid. I'm just, I'm scared—"

"He's not dead," I cut in. "He's not. He can't be."

Chubs pulled back slowly, lifting his glasses to swipe his arm over his eyes. "That's not what I mean. I'm scared of what he'll say when he finds out about . . . *this*." His hands settled again on the wheel. "All of this."

"He'll probably make some stupid joke at your expense," I said, "and give you another dumb nickname."

"No," he said, clearly struggling, "he'll know . . ."

I suddenly felt very still. There was no other way to describe the dread that crept over me when Chubs turned away from me.

"I told you before about all the paperwork that you need to fill out to register as a skip tracer," he said, "but . . . that's only half of it."

"Half?" I repeated.

He nodded, looking miserable. "In order to establish yourself, you have to turn in a kid. There's no other way to put your name in the rankings. You can't cheat the system. Believe me. I tried."

It took an immeasurable amount of time for what he was saying to sink in. With each second that passed, his face became more and more transparent. His thoughts and fears flashed by, unchecked.

"Who?" I asked finally.

"Some Green kid I found in New York." Chubs swallowed hard. "He was . . . He had been living rough for a few years. I could tell by the look of him. Haunted, you know? Hungry. He was practically gaunt. I only saw him because he was trying to break a vending machine at one of those outdoor malls. It was in the middle of the day. There was a whole crowd of people watching him, not getting close to him."

"What happened?"

"He . . . I don't know, he didn't even put up much of a fight," Chubs said, his voice hoarse with emotion. "He just looked at me, and I could see that he had given up. And at the time, I was thinking, you know, that he would at least have food in a camp. He would have a bed. He was only a Green. They would treat him okay if he kept his head down."

"You had to." What else could I say to that? "It was the only way."

"Is that how I'm supposed to explain myself to Lee? Oh, sorry. Your life was more important than his? He's not going to understand." Chubs cleared his throat. "The fact of the matter is, I would have done a lot worse. I would have done anything to find you guys. It scares me. I feel like if there's not someone there to stop me, I'm not sure what I would do."

That was a feeling I knew well—the sensation of freefalling into a dark pit, not knowing how soon you'll hit the bottom of it or if there even is one.

"It won't matter," I said. "In the end, it won't. After we find Liam and get the intel, you better believe I'm going to burn every single one of those camps to the ground."

He looked so uncertain about it, it broke my heart.

"I have to. Will you stay with me on this?" I whispered.

After a moment, Chubs nodded. "All right." He cleared his throat again, trying to force it back to its usual gruff tone. "Where did the others go?"

"They're waiting for us."

"Are we walking, then?" he asked. "I'll have to try to hide the car."

I stared at him a moment, confused. Then, I understood. *He's letting you lead.*

"Yeah," I said. "I think we should try to get into the city on foot."

Chubs nodded, and there wasn't any discussion after that. We took the car a ways down the highway until we found a smaller access road. With the SUV properly masked in the trees and under whatever foliage we could find, we set off into the woods.

"I haven't done this in a while," Chubs said, shifting the pack we had put together of supplies and one of the twenty-five zillion first-aid kits he had insisted on packing. He was smiling, just a faint touch, but it was still there.

"Wish I could say the same," I said, putting a hand on his shoulder to help steady myself as I hauled my legs over a fallen tree.

"Where did you say they were?"

I hadn't even realized we were back in the same small clearing as before until I saw the dizzy array of footsteps pounded out in the mud and mulch. They'd been good on their word, then. They had split, and we'd have to catch up to them.

I looked over at Chubs to tell him as much, but his eyes were focused down on the snow, his eyebrows knit together.

There were more than three sets of tracks here. My brain had taken one look and assumed that Jude had been pacing in his usual way or that Vida had been circling the clearing impatiently. But there were way too many footprints for that.

I saw it then, the way it must have happened. A spiraling circle of steps where Vida had tried to fight, ending in the exposed patch of earth where she had fallen. Across the way, branches broken and littered on the ground—I took another step forward, following the trail until my feet met with a small spray of blazing-bright blood on a melting patch of snow.

No. The wind took on a low menacing growl in my ears. They hadn't gone on ahead.

They had been taken.

THIRTEEN

It didn't even occur to me that Chubs might not be able to keep up with my pace as I ran. The group had cleared a path through the mud and pockets of lingering snow, packing it down to a manageable level with their feet. I took in a deep gulp of the dry air, trying to ignore the snow slipping from the low branches of trees and brush as I tore through them. My pants and coat were soaked through by the time I finally skidded to a stop. The trail of prints, so wide and obvious before, came to a definite end at the lip of a frozen stream.

Chubs panted heavily as he came up beside me, one hand pressed hard against his shoulder. I turned to take the bag of supplies he'd packed, but then thought twice. The one he handed me was just as heavy, and I wouldn't be able to get through the snow with both of them, at least not quickly.

"What now?" he gasped between breaths. "They crossed here?"

"No, it's not possible," I said, kneeling down to test the ice. "There had to be at least ten of them. There's no way they all would have made it across without breaking the ice."

His eyes narrowed at me as I stood. "You can tell all that just by a few prints?"

"No," I said, "I don't know the exact number. Ten or more. Vida wouldn't have let herself be taken by any less."

Chubs looked doubtful, but he didn't deny the possibility.

I walked a ways along the bank of the stream, looking for stray tracks, human or otherwise. They couldn't have just vanished here.

Shit, I thought, threading my fingers through the messy bun I had twisted my hair into. *Shit!*

"Could . . ." Chubs swallowed, shifting the bag uncomfortably on his shoulders. "Do you think they were taken by soldiers? Ones the blockade sent after us?"

I shook my head. "They would have taken the road. We would have seen them." Or at least, that was what I was telling myself. "Skip tracers, maybe?"

This time he was the one to shoot the thought down. "Ten of them? Why would they all be out here, in the middle of nowhere?"

"Then . . ." I began. Chubs's eyes widened as he caught my train of thought.

"The tribe of Blues we're looking for?" he asked. "But why put up a fight?"

I fought back the first sting of panicked tears. *Oh, God. Jude must have been terrified.* "They don't understand how it works. They don't have a life outside of the League—they, we, I mean, were taught to only trust one another."

It was only dumb luck that I turned back to the stream when I did, that the wind pulled back the evergreen foliage of the trees across the way. Otherwise I would have missed the silver glint of gunmetal between its branches.

I threw myself over Chubs, tackling him face-first into the ground as the first shot was fired. I felt something tug on my backpack, and I turned away from the small explosion of snow and dirty leaves when the bullet tore through the ground beside us.

The bullets screeched as they cut through the air following our path as I rolled the two of us back into the shelter of the tree line.

"Keep your head down!" I whispered to Chubs, all but shoving him behind a dense cover of growth. The gun I'd fished out of the glove compartment was warm in my hand as I pulled it up from the waistband of my pants. I fired one shot back, aiming for the spot I thought I had seen the person before, across the stream. The shooting from his or her end came to a sudden, unexpected stop.

The afternoon air was pale and still between us. It had a sharp quality to it; it smelled like snow.

"Ruby!"

A dark blur dropped out of the tree behind me. I spun, without thinking, and launched my elbow out. It connected with something soft that made an audible *crunch* as I threw my full weight into the hit.

There was a sharp cry of pain, followed by a heavy *thump*. The impact sent up whirling clouds of snow. I turned back for Chubs, reaching out for him through the white haze, and felt a hand close over my forearm. The skin was pale, each knuckle torn open or scabbed.

I pulled back a step, bringing my knee up to throw the next attacker off, but the fight was over before it started. I felt a cold, sharp blade dig into my spinal column, and lowered my arms. I turned slightly to look over my shoulder at Chubs. He was covered in mud, his face ashen.

"Who are you?" I said, coming around slowly to face him, keeping clear of the knife.

"Son of a *bitch*," he hissed. The pitch of the voice had been enough to tell me how old he actually was: my age. A year or two older at most.

The boy I'd hit staggered up from the ground, swiping his nose against the sleeve of his threadbare coat, leaving a long, dark streak of crimson on it. The kid with the knife stepped back but didn't put it away.

Bloody Nose held out his hand and I reached out, acting like I was about to put my gun in it. At the last minute, I dropped it and took his hand instead, driving into his mind. His body twitched under my control. I saw a flash of Jude's frightened face in his mind, and it was enough for me.

"What did you do to those kids?" I snarled. "The boy and the girl from earlier? Where did you take them?"

Chubs had a strange look on his face as he watched me, but he stayed silent.

"The guys—" he said, his voice altered by the sickening angle of his nose. My elbow ached in response. "The guys b-brought them to the Slip Kid."

Of course.

Those were the first words that sprang to mind, that chipped through the ice that gripped me in place. *Of course.* Clancy's system had worked so well the first time—why wouldn't he try it again? *Of course.* It wouldn't matter who the kids were, only that they'd be willing—or easily swayed by his abilities—to go to war with President Gray.

Of course.

I had to release the kid from my grip when four other figures appeared in the woods around us, closing in to investigate what had happened. I could control one person, but I wasn't Clancy; any more than that was impossible, and any attempts to try would have revealed the only upper hand I currently had. I stepped forward, showed them I was unarmed, and motioned for Chubs to do the same.

"We want to see the Slip Kid," I said. "We won't give you trouble."

"That a fact?" one of them asked, glancing down at the dazed kid at my feet. "Michael, you hear that, or did that hit knock your screws loose?"

Blood Nose—Michael—shook his head in an obvious attempt to clear it. A head injury was a decent cover for what I had done to him, but it was taking his little brain so long to recover I was worried the other boys around us would get suspicious. They didn't seem willing or able to do anything without his permission.

"We're taking them," Michael said. "Make it fast. Two of you stay on this post. I'll send someone back for you."

This guy is the leader? I thought. It wasn't unreasonable. His size alone would have inspired fear, if nothing else.

They pushed Chubs toward me as we made our way back to the stream. I looped one arm around his waist to keep him close. They took our bags and hauled them up onto their shoulders.

"Well," Chubs muttered, "shit."

We were out in the open again, near the frozen stream—and, more importantly, in the line of sight of the gunman in the tree.

There were hands on me, patting me down, feeling around the insides of my boots. I tried not to react as one took my Swiss Army knife from my boot. The freezing air stung my face, but it was the thought of what they might find in Chubs's pockets that made me go cold to the bone.

Chubs must have read the question on my face, because he shook his head ever so slightly. The kid searching him only found his knife and a pocket full of candy wrappers. He had been with it enough to dump his skip-tracer ID in the woods during the attack or leave it behind in the car, then. Thank God.

I turned to look across the river, narrowly avoiding Chubs's kicking feet as he was lifted off the ground and out of my reach.

He thrashed into the air in the half second it took for the kid with the outstretched hand to lift him up and, using nothing more than his freak abilities, toss him onto the opposite bank.

I felt the warm tug at the pit of my stomach and recognized the sensation. I didn't have the chance to protest before I was hauled up and over the stream, too, dropped onto Chubs with a total and complete lack of kindness.

The other kids burst out laughing, floating one another over the frozen stream with all the gentleness of calming breezes. Other than that, they didn't speak, didn't offer up a single explanation or confirmation of where they were taking us. Two stayed behind to snuff out our tracks in the soft white powder.

We walked in silence. Snow began to fall, catching on my hair and lashes, and cold crept in through the leather of Liam's coat. Chubs tensed, rubbing his bad shoulder absently. I caught his gaze, and I could see my anxiety mirrored in his dark eyes.

"I can't believe it," he muttered. "Again."

"I'll take care of him," I said quietly, looping my arm through his.

"Since that worked so well last time?"

"Hey!" Michael held up his silver handgun. "Shut the hell up!"

We were on foot long enough that I began to wonder if we were ever going to reach the encampment or wherever they planned on taking us. It didn't occur to me until the large river came into sight that we were moving toward Nashville.

I understood straight off why they had originally closed the city; though the river must have surged past its banks months before, most of the water had yet to freeze or pull completely back to its normal level. The water's edges were bloated, drowning the nearby landscape. The river was a monster that only grew larger the closer we came. It was the only thing that stood between us and a looming white warehouse across the way.

Waiting for us on the bank were three small, flat rafts that looked like nothing more than crates and spare planks stitched together with bright blue vinyl rope. A kid in white stood on each of them, gripping a long pole. With the group of us spread out over the three rafts, the kids with poles pushed and navigated us through the shallow, muddy water in slow, methodic movements.

My fists clenched at my sides. One of the loading docks of the warehouse was open and waiting. With a steadiness I didn't expect, the raft floated the rest of the way to the curled silver door and the dark room inside.

The loading platform was raised enough that the rafts were no longer necessary. I was lifted up by the waist and deposited into the arms of another kid waiting there. The girl who caught me was a skinny, pale thing, her green eyes jutting out of the blunt bones of her face. She let out a wet, rumbling cough that came up from deep within her chest, but she didn't say anything as she took my arm and forced me inside.

The walls and floors were cement, cracked and tagged within an inch of their lives with old, faded graffiti. The warehouse was roughly the size of a high school gymnasium, and it still held a few clues about its past life—signs marking where cables and wires could be left. The back wall, the one we were walking toward, had been painted a light robin's-egg blue, and though someone had tried to cover them with a layer of white paint, I could still read the black letters spelling out JOHNSON ELECTRIC beneath it.

Chubs fell in step beside me, nodding toward the brown line that ran along all of the walls, about halfway up toward the ceiling. So the water from the river had been that high?

Every single step I took, every voice around us, every drip of water from the cracks in the vaulted ceilings seemed to echo. The sounds played off the bare walls and boarded-up windows around us. Despite the fact that we were out of the snow and wind, the building wasn't insulated to keep out the persistent chill. Old metal trash cans had been repurposed to hold bonfires, but most of these were located toward the other end of the warehouse, not near the patches of kids scattered by the entrance we had come through.

This . . . wasn't anything like East River had been.

And the teenage boy sitting on the raised platform in the back, disappearing in and out of a haze of cigarette and fire smoke, was not Clancy Gray.

"Who the hell are you?"

There had been a low murmur of interest as we were hauled in, but at my words, it dropped off to silence. My eyes had gone straight to the kid's face, snapping over to it so quickly that I hadn't even noticed the other teens around him until they stepped forward for a better look. There were girls shivering in T-shirts and shorts, leaning against the base of the stage or draped along the crates stacked behind him with only a few blankets between them. Clusters of boys stood around them laughing, some feeding the cloud of putrid gray smoke with their own cigarettes.

This kid had to be closer to his twenties than the others. His face was fringed with the beginning of a reddish beard, which he was busy rubbing against the cheek of a girl with long, dirty blond hair perched on his lap. She was shaking, but I couldn't tell if it was out of fear or cold. When she turned to look at me, I realized the bruise at the edge of her mouth extended all the way to her jaw.

The kid's blond hair was long but slicked back neatly behind his ears. His standard-issue combat boots and PSF's black uniform jacket were spotted with mud but otherwise looked pristine—a little too pristine to have ever been in real use.

"Excuse me?" A Southern accent.

"Who," I repeated, "the *hell* are you?"

All of the teens who sat on his platform turned to look at him in perfect time with one another, but he was only staring at me. I felt the warm tug in my stomach again, and, despite Chubs's attempt to grab me, my feet slid across the dusty floor toward him. I barely managed to catch myself before I crashed against the side of the platform. Old, stacked crates with water-warped plywood nailed over them—that was all that stage was. His chair was little more than a metal folding one with a fuzzy blanket draped over it, most likely for effect.

The teen stood, throwing the girl off him. When she cried out in surprise, he thrust the bowl of whatever he had been eating toward her to shut her up. I fought the urge to search for Vida and Jude in the shadows crawling up around us.

"Where did you find them?" He crouched down at the edge of the platform to peer at my face. His eyes were green, for the most part—a large blotch of brown covered the upper half of his right eye.

"Up by the creek," Michael answered.

"You," the leader said, turning to one of the girls on the stage, "give him that blanket before he freezes. This guy is a king tonight. Look at the haul he brought in."

The girl didn't seem to understand why or how he could ask her to do something like that. She stared, dumb and mute at his back, until one of the boys grabbed a fistful of her short chestnut hair and shoved her forward to the edge of the raised platform. Underneath the warm brown wool sheet, she was wearing a stained yellow T-shirt and a pair of someone's old boxers. No shoes, no socks.

Michael ripped the blanket from her fingers, clucking his tongue at her resistance. One of the other kids, a small boy, gave him the water bottle he had been holding, watching with hooded eyes as the bigger kid polished off the rest of it before tossing the crushed bottle back to him. Then, he fell into place at the leader's right. How it was even possible for someone to look so smug and proud cocooned in a blanket with dried blood all over his face was beyond me.

The leader tossed his cigarette onto the ground at our feet, one end still glowing a pulsing red. I kept my eyes at the sliver of exposed skin above the collar of the PSF jacket.

An unworn jacket. I had worked on enough of them in the Factory to recognize one at first glance. There were no patches, not even the standard American flag. Unless he had ripped all of the stitching out, which was unlikely given that the material wasn't frayed, he had probably plucked the jacket out of a shipment, rather than off a soldier.

He broke his gaze long enough to glance at Michael. A tight shark's smile stretched across his lips.

"He did that?" A nod toward Chubs.

The other teen used his new blanket to wipe at the crusted blood covering his top lip. He opened his mouth, but then clearly thought better about admitting a girl half his size had given his face an adjustment.

The first let out a low laugh as he turned back to me. "Elbow, fist, or foot?"

"Elbow," I said. "I'm happy to perform a demonstration on you if you need one."

The muttering was back, a few wolfish chuckles rising around me. I set my jaw to keep from saying something else equally stupid. *Curb it,* I told myself. *Feel him out.*

"A fighter?" he asked, raising his eyebrows. "What's your color, baby?"

I didn't realize Chubs had moved at all until he was standing beside me. "She's Green. I'm Blue. And you are?"

"They call me Knox," he said. "The name Slip Kid mean anything to you?"

"If you're the Slip Kid," Chubs said, "I am the goddamn Easter Bunny. This is supposed to be East River?"

Knox stood suddenly at that, his amused smile tightening into a much harsher one. "Not what you thought it'd be?"

"We caught them the same place we grabbed the other two, just off the highway," Michael supplied oh-so-helpfully.

"That girl was a Blue, too. We could have an initiation tonight—"

Knox silenced him with a look. Overhead, the snow had apparently warmed to rain. It slanted down over the metal roof, the only sound aside from the eager whisperings of the kids crowding in around us.

"What do you know about East River?" he demanded.

"Well, to begin with—" Chubs began, crossing his arms over his chest.

"We heard it was in Virginia." I cut him off. "We were heading that way when your friends picked us up."

Here was the thing—this smug kid, whoever he was, wherever he had come from, was clearly not the real Slip Kid. We knew that. Knox knew that. But if he knew that *we* knew, I didn't doubt for a second that Knox would dispose of us before we could let everyone else in on the secret, too. The name was legendary; anyone who could gather this many kids, set up this kind of shop—why wouldn't they believe he was the Slip Kid?

"This is some operation you have," I continued, straining my neck to look behind me. No Jude. No Vida. But this was clearly the tribe of Blues Cate had tried to warn us about. "A nice little place. Is this everyone?"

Knox snorted, motioning to one of the younger teens next to him. The boy, twelve or maybe thirteen, went fire-red at the attention. Knox muttered something in his ear and the boy nodded once, then took a running leap off the platform. The last I saw of him was the back of his navy jacket, stained with soot, disappearing out one of the side doors.

"I'm Ruby," I said, then thrust a thumb toward Chubs. "This is Charles. Like I said, we're just making our way through, heading east."

Knox returned to his seat and, without any sort of prompt, the same girl as before scurried back to him, handing him the bowl of food. Soup, judging by the splatters that hit his jacket. I didn't miss the way the teens around him seemed to lean in, watching as the broth vanished spoonful by spoonful.

Do not look at Chubs, I ordered myself. I wouldn't have been able to hold back. The girl, in her threadbare outfit, was skin hanging off birdlike bones.

Knox waved Michael forward, and he and another teen dumped our backpacks on the platform. Two other girls, younger than the first, sprang to action. Piece by piece, they disassembled the packs of supplies we had so carefully stowed. *Good-bye, food bars; good-bye, first-aid kits; good-bye, water bottles and blankets and matches* . . .

Each item they took out was enough to break the thin control I had on my anger. I shifted my eyes up toward where Knox was watching this process, wondering how good it would feel to take his mind apart in the same way. It would be easy, if I could just get close to him.

When Knox glanced up at us, it was with a completely new expression on his face. One that was . . . hungry. Excited. "Where did you get this stuff?"

"We picked over an old gas station," I said, taking a small step closer. "It's ours. We found it."

"What's yours is mine, baby," he said. "Everyone here has to earn his or her things."

Chubs grumbled something under his breath.

"Take this all to storage," Knox told Michael. "Then you and your guys can eat. As much as you want."

Michael grinned, gathering the blanket more firmly around his coat. His team was jumping all over themselves with excitement, pushing past one another to go out the same side door the boy had earlier, except for one teen, the one who hung at the back of the pack. He was average height, wearing an army green coat that was a size too small and had to be worn open. His hair was as long and wild as the others in his group, but he kept his out of his face with a fleece hunter's hat. Just before the door shut, something must have caught his eye, because he turned back, leaning up against the wall there.

"Are you with the kids my guys picked up earlier?" Knox asked, drawing my attention back to him. A heavy gold chain slipped out from beneath his undershirt and jacket as he leaned forward. "The hot piece and the scarecrow?"

Well . . . that was one way to describe them.

"No," I said. Another step closer. Another. "I have no idea who you're talking about."

"Roo!"

Every head in the warehouse swiveled toward that side door. A river of relief broke through me—Vida and Jude stood there, looking slightly worse for wear but whole. Both of them were without jackets. Jude had given up any sort of pretense of pretending he wasn't freezing, but Vida's jaw was clenched tight, her arms pressed hard against her sides. I saw something flicker in her eyes, but she didn't say anything. I wish the same could have been said for Jude.

"See?" he was saying as he poked her arm. "I told you they'd come!"

I sighed, turning back to Knox and the platform.

"Want to try that answer again, sweetness?" he asked coldly.

I shrugged and said nothing. *Dammit.*

"So a Green, a Yellow, and two Blues walk into my woods. . . ." Knox began. He stood and hopped down over the edge of the platform. Vida and Jude were shoved toward us.

He was pacing in front of us, to the amusement of the other kids. Just out of my reach. "Now, the two Blues—you're mighty welcome here, but, of course, we'll have to figure out which of you is actually strong enough to join the hunting parties in initiation."

Initiation?

"I have to duke it out with him?" Vida asked petulantly. "I thought you said it was going to be a fight?"

Knox laughed—and once Knox laughed, everyone was laughing, too.

"Honestly," Vida said, whipping her mass of blue hair back over her shoulder, "you might as well let him go. He's totally worthless—I'll have him laid out on the ground in three seconds. Just sayin'."

Jude wore his confusion plainly, not understanding that this was her warped way of trying to protect Chubs from a fight he'd never win. I was surprised she cared enough to try.

"She's not lying," I said. "If you want the better fighter, it's her, hands down. But he's trained in first-aid. He's patched me up more than once. Look." I lifted my hair away from the scar on my forehead.

Knox didn't take the bait to examine it closer. He wove his fingers together and rested them on the back of his neck as he seemed to mull this over. "The question is more what we're going to do with you and the Yellow."

I did not like the direction this conversation was heading. And neither did Jude. I felt him start to shake, just a little bit, and I closed one hand over his wrist.

"We don't take on weak ones," Knox said. "This isn't a pity parade or a homeless shelter. I'm not about to waste food on a *Green* or a *Yellow*. No one here can vouch for you, which means you'll have to prove yourself in . . . other ways."

Chubs turned on him, his fists clenched at his sides, but another voice rose up before his had the chance to. It was small, more timid than I remembered, but I recognized it.

"I can vouch for them."

At East River, Clancy had relied on two different kids to run security for the camp—Hayes, the ogre-sized brute who ran hits for supplies, and Olivia, who coordinated watch at the perimeters of the camp. To say I was relieved to see a head of long, honey-blond hair push its way through the crowd was an understatement, but her face—I recognized the pieces of her, but it was like they had been torn apart and reassembled with a careless hand. She limped, badly, as she moved closer to us.

Yes. This was Olivia. But at the same time, it wasn't.

Her round cheeks, always flushed with the run she had taken or the orders she had barked out, had sunk in so deeply that it made her eyes look owlish. The golden tan that had kissed her skin was faded to dull ash—and as she turned to look at me, a bolt of horror raced from my heart to the pit of my stomach. Almost the entire right side of her face was puckered with pink scar tissue; it dragged down the corner of that eye, ran down her jawline. It looked as though she'd been mauled by a wild animal or slapped with a fistful of flames.

"Olivia," I gasped. "Oh my God!"

How— No, I knew that she had escaped. Liam had told us as much. When the fires and PSFs came to East River, a few of the Watch kids had been lucky enough to get away in time, Olivia included. Liam was the only one who had come back to look for us.

"Christ," Chubs said, automatically taking a step toward her. "You—"

"The four of them were with me when we escaped the PSF van that had rounded us up," Olivia said, ignoring the hand Chubs raised in her direction. Out of the corner of my eye, I saw the boy in the green coat push himself off the door and through the crowd, stopping near Knox's side. "We got separated in the escape through the woods."

The Olivia I had known had been so full of fire, she could have brought the entire warehouse down to a pile of simpering ash. Now, she merely bobbed her head with a meekness that didn't suit her at all. "Ruby is the one who planned the escape, sir."

"Oh yeah," said the boy in the green coat. He stuffed his hands in his pockets, rocking back on his heels. "I thought they looked familiar. A couple kids gave us the slip that day."

Olivia's gaze flickered toward his, her brows creased in what was either surprise or confusion. It certainly wasn't gratitude on her face.

"Really." Knox's voice was still flat, but I felt his eyes drift back over to me. "And you spent the last few months just wandering around my fine state?"

"Laying low, gathering supplies, looking for Olivia," I said quickly, risking a glance to the boy. What *was* he playing at?

"Why didn't you mention this to Michael, Brett?" Knox asked. "Or speak up before."

The boy—Brett—shrugged. "Didn't make the connection till now, I guess. Her hair was shorter"—he nodded toward me—"and the other one was dressed different."

"They can help me," Olivia continued, her eyes still on the ground. "At least until they prove themselves to you."

Knox blew out an exasperated sigh. He began to pace again, each step falling like thunder in the silence of the warehouse. There was almost a little skip to his step as he walked. "Fine," he said, looking up. "Take the Yellow and Green. Charles, too."

And just like that, he was out of my reach. I was useless to get us out of there.

"The hot piece will stay and keep us entertained," Knox said, smoothing his hair behind his ears with a grin. He nodded to the boys at his left. "Strip their jackets, take anything valuable they might still have on them, and keep them outside—where the trash belongs."

FOURTEEN

THE SIDE DOOR OF THE WAREHOUSE LED INTO AN extensive parking lot. The sea of black was broken up by a few sullen-looking tents, all near to collapsing under the pockets of water collecting on them. Wood pallets formed a kind of floating platform for each one and connected them in a crooked loop. I saw right away why they were needed—they lifted us those few precious inches out of the murky water that swamped the whole lot.

Smoke drifted up lazily from the smoldering remains of fires, mingling with the sour smell of old water. I crossed my arms over my chest, feeling the last bit of anger and despair at the loss of Liam's jacket shake off me. At the far left end of the lot were two small gray buildings—one of which Michael and his team were streaming out of, clutching armfuls of bread and chips. They crossed paths with Brett on their way back to the warehouse, slapping his shoulder, trying to turn him back. He simply waved them on and kept walking toward the building they had come from and the one next to it marked with a spray-painted red *X* over the door. Judging by the locks on the door, no one came out, and no one went in.

Olivia waited until the hunters ducked back into the warehouse before she turned sharp on her heels and gripped my shoulders.

"Oh my God," she was saying, her voice shaking madly. "Not you, too— He's—"

"What happened?" I whispered. Chubs was there in an instant, looping one of Olivia's arms over his shoulder. "What the hell is going on?"

"Wait, you actually *do* know each other?" Jude cried. Chubs yanked him forward, pulling him into our huddle.

"After I left East River . . . I was, well . . ." There was no small amount of fury tucked into her words. "I found a car with a few of the others and we got all the way to Tennessee."

I nodded, waiting for her to continue.

"Of course the car gave out. The PSFs were on us the entire time, and we didn't really have a choice. We split up and ran. I took to the woods and got pulled in by one of the 'Slip Kid's' hunting parties."

"But I thought Fancy was the Slip Kid?" Jude wrapped his arms around himself in a vain attempt to stay warm. I elbowed him hard.

"Fancy?" Olivia asked, startled.

"He nicknamed Clancy," I said, blowing out a long sigh.

The slightest smile curled her lips, only to be replaced by a burst of intense, dark pain. Her hand floated up to her neck and pressed hard at her collarbone, as if she were trying to keep something in by force.

"You know what happened, right?" I whispered. "You know he was responsible?"

She nodded. "I didn't want to believe it at first, but that night, when you guys tried to leave . . . I could see the way he had manipulated us. Controlled us. Our security system was near perfect, and we always knew Gray would leave Clancy alone rather than risk exposing him. The only way they could have found us was if someone leaked the coordinates or provoked him, and the only one with a way to do that was . . . was . . ."

She slid her hand up the length of her throat, hiding the tremor there.

Before, at East River, I'd only had a kind of passing acquaintance with Olivia. Most of our interactions were colored by whether or not Clancy or Liam were around; if they weren't there, we barely acknowledged each other. She had been invested in both, in different ways. Liam was someone who had been easy to work with, who challenged her to think about what they could do for the camps instead of just biding their time deep in the woods. But Clancy—Clancy had been the one she had wanted to protect, impress.

Like every other kid at that camp, he had been her savior. Her everything.

"Fancy sort of suits him," she said finally, stepping out of my grip.

We made our way carefully over the pallets, walking along the swaying trail of them. "When their hunting party found me, I only went with them willingly because I wanted to get to Clancy," Olivia muttered. "I wasn't even thinking it was strange he could set up another camp so fast or that he had gotten away at all. I just wanted to ask him why he did that to us. I think I would have killed him."

"A totally reasonable response," Chubs assured her. "Even more reasonable if you had done it slowly, with much fire and ice picks."

Somehow, Olivia didn't find that funny.

"Imagine my surprise when they dragged me in front of that hick," she said. "The very first thing he told me was that the only way I'd get out of his tribe was if they decided to dump my body in the river."

I shook my head, trying to dispel the angry buzzing between my ears and focus on the here and now, rather than what I was going to do to the bastard. "What's his story?"

"Knox's?" Olivia glanced around, but we were alone. "I can't get a straight one. Supposedly, he broke out of PSF custody a few years back and was holed up in different parts of Nashville until the flood. I don't know how he convinced the first kids here to join up, but I can tell you that most of us didn't join the tribe by choice."

Jude's thick eyebrows were drawn together. "Why does he hate the other colors so much? What happened?"

Olivia lifted a shoulder. "Who knows? No one's willing to risk his anger by asking. We already have to fight for every scrap of food as it is."

"I was wondering about that. It seems like he doesn't

even treat the Blues he has here all that well," I said. "Are they staying because they're scared?"

She nodded to the trees at the other end of the parking lot, past the tents. "If you were to try to make a run for it, you'd run into the patrol he set up, and if you run into the patrol, you don't come back. It's already hard enough that he takes everything you own and forces you to 'earn' it back, but if you don't work hard enough, or suck up enough, or *entertain* him, you get sent out here. Or you get traded."

"Traded . . . ?"

Olivia was as close to tears as I had ever seen her. "He . . . That's how he gets food. You saw the blockades around the city, right? All the soldiers? He brings in the kids he considers worthless, and he trades them for smokes and food. Only now they've been asking for more kids and giving him less and less stuff to balance it out. I'm surprised they haven't just raided us, but I guess he's managed to keep this place a secret."

I thought she was the one trembling until I looked down at my own hands.

Olivia bit her lip. "And of course—*of course*, he takes the kids in the White Tent, the ones no one would know to miss. He knows I can't do anything about it and that they can't fight back. The one time I tried, he took two kids out instead of one."

"What about that kid—Brett?" I asked. "He stood up for you. Could you . . ."

"It doesn't work that way," Olivia said. "He's different than Michael, but Michael's second in command. Brett might bring me things for the kids here every once in a while, but if Michael were to catch him . . . he'd be the next one gone."

The White Tent was exactly that—a large, crooked tent strung together with stained white tarp, set off from the others. The stench of it reached us almost before the sight of it did. Olivia lifted the red bandanna hanging around her neck to cover her mouth. The air was heavy, so thick with the stench of human waste that breathing became almost impossible.

"You just have to take him and get out while he still has a chance," Olivia was saying. "As long as your friend is in the warehouse, you won't be able to get her. But you can take him, at least. I can help you. You might be able to overpower the patrol together."

Jude's hand clenched around my upper arm. "It's okay," I told him. "It's not an option. We won't leave her behind."

He nodded, his face pinched with worry as he glanced back over his shoulder to the warehouse. "Are they going to hurt her?"

I raised an eyebrow. "I'm a lot more worried about what she could do to *them*."

"Olivia?" Chubs called softly. "Are you okay?"

She had stopped just outside of the tent, her hands bunching up the fabric. She bowed her head forward, resting it against the flap.

"He's . . . I'm sorry, I tried, I've tried so hard, but . . ." Olivia's voice was anguished. "I'm the only one who will help them. He tried for a while, but . . ."

"He," I repeated, feeling my heart go very still. "Who?"

Olivia blinked, her confusion marred by the scars on her face. "Aren't you . . . You aren't here for Liam?"

I don't remember pushing past her, but I do remember my hands, as pale as the fabric of the large tent, shoving aside the old bedsheet serving as the door. The stench intensified inside, combined with the sickening scent of mold and foul water. I blinked, forcing my eyes to adjust to the low light. The pallets underfoot creaked and groaned as I stepped inside, one snapping altogether.

There were so many of them—at least twenty-five kids, in rows on either side of the tent. Some were curled up on their sides, others tangled up in the thin sheets around them.

And there was Liam, right in the center of them all.

I lied before.

To Cate. To the others. To myself. Every day. Every single day.

Because here was the truth. Here it was, tearing up and out of me, drawing my feet toward the far corner of the tent, rising like a whimper.

I regretted it.

Seeing his face now, the way his cracked and bruised hands curled softly around the pale yellow blanket draped over him, I regretted it so much, with such a sharp ache, that I felt myself begin to double over before I had taken a single step toward him.

For months, his face had lived only on computer screens, his scowl captured forever in digital files. It was locked in my memory—but I knew firsthand how memories warp and fade as time passes. It was so selfish of me, so terrible and sick, but for three long heartbeats, all I could think was, I should have kept him with me.

I missed him. I missed him, I missed him—oh my God, I missed him so much.

The tent was still and so quiet around us. I brushed a finger against the edge of his blanket's pilling fabric. Someone had stripped him down to a gray T-shirt. His bare feet stuck out toward me, pale, tinged the faintest blue. I felt my breath go out of me in a single blow. The last time I had seen him, his face had been mottled with bruises and cuts courtesy of one bad escape attempt from East River.

But this was the face I remembered, the one I had seen that first day in the minivan. The one that could never hide a single thought. My eyes drifted aimlessly from his broad, clear brow, along the edge of his strong, unshaved jaw. That full bottom lip, chapped and cracked from the cold. His hair matted and darker—too long, even for him.

The air that filled his chest went out in a terrible, wheezing rattle. I reached out, trying to stop my hand from shaking as it settled against his chest. I wanted to count the space between breaths, reassure myself the shallow movement was still movement. It was only a faint touch, but his eyes blinked open. The sky blue had taken on a glassy quality, fever-bright against his otherwise dirty face. They drifted shut again, and I could have sworn the edges of his lips curled up in a faint smile.

If a heart could break once, it shouldn't have been able to happen again. But here I was, and here he was, and it was all so much more terrible than I ever could have imagined.

"Lee," I said, pressing my hand against his chest again, harder. I brought my other hand to his cheek. That was what I was afraid of—they weren't red from the biting cold. He was hot to the touch. "Liam—open your eyes."

"There . . ." he mumbled, shifting under his blankets, ". . . there you are. Can you . . . The keys are . . . I left them, they're . . ."

There you are. I stiffened but didn't move my hand.

"Lee," I said again, "can you hear me? Can you understand what I'm saying?"

His eyelids fluttered open. "Just need a . . ."

The pallet creaked as Chubs knelt beside me. "Hey, buddy," he said, his breath hitching in his throat as he reached over to place the back of his hand against Liam's forehead. "This is some mess you've walked your idiotic self into."

Liam's eyes drifted over to him. The tension in his face seemed to drip away, replaced by a goofy expression of pure joy. "Chubsicle?"

"Yeah, yeah, wipe that dumb-ass look off your face," Chubs said, despite the fact he was wearing an identical look on his own.

Liam's brow wrinkled. "What . . . ? But you're . . . Your folks?"

Chubs glanced over at me. "Can you help me sit him up?"

We each took an arm and tugged his deadweight into an upright position. Liam's head lolled back, his head falling into that curve between my shoulder and neck.

My fingers skimmed the lines of his ribs, catching on the bones. He was so thin; I pressed my fingers to the knobs of his spine and tried very, very hard not to cry.

Chubs pressed his ear up against Liam's chest. "Take a deep breath and blow it out."

Liam's right hand flopped over, giving his friend's face a few clumsy, affectionate pats. ". . . love you, too."

"Breathe," Chubs repeated, "long and deep."

It wasn't long, and it wasn't deep, but I saw his white breath fan out.

Sitting back, Chubs straightened his glasses and motioned for me to help ease him back down. I thought I heard him mumble, "Here?" but Chubs nudged me out of the way to pick up his wrist and count off his pulse.

"How long has he been like this?" Chubs asked.

It was the first time I found myself able to look away from Liam's face. Olivia was hovering behind us, her face splotchy from her scars and the freezing cold. Jude was frozen in the doorway, mouth open in a look of total and complete horror.

"He was caught about a week and a half ago, and he had a really nasty bug he couldn't shake," Olivia explained, her voice trembling slightly. "I knew something was wrong right away. I kept asking him questions about you guys, and he just seemed so disoriented. It turned into a fever, and then . . . this."

"What's wrong with him?" Jude asked. "Why is he acting like that?"

As if to answer for himself, Liam suddenly twisted to the side, his face screwing up with the effort it took to cough.

Deep, wet coughs that shook his entire frame and left him gasping for air. I kept one hand on his stomach, reassured by the slow pulse I felt there. God, his face—my eyes returned to it over and over again.

"I think he has pneumonia," Chubs said. "I can't be sure, but it seems the most likely. If I had to guess, most of the kids here have it, too." He stood on unsteady legs. "What are you treating them with?"

From the moment we had entered the tent until now, my shock and horror at the sight of Liam had been enough to make me forget even my anger. But the bitter reality was solidifying around me, and I could feel the heat rising in my chest, twisting, and twisting, and twisting until it felt like the next breath I released was tinged with fire.

Olivia's words spilled over one another. "Nothing. There's nothing. I have to beg for food, we're surrounded by water, we are drowning in water, and I can't even get a drop of the fresh stuff!"

"It's okay," he told her. "Liv, it's okay. I know you're trying."

"Do you have anything in the car?" I asked, looking up at Chubs.

"Nothing strong enough for this," he said. "We need to get them warm, dry, and hydrated before anything else."

Olivia was still shaking her head. "I've tried so many times, but he won't move the sick ones into the warehouse. Most of them aren't Blues, and they only got this bad because he refused to give them work, and if you don't work, you don't get food. You can't come into the warehouse. I honestly think he's trying to hide them from the others."

Well. He couldn't hide them from me. He couldn't hide what he had done to *Liam*. I felt a pure, unflinching fury grip me. I couldn't have shaken it, even if I had wanted to. I was on my feet, storming toward the flap, and there was only one thought in my mind, streaming through again and again, driving the anger deeper until I felt like I would explode with it.

"Where are you going?" Jude asked, stepping in my way. "Ruby?"

"I'm going to take care of this." It was a stranger's voice. Calm, certain.

"Absolutely not," Chubs said. "What happens if someone catches you swaying him? What do you think he'll do to you?"

"Sway him? Like the way Clancy would have?" Olivia asked. Her eyes went a touch wider at my nod. "Oh. I thought . . . I wondered why he was so interested in you. Why he fought so hard to keep you from leaving."

"Jude," I said. "Help Chubs. You guys need to figure out if there's a way to get a fire going in here without burning the place down. You remember how to do that, right?"

He nodded, his expression still screwed up in misery. "You have to do something. We have to stop him, make him see this isn't right. Please."

"Ruby," Olivia called. Her voice was clear, each word cut from stone. "Ruin him."

My mind was buzzing, waking from a long, unwelcome sleep. It had been a while, hadn't it? My right fist clenched at my side, as if each finger was imagining how it would feel wrapped around his throat. It would be easy—all I needed to do was get close to him.

I knew it was what Clancy would have done. He thought it was our right to use our abilities, that we had been given them for a reason. We have to use them, he had said, to keep the others in their place.

The silky quality of his voice slipped through me, a shudder following like an echo. His dark eyes had been wild when he said that, burning with conviction. I had been terrified of him then. At what he could do . . . and how easily.

I had those abilities, too. For whatever reason—whatever science was locked away on Leda Corp's servers—I had a way to right almost every wrong Knox had brought upon these kids. And Jude, he had turned to me without hesitation, with full faith. Like it was the most natural thing for me to take care of this. I was beginning to see how it was.

Ruin him. I'd do more than that. I was going to humiliate him, bring him low, leave him an empty shell whose only memory was my face. I would chase him into sleep. I would make him regret the moment he'd decided to keep Liam here and leave him outside to die.

"Be careful," Jude whispered, stepping aside to let me pass.

"Don't worry about me," I said. "See if you can find a black coat around here. Check his pockets to make sure he didn't find the flash drive and take it out, too."

"Later, gator," he said.

"In an hour, sunflower," I murmured.

I could feel Chubs's eyes on my back, but I didn't turn around; I couldn't, not without the fear that I'd be forever frozen in this exact spot, watching Liam waste away into nothing in front of me.

I am here, I thought as I stepped out into the rain. *He is here. We are all here.*

And we would be leaving together. Today.

FIFTEEN

THE BOY GUARDING THE DOOR INTO THE WAREhouse couldn't have been older than me, but he did stand a good deal taller and wider. A few months ago, that would have been a real obstacle.

"Stay where you are," he called out, watching me stalk toward him. "You're not allowed inside no more, not until Knox says so."

They had given him a gun, but I could tell by his grip he either didn't know how to use it or he didn't want to. I reached out and brushed my fingers against his outstretched hand. I stopped the memories before they could bubble up; anger made my abilities sharper somehow, more efficient.

"Sit down and stay down," I snapped, and I shoved the door open.

Our combat instructor had once told us that, when you were trying to settle a dispute without violence, the least "productive" emotion you could give in to was anger. No one can reason with another person so furious she can barely see straight. Well. I thought it was pretty productive to getting my way. I let the wind slam the door shut behind me.

I stood in the dark, blinking to adjust my eyes to the light. I felt a movement at my side—a solid, thick shoulder appeared directly in front of me, blocking both my path and line of sight. I followed the line of green coat up to Brett's grim face.

"You can't be here," he whispered. I felt him try to press something into my hands and glanced down. He'd taken his hat off and stuffed it with tiny packages of saltine crackers. "Take this and go back before he sees—"

I had just wrapped my fingers around his wrist when the eyes up on the platform finally picked me out of the shadowy crowd.

"Well, well, well . . ." Knox called. "Look what the wind went and blew in."

I glanced around, surprised to find nearly twice as many kids scattered around the space as before. Most were up near the platform, seated on the ground in circles with bags of chips and cereal boxes out in front of them. They were dressed in shades of gray and white—hunters, back from their hunting? The boys and girls at the far end of the warehouse were stretched out on the cement, moving just enough for me to see that they were breathing. I didn't see any food or fire near them.

I forced a deep breath in, relaxing my face into a fake smile. I had to work this slower, get him to drop his guard so I could get closer. Every nerve in my body was screaming for me to move, run, grab him. My heart throbbed with the refrain: *now*, *now*, *now*. But there were too many bodies between us. Too many hands with guns.

Knox leaned forward in his chair. "Something you wanna say?"

I noticed Vida then, her shock of electric blue hair shining over his shoulder. She moved carefully, long limbs graceful as she swerved and slid through the bodies on the stage.

The look on her face told me everything I needed to know. If Knox made the mistake of leaning back in his chair just then, she would have gladly found a way to break his neck.

Okay? I mouthed to her. Vida nodded, her eyes flicking down to Knox, then back at me. I knew what she was telling me to do.

Michael stood from where he'd been pawing at some poor shaking girl's chest, and he blocked Vida from my sight again.

"I was just wondering what it would take to convince you to let me go out on hunts," I said. I slipped my frozen hands into the back pockets of my pants as I walked up to the stage. "To let me go out and get supplies for everyone?"

Knox threw his head back and laughed. Several of the girls and younger boys sitting on the platform around his feet forced out breathy laughter of their own. My skin prickled; it sounded like a pack of dogs with sliced vocal cords was trying to bark.

I felt a body move behind me, coming up at my back, but I didn't turn to see who it was. These kids weren't about to force me out through intimidation. Michael could hit me, Brett could haul me back outside by force, but what I could do to them went beyond the physical.

"You?" Michael scoffed. "A *Green*?"

"What's the matter?" I asked. "Don't tell me you're afraid I'll prove there's nothing special about you Blues after all. I've always heard you guys were all brawn, no brain."

Just like I thought—he definitely wasn't used to being spoken to this way. The bully in him was fascinated and very, very angry all at once. Most likely because everyone around us looked like they were starting to wonder why I couldn't go out and get them the supplies they obviously needed.

Knox stood slowly, tapping the ash from his cigarette out on the ground.

Come here, I thought. *Come here and let me end this.*

The trickle began at the back of my mind, turning to a full-on roar. I could do this. One step closer, and I'd show him why they ranked my kind as Orange, and his only as Blue.

I would tear him down.

Knox's hair slid forward, past his ears. When he pushed it back, I saw he had woven together bright pieces of paper into rings around each finger. They almost looked like . . . They almost looked like the project a bored kid would make with a candy wrapper. I didn't know what the hell they were or why he was wearing them, but it gave me an idea.

"How about a trade?" I asked. "No work, no food, right? You let me join one of those hunting teams so I can eat, and I provide enough food to feed everyone for the winter."

Knox scoffed, rolling his eyes.

"I'm not lying," I said. "You saw what we had in our packs. That's just what we could fit in our bags. We had to leave tons of it behind."

Vida's full, petal-pink lips parted, a silent question dripping from them.

Of course I was lying. She knew that. *Come on,* I thought. He'd have to accept. I could feel the mood of the kids around us shifting in eagerness. They watched me with a new light in their eyes.

"There was canned food, walls of it—and gallons of clean water. Toilet paper, even," I added, because, let's face it, there are some things you want but don't necessarily need. "Clothes, blankets, you name it. You could stock this place nicely."

By the time I finished speaking, it was so silent I could hear the *plink*, *plink*, *plink* of water dripping from a nearby leak in the roof.

"Oh, yeah? And where is this wonderland? Half past nowhere, straight on into your imagination?" Knox was pacing across the stage again, still blocked by the kids sitting at the edge of it. If he didn't bite soon, I was going to have to jump up there myself.

"Why would I tell you?" I asked. "When you won't give me what I want?"

That was how relationships worked these days. No one did anything for each other unless it benefitted them in some way. Knox had clearly seen enough of the world we lived in to have figured this out, too.

But he didn't like it.

Come on, I thought, fuming. *Come on!*

With one jump, he was off the platform and I was shoved back by an invisible set of hands onto the cement. My teeth clacked against each other, and I just missed losing the tip of my tongue between them. Michael's laughter boomed around me, like it was echoing off the timid, silent figures circling us.

"You think I need to trade you something?" Knox spat. "You think I don't have other ways of making you and your friends talk?"

My hands pressed flat against the ground, wrists throbbing from the impact. This kid had more pride than greed—something I hadn't expected. He didn't even see that more food and supplies at his disposal meant more power for him. All he saw was a little girl who claimed to know better than him, who was giving him a solution to a problem he had created and stirring up unwanted questions in the kids around him. Even if the kids didn't believe me, they *wanted* to.

"Sure you do," came Vida's voice. "But are you willing to risk waiting when the National Guard is going to be back to clear the joint out?"

She had made herself comfortable in Knox's seat, to the visible horror of every kid nearby.

Michael whirled back around, fury rising from his shoulders like steam. "Knox! You gonna take that from her?"

"Don't tell me you're scared of a few little soldiers," Vida continued, inspecting her broken fingernails. "Is that why you keep trying to prove her wrong? Because you're scared of what'll happen if she's right?"

"C'mon," came Brett's voice somewhere near my right. "You have to admit it sounds too good to be true. We've been up and down the river a million times looking for food and never found so much as an empty bag of chips."

"So you'd blow an opportunity like this?" I asked. "After you already saw the proof?"

For his rough exterior, Brett was surprisingly reasonable when it came to hashing things out. "I could go with her—make sure she's not trying to pull a fast one. I'd be happy to take another trip back with a team and get the supplies—"

"Oh, *you* could?" Michael snarled. "*You'd* be happy to? Whose team are you talking about—mine? You think I don't know what you're trying to pull, dickhead? That I haven't been watching your weak-ass attempts to steal my game—?"

Knox held up a hand, stopping them before they could start circling each other like starving feral cats. "The answer is no. Not now, not ever."

"I should have known," I said, pushing myself onto my feet. "You left those kids out in the freezing cold to die. Why would you ever care enough to give everyone here the food and supplies they need?"

You can push someone's button over and over again to get what you want, but there comes a point when your finger slips and you finally hit the wrong one.

"Michael," Knox murmured, suddenly very quiet. Vida had worked enough of a spell over the room that it took calling his name twice to get him to snap out of it. "Take these two . . . pearls of girls outside."

"Knox," Brett began. "What about the supplies . . . ?"

Knox's fist flew out fast, clipping the other boy under the chin. "Take them *outside*. If they're so damn eager to be hunters, then they can prove it at initiation tonight, like everyone else had to."

Vida pushed herself up off the chair and dropped onto the floor next to Knox. Whether he meant to or not, his eyes flicked down over her face and body, over every exposed inch of rich, dark skin. "If you get through it, you're on. But if I see your faces one more time before I send someone to get you, I will burn them off myself."

"Shake on it," I demanded, fighting to keep the smirk off my face.

I stuck out my hand, my head trilling with anticipation of how it would feel, of what, exactly, I would do to bring him as low as he had brought everyone around him.

Knox came toward me, his face steeled, jaw clenched. He raised a hand toward mine, and just when his fingers came into reach, he shifted to grab the ends of my loose braid. It came down to him being just a second faster than my instincts. He pressed the burning red end of his cigarette into my palm, snuffing it out against my skin before shoving me away.

The pain was raw and blinding; I didn't cry, didn't so much as give him a gasp. But I knew, from the moment he glanced back over his shoulder at me with that smirk, I hadn't gotten my hooks into him, either.

They brought us around to the other side of the warehouse, out of sight from the tents and door, to a caged-in area where dead power generators and AC units were locked up.

Vida took one look at our future habitat and began to kick and snarl, struggling against the two guys holding her. With one ear-splitting shriek from her, they lifted Vida into the air and tossed her in. I was in such a state of blind pain, all it took was a nudge from the guy holding my arm for me to walk into the chain-link cage.

I waited until they had secured the locks and were making their way back to the building before dropping to my knees. I pressed my blistered palm into a puddle of freezing slush, swallowing back the whimper. The burn had sliced through every other thought in my head.

Next to me, Vida pushed herself up, dragging her legs over so she could lean against the fence. She took a deep breath in, closing her eyes.

"Let me guess," she said after she had steadied herself. "You found Prince Charming in the White Tent?"

"Him and about twenty others," I said, hating the way my voice shook. My entire hand felt like it was on fire. I tried shaking it out, but the burn felt like it was tearing its way down through each layer of skin.

"Show me," Vida said. When I didn't flip my palm up, she did it for me. I was surprised to feel her vibrating with her own kind of rage.

"Damn. I'll kill him."

She carefully placed my hand palm down in the slush again.

"I blew it," I said. "I was right there. *He* was right there. I should have just . . . used my other hand or . . ."

"Bitch, please," she said. "If you had been able to recover

fast enough to do something, then you really wouldn't be human."

"As opposed to what?"

She shrugged. "A mannequin? An unfeeling, heartless bitch who feeds on others' misery and is physically incapable of crying, unless it's tears of blood?"

I flexed my good hand in my lap. "Is that my rep at HQ?"

"They call you Medusa," Vida said. "One wrong look and your brain turns to stone."

Creative. Also, fitting.

"Where are the others?" she asked.

"In the White Tent outside," I said. I sat back against the steel AC unit so I could look at Vida. "They're all really, really sick. Half of them look like they're already dead."

"They're that bad?" she asked. "Stewart, too?"

"Yeah."

"Damn," she muttered. "That explains why you looked so pissed."

"Yeah," I said, feeling my anger start to prickle again. I'd had him—he was *right there*, and I had been too stupid and too slow to end it. "It does."

"Hey, boo," she said. "I'm in this now, too, and I got a lot of experience playing assholes like they're fucking harps. You need backup, I got you. Stop trying to convince yourself that you're in this alone."

I looked up, surprised.

"But just so you know," she said, sounding like herself again, "if it turns out that we have to fight each other for this initiation shit, I'm still going to kick your ass."

SIXTEEN

WE WERE LOCKED UP LONG ENOUGH THAT WHAT little sunlight there was seeped into winter's early night. Long enough that hunger started to set in, for a fine mist of rain to turn to flurries of snow, and a worried Jude to leave the shelter of the White Tent and come looking for us.

Without any kind of electricity to pump through the light poles in the parking lot, it was damn near impossible to make out anything other than someone's or something's general shape. I gave up looking for a friendly face and turned my full attention back to the kids standing at the corner of the warehouse, about a hundred yards from where we were locked up. I was so absorbed in the horrifying conversation they were having about Knox putting down a wild dog, I didn't see Jude until he popped up at the other end of the cage.

"Roo!" he whispered. *"Roo!"*

Vida whirled around, reaching for a gun that wasn't there. "How did you . . . ?"

"Holy crap, holy crap, *holy* crap. I had to go the whole way around the building to get by without them seeing me."

I cast one last look over my shoulder at our "guards," and then moved toward his glowing face. To his credit, he knew to duck down so Vida and I could block him from the other kids' sight.

"What happened?" The chain-link fence rattled as he pressed himself up against it. "I thought you were just going to chat with him, but you were gone so long, oh my God, why are you in there, what did you *do*? Chubs was—"

"Jude," I tried to interrupt, "Jude—"

"—and then I was all, 'no way; Roo wouldn't let anything bad happen,' but Olivia started saying all of these terrible things that Knox has done, and we couldn't find the flash drive on him, which means it still must be in that jacket—"

"Jude!"

He stopped mid-ramble. "What?"

". . . I need you to go ask Olivia where they store the jackets and stuff they swipe from the kids they recruit," I said.

"Why?" Jude asked. "To try to find Liam's?"

Vida snapped her fingers, cutting him off. I shot her a grateful look.

"No—no, we don't have time to look through them all, and another kid might have grabbed it. We need Liam to be able to tell us what happened to it. What I want you to do is find the jacket *I* was wearing—the leather one, remember? The Chatter is in the inside left pocket. That's all I need you to get."

He stared at me, clearly not comprehending this.

"The Chatter," I repeated. Vida, oh so helpfully, poked him through the fence, directly between his unblinking eyes. "In the inside left pocket. Can you get it for me?"

"You . . . You want *me* . . ."

"Yes!" Vida and I both hissed.

He hesitated for a split second, then broke out into the biggest, goofiest grin I had seen in a long time.

"All right, cool!" he said. "Of course I can do that! Do you think I'm going to have to pick a lock, though? Because I never got that one door open at HQ when Instructor Biglow tried to teach me— Wait." Jude looked from Vida's face to mine, the bright eagerness in his eyes fading quickly with his smile. "Why are you guys in a cage?"

Very quickly, with as few interruptions from Jude as we could manage, I told him what happened.

"Which means you can't go right now, okay?" I said. "You have to wait until tonight, when we're doing the initiation."

"What is it?" he asked. "Some kind of a fight?"

"It doesn't matter," I told him. "You can do this. It's simple. We'll have most of the attention on us, so you just need to find the right moment to slip away. Then you need to contact Cate and have her put Nico on the search for a place we can hit for whatever medicine Chubs needs. Tell them we need it *now* and that it has to be close by. Can you remember that?"

"Okay." Jude took a step back, bouncing on the balls of his feet. His face split again into another quick, nervous grin. "I'll take care of everything."

His hand instinctively went to the place where the solid lump of the compass should have been.

"Where is it?" I asked, startled.

"They took it. When they brought us in. It's cool—it's fine. I'll find it. It's probably in that room."

"Are the others all right?" I asked. "Liam?"

"Umm . . ." He hesitated, biting his lip. "Not good. He won't say it, but I think Chubs is really worried. He said if we don't get medicine, there's a good chance that he and the other kids could die. And I believe him. Roo, it's bad. It's really, really bad."

I pressed my hand against my forehead, closing my eyes, trying to control the rise of bile in my throat. *You had him right there, and you couldn't stop him. Liam is going to die, and you couldn't do anything. After everything, Liam is going to die, and it's on you.*

"Jude," I said. I slipped a hand through one of the warped sections of woven metal, reaching for his shirt to bring him close again. He had a few inches on me, but I had a few years on him and a fair bit more experience when it came to slipping in and out of places unnoticed. "I know you can do this. I *trust* you. But if you think you're about to get caught, ditch the Op, you hear me? We can figure out another way."

"I got this, Roo," he said, his voice thick with promise. "I won't let you down."

He backed away, flashing us a thumbs-up that all but proved to me he had no grasp on how serious the situation actually was. I let out a long breath, watching the evening steal him away in a cloud of white, the swirling paths of the snow altering their course to follow. He was moving fast, with so much unchecked energy, even the wind seemed to shift direction to catch his heel.

I knew he could do it; in training, a break-in was one of the very first simulations they put us through. And, honestly, the awful truth of it was that while the kid was about as sneaky as a pair of cymbals crashing to the ground, he was also the kind of person you wouldn't necessarily notice was missing. Not from a crowd, at least not right away.

"Five minutes, max," Vida said, leaning against the fence beside me. "That's how long I give it before he gets his skinny ass caught and handed to him."

"Then we'd better put on a good show," I said, closing my eyes against the snow, "and give him a fighting chance."

They came for us silently, emerging from the night's cold, clammy hands like ghosts.

"Stop," I muttered to Vida. The kids shoving us forward, six in all, evenly divided between girls and boys in their very best white, didn't speak a word. The old linen sack slipped easily over my head, but Vida wasn't about to let them dull a single one of her senses.

"It's okay," I coaxed, "stay with me here."

Every limb and joint felt heavy and stiff; just walking sent a spike of pain through my shoulders and hips. We made a sharp turn back in the direction of the warehouse. I felt the water from the parking lot splash up over the tops of my heavy boots and grimaced. We'd be inside soon enough. At least it'd be dry.

But the metal door never groaned. It never opened.

Vida's mind must have been guiding her along a similar line of thinking, because I heard her say, "Ruby?" once, a mumble as it rolled past her lips.

"Stay with me," I said again, because what else could I say? It'll be okay?

I remembered, when I was little, my dad used to take me to some of the high school sports games. Football mostly, sometimes baseball. He loved a good game—any game—but what I liked best was just *watching* him. Seeing his whole body turn to follow the path of an incredible pass, the grin that broke out when the baseball blew over the far fence. Dad knew the cheers for each team by heart.

So I recognized the tone when I heard it, the growls of a hungry crowd. The pulsing beat of clapping hands as they finally found the same rhythm. It set my teeth on edge, long before the fire smoke curled in my nostrils.

I stumbled again and again as the kids pushed me forward, dragging me over the crumbling edges of pavement onto the soft, sinking earth, back again onto ground that was harder. Solid. A wave of scorching air brushed my arms as they led me past what felt like a wall of fire.

I couldn't hear my own thoughts over everyone else's voices. I thought, just for a second, I heard Chubs bellow out my name and a softer girl's voice echo it back. *Ruby, Ruby, Ruby, Ruby*—and something else, too.

They herded us right into a small crush of bodies, and it felt like every single one was trying to push back, to keep us from getting in.

The minute my face was clear of the mask, I sucked in a lungful of warm air, trying to shake off the feeling I had a thousand pins pumping through my veins. There were too many faces around me—too many big eyes, cracked lips, scarred faces. The sight of them, the *smell* of their unwashed clothes and bodies combined with the earthiness of the smoke, until it became something else entirely. I craned my neck around, searching for Chubs's face through the hands that were stretched out toward us. Firelight flickered in the dark.

I found him eventually, Olivia by his side. Jude, thank God, was nowhere in sight or earshot, but the wave of relief that washed over me at the thought only lasted until the terror came spilling over their faces, their lips, their entire bodies as they tried to push their way forward. The panic buzzing at the back of my mind drowned my ears with something that sounded almost like white noise.

Olivia had her hands around her mouth, shouting something to us. *Dead*, I thought.

We were in another building, likely the one I'd seen set off to the side of the warehouse. Part of the roof and eastern-facing wall had collapsed in on itself, forcing us to drag our numb, exhausted bodies over the piles of downed cement and twisted metal. It was another, smaller version of the warehouse, nearly burned out by the look of it. The walls and cement floors were bare, with the exception of the black shadows the kids were projecting onto them. At the very center of the room was a large ring of metal trash cans, golden flames leaping up past their lips, stretching toward the kids in white watching from overhead.

In Thurmond, the Factory had been set up in a very particular way to ensure that all of the PSFs would be able to watch a building full of freaks do their work. The floor plan there had been open, much like this, and stacked in the very same way. Hanging overhead were the two remaining metal pathways—low-hanging rafters, really.

It was a sea of white up there, Knox positioned comfortably in the middle of them, sitting at the edge of the rafter. Michael sat at his right, leering down at us with a can of something at his side. At the sight of their grinning faces, my hand pulsed in pain. I pressed it flat against my pants, my mind racing as they pushed Vida and me through to the center of the circle of fire.

Dammit. We really were going to have to fight each other.

I glanced over, watching as Vida ripped the old sack off her head and threw it into the nearest flaming trash can. The veins in her neck were bulging with anger, and she looked as close to tears as I had ever seen her. That was the first moment I actually felt fear. I needed Vida now—I needed her sharp intuition and her refusal to back down, even for a second, from a losing fight.

"Stay with me," I murmured again. Her hands flexed and clenched at her sides, as if she were trying to work her anxiety out that way.

Then, one voice rose above the others.

"Hellooo, ladies," Knox called. "Have you been behaving yourselves?"

The ring took up most of the room on the ground level, but there was enough space that the kids from outside, the ones not in white, could have squeezed in if they had wanted to. Instead they kept their distance—even Chubs, whose shape I could just barely make out through the screen of hot, shimmering air streaming up from the fires.

"I could bring him down here," Vida whispered. "Catch him by surprise and put him right in your hands."

I shook my head. "Too many guns." And all aimed at our backs. Too many Blues, too. We'd have to wait until he chose to come down, then I'd have him. I felt the steady rise of rage and let it fill me, pump through my blood, drive out every single thought of mercy. I felt like a predator, ready to step out of the shadows and make my true face known.

"The rules here are simple," Knox said. "You get pushed out of the ring, you're out of the fight. You get knocked out, you're out of the fight and I get to do what I want to with you. There are no mercy calls. The only way out is to stay standing or throw yourself out to get burned. Got it? Oh—how could I forget? Because it's the two of you, I'm bending my own rules. No powers. This is a fist fight for you, girls, so don't hold back."

Vida and I shared a quick glance. I couldn't tell what she was thinking, but the only thought rocketing through my skull was figuring out the fastest way for her to beat me without cheating. Flat-out refusing to fight would mean the deal was off, but I wasn't exactly thrilled with the idea of Vida literally kicking me through a ring of fire.

"What about the deal?" I called up. "Supplies in exchange for letting me join one of the hunting parties?"

Knox stiffened at the word *supplies*—more importantly, the kids around him leaned forward. A little reminder for them of what their leader was withholding.

"Goddamn," he said, "you are annoying. Win, and maybe I'll think about it."

I took a few steps back, closing my eyes. How hard would she have to hit me to knock me out with one blow?

"Bring him in!" Seeing our reactions, Knox laughed. "What? You actually thought you'd fight each *other*? God, that's hilarious."

Vida spun back toward me to the demolished opening of the building. I didn't; I knew by the look on her face that whatever it was, it was bad.

There was a whisper from above, quickly stifled as new sounds replaced it. A groan, the long, low purr of something heavy being dragged against the ground.

A line of sweat slipped down my back at the grunts of effort, the throaty scream, the jangle of what could only be chains.

The mind is a strange thing, mine stranger than most. It's selective about what it remembers and even pickier about which memories remain as clear and cutting as a shard of glass. Those were the ones that stayed with you, that a single sound or smell could drag out. I had forgotten so much about my life before the soldiers had picked me up, but I would be damned if I ever managed to banish one single black memory from camp.

There was no forgetting the sorting, the test I almost failed.

There was no forgetting the look on Sam's face as I wiped myself clear from her memory.

There was no forgetting the gleam of black guns in the summer sun or the snow falling softly on the electric fence.

There was no forgetting the long line of dangerous ones chained together, their faces hidden beneath leather muzzles.

"What the . . . What the actual fuck?" Vida breathed, her hand reaching out to yank me toward her, behind her.

There he was, pale as a new morning sky, dressed in the tattered remains of camo pants and a shirt that hung off his sunken chest. On first glance, I thought he must have been my age, but it was impossible to tell. He looked shrunken and soft now, but the way his pants were being held up by what looked like a plastic bag threaded through the belt loops made me think he had once been much bigger.

Knox had made sure to wrap him up real pretty in a series of robes and chains. There was a bandanna over his mouth, clenched between yellow teeth, and all I could think was, *I wish they had covered his eyes instead.*

Rimmed with crust and lined with bruises, his eyes pierced through the shadows between us, black and bottomless. He was looking at us, straight through us, into us.

I knew what Olivia had been calling out to me now. I could hear her voice ringing high and clear in my mind.

Red. Red, Ruby, Red.

SEVENTEEN

THERE ARE NIGHTMARES, AND THEN THERE ARE *nightmares*.

The Red lowered his face, a thick curtain of long, dark bangs falling over his brows. But still, it didn't hide his eyes. They watched us through the gaps between his tangled curls. His body gave a sharp jerk, like his muscles were seizing up, and he blinked to ride the spasm out. When his eyes opened again, they were wider, glassy—but another jerk tightened his body, and the hint of humanity was gone.

"Ladies, may I introduce you to Twitch." Knox looked like he was enjoying our stunned expressions. "I picked him up in Nashville after he bolted from the PSF holding his leash. He was stumbling around, jerking like some tweaker. He's come a long way since I started training him." Knox waved a hand toward a kid who, with a look of undeniable terror on his face, walked up and began to cut through the Red's ropes with a knife.

"I think you guys are gonna get along real damn nice," Knox called. "Have fun."

I don't know that I've ever seen two teenage boys run faster than they did once the last metal chain was in a puddle around Twitch's feet. He took one step forward, walking through the wall of flames the trash cans provided. A ripple went through the glowing circle, dimming just for an instant, then flaring up to a blinding white.

"That ass-sucking mofo," Vida muttered. She turned to look at me. "He actually sicced a firebomber on us."

Twitch made good on his name. His head cocked to the right, then jerked to the left in a way that looked painful. In the moments—those precious half seconds—between movements, the only noticeable change was the flash of something like confusion in his eyes.

Knox put his fingers in his mouth and whistled. Then there was no more thinking.

Vida and I dove away from each other as the first kick of fire jumped from the flaming garbage cans to the ground between us. I hit the ground and rolled, trying to put out the smoldering edges of my right pant leg. The burn on my palm felt like it was about to burst open with a blast of fire on its own.

The air above my head grew hot—hotter—then deadly, eating the oxygen and forcing me to roll again. The fire in the barrel I had crashed into flooded over the edge of the metal can and came pouring toward me. It raced along the cement toward us.

The Red lifted a hand in front of him and snapped his fingers. A burst of flame appeared between his curved fingers, and he lobbed it my way like a ball.

Get up, get up, get up, my mind screamed. The sweat on my palms slid against the loose rubble. I pushed myself up and looked for Vida.

She was running, her arms pumping at her sides, charging for the Red's center.

"No!" I cried. The fires from the garbage cans rose up again, crossing the circle to connect in a series of bridges. Vida hissed in pain as a whip of fire branched out and caught her across the shoulder blades.

For an instant, I really thought Vida was going to charge straight through the lines of fire in front of her; there were only two between her and the Red, but they were there, burning, golden red, lighting her skin to a warm, earthy brown.

"Vi—!"

She landed on her hip, sliding the last few feet of distance straight into the Red's legs. He went down with an inhuman roar of protest that was only bounced back to him by the kids in white watching above us. I risked a look up.

Most of the garbage cans were still burning, as were patches of the cement where the lines of fire had collapsed. I stomped one out as I ran toward Vida.

Twitch surged up off the ground, throwing Vida off him with a fierce, pulsing hatred that filled the space between us. I got there to catch her before her burned back could slam into the ground. My vision blanked as her head made impact with my jaw, but I didn't let us fall. I hauled her right back up onto her feet.

I had only ever sparred against Instructor Johnson once, and the "fight" had lasted all of fifteen seconds. It had been right at the beginning of my training, when he needed to "evaluate" my skill level. I walked with a limp for two weeks and had two hand-shaped bruises on my upper arms for twice as long.

Instructor Johnson would have wilted like a daisy under this Red.

Twitch was no longer twitching. His movements were sharp, precise, schooled—something in him had clicked. Vida and I danced away from him time and time again, twisting and bending to get out of the way of his fists sailing toward our faces.

And I had thought the kid looked scrawny.

"Come on, ladies!" Knox heckled. "This is so *boring*!"

I caught Vida's arm before she could launch toward him again, pulling her back a few steps. Twitch didn't follow immediately; instead, he kept to his half of the circle, pacing back and forth like a panther, military-issue boots squeaking underfoot.

It was the first time I had been able to think this entire fight. My body shook with exhaustion and pain. *Think.*

He hadn't been in a rehab camp, not recently at least. Maybe never—but then, where had his gear come from? Twitch didn't seem like he had enough independent thought to rob a National Guard station. In fact, save for the brief bursts of confusion on his face, it didn't look like he had any independent thought at all. Which meant . . .

No way, I thought. *It's not possible.*

But at this point, what wasn't possible?

"Jamboree," I gasped out to Vida.

She blinked. "No shit?"

Vida knew Operation Jamboree the way some kids know about ghost stories, from whispers and the darkest dreaming of her own imagination. President Gray's secret army of trained Reds was common knowledge in the League; they'd been trying to leak information about it for months with no success. The whole thing, apparently, was too "preposterous" for the Federal Coalition to believe, and the Internet watchdogs snagged and blocked any reference to the project before word had a chance to bleed out to international papers.

What Vida didn't know was that the original idea had wormed its way out of the most warped corner of Clancy's mind. He had been the one to plant the idea in the president's, and all of his advisers', minds. Right up until the moment his father had finally realized what his son was doing, Clancy had played a key role in the Reds' training program.

My whole jaw hurt from where Vida had nailed it, and my lip dripped with blood. I spat it out on the ground, swiping an arm over my eyes to clear the stinging sweat away. How had Clancy planned to control them? The Red was acting like his brain had been shattered by rage one minute, while the next he was a carefully trained soldier. He was clearly disoriented, not following anything other than his instincts—all of which looked like they had been reprogrammed to one setting: *kill.*

God, I thought, fury cutting swift and neat through my fear as I watched Twitch. *God, what they did to those kids . . .*

For years, I had been so sure the camp controllers and PSFs took the dangerous ones out to put them down. The knowledge had lived like a devil around my neck, his grip tightening and tightening to the point I couldn't breathe when I thought about it. I had been so relieved when Clancy told me that wasn't the case. But now . . . *now* I wondered if death wouldn't have been the better deal after all. At least they wouldn't be animals. This kid's mind wasn't even his own anymore.

"Hey, boo," Vida said through gritted teeth. "We have to double-team him."

"What good is that going to do?"

"He can create fire and control it, but look at how much concentration it takes him," she said. "He stops the second you go for him, like his brain can't handle both at once."

She was right. For all the damage he could do, he was the same as any of us—using his abilities took effort and practice. But this kid was so damaged, his sense of reality had been warped—whether Clancy had done it through his influence or whoever was running Operation Jamboree had through conditioning, it was clear Twitch had been trained in such a way that when he saw someone, he knew to attack.

"Shut up and fight!" Knox yelled.

"Distract him," Vida said. "I'll end it." Knox only said we had to stay inside of the ring—he never said anything about what shape the ring itself had to be in.

The audience above cried out in alarm as I kicked the nearest can over. The smoldering remains of wood spilled out against the ground, but the fire that raced along the cold cement worked itself through in seconds. Twitch stopped mid-step, staring at the dying flames in confusion. By then, I was already on to the next can. I heard Vida's low cry as she dove for the Red again.

"Stop!" Knox yelled. "You *bitch*! Your friend is gonna have Twitch all to herself—"

A yelp drew my attention back to Vida. She was patting the ends of her hair, trying to put out the flames licking at the strands. Vida dropped to her knees, panting, cussing viciously between her sobs. I started toward them, but the fire from the bins around them surged up and out again, twisting into shimmering webs of intense heat and light.

"Don't, Ruby!" Vida screamed.

Twitch had one hand closed around the back of her neck, the other was raised high above his head. A sliver of fire slipped up from the nearest garbage can, curling around his fingers and wrist like a snake. They were screaming in the rafters, but the one sound we needed to hear, it never came. Knox wasn't going to stop him.

No one is going to stop him. I brought my fingers to my mouth and tried to imitate the noise Knox had made, but I couldn't get a strong enough breath out of my chest. The smoke stung my eyes and burned my throat. . . .

He is going to kill her, he's going to kill her, he's— There was no other option this time.

"Red!" I shouted, my voice hoarse.

The boy looked up, and I had him.

It was almost unconscious, the letting go. It was complete and immediate, like releasing a deep breath I hadn't realized I'd been holding. I felt the tangles of fingers in my mind begin to unfurl—anger, terror, desperation peeling each thread of power apart until I felt a surge of tingling warmth spread out along the base of my skull. The wall of fire in front of me throbbed in time with the Red's frantic twitching. Overhead, I heard Knox start to yell, but the kid was mine now. I was in his head without a single touch.

In a typical mind, there's this feeling of sinking into his or her thoughts. It's a slow, slippery sensation, one that's usually accompanied on my end by a massive migraine. Sometimes I fell slowly, other times all at once. I could tell a lot by the shade of a person's memory, the tint to his or her dreams.

But Twitch was broken. So, so broken.

I didn't slip so much as stab my way through, like a knife driving deep into a pile of shattered glass. His memories were sharp, small, here and gone faster than a blink. I saw a dark-haired girl on the swings, a woman bent over an oven, a line of stuffed green lizards, a name spelled out in block letters on a shelf. Everything sped up then—black boots, wired fences, the green fake leather of a school bus seat. Mud, mud, mud, so much digging, the rattle of chains, the pinch of a muzzle, a fire in the dark burning hotter and hotter. I had to remind myself to breathe. The burning air set my lungs on fire.

I found Clancy's refined face among the fractured images, standing alone behind a glass wall, his hand pressed against it. He only ever came in the dark, like a walking nightmare. Clancy mouthed something, and every thought exploded to white.

I couldn't hear myself over the hollering of the onlookers. I couldn't tell what they were shouting; it was all rabble and noise. But I had this Red in my hands; I had his power at my disposal, and I felt it as deeply as if the fire were running through my veins. I turned back toward where Knox and the others stood stunned, their eyes focused on us from their safe place above.

Not safe anymore, I thought, turning back to the Red. What would Knox do when I turned his little pet against him? What would he do when he felt his skin catch fire?

Twitch stared at me, his pupils shrinking, exploding out to their full size, then shrinking again. His mouth began to work silently, letting out low moans of pain until he finally began to cry. He waited for a command. An order.

Mason.

That was the name I had seen spelled out on his door, the one his mother had whispered lovingly as she tucked him into bed.

His name is Mason. My thoughts were spilling over themselves, trying to comprehend what had just happened. He lived in a house with a blue fence. His mom made his lunch for him every day. He had friends and a dog, and all of them disappeared when the men came and took him into the van. He had White Sox posters on his bedroom wall. He rode his bike in the abandoned lot behind his house. His name was Mason, and he had a life.

I stumbled onto my knees, pressing a hand to my forehead. The connection snapped with the next jagged memory that filtered through his head. He fell a short ways away, near a stacked pile of debris. For a moment, I heard nothing outside of my own harsh breathing and heartbeat. Then, there was an audible snap in my ears—a sickening crack.

"Stop!" I heard Vida scream. "Stop it!"

Even as I watched Mason take the jagged hunk of cement and smash it against his skull, it was like my mind couldn't understand the movement. Vida ripped the stone out of his hand with a cry of protest. The Red lifted his head off the ground, straining his neck, and flung it back again against the ground. He didn't stop, not until I slipped my hands between the heavy bone and the unforgiving cement.

All at once the stink of blood broke through the heady cloud of smoke. I felt it slick and hot against his fine hair.

"Stop!" Vida pressed her hands down against his shoulders, trying to pin him in place. I pried another hunk of cement out of his fingers. The moment it came free and clattered against the floor, he had my hand in his grip.

". . . help me," the boy was sobbing. "Please, please help me, please, I can't—not anymore, oh God, oh God, they're coming again, I see them, they're coming in the dark—"

"It's okay." I leaned down close to his ear.

"Help me," he begged, *"please."*

"It's all right, Mason. It's okay; you're safe." I could dive into his thoughts again—my mind spun with possibilities. I could erase his memory, what he had been through, everything he had seen. I could leave the skinned knees, sunshine days on the playground, his mom's sweet smile. Only the good. He deserved that. Mason needed to be free from this.

"I'm scared," he whispered, his cheeks slick with tears and blood. "I wanna go home—"

The bullet cut so close to my ear, it nicked the edge of it. I felt a stab of pain and a warm rush of blood, pitching forward against Mason to protect him. The shot had come from above—I heard Vida scream something, but I didn't fully register what had happened until she grabbed me by the shoulders and hauled me off the Red, throwing me down to the ground. Knox or whoever had taken the shot at me wasn't going to get another clean one off, not if she had anything to do with it.

My front was drenched in warm wetness. My shirt clung to my skin awkwardly; I tried to smooth it all out, but my hands were frozen as I looked down at myself. Half dazed, I wondered how it was even possible my ear could have bled so much already.

"No, dammit!" Vida's voice rose above the buzzing in my ears. "No, goddamn you!"

I pushed myself upright and turned toward her horrified voice. The faint hum in my ears sharpened, distilling until I could make out the distinct crying and whispers from the kids above us. They were all looking at the Red boy, watching the blood bubble up from where the bullet had lodged in his throat, watching him choke and sputter, his hands clawing at the ground. The space between his breaths stretched longer and longer, until the last exhale came out in a strangled sigh.

I couldn't speak, couldn't hear, couldn't see anything but Mason. My hands rose in front of me with a life of their own, my eyes fixed on the pool of blood that spread across the cement until the edge reached my knees.

"I missed," Knox said. I craned my neck around, watching as he lowered the silver handgun just a tiny bit. "Oh well. Mama did say it was important to throw out broken toys."

The fury rose in me like a fever, burning away every last trace of reluctance. And I didn't even have to think about it; there wasn't a choice to be made. I pushed myself onto my feet, whirling back toward him.

He only had to look at me, flick his gaze toward mine with that arrogant smirk. I felt the rising waves of anger distill to a perfect, piercing strike.

Knox's mind rose in my own like a hot blister, swelling and swelling each time I brushed it until finally it burst, and a gush of liquid memories came pouring out. I didn't have the patience or care to examine them. Ignored the thick, congealed memories of fists, and belts, and angry words that blew up like bombs in his dark world; I pushed through military academies, buzzed hair, beatings—I pushed until Knox dropped to his knees.

It was like the air had been sucked out of the room along with everyone's voices. The fires crackled as they devoured the rest of the wood in the barrels. I heard Vida drag herself toward me, sucking in a sharp, pained gasp. It was like their faces were in orbit around us; there was no one else in the world besides him and me.

“Knox—?” The boy next to him still had his gun leveled at us, but he risked a glance down at Knox. He watched, the same way we all did, as Knox threaded his fingers through his hair and began to rock back and forth.

“Come down here,” I said coldly. “Right now.”

A few of the kids made weak attempts to grab him and keep him in place, but he fought past them. I felt a thrill of power at the thought—the hold I had on him now was so strong, he would have fought them off to get to me. He flipped a rope ladder over the edge of the walkway and began to work his way down.

“What’s going on?” someone shouted. “Knox! What the hell?”

Knox stumbled past Vida, who was watching this all with wide eyes from the ground. I’m not sure if she figured it out right then or just wanted to take advantage of the moment, but she lifted her face, streaked with soot and sweat. Her foot swung around, tripping him, sending him sprawling over himself to the ground at my feet.

“Are you happy?” she yelled to him, to the kids around us. “Did you get off watching that? Did we pass your stupid test?”

Apparently there was only one person who decided whether or not a kid passed, and that was the one who had dropped down onto his knees in front of me.

“I want you to apologize,” I said. “Now. To Mason. To all of these kids for what you did to them, for never giving them what they needed or deserved. For making them fight another kid and pretending like that’s the only way we have to survive in this world." I knelt down in front of him. "I want you to apologize for the kids you left outside to *die*, the ones you said were worthless and who you treated like they were invisible. Because unfortunately for you, they weren't invisible to me."

"Sorry." It was a frail whisper, a shadow of a word. Several kids gasped, but more were stunned into speechlessness. And still, I could tell by the faces around me that a single word wasn't nearly enough. It would never be.

"Tell them your real name," I ordered.

His pupils flared, like he was struggling to fight off my control. I strengthened my grip, my lips turning up in a small smile as he shook. "Wes Truman."

"And are you the Slip Kid, Wes?"

He shook his head, keeping his eyes low to the ground.

"Tell them how you've been getting supplies," I said, letting frost chill the words. "What happens to the kids in the White Tent when you need another pack of cigarettes?"

I could hear footsteps shuffling up through the loose rubble and debris from the collapsed wall, but I kept my eyes focused on the pathetic boy cowering on the floor.

"I . . . trade them."

"With the PSFs?" I pressed.

He bit his lip and nodded.

The silence came crashing down around us—startled cries, wordless screams, weak protests, and one word, repeated over and over again: *Orange*.

"Someone take her out!" a boy shouted. "Take the shot! She'll do that to all of us—"

"You know what I am now," I called up to them. "But that also means you know that every word that just came out of his mouth is true. You've been lied to all this time and treated like you were worthless and incapable of making your own choices, but it stops tonight. Right now." I turned to look back at Knox, who stared numbly at his upturned hands. "I want you to leave tonight and never come back—unless," I began, looking up at the faces above me, "any of you have a problem with that?"

There was some part of me that must have known that a good number of them stayed silent out of fear. The boys who had protested before fell silent the moment my gaze moved across them, their hands strangling the guns in their hands. *You all agree,* I thought. *You do and always will.*

It was so simple. All of it. Those same boys nodded and drifted back into the shadows; all I had to do was push the right images into their minds, shifting quickly among the four or five of them before they knew what I had done. I looked down at Knox, my lip peeling back in disgust as I flooded his thoughts with visions of my own: him struggling out in the freezing snow, him coughing, weak, unable to defend himself as he moved farther west, disappearing forever. I wanted him to experience every bit of disorientation and pain and fever that Liam had. I wanted him swallowed up by the world that created him.

I watched him stand up, cutting his hands on the rough ground. He moved slowly, staggering out through the kids crowded around the collapsed wall. For one brief moment, I thought that they would turn him back and then turn on me, but the girl in front, Olivia, took one giant step aside. She crossed her arms over her chest, watching him go with cold, unflinching eyes. A noise rose from the rest of them as they followed suit, clearing him a path—a hissing, spitting, snarling noise that conveyed what most words couldn't. Then, the ones perched safely above us echoed it back, letting months, even years, of pent-up anger and fear and hopelessness escape with it. The intensity of it was suffocating; I reached up and pressed a hand to my throat. My pulse raced beneath my fingertips.

He was there, and then he was gone. I felt the rage that had powered me follow him out the door, fading like old memory, disappearing into the black night. I thought about it—calling him back in, I mean. It suddenly didn't feel like enough. He deserved so much worse. Why had I even given him a chance when he hadn't found it in his damn black soul to give one to the other kids around him?

Vida limped over to me, watching me with wary eyes. She kept a clear distance between us, her hands fisting her torn pants. Looking at me like she had never seen me before in her life. I was about to ask her what was wrong when I felt an arm loop through mine and turn me around.

Chubs's lips were pressed into a tight line, his eyes hidden by the reflection of firelight in his glasses. It was amazing to me that after everything that happened that night, I still had the strength to untangle myself from him and pull away. He tried to grab me again, to steer me outside and away from the eyes burning into my back.

But I wasn't afraid of these kids or what they could do to me now that they knew what I was. If I could have found the words, I would have told him. I would have said that before I hadn't been strong enough to keep our group together. I hadn't had enough control, enough power, to keep him and the others safe from the world trying to rip us apart. Now I did.

The mood in the room had shifted, was shifting—in that moment, I felt so connected with everyone in that run-down warehouse that I could practically taste their relief like cold, sweet rain on my tongue. It was some time before I realized they were waiting for me to make the first move.

Out of the corner of my eye, I saw Jude push in through the crowd, his chest heaving from his run. The Chatter was lit up in his hand, vibrating loud enough for me to hear. I saw the only confirmation I needed stretched across his face in a grin.

But his eyes shifted then, and it was obvious he wasn't seeing me anymore. Only the wreckage, only the fires still clinging to the cement. Only Mason, his blank, empty gaze still fixed on something beyond our seeing.

"It's okay," I told him, breaking the silence. "We're okay."

And it didn't matter if the others truly believed what I said. They all followed me out anyway.

EIGHTEEN

If you can hear this, you're one of us. If you're one of us, you can find us. Lake Prince. Virginia . . .

The sound of Clancy's voice pouring out of the small boom box's speakers made every single hair on the back of my neck stand at attention. Olivia had set it at the edge of Knox's stage, and Jude had charged the batteries just enough to ensure we would have five minutes of solid listening.

"Why is this still broadcasting?" I asked. "I thought it was being sent out of East River?"

Olivia shook her head. "He set up a couple of signals so the message could be broadcast as far west as Oklahoma. I guess he didn't think it was important to shut the rest down."

This was the first time we had gathered everyone into the warehouse, and it was the first time I was able to get some kind of a head count. Fifty-one kids stood in a half moon around the small device, riveted by the words and bursts of static.

Finally, when it was clear that Olivia couldn't stomach the thought of listening to it play through again, she switched it off. The spell of calm and curiosity went with it. Voices sailed up to the rafters, questions were shot back and forth, ricocheting off the water-stained cement walls. They wanted to know who the voice was, where the boom box had come from, why the kids from the White Tent had been moved inside and the fire barrels dragged closest to them.

"Does this prove it to you?" I asked them. "Knox was never the Slip Kid, at least not the real one, and this isn't East River."

I was annoyed we even had to do this at all; it was clear that most of the kids had believed what I said the night before, but a few holdouts from the hunting parties were clinging stubbornly to their loyalty to Knox. Maybe it wasn't even that—I think they were just afraid they wouldn't get the lion's share of supplies now that Knox wasn't there to enforce his bullshit rules.

Or maybe they really had deluded their hearts into believing that this was East River.

I sat next to Olivia on the edge of the stage. With the spread of kids laid out in front of me, I could see other traces of Knox's cruelty. Burns. That bulging-eyed hunger. The jumps when the wind moaned through the cracks in the roof.

"Is that enough for everyone?" Olivia asked, turning to the kid in white who stood directly in front of the old device. Brett was no longer one of Knox's little watchdogs. He was a seventeen-year-old, born and raised in Nashville, who had never once stepped foot in a camp and, apparently, was slow to process important news.

"Play it again," he said, his voice hoarse. "One more time."

There was a quality to Clancy's voice—confidence, I guess—that made you listen to every last word when he spoke. I rubbed the back of my hand against my forehead and finally let out a breath when he drawled out the final *Virginia*.

"How do we even know *that*'s the Slip Kid?" Brett asked. He had been the one to call in the three other hunting teams and their leaders—Michael, Foster, and Diego. He had also been the one who insisted on watching us when we went through the crushing routine of putting Mason to rest. He hadn't offered help or comfort, even as the blisters on my palms burst with the effort of trying to break the shovel through the frozen ground.

I understood, though. We were outsiders. We'd broken the system. I was only nervous he'd be so put off and angry about our little revolution, he'd convince the others not to make the supply run. Even now, I caught him tossing glances over his shoulder toward where Chubs knelt, tending to the sick kids.

It was becoming clearer to me that he was a key link in the community's chain. If he came our way, the others would follow naturally. But we were running out of time. I could tell by the tight press of Chubs's lips every time he took Liam's temperature.

"I'm not here to give you anything but the truth," Olivia said. "I've kept quiet about it long enough, thinking he'd get better or change his ways. He didn't. He just got worse, and if Ruby hadn't sent him away . . . I don't know what he would have done next, but I know none of those kids over there would have survived it."

"He really traded those kids? Knox said they tried running away, and he took care of them." This from the same girl who had been draped over Knox's lap on the day we were brought in. She had been one of the first kids I gave a blanket to out of the storage room. We'd pulled everything out of the cramped building, laying it out in the middle of the warehouse for everyone to see what was left. Some kids, the older ones, had been brave enough to go reclaim their things, but most had stared blankly at us, not understanding.

The murmurs rose again when Olivia nodded. "There were eleven of them, at least since I got here."

"He did what he had to do to get food," Michael snarled. "We have to make sacrifices. That's what's fair."

"How is it fair for a sick kid to starve because he's too weak to work, and because he can't work, he can never get better?" she shot back. "How?"

Olivia pushed herself up so that she was standing on the platform. She tossed her limp blond hair back and stood straight and tall. "Look—it doesn't have to be this way. I've been to East River, and I've seen all that it can be. I've lived through winters there, and summers, and everything in between, and I never went hungry, not once. I never felt scared— It was . . . It was a good place, because we took care of one another."

I waited for the ax to fall, to see their faces when she told them how that same little slice of heaven was gone and the person behind it all nothing but a mask. But Brett, who'd clearly been struggling to process and accept all of this, was watching her, the tension in his face relaxing with each word until he was nodding.

"We can have that here," she continued. "I know we can. There's room to grow food, ways to set up better security. The Slip Kid doesn't have to be one person, and East River doesn't have to be only one place. We can make our own East River."

"How are we supposed to do that with this?" Michael demanded. He shook his head, the ripped collar of his shirt falling open to reveal the strips of pale pink burn scars bubbling over his neck and shoulders. He jerked a thumb back toward the measly pile of supplies. "You're as stupid as you are ugly, aren't you?"

"Hey!" Brett barked, taking a charging step toward him. Michael backed off with a sneer.

"We start by making sure those kids back there survive," Olivia continued, "that we *all* survive this winter. If you help Ruby and me with this hit, we'll be able to feed ourselves for months. We'll save their lives and, in the process, ours."

"And where's this magical land of make-believe, huh?" Michael pressed.

"One of the hangars at John C. Tune Airport," Olivia fired back, meeting his gaze dead-on. "Does anyone know where it is?"

Brett raised his hand. "It's a couple miles west of here, I think—ten at the most."

"Okay," Olivia said. Her jeans hung loose off her hips, half hidden by the jacket she fished out of the supply pile for herself. "That's doable."

"No," Michael snarled, "it's a *trap*. And anyone who agrees to participate in this shit show deserves what he or she gets."

The kids in white—the hunters—began to shift, their teeth on edge. My mind stirred in response. I had just turned my gaze on him when Olivia spoke again.

"Look, if this is going to work—and it can, and it *will*—things have got to change around here. We can't just be a tribe of Blues. No—*no*, listen to me!" Olivia raised her voice over the startled protests. "This isn't about colors. It should never have been. This has to be a place where we don't separate out by colors. This has to be a place of respect. If you can't respect one another and your abilities, if you aren't willing to help one another understand, then this won't be the place for you."

"And you get to decide this, why?" Michael pressed. "Who are you exactly to try to step up here? We had a system that worked pretty damn fine before. You want us to go soft? There's a reason we only ran with other Blues—the rest of you are so goddamn pathetic you can't do anything, not even protect yourselves."

Olivia hesitated; her own doubts about herself had been simmering below the surface of her scarred skin. The doubt radiated off her, infecting everyone standing nearby. She seemed to wilt in front of me. I felt a small jolt of panic rush through me, like a second, unwanted heartbeat. We weren't done yet. I needed her help—I needed her to be strong.

"Black is the color."

I fought through the press of memory, letting those same words wash over me. Hearing them curled softly by Liam's Southern accent, exactly as they had when he'd first said it all those months ago. "Black is still the color."

She got it. I didn't need pretty words to explain and, really, there were no words to describe what that place had been to us. We had been there together, had worked together, lived together, survived together. East River hadn't just been a camp—it was an idea, a signal fire. A belief. Clancy might have been the Slip Kid, but so was every other kid who dodged the system. Who didn't go quietly. Who wasn't ashamed or afraid of what he or she was.

"Being smart doesn't mean being soft," I continued. "You can stay or you can go, but just remember—if you run, you run alone. And trust me, it's a long, lonely road."

"That's right," Olivia said finally. "If you want to go, now's the time. Just know, though, that from this day on you will never stop running, not until they catch you. Never."

"This is stupid!" Michael shouted. "It's not how it's supposed to work. If you think any of my guys are gonna support this—"

"Then, beat it," Olivia said. "If you don't like it, go. This only works if you want to be here. Take whatever you need and hit the road."

I pushed myself off the small stage and walked right up to him. Michael was all razor edges and steel skin when I had been farther away from him, but I could see the way he was shaking now. He stood a full head over me, outweighed me by dozens of pounds, was armed . . . and none of it mattered. I didn't have to pry inside his head to know that he was replaying last night. That his thoughts were looping on what I'd done to Knox.

What I can't do to him.

The knowing hit me square in the teeth, stopping me dead in my tracks. I could influence him, that wasn't even a question. But he'd been so outspoken and openly hostile that if I flipped him now, his miraculously sudden change of heart would raise suspicions. They would all know that I could and would do the same to them. They'd still be just as afraid of me, only then they'd be motivated enough to do something about it.

Michael stared at me, breathing heavily. Olivia was at my back in an instant, arms crossed over her chest. He licked his lips and started forward, the old hunting rifle at his side clattering with the force of his step.

"No man, come on," another kid in white said, gripping him by the shoulder. "We don't got to stay."

Michael shrugged, throwing the other boy's grip off him. He started toward the loading dock door, then spun toward Brett. "You too, huh?"

"When things go bad, you gotta fix them," Brett said quietly.

Only five of the eight kids in Michael's hunting party followed him out, not saying a single damn word, not taking anything from the pile of supplies, not acknowledging the waves of hands that reached out in silent good-byes. And only one of them turned back to look at me.

I saw the plan unfold in his mind as if he had opened a book and was turning the pages for me. Coming back to camp in the night, *turn*, sneaking back into the warehouse, *turn*, unloading every round in their guns on the kids sleeping in small huddles of blankets, *turn*, the five of them carrying out all of the supplies we'd be bringing back.

My spine stiffened from bone to granite to steel. I shook my head and blasted the plan clear out of his skull.

"Anyone else?" Olivia asked, surveying the huddled masses in front of her. "No? All right. Let's get to work, then."

The former occupants of the White Tent had been laid out beside the supplies, kept in a circle of warmth by the ring of blazing trash cans around them. Chubs glanced up from where he was hunched over Vida's shoulders as I squeezed through the ring, the smell of smoke dragging up one black memory after another. I took a deep breath, pressing a hand against my mouth until Mason's face had cleared from behind my eyes, and stepped over the sleeping kids. He had set them up in two lines again, this time not piled on top of one another.

"You suck at this!" Vida snarled. "What, did you forget your rake in the car? Pour some water on it and leave it the hell alone!"

She was sitting cross-legged in front of Chubs, her elbows resting on her knees and her face pressed firmly into her hands. It was a shock every time I looked at her now, an ugly little reminder of the previous night. When we returned to the warehouse, it had been obvious to all of us that most of Vida's long hair couldn't be saved. She managed to put out the fire before it reached her scalp, thankfully, but the blue ends had been charred and left in uneven patches. With one single, fierce look, she had pulled the small knife Jude had smuggled from the storage room and cut it off herself. Her wavy hair now curled around her ears and chin.

"A rake *would* make this go faster," Chubs muttered. "I'm assuming you enjoy the luxury of having skin on your back, though."

He licked away the sweat from his upper lip. The painstaking process of removing the charred pieces of her shirt from the burn on her shoulders had begun more than an hour ago, and we were all in agony listening to him try to disinfect the area.

"Scoot back!" she hissed. "You smell like unwashed ass."

"How's it going?" I asked, crouching down beside him.

"Could be better," he muttered, "could be worse."

"I am going to straight up murder you," Vida said, her voice trembling with the intensity of the pain, "right in the face."

The tweezers in Chubs's hand stilled, just for an instant. He cleared his throat, but when he spoke again, the heat had evaporated from his voice. "Please. If it means getting away from you for five minutes, I'd gladly let you do it."

"Could be much worse," I amended, looking around again. "I have the list of all the meds you gave to Jude, but was there anything else you wanted me to look for?"

He set the rag back in the water. "Sterile gauze for Vida's burns, any kind of disinfectant like alcohol pads . . . any complete first-aid kits if they have them, really."

"What about other medicine?" I pressed, forcing myself not to look at Liam's still form. "Something else to treat their pneumonia?"

Chubs rubbed the back of his hand against his forehead, closing his eyes. "There's really nothing else, and even then the medicine will only work if it's bacterial pneumonia. If it's viral and it's already this bad, I'm not even sure IV fluid would help."

"There's nothing else . . . not even in your book?"

He'd insisted on trekking all the way back to the car to retrieve some kind of medical text his dad had given him to double-check the list of medicine.

Chubs shook his head.

I felt the scream burning at the base of my throat. NOT HIM. Not Liam. Please don't take him, too. I wondered if this was what all of those parents had felt like once IAAN had gone public and they knew there was a 98 percent chance their kids wouldn't make it through, no matter what they did to help them.

"When are you leaving?" Chubs asked. "Who's going with you?"

"In a few hours," I said. "It'll be most of the hunting groups, but a few of the guys are staying behind. And Vida."

The gunfire flashing through that boy's mind had been enough for me to worry about any other plans they might have for retaking their old home tonight. If they were stupid enough to try something, they'd be guaranteed some serious pain and trauma for their effort.

"And that's comforting, how?" he asked.

Vida reached behind her, trying to punch whatever part of him she could reach.

"You're done," she announced, bolting. The strips of the shirt he had shredded to wrap her burns with fell out of his lap as he lunged after her. We watched her stumble through the ring of fire around us, Chubs's eyes narrowing with every clumsy step she took. Slowly, after she'd disappeared into the kids milling around us, he turned to look at me.

"Yes," I said. "You have to go after her."

He raised his eyebrows in challenge.

"It'll get infected," I reminded him.

"She would drive a saint to murder. Like, ten-stab-wounds-to-the-torso murder."

"Good thing you're not a saint."

He stood at that, thrusting a towel and bucket of warm water toward me, giving some kind of vague motion toward the spread of sick kids behind us. "I'll be back in five minutes. Be useful and try to get them drinking water."

I went down the lines of kids, waking them out of fever dreams, bringing a plastic cup of water to their lips. Short of forcing their mouths open and pouring it down their throats, there wasn't much I could do to get them to swallow. I did the best I could cleaning off their faces with a rag, asking a series of questions that began with, "Are you in pain?" and ended with, "Do you feel worse than yesterday?"

Only one of the kids was able to answer. *Yes*, she had whispered, *yes*. To every question, an aching, soft *yes*.

A sharp cough drew my eyes across the way to where a familiar head of shaggy hair was struggling to escape from the baby blue blanket over him. He was attempting to get up onto his elbows, his chest heaving with the effort. It was his fluttering, shallow breaths that worried me—the way his arms shook supporting his weight.

"Stop," I said, making my way over to him, "please—it's all right, just lie back—"

Liam's eyes were wide, rimmed with red and bruises still fading. His arms gave out under him, and without any thought to it, I caught him by the shoulders and carefully lowered him back down. His eyes never left my face; the blue was paler somehow, brighter and glassy with fever.

"Careful," I murmured. After touching his burning skin, my hands felt as cold as they were empty when I pulled them away.

"What's going on?" Liam whispered, struggling to swallow. "What's . . . happening?"

"Chubs just went to get something," I said softly. "He'll be right back."

Liam nodded slightly, closing his eyes with a soft sigh. I started to reach over to brush the curling ends of his hair off his forehead when he turned toward me and forced his lids open. "You're . . . awfully pretty. What's your . . . name?"

The words wheezed and whistled out of him in a heart-stopping way, but I was caught so off guard by how coherent he was, it took me several precious moments to respond.

"Ruby," he repeated in the warm, caressing tones of his Southern lilt. "Like 'Ruby Tuesday.' That's nice."

Then Liam's expression dissolved completely. His brows drew together in a look of intense concentration, his lips repeating that one word over and over again, soundlessly.

Ruby.

I knelt down next to him, sliding the bucket over. I braced one hand on the ground beside his upturned palm.

"Ruby," he repeated, his light eyes cloudy. "You . . . Cole said . . . He told me we had never met, and I thought . . . I thought it was a dream."

I brought the rag up to his face and began, with gentle strokes, to clean the dirt and soot away from it. It was okay like this, I reasoned. I wasn't touching him directly. The stubble on his chin rasped as I brushed the rag against it. I focused on the small white scar at the corner of his lips. I focused on not pressing mine to that spot, no matter how much it felt like I was fading into him.

"A dream?" I pressed, hoping to keep him talking. "What kind of dream was it?"

It wasn't . . . No, it wasn't possible. I had seen people become confused after I'd messed with their memories, a bit muddled on the details, but I had gone through and picked every instance of me clean from Liam's mind. I had replaced myself with thin air and shadows.

A faint smile formed on his lips. "A good one."

"Lee . . ."

"I need . . . Are the keys . . . ?" His voice was getting

softer. "We'll go get . . . I think Zu is— She's in the aisle with— The one with—"

Aisle?

"I don't want those guys to . . . to see her. They're going to hurt them, both of them—"

I pulled back, but Liam's hand somehow found mine on the ground, and his fingers latched onto it, pinning me there. "What guys? Zu's safe; no one is going to hurt her."

"The—Walmart . . . I told her, I told her to go with . . . She went with— No, where is she? Where's Zu?"

"She's safe," I promised, trying to pull my hand back. His grip was persistent, like he was trying to force me to understand something, and the more he struggled, the harder it was for him to catch his breath. I took my free hand and pressed it to his cheek, leaning over his face. "Liam, look at me. Zu's safe. You have to—you have to relax. Everything will be all right. She's safe."

"Safe." The word sounded hollow. He closed his eyes on it. "Don't go again," he whispered. "Don't go . . . where I can't follow, please, *please*, not again . . ."

"I'll stay right here," I said, rubbing a thumb along his cheekbone.

You have to stop this. You have to leave. Right now.

"Don't lie," he mumbled, at the edge of sleep. "This is . . . a place we don't have to . . ."

My vision blanked out with an array of spots and a pounding rush of blood as I shot up onto my feet. I pressed a hand to my mouth, waiting for my sight to clear, trying not to trip over the kids nearby. I knew what he had been trying to say. I had heard those words before, had said them myself, but there was— It wasn't possible—

This is a place we don't have to lie.

"Ruby?"

Vida and Chubs were standing in front of the fire barrels, watching me with twin expressions of concern. How long had they been standing there listening? Chubs took a step toward me, but I waved him off. "I'm okay, he just . . ."

I crouched down, putting my head in my hands, forcing in two deep, steadying breaths.

Not possible.

"Are you sure?" Chubs repeated, his voice sounding colder than before. "Are you finished playing this game?"

I nodded, keeping my eyes on the ground at his feet. My stomach rolled and heaved. I could hear Liam struggling with the blanket twisted between his legs, my mind suddenly stirring.

"You think it's okay to be all sweet to him like this now and confuse him even more? The plan is still to take the flash drive and dump us for the League, right?" he demanded. "What's going to happen when he wakes up?"

"She's going to mope around and pretend like she's never met him before in all the sad, pathetic years of her life," Vida said, sitting down a short distance away. "Because this is a grab-and-go operation. Ruby *knows* that's all this is, doesn't she? She said she wouldn't let her feelings get all mixed up and twisty about this, didn't she?"

I swallowed hard. "I know. Can you . . . Will you tell him why we're here?"

"The truth?" Chubs challenged, his voice sharp.

It started as a single cough, but I recognized the first sharp gasp behind me for what it was. Liam struggled against his blankets, trying to get his hands up to his throat as he fought for the next breath. He sucked at the air, trying to twist onto his side, but he couldn't get himself over onto his shoulder. There was no way to tell which of us moved first. By the time I reached Liam's side, Chubs was there, too, propping his friend up to keep him from choking.

"It's okay," Chubs said, leaning him forward so he could pat his back. He sounded calm, but a sheen of sweat had broken out on his forehead. "One breath at a time. You're fine. You're okay."

He didn't sound okay. He sounded like . . .

He's going to die. My hands twisted in my hair. After everything, he was going to die here, like this, fighting and failing and drifting away to a place I couldn't reach him.

"Water?" Vida asked as she hobbled over with a plastic bottle in her hand. I hated the hard glint to her eyes. The judgment I saw her pass on Liam's condition and the look of pity she sent my way.

"No," Chubs said, "it might obstruct his airways. Ruby. *Ruby*—he's going to be okay; I'm going to keep him awake and make sure he moves around. I need that medicine. I need fluids, heat packs, anything. Quickly."

I nodded, fisting my hands in my hair, forcing in one damp breath after another.

"Roo!" Jude's voice floated over to us a moment before he appeared at the edge of the fires, holding up a familiar black jacket. "I found it, I found it, I found it!"

The three of us shushed him.

"Come here!" I waved him over, taking the jacket before he could accidentally light it on fire. I had only gotten a quick look at the coat in Cole's memories, and even then, it had been half hidden by the shadows swirling there—but this looked close enough, even if it wasn't black. The jacket was dark gray, waxed canvas with a flannel interior, and even after being separated from its current owner, it still smelled like him. Pine, fire smoke, and sweat. I felt both Vida's and Chubs's eyes on me as I ran my fingers along the seams, until they found the hard, rectangular lump that Cole had stitched into the dark lining.

"He's right." I passed the jacket over to Vida. "Leave it in there for now; we'll cut it out after we go."

My eyes drifted back to Liam's ashen face. It screwed up with the effort of the next cough, but it sounded stronger to me somehow, like he was clearing out the blockage. Jude hovered behind me, taking all of this in, too. The pride beaming from his face drained away. His hand closed tightly around my shoulder, either to steady himself or me. Both, I guess.

"Can you go tell Olivia I'm ready when she is?" I asked. "And—*hey*—" I caught the back of his shirt. "Find yourself something warmer to wear, will you?"

A clumsy salute was all I got in exchange for that. Vida raised her brows as he bounced away, a smug *Good luck with that one!* look stamped across her face. Maybe Vida was right and I should have forced him to stay behind, but there was no telling what kind of tech we were going to encounter. He might not have been able to hit a target a foot away or run more than a hundred feet, but as a Yellow, Jude had been specifically trained to handle electronic locks and security systems.

I helped Chubs lower Liam back onto the ground, but he caught my hands before I could pull back. His eyes slid from his friend's pale face to mine.

"Is this really better than it would have been if you'd just stayed together?"

I flinched.

"You think you *maybe* overestimated his ability to take care of his own sorry ass without us?" Chubs asked. "Just a little?"

It wasn't better, but it wasn't necessarily worse. Chubs could pick at this scab all he wanted, turning and pointing every single time the wound started bleeding again, but he didn't understand. The Liam in front of us was a reflection of the world we were forced to live in, and as cruel and harsh as it was . . . at least it wasn't the Liam the League would have turned out: a violent, unforgiving reflection of how they thought the world *should* be.

"I'm not happy about this."

"I know," I whispered. I leaned across Liam's prone form to wrap my arms around Chubs's neck. If he was surprised by my burst of affection, he didn't show it. Instead, he patted me gently on the back before turning to finish his work with Vida. "You make me as crazy as a bag of cats, but if anything happens to you, I'm going to lose it. Are you sure . . . are you a hundred percent positive you know what you're doing?"

"Yeah," I said. Unfortunately. "I've had training, remember?"

His mouth twisted into a humorless smile. "And to think, when we found you . . ."

Chubs didn't have to finish. I knew what I'd been when I'd found them: a terrified splinter of a girl who had been shattered a long time ago. I had nothing, and no one, and no real place to go. Maybe I was still broken and would always be—but now, at least, I was piecing myself back together, lining up one jagged edge at a time.

NINETEEN

We only waited long enough for the sun to go down before heading out. The quick sunset was one of the few blessings of a rapidly approaching winter. I tried to calculate, in a distracted kind of way, exactly how much time had passed since I set off looking for Liam. Two weeks, if even? It was December; I remembered the digital display in the train station in Rhode Island. I counted back.

"We missed your birthday."

We were hovering at the back of the pack, drifting there almost naturally while Olivia and Brett had taken charge in front.

Whatever Springsteen song Jude had been humming under his breath was bottled back up, mid-note. *"What?"*

"It was last week," I said, reaching out to steady him as he jumped over a fallen tree. "Today's December eighteenth."

"Really?" Jude crossed his arms over his chest and began to rub them. "Feels like it, I guess."

"Fifteen," I said with a low whistle. "You're getting up there in years, old man."

I started to unwind the wool scarf from around my neck, but he waved it away and marched on, his EMT jacket crinkling as he moved. For such a large group, we were moving quietly through the undergrowth—snapping a few twigs here and there, breaking through pockets of ice. We were still too deep into what Brett had called the Cheatham Wildlife Management Area to attract much attention anyway.

"Oh! You found it?" I asked when I caught the flash of silver gripped in Jude's palm.

Jude held it out for me to see. It was a circular, nearly flat disc. The silver coating glinted in the single strand of moonlight that cut through the tree branches. I plucked it out of his hand and put the warm metal at the center of my palm. The compass's glass had cracked in two places.

"Yeah," he said, taking it back. "For a second there . . . never mind."

"Never mind?" I repeated in disbelief. "What's wrong?"

"It's just that, for a second, I was really happy I found it, you know? And then I started to think that maybe I shouldn't take it with me."

"Because . . . ?"

"Because Alban gave it to me," he said. "A few days after I came to HQ. He kept saying how proud he was that I was part of the League, but it's like . . . now I don't think I'm so proud of being part of it."

I let out a long sigh, trying to find the right words. Jude only shrugged again and slid the string over his head. The compass disappeared under his jacket, and I thought, *That's the difference.* That was the fundamental difference between the two of us. Once I woke up to reality, I couldn't go back to the dream—but Jude was still able to hold out hope in his heart that it would be there waiting for him when he was ready to return. After everything, he still believed that the League could be different, better, healed.

I wasn't out of shape by any means, but hiking over hill after hill, fighting through the thick mulch of newly dead leaves on an empty stomach, all the while trying to keep my brain from circling back to Liam, was beginning to weigh on me. Jude's stomach had growled no less than four times in the past half hour alone, and while he seemed immune to getting cranky like the rest of us, I felt him start to sag next to me.

"Almost there," I assured him, shooting a dirty look at the back of Brett's head. It wasn't his fault; we didn't have cars to transport everyone. There'd been some discussion about trying to navigate down on the Cumberland River, but even months after the flooding, Brett felt like its current was too unstable for their rafts. So we were walking, using fabric cut from the tents as makeshift bags for the supplies.

We were walking ten miles, eleven, twelve. My fingers were frozen stiff; not even pressing them up under my armpits could get the blood flowing back through them.

Jude pursed his lips together, reaching up to adjust his cap. With it pressing down at such an awkward angle over his curly hair, it bent his ears out, making them look bigger than they actually were. For a bizarre second, I felt my heart swell just the smallest bit at the sight.

"Annnnnnyway," said Jude, master of awkward transitions. "This is going to be so great. So, so great. We'll be in like this"—he snapped his fingers—"swipe the meds and some food, and out, like, bam!" He clenched both fists and flashed his fingers out. "They won't even know we've been there until we're gone. We'll be freaking legends!"

Jude kept saying "they" this and "they" that, but that was the problem—we didn't know who was in charge of the airport or why they were hoarding supplies. I'd tried to send a follow-up message to Cate and Nico to ask, but they hadn't responded before we left.

We were still heading east, toward Nashville's center, but the river didn't follow a straight path. It had looped down again, directly in front of us.

I nudged my way up to the front of the group. My outstretched hand eventually found Olivia's shoulder, and she reached back, pulling me to the edge of the Cumberland River.

"Whoa," was Jude's only comment.

Until we hit that first barrier, I hadn't really understood why, months after the floodwaters receded, the city was still closed. But it was like with any disasters; the cleanup was almost always worse than the stress of the disaster in progress. No wonder the ground had become little more than a swamp under my boots, no wonder the river was still flooding out. The initial storms had been powerful enough to carry whole sections of homes back into the river, to upend massive river barges and leave them stranded and rusting under the sun. It was like a terrible drain clog. The water couldn't flow naturally down toward the city, which meant it was still bleeding out into the nearby fields and forests.

"It's right over there," Brett said, pointing to distant white shapes. As if on cue, a red light on one of them began to pulse slow and steady. "Nice to see Gray and his boys got around to cleaning this mess up like he swore he would."

"Are we . . . swimming?" I asked, trying not to grimace.

Olivia turned toward me, holding up our one lone flashlight. The scarred half of her face stretched into a genuine smile. "Nope. We're going to play leapfrog."

It turned out that "playing leapfrog" with a bunch of Blues essentially meant resigning yourself to being flung from floating object to floating object like a rag doll. The system they'd worked through was impressive; the river was too wide for the Blues to lift another kid with their abilities and send him cruising the whole way across it. Instead, Brett took advantage of the flood's wreckage, lifting Olivia and setting her down, with impressive accuracy and care, on the upturned corner of a half-sunk barge. She, in turn, sent the next Blue a little farther, onto the roof of what looked like a large mobile home. With the three of them in position, they were able to pass each of us along without much trouble at all. I landed on my knees, finally on the other bank.

We cut another path through a thicket of trees, emerging muddy and slick with the fresh rain falling overhead. The runway was shorter than the ones I'd seen at bigger airports, jam-packed with planes of all sizes and shapes. Mixed in between the helicopters and one-seaters were green-and-tan military vehicles. The airport wasn't in use after all, then—and if the planes and trucks were out here, it meant there really was a good chance that Cate and Nico's intel *was* good, and something else was being stored in the hangars.

Someone—the National Guard by the look of the vehicles—had halfheartedly put up a chain-link fence around the perimeter of the runways and hangars, along with signs that read things like NO TRESSPASSING and HIGH VOLTAGE. Olivia threw a rock, which bounced back and hit the mud with the tiniest rattle. Jude twisted out of the grip I had on his shirt to belly crawl through the grass.

"Hey!" I whispered. "Jude!"

He tapped the fence with his finger, then again for good measure before he hustled back over to us. "That has about as much electricity as my shoe," he whispered.

This isn't right, I thought. If there was something worth having here, there'd be people to protect it . . . right?

I scanned the field in front of us again, Instructor March's voice ringing in my ears: *If it looks too good, too easy, it never is*. And the simulation we'd run after—with Vida and I storming a warehouse—had proven that point. Sure, it had been all clear on the outside. The agents playing the roles of the National Guardsmen had been waiting for us *inside*.

"Roo." Jude groaned. "Come *on*."

There was no real cover between the trees and the hangars, but that didn't stop Brett and some of the others from blowing past us to continue forward. Even Olivia looked over at me, exasperated, before she stood and jogged to catch up to them.

"All right," I told Jude, "stay close—"

But he was already up and running, too, weaving through the vehicles and planes on the runway. I finally caught up with them when they stopped at the edge of the asphalt, crouching down behind the last line of vehicles.

"I'll take Brett and Jude with me," I said, taking the flashlight from Olivia. "Two flashes for all clear, one for turn back. Got it?"

"There's *no one here*, Ruby."

"And that doesn't strike you as odd?" I hissed back. There were tire tracks and footprints all around us; if they were old, they would have been washed out after days of rain.

The nearby parking lots were mostly empty or filled with large shipping trucks. Now and then a light above them would flicker, but aside from that, the airport was dark.

Every nerve in my body was tingling by the time I met up with Brett again after we'd lapped the buildings. I jerked my chin back in the direction where we'd left Jude waiting.

"This is too easy," Brett finally admitted, shifting his old rifle to his shoulder. "Where the hell is everyone?"

Please not in the hangars, I thought. *Please.* This was my idea—I'd pushed them into this, and it would be on me to get us out if everything blew up in our faces.

Cate wouldn't have sent us here if she thought it was too dangerous, I told myself, not if there was a chance we could be caught.

"Call the others over," I told Jude, silencing the small voice before it could send me spiraling into true fear.

I counted them again as they ran toward us. One, two, three, all the way up to twenty-one.

The hunting party shrank into the shadow of Hangar 1, backs pressed to the wall, eyes scanning the dark field. The hangar door was locked with a series of imposing chains we had no way of slicing through, but there was a side-access door that, like I'd predicted, had some kind of electronic lock that looked like it had been beamed back from the distant future.

"Step aside," Jude said, shooing me away with his hands. "The master is here."

"Careful," I warned. "Frying it completely will probably trigger it, too."

"Honestly," he said, squinting at the display. It lit instinctively when he stepped in front of it, pulling up a digital number pad. "You're acting like I've never done this before!"

"You haven't," I reminded him. "Nico usually disables the alarm systems remotely."

"Details, details." Jude waved me off with one hand and brought his other palm up against the screen. "Be silent so the master can do his work!"

"Can the master hurry the hell up?" Brett hissed, hopping from foot to foot, arms crossed over his chest. I was starting to feel the winter bite, too. The sweat gliding down my face felt like it was two degrees away from freezing into solid crystals.

"Count of three," Jude breathed out, "push on the door handle. Ready?"

I slipped around him, getting a good grip on the metal bar. "Go for it."

At three, the system's screen flickered black, and I waited only long enough to hear the lock pop before shoving it open with my shoulder. When the system's number pad flashed back up, it cast an eerie red halo on the drifting snowflakes.

I waited for the shrill cry of an alarm, the blinding flash of floodlights spotlighting our small group. I waited to feel Jude shrink against the wall behind me in terror. I waited, waited, waited. But there was nothing to wait for.

"Okay!" Jude called. "I tricked the system into thinking that the door is actually closed—we just have to keep it open, and then we won't run into any problems."

"Nice job!" I whispered. The others streamed in past us, leaving a trail of mud and slush on the concrete ramp. We smelled like wet dogs that had rolled around in an ashtray.

Jude grinned as he dashed in after them. Someone hit the overhead lights and flooded the room with pristine white. I covered my eyes with a hand, trying to adjust to the glare.

There was a strange charge to the air now; I felt Jude's mood shift from a sparkling excitement to the kind of shock that only ever comes like a brick to the face. The shift was so fast, and so sudden, that I was almost too afraid to see the hangar for myself.

"Holy . . . shit."

There were rows of metal shelves lining the echoing room; they'd been set up almost like the stacks in a library but had to be a good two or three times the normal size. The soldiers had dragged them into tight, neat rows. The thick layer of faint peach paint someone had coated the cement with still had the gouges and scuff marks to prove it. Stacked on top of them were pallets and pyramids of boxes. Many were unlabeled, even more wrapped up tightly in a nest of clear plastic.

"What language is that?" Olivia asked. She kicked at the nearest one, knocking the dust and clumps of dirt from it with the toe of her boot. It was buckled on one side, the thin wood cracking as if it had fallen from a great height and landed wrong side up in a field.

"Chinese?" Jude guessed. "Japanese? Korean?"

I didn't recognize the words printed there, but the simple red cross that had been stamped over it—that I *did* recognize.

The American Red Cross branches had, if you believed the news, run out of funds and supplies once all shipping to and from the United States was halted. People were afraid that IAAN was contagious and could jump ship, riding shotgun on a package or in a person to go plague another, healthier country. Once the economy was gone, the organization barely had funding to stay afloat for two more years.

So what the hell was this stuff?

"Liv—check it out!" one of the guys called. He and a few of the others had sliced through the plastic and were levitating boxes down to the ground from the upper shelves. One of them was already gutted, its fire-engine-red innards sliding across the floor. I picked up one of the red packages that had spilled out, surprised by its weight and rectangular shape. There was a sketch of a man lifting food to his mouth, and a flag, both printed under the words HUMANITARIAN DAILY RATION.

"'This bag contains one day's complete food requirement for one person,'" Olivia read. There were more lines beneath it—in French and Spanish, maybe?

"'Food gift from the people of China,'" I finished, passing the package back to her.

There were several sharp intakes of breath around us, but most of the others had been driven onto the next shelf, pulling down cardboard boxes printed with TEN 24-HOURS RATIONS GP NATO/OTAN APPROVED.

"This stuff is from the UK, I think." Jude had ripped into one of the boxes and was examining a pamphlet that had been left inside. "There's . . . there's so much stuff. Matches, soup, *chocolate*—oh my God, there's even tea!"

"Take what we need," I said, "but look for the medicine. Do you see any of it?"

"This stuff is from *Russia*!" I heard Brett call from the next aisle over.

"Here's Germany, Canada, and I think Japan," Olivia called back.

"France and Italy, too," came another voice. "They all say daily rations!"

I slipped the thin piece of notebook paper Chubs had scribbled out his list on, holding it up to catch the light. His handwriting was as dark and smudged as ever; whatever pen he'd managed to dig up out of the supply pile had started sputtering ink when he hit *penicillin*. He branched out all of the different kinds beneath that word: *Amoxicillin (Amoxil), Ampicillin (Rimacillin), Benzylpenicillin (Crystapen)* . . .

I jogged down the aisles, scanning the boxes and crates with wary eyes. More food, trash bags of what looked like wool blankets, all boxed up, all stamped with flags I didn't recognize. There were red crosses everywhere, on everything. Dirt and clumps of dead grass clung to their edges. It had all been outside once, I realized. Dropped by planes passing overhead, maybe? Cate had mentioned rumors of foreign aid being left in parts of the country, but those same rumors had died out when no one turned up any evidence to prove it.

"One minute!"

My heart jumped from my ribs to the back of my throat; the air whistling in between my teeth sounded loud to my ears. It was quieter back here under the towering plastic tubs that were stacked against the hangar's back wall. I leaned down, brushing away the dust from its clear side. More of those strange red packages. I moved onto the next tub, half listening to the anxious whispers carrying over from the other side of the hangar.

I didn't stop searching, not until my eyes drifted over the familiar curved neck of Leda Corp's golden swan. Chubs's list fluttered to the ground as I stood on my toes, trying to see what was inside of this one. Leda Corp meant medicine; my experiences riding in the back of cargo planes had taught me that much. I got as good of a grip as I could on the plastic lid and began to yank it out. Jude was calling for me, his voice drifting above the others'.

"Come on, come on," I grumbled, my arms shaking with the effort.

The tub exploded open as it hit the ground; I dug into the clear packets of vials and sterile needles until I recognized one of the penicillin names that Chubs had written down. I took as many as I could, scooping them into my bag. Another tub was labeled VACCINES, but the one below it had wound-up ribbons of gauze, cotton pads, and rubbing alcohol.

"A little help over here!" I called. One of my bags was already full, and the second one was quickly going the same way. We needed more. Liam needed more.

Footsteps fell fast and heavy on the cement. I felt someone rush behind me, muttering something under his breath that I didn't quite catch—one glance over my shoulder told me that half of the group, struggling under the new weight of their packs, was doing one last loop through the different aisles.

"Ruby!"

It wasn't the crack in Jude's voice that sent me spinning back—it was the sudden, overwhelming stench of stale cigarette smoke.

I wasn't fast enough. I shifted, meaning to throw up an arm to block the blow, but the knife found me a moment before the punch to the back of the head did.

I don't know if I screamed. My jaw dropped with the burst of pain. I tried to catch myself as I pitched forward into the tubs, but a hand fisted around my ponytail and wrenched me back. I didn't have a chance to regain my balance. The gun was ripped out from the back of my pants before I could think clearly enough to pull it.

Michael was breathing ragged and uneven, more with fury, I thought, than the effort of the attack. The knife, or whatever he'd used, twisted in my lower back, and that time I *knew* I screamed. The arm across my chest slid up to press against my throat, my gun fisted tight in his hand. He pressed it up under my chin, forcing it as high as the bones in my neck would allow without snapping. I couldn't breathe, couldn't swallow, couldn't move.

"Miss me?" he hissed.

I tried throwing my head back, twisting, anything to get away. *You're okay,* I told myself. *Not your spine, not your kidney, just—*

"Thanks for finding this place," he continued, slamming me forward against the tubs. Michael leaned down low, bringing his lips up to my ear. "You and the others can get your sweet fill until the PSFs get here, yeah?"

The force of Jude ramming into us shoulder-first wasn't enough to throw Michael off me completely, but it was powerful enough that I could turn and drive my knee up into his center. I heard the knife give way from my skin with a sucking sound and clatter against the floor. Jude's mop of curling hair dove for it at the same time Michael did. My entire right side screamed in pain as my foot went flying toward his face.

"Bitch!" he screamed, and then I was flying back, slamming into the shelves opposite us. Jude was sent flying in another direction, back toward Brett and Olivia, who were coming down the aisle to see what was happening. One shot fired—another one—and the lights changed from white to a flashing red, and everything after was swallowed by a pulsing screech.

TWENTY

I DON'T KNOW HOW I GOT FROM THE BACK OF THE hangar to the front, only that when the black fuzz lifted from my brain and the nauseating brightness of the overhead lights warmed to an unbearable glow, Jude had me propped up at one shoulder, Olivia at the other, and we were watching as Michael and four others collected our guns and sacks of food rations.

To the right of them, shaking like the last leaf on an autumn tree, was a blank-stared Knox.

So that was where Michael and the others had gone—to find their old pack leader. A lot of good it seemed like it was doing for them now, though. Knox muttered to himself, rocking back and forth on his heels, the same word forming on his lips: *Leave*, *leave*, *leave*.

"—your choice," Michael shouted. The noise had cut out, but not the flashing lights. "You chose strangers over Knox! Over *me*! You wanna take everything from us and kick us out? We found that damn warehouse! We set everything up!"

Jude was shaking—not from fear or the cold but from blistering anger. "So if you can't have it, no one can—is that it?" he said, his hand tightening around my waist. "You hate your life, so you have to make everyone else just as miserable and hungry and pathetic as you are?"

"I am *not* pathetic—none of us are! If she hadn't messed him up, Knox would be telling you this! Look at him—*look!* You want her to do this to you? You want another performance of her freak show?"

"Believe me . . ." I shook my head in a weak attempt to clear the spots from my vision. "If you don't drop those bags and get the hell out of my sight in two seconds, you'll be next."

He raised his gun, but Olivia and Brett both stepped directly in front of me.

There was a quick movement to my left. I looked over just in time to see one of Michael's team yank the door to open it again. One of them must have shut it, I realized. That's why the alarms had gone off in the first place.

"Time to go," the boy shouted. "They're pulling up!"

My core settled to stone. If *they* were here, it was already too late.

"Don't—!" Brett warned, but Michael grabbed Knox and followed the others out into the night anyway. There were two beats of silence. I closed my eyes and turned away from the shouting, the whining of cars, and guns and uniforms. One shot was fired. A hundred answered.

“Down!” I commanded, tackling Jude. For the most part, the bullets pinged off the large hangar door, just to the right of the smaller side access door we’d come through, but some passed through the thin metal and buried themselves in the same shelves of supplies we had just ransacked.

My mind was fraying at the edges, a pounding headache echoing every throb of pain in my lower back. I swiped at the sweat beading on my upper lip. I didn’t need to get up with Brett, or find a way to look outside. I knew what I’d see—four dumb, dead kids and a swarm of black and camo setting up a line of defense.

“I count thirty of them,” one of the Blues said. *I don’t even know your name,* I thought numbly, *and you followed us here anyway. I am going to get you killed.*

I felt the overpowering urge to throw up as I stood. *We are dead. I killed us.*

“This’ll be cake, right?” Brett said, clearing his throat. He turned back to the others. “They got guns, but we got brains. I like those odds.”

“One big push should do it,” Olivia agreed. “I can take half back over the river the way we came, but someone else should try to take the other half the long way.”

Brett rubbed a hand through his dark hair with a light laugh. “By *someone*, you mean me? That eager to get rid of me?”

The Blues were dividing themselves up, falling in place behind Olivia and Brett, and the absurdity of what we were about to do—shove them like playground bullies, then try to outrun the bullets that followed—made me want to scream.

I stood at the edge of the noise and movement, feeling strangely disconnected from what was going on around me. But Jude—he cut right through the panic, shoving his way through the bodies to reach the fuse box on the wall.

"Everyone line up at the door," he said, smashing the small lock on the electrical box with a nearby fire extinguisher. He tossed the broken metal behind him and pulled the gray cover open. Jude bit the tip of his right glove and pulled it back off, placing his bare hand against the assortment of switches. The dials at the top began to spin at a crazy speed, their tiny red arms blurring.

"You guys throw them back, and I'll follow up with a punch." He sounded calm—way too calm for him.

"What are you doing?" I asked. The air felt warmer, tickling my face. The mop of chestnut hair in front of me started to rise and crackle with static. I took a step back, but it wasn't until the lights snapped off and the alarm went dead that I could see the blue lines of sparks racing along his hands and arms.

"Ruby, you have to hit the button for the door," he said. Just standing close to him made the hair on my arms rise.

"What are you doing?" I asked again. He seemed to be splitting into two in front of my eyes. I blinked, but the halo of light around him didn't vanish with it.

"Trust me," he said, his voice carrying that unnatural calmness. "I got this one."

He counted down from three, forcing the Blues to scramble into the line he had ordered. Jude took care not to touch anyone at the very center of the line; the others seemed to curve around him, responding to his charge and the shift in mood.

No, I thought, biting the word back. *No, not there.* Not where they can hurt you—

"One!" Jude's voice rang out. My hand slapped against the button.

The snow had changed to a heavy rain while we were inside. It fell in sheets, distorting the lights the soldiers had set up. The white beams flooded in at our feet and traveled upward over our legs as the enormous door continued to rise. Jude waited until the light hit him square in the chest, and then he clenched both fists.

They weren't floodlights, I realized. Just the headlights of the four trucks that had parked in a half ring around the hangar's door. Most of the soldiers had taken up behind the green vehicles, bracing their guns over the hoods for a steadier aim. A good two dozen soldiers knelt on the ground in front of them, rifles raised, helmets strapped on.

The door came to a screeching stop overhead.

A few of the soldiers in camo sat back on their heels or pulled back from the sights of their guns. Surprised, I'm sure, to see nothing but a small cluster of freaks. One of the men in front turned and shouted something back to the others, but the rain swallowed his words.

A burst of whining static cut in. Someone had retrieved a megaphone for one of the older men in the back. "You are to come with us," he said, "on authority of the Psi Special Forces commander, Joseph Traylor. If you do not cooperate, we will respond with force."

"Yeah?" Brett called. "You can tell Joseph Traylor that, on our authority, he can suck it!"

That was the cue, whether he had meant it to be or not. The Blues took one single step forward and threw up their arms. Even the soldiers who recognized what was happening were too slow to fully respond. The *pop-pop-pop* of an automatic weapon was swallowed by the startled screams as the whole cluster of the soldiers and their trucks were lifted and thrown back, as if by an invisible tidal wave.

And then, Jude stepped out into the rain.

It was both horrible and beautiful to watch—familiar, somehow, to see the roaring electricity he had collected from the hangar hover around him like a blue sun. The light swelled out, bursting past the walls of his skin and raced out along the pooled rainwater on the pavement in rivers of searing light. Jude's shape became a shadow, a simple silhouette, as the electricity billowed out in front of him, growing like a silent, blinding explosion.

The night lost the fresh smell of rain, carrying a new stench of burned skin, and hair, and the unmistakable gut-churning odor of white-hot rubber instead. The electricity sizzled as it lashed out. It jumped up past the rubber-soled boots. It lit clothes and bones and skin, heating the metal canisters of pepper spray until they exploded. The soldiers that hadn't been knocked out by the Blues' hit began to writhe on the ground. One managed to lift his gun, aiming in the general direction of Jude, only to be shoved farther back by Brett.

Jude stayed on his feet as long as he could, shaking and trembling like a wet rabbit in the blistering cold. Then he collapsed, knees to pavement, chest to pavement, face to pavement in such a boneless way that I screamed, pushing past the others to get to him.

I flipped him over onto his back, ignoring the sharp pricks of static stabbing my fingers. His face felt burning to the touch, even under a blanket of freezing rain. When he had fallen, so had the charge, the popping blue rivets of electricity evaporating like steam.

Olivia's group came out next, scrambling for whatever guns they could reach, kicking aside prone soldiers to get to them.

"Olivia!" Brett shouted. I looked up as he and the others came rushing out after the first group. She stopped, her feet sliding against the pavement as she turned. He had one hand around her upper arm, another in her loose braid. He drew his face down to her scarred one and kissed her. It lasted no longer than a heartbeat. A firm, exact message.

"Now run!" he said, pushing her toward the others.

I struggled under Jude's awkward length, trying to lift his prone form. Brett shoulder-checked me aside, not having the patience or, clearly, the time to waste on trying to rouse the kid out of his exhausted stupor. He hoisted Jude up onto his back. The pack he had carried out was kicked to another Blue, who scooped it up mid-stride.

"This way!" he called.

The running was so much worse, so much harder than I expected. Car engines came rip-roaring alive behind us. I saw more speeding down the nearby road, but only the last two in that caravan saw us quickly enough to turn off into the field before entering the small airport. The headlights bounced as the SUVs took each hill and pit. The trees, though, the trees were up ahead, their dark, thick line lit—

A hand closed around my wrist, wrenching me back. I fell hard, my feet slipping out from under me with the combination of mud and frost and ice. An explosion of gray spots bloomed behind my eyelids as my head slammed back against the ground.

The soldier shined a flashlight in my face, close enough to my eyes that I had to shut them again to escape the brightness. Her knee came down on my chest and pushed that last breath of air out of it. I twisted and kicked, a frustrated scream ripping out of my throat.

Then the light dropped away and I could open my eyes again. She was young—but, more importantly, she was furious. The soldier tugged an orange object off her belt and held it directly in front of my face. She shouted something I couldn't hear. The rain—it was only rain, filling my mouth, my nose, my eyes, my ears. The orange device swam in my vision again, disappearing in another burst of white light.

I knew the moment the device pulled up my profile. The PSF's face went slack with horror, her eyes drifting back down to my face.

I turned my head and sunk my teeth into her wrist's burned pink flesh. She shrieked, but I was already in her mind. A car's bright headlights slashed through the dark, highlighting the shapes running toward us, heading into the woods.

"Get . . . off!" I kicked one last time, with enough force that even Instructor Johnson would have approved.

The soldier slumped off me, landing hard in the dirt. Her eyes were open and vacant, staring at me. Waiting for an order.

I didn't bother unhooking my mind's claws from her. I didn't care. Every part of my body felt slow and heavy. It took all my focus to get to the trees without falling, and more than even that to haul my limbs through the crunching underbrush and ice. The land was rising; every hill seemed to set me back from the pack that much farther.

I ran. Or I tried to. I tried everything I could to push myself past the haze settling over my mind and the trembling that started in my legs and rose steadily with each drop in the landscape. I thought of Liam, of Chubs, of Vida, of Jude. We had to get back and tell the others; we had to move them in case any of the soldiers traced our path.

"Jude . . ." I mumbled, my foot slipping out from under me. Something boiling hot raced down over my hip. "Jude . . . Vida . . . Chubs . . . Liam . . . Jude . . ."

Brett had taken him, hadn't he? If he could navigate through the twisted tree branches with the kid's full weight on his back, I could do this. I could stand back up.

You did this. We were done. They would take us, and I would never see any of them again.

I breathed out their names until there was no air in my chest. I walked until my legs disappeared from under me. I watched as the last trace of the kids up ahead faded at the crest of a hill, bleeding into the deep dark of the woods. I didn't remember falling, only the sensation that I had somehow lost half my body and left it behind under the cover of the trees.

I pushed myself onto my back, my hand flopping around my waist, looking for a gun that wasn't there. *Accept, adapt, act.* With a sob of pain, I hauled myself back up against a tree trunk, propping my back up. I'd be able to see anyone coming. I could rest now.

I could look up through the bare bones of the old trees around me and watch the rain tear the sky down piece by piece, until there was nothing left but darkness.

TWENTY-ONE

I WAS BORN IN THE DARK HEART OF A FIERCE WINter.

My parents' and my Grams's words, not mine. She and Dad loved to pull out the story of the death-defying trip home from the hospital when I wouldn't settle down at night or I got fidgety and bored at family dinners. The blizzard got me every time. I'd let myself be wrapped up in the way their words seemed to drip with danger, how they used their hands to try to show how high the snow rose. I could barely keep up; each time, I tried to absorb every word, take the words in so deep I'd dream about them when I finally fell asleep. Now, there was just an overwhelming sense of embarrassment. I hated how stupid I'd been to think that surviving it meant I was somehow special. That I ever thought it was undeniable proof there was something I was supposed to live to do later.

"The sky was the color of ash," Dad would say, "and the minute I left the parking lot, the clouds seemed to drop. I should have turned back right away, but your mom wanted to get home to Grams. She was throwing a whole welcome-home shindig for us, you know."

They had made it as far as they could, Dad in the driver's seat trying to force his way through a suffocating curtain of white, Mom in the backseat with me, yelling at him to pull over before he drove us off some nonexistent cliff. He liked telling that part of the story the best—Dad was the only one who could nail the high, breathy quality that Mom's voice got when she was hovering at the edge of a meltdown.

The car's headlights were no match for the snow, but there were still people fighting to get down that stretch of highway. Dad did pull over, but someone coming from the complete opposite direction jumped lanes and smashed into the front of our car. I don't know where they were going or why they were speeding blindly through high winds and no visibility, but they totaled our car, forcing us off the shoulder and into an ever-building snow bank. They killed the engine and the battery.

There was no cell phone reception—they couldn't even pick up the radio. Mom always told that part of the story in a tight voice, her imagination fixed on everything that could have happened to us if the storm had gone on much longer than it did. The three of us huddled in the backseat together for three hours, trying not to panic, pressing together for warmth. I slept through the whole thing.

I think Grams liked the story because she got to play the hero. She'd mobilized the neighbors into a search party and used her truck to haul my parents' car back onto the highway.

"It's just life for you, Little Bee," she told me years later. "Sometimes you're the one speeding along in a panic, doing too much, not paying attention, wrecking things you don't mean to. And sometimes life just happens to you, and you can't dodge it. It crashes into you because it wants to see what you're made of."

Despite how terrifying the story was to me as a kid, I still loved winter growing up; the cold didn't bother me, because I knew that in the span of months, weeks, days, the season would change again. It's easy to ride out the coldest of days with nothing more than that promise and the warmth of the people around you.

But this chill, the one I felt now, sank down to my bones; it was a numbness that wasn't about to be shaken off. There was no escaping it.

The ground slid under my back, patches of mud gave way to ice, and then again to rocks that dug into my tailbone and ripped up the length of my spine. I heard the crackle of frostbitten leaves as they passed by my ears, felt the sharp tugging as my hair caught on something. One hand tried to close around a passing root, to anchor myself against the river of dirt, but I was moving too quickly. The sun flashed red behind my eyelids, stabbing through the pounding pain inside my skull. I couldn't feel my right leg—I actually couldn't feel much of anything on my right side. It wasn't until the light receded and I could open my eyes that my mind finally made the connection that I was moving, not the ground.

The sky overhead was blue behind the patches of towering white clouds. I could just make it out through the naked gray arms of the trees. I drew my brows together, taking in the sharp stink of body odor. There was a grunt of effort as a large, rough surface passed under my back. Then it was smooth earth, a dip that came quickly, without warning, like the initial dive of a descending airplane. My stomach and eyes shifted down.

The man wore a deep red puffer jacket, one that had been worn and frayed by the decades. The hem by his hip was torn, the white stuffing pushing through the hole. His jeans were too tight. They protested every time he turned to get a better grip on my leg.

"D-Don't—" My voice was gone. I tried to bring my other leg up to kick his grip off, but none of my limbs were responding.

The man must have felt me strain, because he glanced back over his shoulder. "Awake, are you?"

I was seeing two of him, then three, then four. Focus, I ordered myself. The guy looked about as threatening as a mall Santa—he wore his beard long and patchy, but the gut was there. Dad used to read me books that talked about the twinkle in Santa's eye and his rosy red cheeks. Well, this one's eyes were glinting, all right. With dollar signs.

"Try anything funny and I'll snap that neck of yours. You hear me?"

Move. I tried to lift my hips. Instructor Johnson had taught me how to break out of a hold like this, several times over. I tried feeling for a rock I could throw at the tender spot where the base of his skull met his neck, for the Swiss Army knife that was no longer stashed in my boot. My body wasn't responding. I had hit my head—not that hard, right? The night before was cast in shadow. I remembered the long walk, Jude resetting the security system, all of those boxes and crates stamped with flags and strange languages. And Knox. Knox had been there, hadn't he?

The headache exploded behind my eyes, and I squeezed them shut again. The sun was shining—why was I so, so cold?

"There's someone here who'll be *super* interested in meeting you," the man continued. "Came nosing around this morning askin' questions 'bout whether or not we'd seen any kids. Said there was a big bust up by the airpark, a few might have gotten away. And I thought to myself, Joe Hiddle, this man could be crazy or he could be right. So I went out hunting, like usual, and what do I find!"

I dropped my hips, trying to create as much drag as possible going down the next hill. Maybe I couldn't fight back, but I wasn't going to make it easy on him.

"What," he began, twisting my ankle at an unnatural angle, "did I just say?"

I used what little mobility I had in my neck to crane it forward as we came down that last hill. Tents, more than I had even seen back at the warehouse. Most were white or printed with the words PROPERTY OF THE U.S. ARMY. A jolt of terror went through me, powering one solid kick to the back of the man's kneecap. The burst of pain that ripped down my right side was nothing compared to the man kicking me square in the ribs.

I went quietly because I had to. That barest hint of energy I had felt dripped out of me, and I could almost imagine it trailing behind us like a smear of blood.

"Sandra!" the man shouted. "Sandy, that guy still here?"

There were feet and faces around us from the moment we entered the line of tents. The smells here came in bursts—smoked meat, dirty laundry, stale water. It was all mud around the entrances of the tents, but inside were rugs and candles and piles of old mattresses and bedding.

"Joe, is that . . . ?" someone began.

"Back off, Ava," Joe warned. "I found her. *Sandra!*"

"He just left," came another woman's voice, her accent almost undecipherable. "I'll go see if his truck is still on the highway. You—you just keep that one here."

My sweatshirt had pulled up in the back, and the mud there felt as slimy as it was freezing. Something—someone—touched my left hand with the side of his foot. "Is she . . . Is that kid . . ."

A middle-age woman's flushed face leaned down close over mine. She pulled one of her mismatched gloves off and started to put the back of her hand to my forehead. Joe all but growled at her, forcing her back a step. My eyes drifted shut again, and by the time I had worked them open, there were other faces in place of hers. It was a gallery wall of unrestrained emotions. Portraits of weary fear, landscapes of sadness, miniatures of curiosity. I tried shifting again, but I couldn't ease the gripping pain in my head.

"She's shaking," one of the men said. I saw his yellowing Nikes, not his face. "Let me get her a blanket."

"Is she sick? She's so pale!" A woman this time. "God, she can't be older than sixteen—*look* at her, Joe. You're going to give her to that man?"

Here's the thing about guns—they were like the talking stick my first grade teacher used to pass around during class. Whoever held it was the only one allowed to speak. "Get back to your damn tents." Joe's gun was a shiny silver revolver, and no one was willing to test to see how many bullets were left in the cylinder.

A woman—Sandra—let out a shriek of "Here he is! Here he is!" and it was carried straight to us by the wind. The unmistakable sound of a car engine followed, the growl of its engine louder and louder as it drove around the sunken perimeter of the tent city.

I licked my chapped lips, trying to drag in a deep breath that wouldn't come. This man, whoever he was, was like a stone thrown into a lake of still water. Even the people who had questioned Joe scattered. My leg was dropped back to the ground. The blood that rushed back into it felt like it was filled with glass.

"And *my* money?" Joe was saying. "I wanna know how I'm getting reimbursed by Gray. He sure as shit didn't do anything when the river took everything I owned!"

"Your name goes into the skip-tracer system. They find you. I'm just transport. Hold her there, will you?"

The fog ripped back from my brain. A foot came down on my wrist, pinning me.

"No!" I choked out, eyes searching the tent fronts for a sympathetic face, an indecisive one—anyone who wasn't Rob Meadows.

They watched. All of them, every single person in that tent city. Their anxiety pawed at the air and stirred in my mind. But their silence—that was deafening.

Opening my eyes again would make it real, but that was the way he wanted it. His hand fisted in whatever was left of my ponytail, tightening and wrenching my head back to get a better look at me. He smiled.

"Hiya, *Gem*," Rob snarled. "Been a while."

I choked on the word *no*.

"Here." Rob absently shoved a tablet toward the man. "Type in your name and social security number—reward is split sixty-forty."

"Sixty-f-forty!" Joe sputtered. "That's—holy *God* . . . that figure's right?"

"How much?" someone shouted from down the way. "Don't forget I let you borrow my gun—you owe me for last month's rations!"

"*Hold* her!" Rob barked. "She needs proper restraints!"

My hands were drawn together and kept there, not by plastic but by the press of metal. I heard the chain rattle and felt him lift my head, sucked in the scent of leather.

I screamed. It was a ragged, ugly noise that shattered my throat. *"No,"* I begged, tossing my head, twisting my neck to get away. Rob's knees dropped onto my chest, and my next breath came out as a sob.

"Oh yeah, you remember *this*, don't you?"

"No!" I sobbed. "Please—"

In the end, all of that training came to nothing. I could shift and cry and try to scream, but my ribs felt like they were caving in. The whole world was collapsing, crushing, and dissolving the faces of everyone who stood there watching. Rob snapped on a pair of thick rubber gloves before shoving the muzzle over my mouth and tightening the strap behind my head, and I was a little girl again. I was the monster of the story.

My breath was hot, steaming. Joe passed the tablet to Rob and took several steps back. He looked at the white-haired woman to his right and said, "God, if I'd known . . . I wouldn't have touched the thing at all."

Rob bent and tried to haul me out of the mud by the chain that connected the handcuffs to the muzzle. I got no farther than my knees; the rest of my body still hadn't solidified under me. With an ear-scorching curse and a grunt of disgust, he picked me up and carried me under one arm, letting my feet drag and bounce along the ground. I reared back, trying to knock my head against the knots of muscles in his arm, but he only chuckled.

"I don't always get the world," he said. "But sometimes it treats me right. That look on your face when you saw me—I tell you, that was something else."

I twisted as he dragged me up into the back of his old red Jeep.

"I knew if I watched the skip-tracer network, you'd screw up eventually. I'd get to ask you myself about the real reason you dodged out of the Op—what Cole and Cate have to do with it. I wanted to be the one to pick you up, to drive you straight back to that little camp of yours and watch them drag you in."

I screamed into the leather, kicking at the back of the seat.

"You and me?" he said, pulling a long strip of plastic from the backpack he was wearing to bind my feet. I tried to kick, which earned me another laugh. "We're gonna have such a fun trip back to West Virginia. I won't even ask for the reward."

The door slammed shut on my face, finally blocking me from the cluster of adults that stood in a single line in front of their homes, watching. The car rocked as he opened the driver's door and sat down.

"You wanna know why I killed those kids, bitch?" he called back. "They weren't fighters. None of you are, but you're the ones with all the power in the League these days. You get to overrun us, decide the Ops, turn Alban into a worthless pile of cooing shit. But you don't understand; none of you does. You don't get what this world has to be if we're going to survive this. Even these skip tracers, they just don't understand that you're worth a lot more to this country dead than alive."

Rob was speeding despite the Jeep's shuddering protests, blasting ZZ goddamn Top as loud as the stereo would go. He shouted back that he was tired of hearing me snivel and sob. What a coincidence. I was pretty damn tired of "La Grange" and the smell of exhaust.

I tried everything I could think of to get the muzzle off. The strap around the back of my head wouldn't budge. He'd tightened it to the point of pain and, from the sound of it, had used a smaller plastic cable tie to reinforce it. I grunted, shifting to try to get to my boot.

Something pulled at my lower back, and there was a feeling like a tear. I bit my lip, ignoring the warm flush of liquid soaking into my jeans.

Michael. I'd forgotten about him getting the jump on me. No wonder it felt like I'd been dragged under a truck. I'd seen the blade—it had been small, about the size of the one on my Swiss Army knife. I needed to push through the pain—keep riding the adrenaline to keep from passing out again.

The space was tight and almost too narrow to work, but I could be small when I wanted to be. I slid my fingers past the laces into the tight leather. I curled myself around my knees to better my reach before remembering there was nothing to get—I'd never gotten my Swiss Army knife back. I hadn't been able to find it in the supplies. I swallowed hard. *It's okay. It's okay. Don't panic*—but I was. I could feel it bubbling up in my chest, and I knew if I let it get out of hand it would suffocate me. *You're okay.*

The song finally—*finally*—faded out.

"Preparations for the Unity Summit are ongoing," came President Gray's eerily calm voice. *"I look forward to sitting with these men, many of whom I greatly respect, and—"*

Rob punched the station off. "It's funny, isn't it?" he called back. "That the president all of a sudden is that much more revolutionary than Alban? That he wants something *new*?"

Yeah, I wanted to say, *hilarious.* The guy had the misfortune of heading up an organization that had gone and grown itself another head, one with sharper teeth.

"It took Alban forever to see what a mistake it was to bring you in, and he still sent you shitheads out to do jobs *any* of us could have done. He can have his past, but he's not going to change *my* future."

I looked around, trying to find something potentially sharp enough to saw the plastic zip tie around my wrists.

"And *Conner* . . . she just wanted to babysit you, but we got no time for that. We got no place for you, here or anywhere. The only place for you is in those camps or buried with the rest of them. You hear me?" He was shouting now. "I don't need an excuse for what I did! I joined to get Gray out, not play house with a guy who's too damn scared to even go aboveground. He thinks we joined up because of you? He wants to know why we can't *respect* you? But he won't let us use you for the one thing you're good for?"

Dying for people like him, I thought, *that's what he means.*

"I did what I had to do, and I'd do it again. I'll do it to every damn kid in the League until they get their heads straight again, and I'll start with your team."

Anger pulsed through me, warring with disgust.

Keep it together, I commanded myself. *He doesn't know.* I didn't need to touch him. He could silence me, but Rob had no power over my mind.

"What would Jude make of the electric fence at your old home, Ruby?" he wondered aloud. "What would the guards do to Vida when they saw just how *pretty*, just how *built* she is for a girl her age? And Nico—he's a pretty easy target, isn't he?"

I closed my eyes. I forced myself to relax, to remember that here, now, and always, I was the predator. This was what Clancy had meant when he had claimed I'd never be able to control my abilities because I was too afraid of what they would make me. I hadn't been able to do it before—not from lack of wanting or trying, but because I couldn't let go of needing to control where it would take me.

I hadn't needed to touch Mason or Knox to slide into their minds. I hadn't tried to restrain my abilities out of fear, and, in exchange, they'd given me what I wanted.

All I wanted now was to get out of this damn car. I wanted to show Rob what a terrible, terrible decision it had been to come after me. To threaten the people I cared about.

I was coming to find out that once I had been in someone's mind, the pathway to get back in was slicker, easier than before. All I needed now was to channel the *want* I felt burning a hole in the center of my chest, and picture Rob's face, and the invisible hands peacefully unfurled, slithering under the seats that separated us like wisps of smoke. I had him; I dropped into his mind with the grace and steadiness of an anchor through water.

Before, his memories and thoughts had been slow to bloom, velveteen and expanding with every turn. Now they burst like splatters of black tar, a jumbled mess of faces, numbers, hands, and guns.

I remembered what those kids looked like—I didn't have to imagine the details. I just had to push the image of them sitting in the car with him. The girl sitting next to him in the front seat and the boy behind her.

"What— What the—?"

I forced the image of her staring at him, exactly as she had the moment before he pulled the trigger. The car swerved to the left, to the right, as Rob swore. I focused on the boy now, bringing him to the front of both of our minds.

More.

This wasn't enough, not for *him*. Murderer, killer, animal—someone who took sick pleasure in the hunt but got even more out of the actual gutting. I'd seen his face that night, when he killed those kids. A satisfied smirk, tinged with a hunger I hadn't understood until now. *More.*

What would he have done to Jude if I'd let him? Would he have shot him like the others? Slit his throat? Suffocated him with his huge hands until, finally, he'd see that he'd smothered the last spark of his life?

I made the girl reach for him, and he saw it happen all over again, just like I had. The way her right eye socket had cracked as the bullet tore through it. A spray of blood came up to splatter his face and the windshield, and the hallucination was so strong, so deliciously powerful, that the car swerved and I heard the windshield wipers turn on.

"Stop it!" he shouted. "Goddammit, stop it!"

I pictured the girl reaching over, running a hand along his arm, and because his mind told him he felt her, he did. The car jerked wildly to the left again as he tried to get away from her. *More.*

He'd killed those kids, but it wasn't even just that. First, he'd broken them out of their camp. He'd given them the hope of freedom, of seeing their families again one day. He'd taken their dreams and crushed them.

"I know what you're doing!" he snarled. "I know it's you!"

A thrill of satisfaction sang through me with his first ragged gasp. I sent the boy crawling out of the backseat, over the armrest, wrapping his arms around Rob's neck. He smeared blood down the front of the man's shirt, and he nuzzled into it. Rob needed to feel the warm pulse of it, a sticky, burning fluid that would never wash out of the fabric, never mind off his skin. The boy and girl began to sob, wail, thrash—I poured every last ounce of my fury and fear and devastation into it.

A gunshot from the driver's seat blew out the passenger side window; Rob tried unloading his entire cartridge into the girl sitting there, but with every shot, I brought her that much closer to him until her hand was on the gun, on his hand, and she was turning both back to his chest.

I can end it like this, I thought, *by his own hand.* It would be right. I had the power to punish now. Not the man with the gun, not the trained killer, or the soldiers, or the guards walking the length of the electric fences at Thurmond. Me. The thought was enough to pump electrified blood through my veins; I didn't feel the pain in my back or my head anymore. I felt light, and high, and floating free. I could end his life with his own hand, a single shot to the heart. The same hand, the same heart, that had shattered so many lives and brought me to this—to this place of pain and excruciating fear. The one that had tied me up like an animal.

He was the animal. A stupid brute, just like Knox had been. They needed a handler, someone to make decisions for them, to make sure they could never hurt anyone ever again.

"Stop—*stop*," he sobbed, sounding like a kid himself. "Please, God, please—"

His terror seeped out through his pores, the smell of his sweat sour, panting breath overpowering even the leather. My nose burned with it as I tightened my grip on him, bringing the girl closer again and again until her ghostly, pale hand floated up and stroked the side of his face, tracing childish patterns in the imaginary blood and grime.

We have to use them to keep the others in their place.

"You are—you are a monster," Rob choked out. "All of you are going to ruin us; you're going to ruin everything, damn you, damn you, *damn you*!"

An explosion of noise and movement rocked the back of the car, throwing me against the seat. Then the small explosion came, and then we were spinning—*spinning*—until we weren't.

The force of the crash blew out the back windows and showered me with glass. I heard one last scream from Rob, before the impact and nothing but a grating crunch of metal as the front end of the car plowed into the thicket of trees beside the road.

I rammed against the back of the seat, my teeth clacking. The blow to my forehead blanked every thought to a blinding white. The images of the boy and girl were ripped out from behind my eyelids. They vanished, Rob's face disappeared, and it was just me—just me and what I'd done.

Oh my God. I tried sucking in air through the muzzle, but in the last few minutes it'd tightened, and tightened, and tightened with the shrill screaming inside of my head. I banged my face against the carpet, the first sob working its way out of me like someone had reached in and ripped it out of my throat. *Oh my God, oh my God, oh my God.*

Clancy would have been so proud of me. The way I'd used those kids, twisting them, manipulating them, ripping into Rob's mind until it shattered. Clancy would have looked into my face and seen his own reflection there.

We have to use them to keep the others in their place.

My stomach heaved, the bile burning its way into my mouth until I was choking on it. I wanted to be sick, I wanted to get the blackness out of me, I needed air, to get away from Rob, from this, from what he'd made me and what I'd done.

Monster, monster, monster, monster, monster. I slammed my foot against the trunk door over and over until the plastic began to crack. Where was Rob? Why wasn't he saying anything?

There was the screech of brakes and the sound of slamming doors. I only kicked harder, a steady *bang, bang, bang* like the beat of an old rock 'n' roll song, like guns firing in the night.

I was still sobbing when the back door finally burst open. I rolled out, hitting the dirt facedown with a low cry of pain. Even in the open air, the muzzle was suffocating, and it wasn't coming off; I was never going to get it off—

"Busy day, girlfriend?"

Vida stood over me, her shadow flat against the ground near my face.

I was struggling as hard as I could to get the damn muzzle off, tasting leather and my own salty tears. I knew I was hyperventilating, but I couldn't bottle up the swelling panic that had finally burst forward when the Jeep crashed. I didn't want her to see me like this. I didn't want any of them to see me like this. *Please leave, please leave me alone; I can't be around you, please, please, please just leave me here. . . .*

"Ruby," she said, flipping me over. "Okay, *okay*, Ruby—just let me take it off—"

Her knife snapped the plastic zip tie around my wrists, but I felt her fingers fumble as they tried to work the straps on the muzzle. I was screaming at her, begging, *Leave me! Leave me!* and it came out as nothing more than a low moan.

"Shit!" She had to use a knife on the leather. It snapped under her careful fingers, one strap, then the next, and then the air was in my mouth, cold and tasting like car exhaust.

"No," I cried, "I can't— You have to—you have to . . ."

"Vida!" Jude sounded far away. "Is she okay?"

My vision bobbed in and out of a foamy sea of gray. The cold was a snake that slithered along my limbs, wrapping tightly around my chest as I tried to catch my breath. There was a scramble of shoes against the loose asphalt on the highway's shoulder. A new set of hands on me, a new face hovering over mine. "Check on him!" Chubs barked.

"Oh, *gladly*," Vida growled, circling around the back of the Jeep.

"Can you stand?" Chubs's face appeared right over mine, his hands pressing against my cheeks. "Are you in pain? Can you speak?"

I tried to drag myself away from him, coughing up the bitter, burning taste draining down the back of my throat.

"Ruby, Jesus." Chubs grabbed my shoulders, holding me in place. His voice cracked. "You're all right. You are, I promise. We're here, okay? Take a deep breath. Look at me. Just look at me—you're all right."

I pressed my forehead against the asphalt, trying to get the words out, the warning. My vision flickered black at the edges, but my head felt like someone had split the back of it open. My fingernails dug into the road, like I could dig in deep enough to bury myself there. I was hearing voices, shouting nearby and far, but I was also hearing Clancy, his silky voice whispering in my ear: *You're mine now.*

"Well?" Chubs asked. My eyes drifted up to Vida's face, which had gone a shade of sickly gray. She swiped the back of her hand over her mouth.

They got me off the ground together, Vida all but lifting me over her shoulder. "Can you get the cuffs off?" she asked Chubs. The chain was still attached to the muzzle, and both dragged along the ground, marking our path.

"Not important—you can drive?"

"Like a fucking boss," she shot back modestly, "why?"

"No . . . !" I bawled. I clawed at the collar of my shirt, trying to keep the fabric from tightening into a choking collar. "No, you have to . . . Have to leave me . . ."

"Roo!" Jude was shouting. "What's wrong with her?"

"Get the door!" Chubs ordered. "No, not you, idiot—you stay in the car!"

"Is she okay? Chubs?"

Liam . . . That was Liam, wasn't it? It sounded like him, the old him, at the other end of a tunnel. How was that possible? The medicine?

The back door opened and Chubs crawled in first, dragging me across the seat after him. I clenched my teeth against the pain, my vision blurring at the sight of Jude jumping in, sliding under my stretched-out legs. I tried to lift a hand to drag my hair out of my eyes, but I couldn't feel anything below my shoulders.

My vision flashed white again. Pain was alive, screaming, drowning out the guilt, the devastation, even the fear. And I knew I was going, I was gone, because it sounded like Liam was screaming, too.

"Chubs!" I turned my head, watching as a white hand smashed against the metal grating. Liam's pleading voice was as agonizing to hear as the rough coughing that followed. "Stop it, you're hurting her!"

"Oh, hell *no* you are not opening that door!" Vida yelled. "Sit your ass down, blondie, or I'll tranq it!"

"Where?" Chubs was asking, his hands smoothing the hair off my back and neck.

I didn't understand what he meant until Jude said, "In the back—I don't know how bad it is, but he got her."

The car zipped back, bouncing until it hit the smooth surface of the highway, and then we were flying forward with a startled protest from Chubs.

"Is she okay? Is she hurt? Jesus, Chubs—just tell me!"

Chubs shoved my sweater and shirt up, exposing my back to the warm air blowing out of the vents. There was a surprised hiss, but I wasn't sure if it had come from him or me. His fingers felt like ice as they pressed down at the beating center of the pain.

"Oh my God," Jude cried. He was holding my legs across his lap, hugging them to his chest. "Roo, I'm sorry, I didn't know—"

"What?" Liam begged. "Is she okay?"

Chubs didn't lie—or at least, when he did, they were important lies, usually to protect one or all of us. But we were Team Reality, the two of us, and we generally didn't sugarcoat things. It must have been bad, then, because he decided not to answer at all.

"What about the guy?" he asked. Whatever he put against my back was freezing, and then, without warning, began to sting. Cleaning the wound, I thought, my vision swimming.

"He won't be causing problems," Vida said thickly. "Not anymore."

"What do you mean?" Chubs demanded.

"Jackson Pollock don't got nothing on that windshield," she said simply.

"You didn't . . ." Jude began.

"No," she said, and I could hear the regret in her voice, "the trees and steering wheel get credit for that masterpiece."

"You know Jackson Pollock?" Chubs's hands actually stilled, just for that instant.

"Surprise, asshole," she said, "I can fucking read."

"Chubs!" It sounded like the word had been ripped raw from Liam's throat. It was naked with fear, and my heart actually lurched at the sound of it. *"Tell me she's okay!"*

"O . . . kay," I rasped out.

I felt myself drifting, gliding out on a wave of numbing ice that stole the feeling from my hands, my legs, my spine. All it took was Chubs pressing the tip of the needle to my skin for the pain to reach up and drag me back down into the dark.

TWENTY-TWO

It felt familiar and wrong all at once, waking up. Like one memory had become tangled up in another, and both were struggling under the strange weight of déjā vu. Solid, flat, cold—I was on the ground. Hard, solid earth. It was all damp earth and something uniquely human that filled my nose, not the fake lemon smell from Black Betty's past life as a cleaning service's van. It wasn't the drone of a radio host reporting the day's horrible news drifting to my ears, but the steady, deep breathing of four others fixed fast into sleep.

Finding consciousness was like hauling myself up from the bottom of a thick-slimed swamp. It was only when I broke the surface that the pain hit me. It started in my lower back and shot up and down my right side, tightening every muscle and tendon to the point of snapping along the way. All at once, the ground, the blankets, the dark became too much. I felt the phantom grip of the leather band around my head, tasted the bitter tang of metal in my mouth. I realized then it was possible to choke on a memory, to feel it close tight and fast around your throat. Leather. All I could smell was leather.

Chubs's tent, I realized. It had been real. They had found me.

Jude, Vida . . . I pushed myself up, ignoring the protest of stiff muscles and the wailing pain in my back. There they were, sleeping lengthwise over our heads, practically on top of one another. *Chubs. Liam.*

A freezing wind blew up the back of my shirt, but it felt refreshing compared to the stale, warm air inside the tent. I had the dim thought that I needed to find my boots, but it didn't seem half as important as just getting away. Finding a place to be alone, to release the scream working itself up from my core. Just ahead were the smoldering remains of the campfire at the center of the clearing—an old, public campsite, maybe—and a clothesline scattered with shirts and sweatshirts that were strung up and frozen into stiff clumps.

It felt colder than it had been when we first arrived in Tennessee. They had found a flat clearing to park the car, but a quick glance around told me the hills here were more ragged than they had been before. The dead grass was finer, longer, buried beneath old, browning clumps of stone. Definitely not Nashville, then.

I took several deep breaths in through my mouth and circled back around to the pile of charred wood and ash that had been their campfire. Chubs had left a canteen out, but both it and the plastic water bottle next to it were empty.

My socks were wet and grimy, slick against the mud. I stumbled forward, muttering a few choice cuss words under my breath when my legs decided to give out. It took me longer than I would ever admit to reach the SUV, but once I careened into the passenger side, I had a chance to catch my breath. I had left a water bottle under the front seat. I remembered feeling the plastic butting up against my heels every time Chubs made a sharp turn. I just needed a sip. One single sip to get rid of the disgusting taste coating my tongue.

The doors were locked. I stepped off the car rail, shaking my head as I moved back toward the fire pit. There was a thin gray wool blanket draped over a well-used tree stump, and I claimed it, wrapping it tightly around my shoulders.

We got no place for you, here or anywhere. The only place for you is in those camps or buried with the rest of them.

I shook my head hard to clear the unwanted voice, throwing my loose hair around my cheeks and shoulders. It felt clean. Soft, even, against my cheeks. I slipped a hand out from under the blanket and felt for its straggly ends. No leaves or tangles. Someone had brushed it.

Jesus, I thought, wrapping the blanket tighter around me. That guy . . . He had dragged me after him, had dragged me straight to—

My throat ached. I could hear the blast of static stronger now over the rising pulse in my ears. For one terrifying second I was sure Rob was back, that he'd brought a White Noise machine with him. But this sound was low and distant, not at all painful.

I followed its rushing noise out from the clearing, spotting the old hiking trail immediately. Snow blanketed the uneven ground, hiding sharp rocks and unforgiving holes, but I saw the curved path, clear of trees. I braced my hands against the steady bodies of white oaks and maples. The sun was just beginning to touch the horizon; the first rays of pale yellow light fanned out against the snow.

By the time I made it down to the pool of water, I felt stupid for ever having thought it could be something so terrifying and awful—something as unnatural as White Noise.

Waterfalls. Tumbling, roaring waterfalls in what looked like a miniature canyon. The water jettisoned over the curling lips of the rocky cliff, branching out into smaller falls alongside the bigger one. The dark rocks circled in around the pool and leaned forward, almost like a body hunching its shoulders against the cold.

The path connected with what looked like a wooden deck, which had been built out over the edge of the small body of water. I stepped over a small creek that had split off from the pool, breaking the crust of thin ice that lined either side of it.

The deck was damp, covered in scattered patches of snow. I brushed aside a small glittering pile of it and planted myself right at the edge, where I'd have the best view of the wild, roaring water as it came tumbling down.

The waterfall cast a fine mist over the pool's glinting surface. I reached down and scooped the blisteringly cold water into my hands and splashed it against my face.

I slipped a hand up under the blanket and the sweatshirt, trying to find the one source of white-hot pain. The lump of neat, even stitches only stopped stinging when my stiff, icy fingers were there to numb it.

I thought, at first, that it was only the mist clinging to my cheeks. That the wind might have carried over a spray of water from the falls. But the ache in my throat was still there, solid and unmoving, and something very much like a sob started to bubble up from my chest. There was no one there to see me cry and no point in trying to stop the tears from coming.

I pressed my face against the blanket, balling it up against my mouth to smother the scream. And it was like once I started, I unlocked that gate, the rest of it came flooding out, and I couldn't stop. Every thought that raced through me was tainted by blood; I could actually taste it at the back of my throat.

I killed that man.

No, it wasn't just that. I had tortured him with fear. It wasn't that he didn't deserve to be punished for the crimes he'd committed, it was how I had done it—how I had used those kids, manipulating them and their memory, when they were already victims. And I had liked doing it. I had relished how easy it was to consume his mind, filling it bit by horrifying bit with terror until I had felt it snap completely. The darkness that had reached out for me then had been warm. Exciting. The rush of it had left a tingling, jittery feeling in my limbs that I still couldn't shake.

I had kicked Knox out for what he'd done to Liam, but I'd stubbornly ignored the reality that Liam would never, ever have considered it the right decision to make. I had assumed he was unredeemable, but he was a kid—Knox, or Wes, or whatever he wanted to call himself, was one of us. How was turning him out to the cold to die any more forgivable than turning other kids over to get food? And Mason . . . I could have helped Mason. I could have taken away his painful memories, but my first instinct had been to use him as a weapon. Like he wasn't human at all and didn't deserve to make his own choices.

Maybe . . . maybe the camp controllers had been right to do what they did to the dangerous ones. Maybe we needed to be muzzled, chained, conditioned to follow orders—it had felt so natural for me to command Rob, and Knox, and every other kid who challenged me at the warehouse.

And it made me Clancy. It made me Martin. It made me the Orange on the bus into Thurmond, who'd compelled that woman to kill herself with her own gun. It made me the countless others who tortured the PSFs and camp controllers by flooding their brains with horrifying images.

I wasn't any different than them. I wasn't any better. All along, I'd thought that gaining more control over my abilities would mean reclaiming my life. But that wasn't the case at all, was it? It was entirely possible that not being able to control them—being afraid of them—was the only reason I hadn't followed the other Oranges down that path earlier.

I saw now how the League had been good for me. They'd given me discipline, focus, and direction on how and when to use my abilities. It only proved I'd been right when I told Cate I shouldn't be Leader—we needed people who were stronger, people who still had good left to their names. Or, at the very least, people who could still trust that their instincts wouldn't take them into this kind of darkness.

Murderer. Just like all the other agents in the League.

The blanket was hot and damp with my tears. I lifted my face again, trying to cool my aching face and lungs, but nothing helped. Nothing erased the images of what I imagined Rob must have looked like to Vida when she saw him that last time. Nothing eased away the final thoughts that had blazed through his mind in the seconds before his life ended. A beautiful woman in a checkered dress, a red bicycle, an open field, the sunset over Los Angeles—

"Stop it," I choked out, *"stop."*

And I hurt. Every part of me, from the blinding headache behind my eyes to the cuts and bruises along my back. There wasn't enough space in my lungs for the air I needed. No matter how hard the sobs shook my body, I couldn't ease the pressure there. It felt like I was being folded, and folded, and folded again, until there was nothing left to do but break.

The rushing water swallowed every other sound, including the footsteps that tapped out a slow, hesitant trail over the wood behind me. But I knew he was there.

"Hey," Liam said, his voice soft.

The mist from the falls passed between us, spinning the large snowflakes into a pure white screen. When it pulled away with the next freezing breeze, he was still standing there, still clutching my black boots to his chest, still with that tortured look on his already worn, ashen face. He opened his mouth, taking a small step forward. His legs were still unsteady, but it was the way he was openly looking at me, searching my face, that had me anxious.

But he was alive. He was standing on his own two feet. The glaze over his eyes had passed. His breathing was shallow but consistent—a steady in, a steady out, with only a small interruption for him to cough.

Liam had always been an easy read. He couldn't hide any of his thoughts or feelings, no matter how many smiles he forced. His face was as open as it always was, so heartbreakingly perfect even with pain tightening the line of his mouth. His eyes were—they were so pale in this light, jumping from my eyes to my nose to my lips like he had never seen me before but never wanted to stop looking. An ache started at the center of my chest and worked its way out, twisting my insides until I finally forced myself to look away.

"I don't . . ." he began, the words edged with soft desperation. "How can I help? What . . . what can I do to make it stop hurting? Make it better?"

Liam, you can't. Not this time. The thought made me feel displaced somehow, like I was watching him come toward me from the top of the falls.

"Just don't tell them about this," I whispered. "Please."

I wiped at the tears on my face. They stung as they dripped down my cheeks, my chin, onto my neck. It was embarrassing and overwhelming but somehow right that he was the person who found me.

Out of the corner of my eye, I saw Liam nod. Of course he understood—he'd gone off a number of times by himself because he didn't want us to see him fray and unravel. When you have people relying on you, you can't put on anything other than a brave, determined face, otherwise you chip away at their confidence, too.

"There has to be something in the medicine . . . in the

bag," he was saying, "something to help you rest or to . . . to . . ."

They had gotten the medicine back to camp, then. Chubs had administered it. The fact that Liam was even as coherent as he was now meant that the hit hadn't been for nothing—some small good had come out of it.

I took my boots when he offered them, slipping them on. The numbed sensation was working up from my toes to my ankles to my calves, and I was waiting for it to spread. I was so tired; I hurt so badly. I felt myself slipping under a flat, gray ice, and I didn't have the strength to pull myself up from under it. I sucked in a deep breath, tilting my head back—like that would be enough to stop the tears.

"Tell me," he pleaded. "I can't— This is . . . It's too much."

Too much. My mind latched onto that single phrase. *Too much, too much, too much.*

He knelt down next to me, his Adam's apple bobbing as he swallowed; I couldn't tear my eyes away from it, not until he reached over, his finger running along the scar on my forehead. When I didn't flinch away, I felt it trail feather-soft down the side of my face, across my cheek. His hands were rough and chapped from the unforgiving weather as they slid back through my hair to the hollows behind my ears. I closed my eyes, letting his thumbs brush away the tiny flakes of snow that had caught in my lashes.

Move, I told myself as I forced my eyes open. *Move*—because he wasn't. I could feel him leaning toward me, dipping his head closer to mine, and I mirrored him, tilting my face up to meet him halfway. Liam's eyes were closed, and it seemed, just for a second, almost like he was trapped in some kind of a dream. I felt his breath warm my lips.

The touch was so assured, and I had wanted it for so long, that in that tiny slice of morning, it was almost easy to forget what I had done.

That he wasn't supposed to know me at all, let alone care enough to try.

Too much.

"What are you doing?" I whispered.

Every part of him seemed to seize up, and I recognized the alarm in his face when I saw it. Liam jerked his hands away, falling off balance in the process. He tried to scramble up onto his feet, but he was slow and weak, and the best he could manage was looking away as the tips of his ears went bright red. He was on his feet and moving before the feeling of his touch disappeared from my skin.

He muttered something, tucking his hands up under his arms as he shook his head. He backed away two steps at a time, and I wondered what kind of expression I must have been wearing for him to mirror such a lost one back to me.

"It's okay," I told him, though it was so far from the truth, I would have laughed if I wasn't already crying. It was amazing—I had no idea you could keep sinking, even after you'd hit the dark bottom of your life. But letting him get that close, letting him comfort me after everything I had done, was a bruising low.

Before I could finish, Liam was talking again, and that strange tone was back in his voice. Even as he spoke, he was shaking his head. "Ruby—you're Ruby. Chubs said that you and Vida and Little Buddy there were helping him look for me. He said that you and me, we never met before, but we had to have, we had to, because I know your face. I know your voice. How does that work?"

"I talked to you while you were sick," I said, feeling panic grip at my stomach. "In the warehouse in Nashville."

"No—*no*—I mean, yeah, I know you did." Liam was rambling in a way that was almost agitated. Pacing, too, the small width of the wooden deck. "That's not it; I know it's not."

End this now. Don't twist it any further. A clean cut and you can go and finish this.

"I'm League," I blurted out, because it was the one thing I knew would stop him from coming closer—the one thing that would change his look of compassion to one of total and complete contempt.

"You—" he began. "What? That's not . . . that's not possible."

The camps. I needed to think about the camps we'd free as soon as I brought the intel back to Cole and Cate. The good work that would come from this, rising up above the blood pooling under my feet and the trail of smoke and fire my footsteps left behind. That was my future now. That was the only thing there was for me.

"You're right, though. We did meet before," I said. "At a safe house in Maryland. I handed you the money from your brother, remember?"

He did now. I could see it in his face, the way he squared his shoulders. I kept my eyes on the trees behind his head, my arms wrapped tight around my center to try to trap in that last bit of warmth. He looked like he was about to be sick.

"But you got out, right?" Liam said. "Because Chubs would have told me. He wouldn't have kept that from me. You were League, but now you're—"

"I'm League, and so are Vida and Jude." I knew Chubs well enough to know exactly why he hadn't let that piece of information slip. "He didn't tell you because he knew that you'd want to split. But he and I have a deal."

"I—I don't get it," Liam managed to squeeze out. He was backing away again, running a hand over his face. "A deal?"

I'd already driven the knife into his chest. Twisting it now would finish things forever. *Don't,* a small voice whispered. *Not again.*

He stared at me, waiting, shaking from the cold or anger, I couldn't tell. I came toward him, and he let me. Liam was breathing harder now, a wheezing, wet whistle, as I reached for the bottom hem of his brother's jacket and ripped the stitches Cole had hastily sewn in place.

The flash drive was a simple black rectangle, stamped with Leda Corp's golden swan. It was warm from having lived so close to his body for the past few hours—days, maybe.

Liam stumbled back, his every thought crashing over his face. "What the hell is that?"

"Your brother," I said. "He sent us to find you. You took his jacket instead of yours when you ran in Philly. And you took this with you."

“What is that?” he repeated, trying to reach for it. I closed my fist and shoved the damn thing in my pocket before I was tempted to do something stupid. All of this for a tiny piece of cheap plastic.

“It’s classified intel,” I told him, forcing my feet forward, up the path. “From the Op your brother was running.”

I half hoped he wouldn’t come after me. That he’d stay down there, and I could go back and walk through the camp, through whatever woods we were in, and just disappear. But nothing in my life was ever going to be that easy. Instead, he pushed past me on the trail, taking those first few steps like he was staggering out of knee-deep water, unsteady and coughing up the fluid trapped in his lungs. Instinctively, I put a hand out to steady him, but he ripped his arm away and kept pressing forward, calling Chubs’s name.

He must have already been out looking for us. We met him on the path, just as it curved into the campsite. The kid was a mess of sleepy eyes and rumpled clothes; his brain must not have fully warmed up yet, because he hadn’t thought to put on a coat or shoes despite the frigid temperature.

“What?” he cried, looking between us. “What’s going on?”

“I can’t even believe you,” Liam rasped. “What the hell kind of game are you playing here?”

Chubs blinked. “What are you . . . ?”

“I know everything!” Liam stalked over to him, still breathing hard from the climb back up the trail. “How long were you planning on keeping this from me? The League. *Really?* Jesus—you’re supposed to be the smart one! You made a deal with *them*?”

"Oh." Chubs rubbed a hand over the tufts of his dark hair and blew out a long, exasperated sigh. I had about three seconds to deflect Liam's anger back on me before Chubs said something he'd really regret.

"Yes, *that*!" Liam charged up into the campsite, stalking over to the smothered fire. He wouldn't let me get close enough to so much as share his breathing space.

"Will you please listen to me?" I asked. "It was all my idea—all of it. Your brother sent us to find the flash drive, and in the process we found your friend. We agreed that if we helped him find you, we wouldn't turn any information about you over to the League. And we'd help you get to California to find Zu."

At first I assumed the wide-eyed look Chubs flashed my way was because he'd been shocked at my ability to turn out one lie after another. But some part of me must have known, even as I said it, that I'd picked the wrong nail to hammer home.

"And you know that *how*?" Liam demanded. "And you know her *how*, exactly?"

I swallowed, wrapping my arms around my center, my mind spinning through excuses, each one worse than the next.

"Answer me!"

I flinched. "I just . . . have heard stories—from Chubs, I mean."

Liam spun toward Chubs, his face burning with anger and disbelief. "What else did you tell her?"

"Nothing! Lee, you have to calm down—please, sit down. *Listen.*"

"I can't believe you! Don't you realize they have ways of tracking her down? Do you *want* them to take her in? *Zu*—we promised that we'd— I thought—"

"He didn't tell me anything about her, other than you were traveling together for a while," I said calmly. Liam had been protective of all of us in different ways, but Zu had been a special case.

"Stay out of this, Green!" He was still wholly focused on Chubs. "What else did you tell her? What else did she get out of you?"

I jerked back, one single word throwing me off balance.

"What did you just call her?" Chubs interrupted. Of course he had caught it, too.

"What? I'm not allowed to use her name now?" he demanded. The look on his face was ripe with derision. "What do you want me to call you? What clever codename did the League think up for you? Pumpkin? Tiger? Tangerine?"

"You called me Green," I said.

"No I didn't," he said. "Why the hell would I call you that? I know what you are."

"You did," Chubs insisted. "You called her Green. You really don't remember?"

My heart shattered the ice around it, slamming against my rib cage, beating harder with every minute of silence that followed. The anger had left him quickly, replaced by confusion that bloomed into an open, barefaced fear as he looked between us.

"It's okay," I said, holding up my hands in a weak attempt to placate him, "it's fine. You can call me whatever you want; it really doesn't matter. . . ."

"Are you messing with him? Are you forcing him to play nice with you?" Liam asked. His face was flushed, and it almost seemed like his anger was edging into anxiety. He was looking at his friend and seeing a stranger.

I couldn't keep up with his flip-flopping moods, and I suddenly wondered if it was even worth the energy to try. The memory of what had happened when he'd found me down by the falls evaporated like mist in the sunlight. Maybe I had imagined it altogether.

"Are you freaking kidding me?" Chubs said. "After what happened at East River? Do I need to remind you that while Clancy Gray turned you into his little poodle, he couldn't even touch me?"

"I don't . . . What?" Liam's breath exploded out of him. "What are you talking about?"

Oh, I thought, *damn.*

When I had gone in and pulled myself out of Liam's memories, I'd had to . . . tweak a few of them, otherwise they wouldn't have made sense. The night we tried leaving East River had been one of them, because the whole terrifying episode had been sparked by my letting my guard down and trusting Clancy when I shouldn't have. I was a crucial part of that story.

But now—what had I slipped into its place? Had I just erased that night completely? My mind was spinning, trying to dig up what images I had pushed into that vacant space, but everything was black, and black, and black.

Chubs turned to look at me with a glare that could have incinerated a mountain.

"What are you looking at *her* for?" Liam exploded. "I don't even know what you're doing here, and with them!"

"We were trying to find *you*!" Chubs said. "All of us just wanted to help *you*!"

"Oh, for fuck's sake," came Vida's shrill voice from inside the tent. "Can you two shut the hell up and just go back to spooning? We don't need to hear this same shitty argument for the tenth fucking time before five A.M.!"

Jude made a very valiant effort to shush her, but the damage was done.

"*You*—you— I can't—" Chubs sputtered, too furious to form an actual sentence. "Come out here. *Right now!*"

"Come and get me, big boy," she sang back. "I know I don't have the parts you like, but we can always make it work."

"Oh, like a functioning brain?" he shouted.

"Chubs!" I snapped. He knew what she was like—he was only playing into her hands. "Vida, please come out. You too, Jude."

She exited the tent with a blanket wrapped around her like a queen's flowing robe. The effect was soured by the fact her fading blue hair was sticking straight up on either side of her head like horns. Jude didn't look much better—I don't know that I had ever seen such dark rings under his eyes. He slouched out after her in his EMT jacket, taking a seat on the opposite side of the fire pit.

"I'm not gonna change my mind, so don't even start spinning your little yarn about how *great* the League is, how *wonderful* the agents are," Liam said, crossing his arms over his chest. "Tell Cole to go screw himself. I don't need him—or *you*—to take care of me!"

"Says the kid who was two steps away from death's grasping fingers when we found him," Vida said, rolling her eyes. "You're fucking welcome, by the way."

"I promise that we don't have any other motivation beside getting the flash drive and seeing our end of the deal through," I told him, watching his chest heave with the effort to get enough air in. It was easier to talk to him like he was a stranger. And as pale, as thin, as unshaven and dirty as he was, it wasn't hard to imagine him as one.

This is not Liam, I thought. *Something's wrong.*

"Is that a fact?" Liam said coldly. "I didn't ask for any of this, and the last thing I'd ever want is to be babysat by someone like *you*."

It took me a second longer than the others to realize that last zinger was for me.

"Hey!" Jude cut in. "We're just trying to help. You don't have to be mean about it."

"Lee, you're being dramatic," Chubs began.

"And you—God, it's like you get a new pair of glasses, a car, and some tech and you think you're Rambo in the jungle. I never thought *you* would play along with this."

"If he trusts us," Jude tried again, "why can't you?"

"The League?" Liam let out a single bark of laughter. "Are you all really that stupid?"

He held up a hand to silence whatever Vida was about to say. "They talk about rehabilitation and do nothing but hold kids hostage. They talk about training kids to defend themselves, and then turn around and send them off to be killed. Either we're in camps, or we're with the League, or we're on the run, and it's not even a choice. You wanna know what I want? A choice. Just *one*. And this is me making it. You might be okay heading back into the arms of those murderers, but I'm staying the hell away from them. From *you*."

With that, he shouldered past Chubs and me and started heading back down the same path to the falls. Chubs glanced sideways at me, but I kept my eyes on Liam as I lowered myself down onto the stump, rubbing absently at the row of stitches on my lower back.

"You really think he wants me going after him this time?" I asked.

Chubs sighed, rubbing his hands briskly over his arms, and followed his friend down the trail. Neither of them got far; if I stood on my toes, I could see where Liam stood, leaning heavily against a tree. At first, it looked like Chubs was keeping a careful distance, not wanting to provoke Liam's temper again. But he must have said something, apologized, because in the next moment, Chubs was standing close to him, one hand on Liam's back, the other pointing back in our direction.

"I can't believe he said all that bullshit," Vida groused. "This kid has more mood swings than a toddler's birthday party."

"I didn't realize he hated us that much. . . ." Jude said.

"He doesn't hate you," I promised, still watching the boys. "He hates the League. He thinks we're better off without them—that we don't need them."

"Well, he needed us," Vida said, "right around the time when he was drowning in his own mucus."

Jude was quiet, even as he watched me watch the others. When I glanced back to ask him what was wrong, he only looked away and busied himself with digging Chubs's coat out of the tent. I forced myself to sit on one of the tree stumps around the fire pit, my entire brain throbbing in time with my pulse.

It was ten more minutes before Chubs and Liam made their way back over to us. Chubs was still shaking his head, clearly frustrated. Liam kept his own face down, avoiding all of us. The biting wind or embarrassment had turned the tips of his ears red. He kept his hands shoved in his pockets as he shuffled forward, past us, toward the tent.

"He agreed to stay for now," Chubs said. "He does want to go to California to find Zu, but he doesn't want any of you to be able to tail us—we'll probably have to split up before we hit state lines."

"That kid's a few colors short of a rainbow, isn't he?" Vida said, rolling her eyes. Jude huddled in close to the two of them, passing the coat over to a grateful, shivering Chubs. "Be sure to send us a postcard when you get your asses caught and hauled back into a camp."

"I'll keep working on him," Chubs promised. "He just needs to cool down."

"I know," I said. "Thank you."

But I knew it wasn't going to be enough.

TWENTY-THREE

NATURAL FALLS STATE PARK WAS LOCATED IN Oklahoma, in what most considered the highlands of the Ozarks—right up in the northeast corner of the state, where it was really freaking cold in December. Chubs gave me a brief tour of the campsite as we made our way back to the others. A few picnic tables here and there, RV parking, a number of hiking trails that looped around one another. The only thing that really mattered was that the campsite was deserted.

"Are you in any pain?" he asked, tossing another branch on the growing fire.

"I'm fine. I just want to know what happened."

I scooted, giving him half of the stump so he wouldn't have to sit in the snow, and threw one end of the blanket over his shoulder, drawing him in close. He still smelled faintly of laundry detergent and hand sanitizer, only now I could pick up earthy scents, too—the kind that gave away just how many nights he'd slept on the ground without a shower in between. The poor kid probably felt like he was dying.

"Okay," he said, taking a deep breath.

They knew, right away, that something was wrong when Olivia's half of the team came back alone. She and her group of ten had made it back mostly unscathed, with as many supplies as they could carry over the water. Brett didn't appear for another two hours, struggling through the soaking parking lot with Jude still draped over his shoulder. His team hadn't fared so well—only five of them had made it back, and I wasn't included in that total.

"I showed Olivia how to give the kids the medicine the right way, dosed Lee, and then we carried him out to the car. We spent most of the night driving around, trying to pick up an Internet signal to download an update from the skip-tracer network. We all were so sure the PSFs had grabbed you."

"Almost," I whispered, but didn't think he could hear me.

Even before they found a connection to hook into, Cate had sent a message through the Chatter. It turned out that when you got snapped by a profiler, the device the PSF snapped in my face, it not only brought your listing up for the PSF or skip tracer's viewing pleasure. It *also* automatically updated that same listing with time and location stamps on both the PSF and skip-tracer networks.

That's how Rob knew to look in that area, I thought.

"But how did you know to look for Rob in the first place?"

"We didn't at first. He was under a fake name." Chubs glanced down at where his fingers were laced together. "He updated the skip-tracer network to say that you were *recovered*. Once that happened, I could look up his profile—see what car he'd registered and the license plate. We weren't too far from the area, but I'm still amazed we kept it together long enough to find you. After we found you we came here—we've been camped out for almost four days."

"Thanks," I said after a small stretch of silence, "for not giving up on me."

"You seriously thought we would?" he asked. "That we wouldn't have done everything and anything we could to find you?"

"That's not what I meant," I said. "It's just . . ." *Maybe it would have been better if you had let them take me.* The buzz in my ears drowned out the world, and I felt the first touch of panic creep back in. "If he's this unhappy with us around, it might be for the best to split up."

"No. It doesn't make sense," Chubs said. "I can't keep up with his moods. He was freaking out when we found you—it was a full-on meltdown. I've never seen him like that before. Maybe some part of him figured out you guys were League before you told him . . . that's the only thing I can think of that would explain why he's acting like this. The Liam I knew wouldn't have wanted to abandon a bunch of kids if he thought we all could get along—I mean, you're proof of that. But it's like, ever since he started feeling better, he's been jumpy. Irritable."

"He has no reason to trust us," I said. "I understand why."

"Look, I'm not going to choose," Chubs said. "I can't let him go on his own again, but I'm not going to leave you, either. So you have to find a way to make this work, got it? You have to get him to trust you. Wait—why are you shaking your head?"

"I meant what I told him," I said. "It wasn't the full truth, but it's the best I can do. I'm going to help you guys get wherever it is you decide you want to go, then head back to Cole to finish this."

Chubs's grip on me tightened, but it was the shock and hurt and fear he let off that choked me up while I struggled to speak.

"You know . . . *you know* how important this is. I feel like if I'm not there to make sure it happens, if I don't see for myself what caused *this*"—I motioned between us—"I'll never forgive myself. If I can't . . . if I can't be around Liam anymore, I can at least do that for him. That was his dream, remember?"

"No," he whispered, "I can't do this again—it can't be the way it was with Zu, the way it was the last six months. I know it's selfish, but I have to know you're safe, and you'll never be safe with them. At least think about that, okay? Give me a chance to change your mind, too."

No, I thought, giving him a weak, reassuring smile. Even if Liam didn't look at me with such hate in his eyes, even if he had kissed me down by the falls, none of it would have mattered. I wasn't the blank slate I'd been when Liam, Chubs, and Zu found me. I had done things I was ashamed of then, sure, but now I'd gone to a place I couldn't come back from, and there was too much light in them to drag them there with me.

"We'll see," I said, squeezing his fingers, "we'll see."

Despite the fact he had no maps and no way of downloading any kind of update from the skip-tracer network to navigate us, Chubs still pushed to have us move out of the park as quickly as we could. We'd have one more night to rest, then start driving west again first thing in the morning.

I doubted it was because he was in any hurry to get to California. Chubs had reached his absolute breaking point for being able to handle this kind of cold—both physically and on an emotional level. I wasn't sure what Vida was going to do if she got one more lecture about hypothermia, but I imagined it probably involved holding Chubs, the fire pit, and one well-aimed push. She hadn't figured out that it wasn't himself that he was worried about.

The cold weather was wreaking havoc on Liam's lungs. He was huffing, and puffing, and hacking, and coughing every time he tried to increase his pace above a hobble. Instead of trying to gather the scattered supplies, he crouched down next to Jude and helped him stoke the fire, debating whether Bruce Springsteen's *Born in the U.S.A.* was a better album than *Born to Run*.

Finished with that, they went to the backseat of the SUV to fish out more layers to pile on. Without a second thought to it, Liam reached down for his old leather jacket and slipped it on over the thinner dark gray one.

"But that's—" Jude started to protest. I shook my head

sharply in his direction and ducked away before Liam could turn and see what caused him to clam up. I made it a point to give him space after that, going right when he'd go left, always keeping the fire between us. By the time Jude started hinting strongly he needed to be fed dinner, Liam seemed to have relaxed. Enough, at least, to crack a smile when Chubs tripped and went down with a squawk, sending the food rations in his arms flying.

"I was wondering what happened to this stuff," I said as I helped him gather up the foil packets again.

"We had to leave most of it behind," Chubs said as we made our way back to where the others were hunkered down around the fire pit. "It was mostly what we could stuff in our pockets. It's been enough—okay, who wants what?"

"I'll take one of the Chinese fig bars if you see one," Jude said.

"The French trail mix," Vida said. "Silver packet."

"Did anyone ever figure out where this stuff came from?" I asked. "Or why it was just there, going to waste?"

"We decided to chalk that one up to the president being a sneaky asshole and the rest of the world not sucking half as badly as we thought it did," Vida said. "The end."

All along, President Gray had been insistent in his weekly addresses that Americans were pulling themselves up by the bootstraps and taking care of themselves and their countrymen. He made it a point, time and time again, to nail the United Nations for the economic sanctions they put on the country. No one did business with us, so we would have to do business with one another. No one would send in financial relief, so the few people who hadn't lost the bulk of their fortunes when the markets crashed were the ones who would have to donate. Americans would help Americans.

The United Kingdom, France, Japan, Germany—*they just do not understand the American way*, he once said. They weren't affected by IAAN; they didn't feel the razor's edge of our pain. I watched him on one of the TVs in the atrium, back at HQ, his face looking older and grayer than it had just a week before. It looked like he was sitting in the old Oval Office, but Nico had pointed out the glow around the edge of the image, which pointed to the use of some kind of green screen. For a guy with endless opportunities for protection, he hadn't been back in DC since the first bombings—he just moved from one Manhattan high-rise to the next.

They do not understand that certain sacrifices must be made in times like these, Gray had continued. *That we can rise above it, given time and dedication. We are Americans, and we will do it our own way, as we have always done. . . .* And it was like the longer he talked, the more words he used, the less they came to mean anything. It was an endless stream of ideas that were as flat as his voice. All they did these days was spin, and spin, and spin us around in circles until we were too dizzy to listen to what they were really saying.

"What about you?" I asked Liam. "Hungry?"

Time and silence and obvious embarrassment about his earlier breakdown had softened Liam just a tiny bit—first toward Jude, who, despite everything Liam had flung his way earlier, was watching Liam the way a kid might gawk at his favorite baseball player. Then toward Vida, whose charming personality didn't let anyone ignore her for long. I could see he was still angry with Chubs, but even that was draining away now that the initial shock had faded. I was glad Vida and Jude were getting a glimpse of who he really was—without the strange, battered armor he'd sewn himself into.

"Yeah . . . whatever is fine." He didn't glance up from the small black booklet in his right hand.

I reclaimed my seat next to Chubs, letting him fuss over me without hearing a word of what he was saying. To my right, Jude was building a miniature snowman, using the M&M's from his own trail mix to make its grin—though it was lopsided enough to look more demented than cute. He was humming a soft, breathy version of some Springsteen song.

"Joseph Lister?" Liam said suddenly, cutting through the silence. "Really? *Him?*"

Chubs stiffened beside me. "That man was a *hero*. He pioneered research on the origins of infections and sterilization."

Liam stared hard at the faux leather cover of Chubs's skip-tracer ID, carefully choosing his next words. "You couldn't have chosen something cooler? Someone who is maybe not an old dead white guy?"

"His work led to the reduction of postoperative infections and safer surgical practices," Chubs insisted. "Who would you have picked? Captain America?"

"Steve Rogers is a perfectly legit name." Liam passed the ID back to him. "This is all . . . very Boba Fett of you. I'm not sure what to say, Chubsie."

Say it's okay, I thought, remembering the fear in Chubs's voice when he'd confessed about turning that kid in. *Tell him you understand that he had to do this, even if you don't.*

"What?" Chubs scoffed, his voice just that tiny bit too light. "For once, you're speechless?"

"No, I'm just . . ." Liam cleared his throat. "Grateful, I guess. That you came looking for me and you had to do . . . *this*. I know it wasn't . . . I know it couldn't have been easy."

"Just shut up and start sucking each other's faces already," Vida grumbled, leaning awkwardly against the stump. She would never admit it aloud, but I knew the burns on her back were eating her alive with pain. "I'm trying to make up for the sleep I lost when you started screeching at each other like cats in heat."

"Miss Vida," Liam said, "has anyone ever told you that you are positively the whipped cream on the sundae of life?"

She glared at him. "Anyone ever told you your head is shaped like a pencil?"

"That is physically impossible," Chubs groused. "He'd be—"

"Actually," Liam began, "Cole once did try to— What?"

"Oh, I'm sorry," Chubs said, "apparently the middle of my sentence interrupted the beginning of yours. Do continue."

"I'm going to guess you probably don't want to hear about the time he pushed my head through the neighbor's fence. . . ."

"Was there a lot of blood?" Vida asked, suddenly interested. "Did you lose an ear?"

Liam held his hands up next to his ears, indicating both were still firmly attached to his skull.

"Then, no," she said. "No one wants to hear your boring-ass story."

Night settled in quickly overhead. I tracked the movement of the sun through the trees overhead. The faint orange glow swept across the forest's snowy floor until it finally faded away into a sleepy gray, and the cold forced us back inside the tent.

Vida lay on her back, holding the Chatter up in the air, moving it around to find that exact right position to catch a signal. She'd been trying to send an ALL CLEAR // OBJECTIVE ACCOMPLISHED in response to the ten REPORT STATUS messages that had been waiting for us when she turned it on a few days before. If Cate was half as anxious as Vida was to make contact, I had a feeling there'd be ten more messages waiting once the device reconnected with the Chatter network.

"Nothing?" I asked.

She let it fall onto her chest with an annoyed sigh and shook her head.

"Maybe once we get out of the mountains," I said, but she didn't seem comforted by the thought. Vida squinted at me from across the dark tent.

"Since when did *you* start drinking from the half-full glass?"

I grunted, pressing my face back down against my arms at the next sharp stab of pain in my back.

"Does this hurt?" Chubs asked. He kept one hand flat on

my shoulder blades to keep me down while the other poked and prodded at my stitches.

I managed another grunt in response.

"I'm going to disinfect it again," Chubs warned.

"Super."

We settled into a quiet little calm that was at odds with the billowing winds outside. Once he was finished with me, Chubs picked up a book, *White Fang*, and settled down on his sleeping bag to read. I stayed on my stomach, trying to force myself to sleep.

Jude reappeared at the tent entrance with the flashlights he'd been sent to find in the car. His curly hair was coated in a thick layer of snow that he then decided to shake out all over us. It was the first grin I'd seen him crack in . . . days? Weeks? But when he caught my eye, Jude looked away, sitting next to Liam to resume their game of war.

The longer it stayed silent between us, the more overwhelming the awkwardness became. Vida was starting to get that dangerous gleam in her eye, too: a smile that got progressively more wicked the longer she stared at the side of Chubs's head.

"So a thought crossed my mind," Liam said suddenly.

"That must have been a lonely journey," Chubs said, flipping the page of his book.

Liam rolled his eyes. "It's getting late, and I was just thinking that we should take turns on watch. Set up shifts. That sound good?"

I nodded.

"Young Jude here and I can take the first one," Liam said. "Ruby and Chubs the second, and Vida can bring up the rear."

I thought about protesting the lineup, but Liam looked like he was ready for a challenge and I just didn't have it in me.

I faded in and out of sleep all night, twisting and turning against the blankets serving as bedding in the tent. I was awake to hear Liam tell Jude, in quiet tones, about some horror flick he'd watched religiously as a kid.

The blankets rustled as they shuffled back over to the bedding. Jude had all but dropped to his knees between Chubs and me in exhaustion, patting us on the shoulders until we were both awake and sitting up. He let out a blissful sigh as he curled up under the blankets. But Liam was slower in his approach, almost hesitant. I felt his eyes fix on me the way you feel a beam of sunlight cut through a window. Warm. Focused.

I got up as he slid under the other end of the blanket, positioning himself as far away from me as he could without giving up the warmth or comfort of the fleece padding under us.

To stay busy and keep our blood flowing, Chubs and I did a quick walk around the camp, glad to have the wind and snow die down, if only for a few minutes.

"Is that where you drove in?" I asked, pointing to a trail that seemed wider than the others.

Chubs nodded. "It winds around and connects to a highway. This section of it was closed off, I think, because there's no one to plow the roads. I'm hoping the snow starts melting tomorrow, otherwise I have no idea how we're going to drive out of here."

A few hours later, just shy of dawn, it was Vida's turn. She stood up in the tent, physically trying to shake the sleep off her, before stumbling out into the cold morning. I stared at the tiny sliver of space between Chubs and Liam and promptly turned on my heel, following her back outside.

Vida broke the intense gaze she'd fixed across the clearing when I sat down next to her, but she didn't seem surprised.

"I slept too long in the car," I lied, warming my stiff hands near the fire. "I'm just not tired."

"Uh-huh," she said, rolling her eyes. "Want to tell me what's really on your mind?"

"Why?" I asked. "You actually care?"

"If it has to do with Prince Charming, then, no, not really," Vida said, leaning back. "But if it has to do with you ditching out with Tweedle Dee and Tweedle Dumbass and leaving me and Judith to finish out the Op, I want to hear about it."

I shook my head. "Sorry to break it to you, but I'm not going anywhere."

"Really?" Now Vida actually did sound surprised. "Then what was all that whispering between you and Grannie?"

"He asked me to go with them," I admitted, "but I can't."

"Can't or won't?" Vida asked.

"Can't," I whispered. "Won't. What does it matter?"

Vida sat up straighter at that. "What's going on with you?"

I shrugged, rubbing my fingers along the worn edge of the blanket I'd wrapped around myself.

"You've been acting like a spooked cat since we picked you up. . . ." I saw her mind working behind her dark eyes, narrowing as she made the connection.

I'm not sure why it was easier to tell Vida this, or why I wanted to, when I hadn't been able to speak a word of it to Chubs. Maybe it was because I knew she already had such a low opinion of me that it didn't matter either way if it made her hate me that much more.

"I went too far," I said. "With Knox, the kids at that warehouse—with Rob."

"How?" she asked. "You mean the fact that you don't have to touch people to use your brain voodoo?"

"It's complicated," I mumbled. "It won't make sense to you."

"Why? Because you think I'm stupid?" Vida kicked at my foot. "Give me an answer, straight, and if my little-bitty brain has questions, I can ask them."

"That's not—" I stopped myself. I needed to stop fighting with her over every damn thing. "It's just . . . you're okay with your abilities, right? Okay as you can be, I mean," I corrected, seeing her sharp look. "But I hate what I can do. I *hate* it every day, every minute. And it's better now that I have a grip on it, but before . . ." Every minute had been a waking nightmare. I had lived life second to second, holding my breath, waiting for the inevitable slip that would ruin everything again. "It's not right, okay? I know it isn't. I don't like how it feels to compel people to do things, especially when I know it's the opposite of what they would normally do. I don't like seeing their memories or their thoughts or the things they wanted to keep to themselves."

Vida didn't break her gaze for an instant. "I'm not seeing the problem . . . ?"

"I just . . . got in too deep," I said. "I could feel myself digging deeper and deeper, but it didn't matter to me. I was in control. I could get anyone to do anything I wanted. I got to punish the people who hurt me, and you, and Liam—and I still wanted more. Once I didn't have to touch a person to use him or her, it was like taking away that last roadblock."

She sighed. "Not that it'll make you feel any better, but that Knox kid got what he deserved in the end."

"It wasn't just him," I said. "I was in Mason's head—and I thought, I really thought about turning him on Knox. *That* was my first instinct, not helping him. And then, with Rob . . ."

Vida didn't react as I laid out exactly what had happened in the car—what I had done to him—in vivid detail. I confessed it all to her, the words flooding out, releasing the knot that had been tightening in the pit of my stomach since it happened.

"I don't want to be him, Vida," I heard myself saying. "I don't want to use my abilities unless I have to—but then how do I stop myself?"

"Is that why you were screaming at us to leave you?" she asked. "Which, by the way, screw you. You think I'm *that* big of an asshole?"

"What if I can't stop," I said, "and something happens to you? Or Jude, or Nico, or Cate, or Chubs, or . . ."

Liam. The thought turned my stomach over.

I was surprised by the quiet that followed. Vida drew her hands into her lap, fixing her gaze on them as she went to work picking at her bloody cuticles.

"That other Orange," she said after a while. "He was a grade-A freak."

"Yes," I agreed, "he was. He was never shy about taking whatever he wanted from whomever he wanted."

"Gave me the fuckin' creeps," she muttered. "Wormed into my head and whispered all of this disgusting shit. Tried to get me to . . . do things."

"I know, he—" I started to say. My mouth finally caught up with my brain. "Hold on—what?"

"That kid. *Martin*," she squeezed out. "I wanted to tell Cate, but he never let me get close enough to her."

I don't know what it was that rose up inside of me then—surprise, maybe, that I had never once pictured Martin positioned at the center of my team, talking with Nico, battling Vida at every turn, teasing Jude. The tiniest flash of jealousy that he had had them, even if it had only been for a few weeks. Horror, mostly, that Cate had subjected them to that monster.

I still had nightmares about riding in that car with him, feeling the first brush of his influence spike through my blood. He had played with me, batting at me with his claws, and I hadn't been able to do one damn thing about it.

"I just figured that you would be the same way." Her dark eyes found mine. "But you're okay . . . I guess."

I let out a humorless laugh. "Thanks . . . I guess."

"The president's kid was like that, though?" she asked. "Man, what the hell?"

"It does something to you," I said. "The thing that scares me is that some part of me understands where they're coming from. They took everything from us, you know? Why shouldn't we be able to take it back if we have the power to?"

"Are you shitting me?" Vida said. "The fact that you can even ask these questions means you haven't fallen to their level and you probably never will. I get it—I mean, I understand why you're afraid. I do. But you're missing the key difference between you and those two."

"What?"

"You are *not alone*," she said. "You aren't, even if it feels that way sometimes. You have people who are in your corner, who care about you like crazy. Not because you forced them to feel that way, but because they want to. Can you honestly tell me those other two shitheads have that? Do you think they would have been half as bad if there had been people there to step in and tell them when to stop?"

"I can't stop thinking about those kids," I said, tears pricking the backs of my eyes.

"Good," Vida said. "It's on you to remember them and what that felt like to come up out of the dark and see what you'd done. Forgive yourself, but don't forget."

"And if it's not enough?"

"Then *I'll* stop you," she said. "I'm not afraid of your crazy power. Not anymore, at least." Vida stood up, brushing her pants off. "I'm going to go take a walk around. When

I come back, you better already be asleep, or I'll knock you out myself."

"Thanks," I said. "For listening, I mean."

"Don't mention it."

I waited until Vida was heading down a trail before I turned back to the tent and crawled between Liam and Chubs. I was too tired and too drained to wonder or care if it was a bad idea. I settled down and closed my eyes, letting my thoughts slow and spill into a soft, pale blue dream.

TWENTY-FOUR

I WAS SO USED TO THE STRANGE ON-OFF SLEEP schedule of my life now, I'm not sure what it was that actually woke me up. Not a noise. Vida was back in the tent, humming softly, some old song I half recognized. I watched, disoriented, as she gleefully tore out scraps of *White Fang*'s pages, rolled each into a tiny ball, and threw them one by one into Chubs's mouth, which had fallen wide open in sleep.

I sat up and rubbed my face, trying to clear the crud from my eyes. "What time is it?"

She shrugged. "Half past who the hell knows? Go back to sleep."

"Okay," I said, lowering myself down onto my elbows. Chubs's rattling snores kept time with the persistent rip of each page. Both he and Jude were sleeping flat on their backs, shoulder to shoulder. I slid back down under the covers, turning onto my left side again. The blanket twisted with me, leaving Liam without an inch of it.

I sat up again, heavy limbs and all, and untangled myself from the soft wool. With Liam's half of the blanket finally freed from under me, I tossed it carefully back in his direction, watching, with disbelieving eyes, as the pale peach fabric fluttered down through empty air and settled on the ground.

"Where's Lee?" I hadn't been awake before. I was now.

"He went out," Vida said, not looking up from her work.

"Out," I repeated, the word tasting like blood on my tongue. "Out where?"

"To walk around for a while," she said. "He said he couldn't sleep."

"You let him go alone?" I scrambled for my boots, hands shaking as I pulled them on. "How long ago did he leave?"

"What's going on?" Chubs mumbled.

"Liam left," I said.

"What?" His hands smacked around on the ground until they found his glasses. He shoved them onto the bridge of his nose. "Are you sure?"

"I'm going to bring him back," I said, tugging on the navy sweatshirt and an oversize dust-smeared black peacoat they'd grabbed by mistake as they left the warehouse in Nashville. "Vida—did he tell you where he was going?"

"Leave him alone, boo," she said, not turning around. "He's a big kid. Wears the underwear and everything."

"You don't understand," I said, "he's *not coming back.* He's leaving for good."

Vida's lips parted as she glanced around, the full weight of realization knocking the breath out of her. "Well . . . you have the flash drive, right? It's not a total disaster. . . ."

"Are you kidding me?" I shouted. Jude sat straight up, blinking, but I didn't have time to answer any of his questions. "Where would he go? He'd need a car or a bike—did he mention anything to any of you?"

"No!" Chubs said. "I would have told you!"

"Definitely not," Jude said. "He kept talking about all of us going together tomorrow. Maybe . . . I mean, he could come back, right? If we give him a few minutes?"

He could be right. I forced myself to gulp down a deep breath. I pressed a hand, hard, against my chest, trying to ease the fluttering beat of my heart. He could have just gone down to the falls. That was possible, wasn't it? Liam would never have left without Chubs or some kind of—

I stopped mid-thought, noticing for the first time the tiny sliver of paper sticking up out of his shirt's front pocket. The button there had been undone, making room for a folded note. I reached over and plucked it out before Chubs could stop me.

Gas station off highway, 2 miles south. Come by 6.

I crumpled the note in my fist, throwing it back at him.

"I didn't know!" he said before he'd even read it. "I didn't!"

We had a total of two guns that Vida and I traded off carrying, since both Chubs and Liam refused on moral grounds. The revolver was on the ground at Vida's feet, and the black semi-automatic was resting on top of the deflated backpack. Which meant Liam had neither.

Of course—*of course* he would go to the one place he had the best chance of being spotted by someone else. What was he thinking? That he'd be fine under the cover of night?

I took off at a stumbling run, shoving the tent flap open. The thick soles of my boots smashed through the snow.

"Wait for me!" Vida shouted. *"Ruby!"*

Outside of our small shelter, the freezing air hit me like a bat to the face. In the precious few seconds it took for me to get my bearings and head toward the small road Chubs had pointed out earlier, large flakes of snow had already managed to work their way along my loose hair, down into the collar of my coat. But they weren't nearly heavy enough to cover the careless footprints he'd left behind.

I ran. Through the flurries of snow, the morning misty haze, the overgrown trails, until I found the highway. The blanket of snow on the road wasn't nearly as thick-skinned as the layer covering the forest floor. I lost sight of his trail just as I skidded onto the icy blacktop, the stitches pulling so tight in my back it momentarily knocked the breath out of me. I staggered forward, lungs burning. The sun was rising in the east; it was the only reason I knew how to set my feet toward the south.

It was another twenty minutes, a whole lifetime of poisonous terror, before the small strip of businesses took shape down the misty highway and I spotted the gas station they must have passed on the way in.

I was out of breath, my lower back screaming in pain each time I swung my leg forward. The paved road disappeared into slushy dirt that splattered up onto my shins. The half dozen gas pumps had been knocked face-first into the torn-up pavement.

There were a couple of vehicles parked behind the station, one—a truck—with its hood propped open, as if someone had just taken a look. If he had found something wrong with it, there was a chance he was looking for a part in the service garage. *Or food,* I thought, turning back toward the building. *Stocking up before he runs.*

The back door of the station was unlocked; if I were being technical about it, the lock and handle had both been blown right off. It creaked as I opened it, and I slipped inside.

The store was bigger than I was expecting it to be but in worse shape. Someone had done a fairly thorough job of cleaning the joint out, but here and there were jumbo bags of chips, and a soda dispenser was still glowing and buzzing with last gasps of electricity. The gun stayed in my hand, cold and solid, trained on the glass doors of the drink refrigerators and the endless graffiti tagging that masked from view anything still inside.

I followed the line of the shelves as they flowed past the cash register and empty cardboard candy containers, around the front of the store to a fairly new-looking section of the building labeled FULL SERVICE.

The short hallway between the store and the mechanic garage was decorated with photos and posters of old cars with bikini-clad girls perched on top of them. I took in a slow, steadying breath. It was all rubber, gas, and oil; no amount of time or bleach was going to scrub that stench from the air.

There was another entrance into that section from the outside. The sign on the glass door was still flipped to OUT—BACK IN 15, and it directed visitors to kindly inquire at the back garage if it was an emergency. There were chairs, photos of vacant-eyed employees lining the wall, and model tires—but no footprints, no noise, no Liam.

A spike of fear cut through me as I shouldered the door to the mechanic shop open. I turned, trying to catch the heavy thing before it could slam shut, and that was the mistake—I knew it even as I turned, even as Instructor Johnson's favorite saying rang out in my ears: *Don't turn your back on the unknown.*

There was a tingling sensation at my back that I recognized a second too late. A burst of pressure slammed into me, throwing me forward as if someone had tackled me from behind. My forehead cracked against the door frame. My eyes flashed black, white, black as I crumpled. The gun clattered away, skimming across the cement, out of reach.

Then, a warm, familiar voice, pitched with fear: "Oh my God! Sorry, I thought—" Liam's pale form burst out behind the hollowed-out car frame in the middle of the garage. "What are you doing here?"

"What are *you* doing here?" I demanded, looking around for the gun under the workbenches and tables. There were tools and parts scattered everywhere, collecting dust and even more grime. "You came out here alone, without any kind of way to protect yourself—"

"No way to protect myself?" he repeated, raising a brow.

"You know what I mean!" I crouched down, blinking back the dark spots in my vision, and felt under the metal table until my fingers closed around the barrel. I waved it toward him for emphasis. "What were you going to do against one of these?"

He turned back to the car, his mouth pressed tightly into a line of disgust. "I disarmed you pretty easily. What would the instructors say about *that*?"

It stung more than I expected it to. I watched in silence as he flipped the hood of the skeletal car back open, the tool flashing silver in his hand. But he wasn't working; instead, his hands were braced against the green frame. The leather jacket clung to his shoulders as he leaned forward, hanging his head. I kept my back flat against the door, a silent guard against anything that might come in.

"So you found me," he muttered, his voice strained. "I suppose I have Chubs to thank for that?"

His mind was turning through a wild range of emotions, flipping between what felt like hot anger and murky guilt and crushing hopelessness in a matter of seconds. It felt like his mind was calling to mine, like it was screaming for me.

I pressed the back of my hand against my forehead. Ever since I'd given in and stopped trying to fold them away, my abilities had been quieter. Settled, even. Now was not the moment to lose that bit of calm.

"I know—" I began, licking my dry lips. "I know you can take care of yourself. But we don't know anything about this town. We don't know who could come by, and the thought of you out here alone . . ."

"I *wanted* to be alone," he said, his voice gruff. "I just wanted . . . I just needed to clear my head. Away from them. Away from *you*."

I stared at him, trying to take what he had just said and align it with the look of all-out desperation on his face.

"Look," I began, "I get it. You don't like me, but—"

"I don't like you?"

He let out a low, flat laugh. One fell into the next, and it was awful—not at all him. He was half choking on them as he turned around, shaking his head. It almost sounded like a sob, the way his breath burst out of him.

"I don't like you," he repeated, his face bleak. "I don't *like* you?"

"Liam—" I started, alarmed.

"I can't—I can't think about anything or anyone else," he whispered. A hand drifted up, dragging back through his hair. "I can't think straight when you're around. I can't sleep. It feels like I can't breathe— I just—"

"Liam, please," I begged. "You're tired. You're barely over being sick. Let's just . . . Can we just go back to the others?"

"I love you." He turned toward me, that agonized expression still on his face. "I love you every second of every day, and I don't understand why, or how to make it stop—"

He looked wild with pain; it pinned me in place, even before what he had said registered in my mind.

"I know it's wrong; I know it down to my damn bones. And I feel like I'm sick. I'm trying to be a good person, but I can't. I can't do it anymore."

What is this? The look of open pain on his face was too much to process. My mind couldn't work fast enough.

My hands fisted in the pockets of my coat. I felt myself backing away toward the door, trying to escape that look, trying to stop my heart from tearing out of my chest. He's confused. Explain it to him. He's only confused.

"Look at me."

I couldn't move; there was nowhere to go. He wasn't hiding from me anymore. I felt his feelings unravel around him, a flood of warmth and a piercing pain that cut through the daze I felt when he stepped in close to me.

My hands stayed in my pockets; his were at his sides. We weren't touching, not really. I had the sudden, sharp memory of the way his fingers had brushed against mine a few hours before. He bent his face down to my shoulder, his breath slipping through three layers of cloth to warm the skin there. One of his fingers hooked a belt loop on my jeans and inched me just that tiny bit closer. His nose skimmed up my throat, along my cheek, and I saw none of it. I squeezed my eyes shut as his forehead finally came to rest against mine.

"Look at me."

"Don't do this," I whispered.

"I don't know what's wrong with me," he breathed out. "I feel like . . . I feel like I'm losing my damn mind, like your face has been carved into my heart, and I don't remember when, and I don't understand why, but the scar is there, and I can't get it to heal. It won't go. I can't make it fade. And you won't even look at me."

My hands slipped out of the safety of my coat and gripped his jacket's soft leather. He was still wearing Cole's beneath it. "It's okay," I choked out. "We'll figure it out."

"I swear," he whispered, his mouth hovering over mine. "I swear, I swear . . . I swear we were on that beach, and I saw you wearing this light green dress, and we talked for hours. I had a life, and so did you, and we lived them together. It doesn't fit. That piece doesn't fit. Claire was there, and Cole promised we'd never been. But then . . . I see your face in the firelight, and I remember different fires, different smiles, different everything. I remember you in the green dress, and then it becomes a green uniform, and it doesn't make sense!"

Green dress—the beach? Virginia Beach?

One tear escaped my lashes, then another. It had happened so fast; I'd had to work so quickly in that sky blue room. What he was saying now—none of it had happened, not really, but the way he had told it then had felt real to *me*. We could have met that summer, on that beach, with nothing but a tiny stretch of sun and sand to keep us apart. I must have been thinking about it, even as I pulled myself out of his thoughts and memories. I must have missed that one tiny sliver of myself, or pushed it, or—

"I'm . . . It's—it's like torture." His voice was strained, hardly even a whisper. "I think I'm losing it—I don't know what's happening, what happened, but I look at you, I look at you, and I love you so much. Not because of anything you've said, or done, or anything at all. I look at you, and I just love you, and it terrifies me. It terrifies me what I would do for you. Please . . . you have to tell me . . . tell me I'm not crazy. Please just *look at me*."

My eyes drifted up to his, and it was over.

His lips caught mine in a hard kiss, driving them apart with the force of it. There was nothing gentle about it. I felt the door rattle against my back as he shifted, pressing me against it, taking my face between his hands. Every thought in my head exploded to a pure, pounding white, and I felt the dark curl of desire begin to twist inside me, bending all my rules, snapping that last trembling bit of restraint. I tried one last time to pull away.

"No," he said, bringing my lips back to his. It was just like it had been before—I slid my hands under his jacket to press him closer. The low groan at the back of his throat, a small, pleading noise that set every inch of my skin on fire.

Then, it changed. I pulled back, gasping for a breath, and when I found him again, it was deeper, and softer, and sweeter. It was a kiss I remembered, the kind we used to have when it felt like we had all the time in the world, when the roads stretched out just for us.

I gave in to that feeling. I didn't care what it made me—weak, selfish, stupid, terrible. I remembered that tiny bit of warm peace before I had ruined him, throwing his mind into a jumble of desperate confusion. There was so much darkness to it now; the clear, bright corridors of memories had collapsed in on themselves. I fought my way through, tearing down filmy sheets of black and burned brown. I was drowning in it, in him, and it was so different, so strange, that I didn't recognize the fact I was in his mind until it was too late.

Stop, stop, stopstopstop—

I shoved him back, breaking the physical connection between us. We both stumbled, my head screaming with pain as I crashed down onto my knees. Liam fell back onto the nearest work table, sending the hundreds of little tools and bolts stacked there tumbling to the ground in a shower of piercing noise that seemed to go on and on, echoing the final *snap* that whipped through me as my mind broke away from his.

Shit, I thought, gasping for breath. I felt sick, physically ill, as the world bobbed up under me. For several terrifying seconds, the burning in my mind was bad enough that I couldn't see at all. I all but crawled, feeling for the gun I had dropped as he grabbed me. I tried to haul myself back onto my feet using one of the shelves of hubcaps, but I only succeeded in tearing it down off the wall and sending them showering down over me.

Finally, I just gave up, leaning back against the wall, drawing my knees up to my chest. The ache had trickled down the back of my neck, dripping bit by bit into the center of my chest. *Shit, shit, shit.* I dug the heels of my palms against my eyes, sucking in another ragged breath.

"Ruby."

I looked up from my hands, searching for his face in the darkness.

"Ruby, you . . ." Liam's voice had an edge of panic to it now as he reached for me and pulled me up toward him. I fell against him, too stunned to move as he wrapped his arms around my shoulders, buried his face in my hair. "We— That safe house—"

Oh my God.

"You did something—you—oh, God, *Chubs*!" Liam pulled back, trapping my face between his hands. "Chubs was shot! They took him, and they took us—we were in that room, and you—what did you do? What did you *do* to me? Why would I leave? Why would I leave without you?"

The blood drained from my face, from my entire body. I ran my fingers back through his hair, forcing him to look me directly in the eye. Every one of his muscles shook. "He's okay. *Liam!* Chubs is okay; he's fine. We came to find you in Nashville, remember?"

He looked over at me again, and for the first time in weeks, his eyes were sharp. Clear. He was looking at me, and I knew the exact moment he realized what I'd done to him. His hair fell into his face as he shook his head; his lips worked in silent disbelief. I couldn't bring myself to say one thing.

This isn't possible.

How many memories had I wiped clean now? Dozens? A hundred? And from the beginning, from that look of pure fear on my mom's face, I knew there would be no going back. When it happened again to Sam, it only confirmed it. Slipping into her mind, trying to fix what I'd done, had only ever proven there was nothing I *could* do. That there wasn't a trace of myself left to draw out to the front of her mind again.

But now—I hadn't pushed the memories into his mind. I knew what that felt like. This was something different; it had to be. All I'd done was pull myself free before I could sink in too far and do real damage. There was no way that this was happening. No way.

He stepped back, out of my reach. Away from me.

"I can explain," I started, my voice trembling. But he didn't want to hear any of it. Liam turned back to the car at the center of the damp garage, scooping up a small backpack I didn't recognize and swinging it over his shoulder. Panicked movements brought him back to the door. He needed to see it for himself, I realized, that Chubs was all right. That everything that had happened since we found him had, in truth, actually happened.

"Wait!" I called, starting after him. *"Lee!"*

I heard his footsteps pound against the linoleum of the front office, and his frustrated grunt as he knocked into the desk.

I heard the gunshots. The one-two punch of explosive sound that shattered a wall of glass and brought my world down with it.

TWENTY-FIVE

I SCRAMBLED THROUGH THE FRONT WAITING ROOM, the gun swinging up in my hands as I ran. Liam had just turned the corner back into the store—I saw him on the ground, flat on his back. The glass was scattered thickly over him; on first glance, it almost looked like someone had broken a solid sheet of ice against his chest.

That was all it took. Something cool and collected slipped into place. The terror that had almost brought me down to my knees distilled into something useful, something calculating, something the Children's League had been careful to grow and nurture.

Controlled panic.

I wanted to run straight into the store, but I knew from countless simulations how that scenario would play out. Instead, I stuck my head out just enough to see which drink coolers had been blown out. Only the very last one, the one closest to me was shattered.

The shooter was likely by the back door—he or she must have seen a flash of Liam coming around the corner and fired.

I glanced down, long enough to see his chest rise and fall. His hands rose and settled down over it as he gasped for breath. Alive.

Where was the shooter?

I swallowed the burning anger, fingers choking my gun as I searched the front wall for something reflective. There was one of those round security mirrors just behind the cash register stand, and as grimy as it was, as narrow as my vision had become, I would never have missed her. The woman was thick around the center, in her late fifties, early sixties, if I had to pinpoint it. The wiry gray hair that was only half tucked under her hat and green hunting jacket's collar gave her away.

She was shaking hard, cussing as she dropped the shells she was trying to reload, and she disappeared behind the shelf of ChapStick to retrieve them. I positioned myself over Liam and took aim through the gold frames of the coolers. When she popped back up, I was ready—squeezing off two shots that lodged into the wall behind her.

I don't think she even looked at me before she fired that one last shot and bolted. I ducked on instinct, though it was obvious she had aimed wide. The front window of the store shattered as the shotgun's slugs tore through it. And it was all thunder and noise, anxiety and terror, and glass. So much glass.

Liam groaned at my feet. I dropped down, brushing the shards from his hair and front. My hands slipped inside his jacket again, feeling for blood. The floor was clean and my fingers came away the same. Not hurt. The thought was fleeting as I hauled him up into a sitting position. He slumped against the cooler's frame, clearly stunned. His ears must have been ringing something terrible.

I cupped his face between my hands in relief, pressing my lips to his forehead, to his cheek. "Are you okay?" I breathed out.

He nodded, pressing a hand over mine. Falling had knocked the breath out of him. "I'm okay."

A car engine roared to life outside. I pushed back, sweeping the gun off the floor.

"Ruby!" Liam called after me, but I was already running, ramming my shoulder into the broken, swinging back door. The taillights were burning bright red, growing smaller and smaller with the distance the woman put between us. I ran after her as long as I could, surging forward on a tide of anger. She'd come *this close* to hurting him, to killing him.

I planted my feet and raised the gun one last time, my aim fixed steadily on her back left tire. If she *had* seen one of us and still had enough wits left to report us—

No. My arm dropped heavily back to my side, and I switched the safety on with my thumb. Even if she had seen us, even if she had figured out what we were, this was the beating heart of the Middle of Nowhere. It wasn't a town, let alone a place skip tracers or even PSFs would think to haunt. She could call, but it would be hours, maybe days, before someone responded.

I rubbed the sweat off my forehead with my wrist. God. That woman had probably come in looking for food, maybe shelter. She hadn't been trained, and the sloppy way she'd held that gun made me wonder if she hadn't fired those first shots by mistake. Liam and I hadn't been quiet in the garage. Maybe she'd heard us, heard him coming, and panicked at the thought of being caught stealing?

It wasn't worth it to try to puzzle it out, and I didn't have the energy to. My problems weren't up ahead anymore. They were standing right behind me.

I turned on my heels slowly, walking back toward the gas station where Liam was waiting. With the sun rising steadily at his back, his face was thrown into shadow. There was still crushed glass dusted across his shoulders, but I kept my eyes on the backpack clenched between his fingers. His cracked, white-boned knuckles.

There was a new cut across the bridge of his nose, and blood oozed from an open gash on his chin, but that was the worst the flying glass could manage. I only had to take one look at his face to know that what I'd done had cut him to the core.

He waited for me to reach him, one agonizing step at a time. I felt a flood of hot shame wash down through me, tightening my throat, pricking my eyes with tears. A flush of red swept up his throat, over his face, to the very tips of his ears. Liam watched me, the longing on his face etched bone deep; I knew how hard he was struggling with it, because I was fighting with everything I had not to reach out and take his hand, run my thumb over the warm pulse in his wrist. It was unbearable, that thing between us. How much I wanted to pretend we'd never lived a life outside of this moment.

"Did . . ." Liam pressed a fist against his mouth, struggling with his next words. "Did you just not want to be with me?"

It was almost too much for me to take. "How could you think that?"

"What else am I supposed to think?" he demanded. "I feel like I've been . . . underwater. I can't get a thought straight, but I remember *that*. I remember the safe house. We were together; we were going to be okay."

"You know we weren't," I told him. "It was the only thing I could do. It was the only way they'd let you go, and I couldn't let you stay."

From almost the beginning, Liam and I had a kind of understanding between us that lived without words, only looks and feelings. I knew, instinctively, why he made the choices he did, and he could trace my lines of thought as easily as one would follow a lit road. I'd never thought this moment would come to pass, but I also never believed he wouldn't just *know* why I'd made that decision.

"You're not even sorry," he breathed out.

"No," I managed to say around the stone lodged in my throat. "Because the only thing worse than being without you would have been watching them break you day after day, until you weren't yourself anymore, until they sent you on an Op that you didn't come back from."

"Like they did to you?" said Liam harshly. "And now I just have to accept it? You took away my choice, Ruby—and for what? Because you thought I wasn't strong enough to survive being with the League?"

"Because *I'm* not strong enough to survive seeing you with the League!" I said. "Because I wanted you, after everything you went through, to have a chance to find your parents and live your life."

"Dammit—I wanted *you*!" Liam seized my arms, his fingers tightening like he could make me understand his pain that way. "More than anything! And you just . . . crashed through my mind and sealed everything away, like you had the right to, like *I* didn't need *you*. What kills me is that I trusted you—I was so sure you knew that. I would have been okay, because you would have been there with me!"

How many times had I told myself a version of that? Hearing it, though—that was a knife to the throat, a razor's edge I had no choice but to lean into.

"My head is so damn muddy, nothing is lining up." He took a step back, letting himself drop down in a crouch. "Chubs was shot, and Zu is still out there, and East River burned, and—everything after that is like a nightmare. And you . . . you were with those people this whole time. Anything could have happened to you, and I would never have known. Do you know what that feels like?"

I dropped down to my knees in front of him, hitting the ground hard enough to finally jar the tears clinging to my eyelashes. I felt exhausted. Empty.

"I can't fix this," I said. "I know I've messed everything up, and there's no way back from this, okay? I do. But your life was worth more than what I wanted, and it was the only way I could think of to make sure you didn't get it in your head to come find me."

"Who says I would have?" I knew he meant it cruelly, that it was a weak moment and all he wanted was for me to feel as much pain as he did, but there wasn't enough venom in his words for them to sting. He just wasn't capable of it.

"I would have torn this whole damn country apart looking for you," I said softly. "Maybe you really would have left. Maybe you wouldn't have come looking for me. Maybe I misread everything. But if you even felt a quarter of what I did . . ." My words wavered. "I used to wonder, you know, all the time, if it was all because you felt sorry for me. Because you pitied me or were looking for another person to protect."

"And you could never see another reason?" he whispered in a fierce voice. "It couldn't have been because I respected how hard you fought to survive? Because I saw how kind your heart was? Or that you were funny, and brave, and strong, and you made me feel like I was all of those things, too, even when I didn't deserve it?"

"Liam—"

"I don't know what to say or what to do here," he said, shaking his head. "It feels like it never ended for me. Do you get that? I can't forget it ever happened. I can't hate you—I can't, not when I want to kiss you so damn badly." Then, so brokenly, I almost couldn't understand him, he continued. "Why couldn't you have taken everything? Not just the memories but the feelings, too?"

I stared at him, my mind blanking in confusion.

"It's terrifying—*terrifying*—to meet a stranger and feel something for her so intense it actually stops your heart, and you don't have *any* basis for it. No context. The feelings are there, and it's like they're clawing at your chest, needing to get out. Even now, even when I just *look* at you, it feels like they're crushing me—with how much I want, and need, and love you. But you're not even sorry; you just expect that I'll be okay with the fact you threw your life away for mine."

The world around us had retreated so far back from our pocket of misery, I'd forgotten it even existed. That we were out at the edge of an open highway, exposed to the freezing cold and any passing eyes. Reality came roaring back in the form of a car engine, a blaring horn, and headlights aimed directly at us.

I pulled Liam up onto his feet, reaching for the gun tucked into my coat pocket—but I saw the car now, the familiar dusty tan of Chubs's SUV. The car skidded to a stop a few feet away, kicking up an explosion of snow.

Chubs jumped out of the driver's seat, leaving the engine running. "Oh, thank God. I saw you both on the ground and I thought you killed each other."

I turned my back to them both, wiping my cheeks against my coat sleeves. Behind me, I heard Chubs suck in a sharp breath, but Liam was the one to speak, his voice frighteningly calm.

"Come inside for a sec. There's some food left we can take."

I didn't want to follow them, and I didn't want to get into the car. I couldn't move; the fight, if I could even call it that, had drained me to the point that I was seeing two of Jude as he jumped out of the car and came toward me.

"Roo?" He sounded scared.

I physically shook myself to clear my head. "It's okay."

"What happened?" he whispered, pressing a comforting hand to my back. "Did you guys fight?"

"No," I said. "He remembers now."

We turned, watching as Chubs stumbled over himself, trying to keep up as Liam dragged him over to the gas station. He looked back at me with wide eyes as Liam kicked the door open with his foot. The *bang* as it slammed against the opposite cinderblock wall was enough to draw Vida out of the car, too.

It took two, maybe three full seconds for the shouting to start. They'd moved far enough into the store that we couldn't tell exactly what they were saying; particularly hot words jumped out now and again—*How could you?* and *Why?* and *Her, her, her.*

"Holy shit." Vida turned back toward me, her hands planted firmly on her hips. "I told you to leave the kid alone. What did you do to him?"

My skin felt tight and hot over my face with the effort it took not to burst into tears.

"—a damn idiot!" Liam was shouting. "Because I feel like a goddamn fool!"

"He knows?" Vida asked. "You told him?"

"No . . . I think he remembers. I think I undid it. Or I never really did it. I don't know. He won't talk to me. He's never going to talk to me ever again."

"I don't think that's true," Jude offered. "He's probably just overwhelmed. It seems like . . ."

"Like what?" Vida asked.

"That some part of him remembered you. He got so upset when we found you, and he thought you were going to die, remember?"

"Why was he acting like such an ass, then?" Vida asked.

"Think about it—he knew that Roo was League, but he treated her differently than he treated us, right? Maybe being around you made him feel confused—his brain was telling him one thing, but his instincts were telling him another?"

That was the way Liam had explained it; Jude had been perceptive enough to pick up on something I never would have imagined possible. With my parents and Sam . . . they had been cold after I'd erased their memories—sealed their memories, or whatever it was I was actually doing. I had been so young then, I'd just assumed that some part of them recognized what I was, and they hated me for it.

Maybe I wasn't completely wrong, then. If I had taken their memories of me but none of the feelings they had, was it the same for them as it was for Liam? They were scared and just confused by what they felt? My mom hadn't exactly been stable then—she had panic attacks if I was even a second late coming home from school. Maybe she saw me that morning, and it was too much for her. And Dad, calm, reliable Dad—he could have been worried about what she would do, and that's why he didn't have me come back inside.

Maybe I could fix them, too. The voice was small, but it was there, tugging at my ear.

"It doesn't change what Lee feels now, though," I said. Or how my parents would feel to find out what their daughter really was.

I let the others lead me back to the car and slid into the backseat. They had packed up the tent and cleared the campsite before they'd come to get us, not only because they were worried, but because Vida had finally been able to send her message to Cate.

And she'd gotten one in reply.

Instead of taking one of the front seats, Vida slid in next to me. Jude was starting to climb in after her when she pushed him back out with her foot and said, "Will you go get Grannie and tell him to hurry his ass up?"

Jude started to protest, but Vida was already shutting the door.

"What's wrong?" I asked, feeling much more alert seeing the Chatter in her hand. "What did she say?"

"I don't know . . . Something feels off," Vida said. "Read it yourself."

The Chatter's blue-white light flooded the backseat as I scrolled up through the latest conversation.

GLAD YOU ARE SAFE // WE NEED TO SET MEETING ASAP // CURRENT LOCATION?

Vida had written back:

CURRENT LOCATION OK // CAN BE IN CA TMRW

The response was instant:

WILL MEET AND ESCORT YOU // PUEBLO, CO // DITCH TARGET

I knew you lost a person's voice through short, abrupt messages. And that was the whole point of the Chatter: to relay information or media as quickly as possible. "Ditch Target" seemed especially terse, though. Not only that, but why would Cate—or Cole—risk leaving HQ and drawing attention to their plan?

DO NOT TELL TARGET OF MEET LOCATION

Below that was a street address.

"Do you think something happened?" Vida pressed. "Why the hell would she risk leaving HQ when it could blow the whole Op?"

"Maybe she thinks we won't be able to cross the California border without her help?" It was a weak explanation but a plausible one. "Vida, did she give the Chatter to you directly? Like, physically handed it to you?"

"Yeah," Vida said. "Nico set up the link between them himself." I watched her dark eyes go wide as she finally came upon the same horrible possibility I had. "You think someone took the Chatter from her? That something happened to her? Or Cole has it?"

"I think it's possible someone broke into our link between our Chatters," I said, my voice sounding much calmer than I felt. "And they've been intercepting all of our messages back and forth."

"No way," Vida said. "The whole point is that you can't hack the line. Is there any way to test?"

Maybe—one. I clenched my jaw, typing out each word carefully, deliberately.

WILL CONTACT ON ARRIVAL // LATER GATOR

The seconds dragged on and the screen dimmed from inactivity, but I didn't shut it off and Vida didn't pull away until it flashed back to full glow. The vibration seemed to race up the length of my bone, sending a wave of goose bumps after it.

GOOD // AFTER A WHILE CROCODILE

It was another ten minutes before the boys appeared at the entrance of the convenience store, each with something different in his arms. Chubs was all but nuzzling a package of toilet paper, Jude was balancing five different jumbo bags of chips, and Liam was struggling not to drop his ten soda bottles.

"Breathe, boo," Vida said, "play it cool. We just gotta get to Colorado."

And lie the whole way there, I thought, leaning my forehead against the door. It hadn't been much of a decision at all. If it wasn't Cate or Cole waiting for us, it meant something had happened to them—either their plan with the flash drive had been discovered, or someone found out they knew exactly where we were, and they were doing nothing to bring us back in. So many possible suspects flashed through my mind: Alban, his advisers, Jarvin, all of his friends. I couldn't shake the feeling that it all came down to the flash drive, couldn't shake the thoughts of how someone like Jarvin would use the intel for his own agenda, rather than to help us. And the worst of it was, we wouldn't know if it was safe to bring ourselves and the flash drive back to HQ unless we confirmed it first with whoever was waiting in Colorado.

And if it was really Cate, then fine. Pueblo, Colorado, was as good a place as any to go our separate ways from the boys. It was like Vida had said—no use clinging to them when I'd have to snip the cord eventually.

A blast of cold air hit us as they opened the trunk and dumped the supplies there. Jude crawled in beside Vida, trying to rub some feeling back into his hands. Cold air escaped from the folds of his jacket as he leaned toward the vents and pointed them all in his direction.

Chubs reclaimed the driver's seat, glancing back like he was surprised to find it still vacant. I met Liam's eyes just before he opened the passenger door and hauled himself in.

I had no idea what Chubs was waiting for, but we must have sat in silence for a good five minutes before Liam finally said, "Can we pretend for a few minutes that this isn't soul-crushingly awkward, and can someone please explain to me what's really going on?"

Chubs finally released the parking brake. "Later. I can't safely and successfully navigate the roads if I don't have quiet."

"Grannie," Vida said, "that's pathetic, even for you. You want one of the big kids to drive?"

"I'll do it!" Jude offered, snapping the cover of his compass shut and sitting straight up. "I had a few lessons at HQ."

"You had one lesson," I said, "and it ended when you side-swiped three other cars while trying to park."

"You killed that beautiful Mercedes," Vida said. "That beautiful, beautiful car."

"That wasn't my fault!"

Chubs ignored us, and we made our way back onto the highway as he proceeded at his usual careful speed. I settled in to tell the story again, the best I could, about what Cole had planned to do with the flash drive once he had it. Everything came tumbling out, from the moment they had brought Blake's body in, the escape in Boston, meeting with Chubs, and finding him in Nashville. Liam had questions—good ones—about how Cole and Cate were going to try to use the research as leverage for turning the League onto the right course.

"Okay," Liam muttered when I was finished, more to himself than me. "Okay . . . It's just, I have one more question. If you were going to risk your neck escaping that Op and trying to find me, what was in it for you?"

Wasn't it obvious?

"I told you. Cole said if I brought back the flash drive, Alban would give him anything he wanted. Including working on freeing the camps," I said. "And, in the meantime, I'd be able to make sure you were safe and that Alban would have no reason to come after you and bring you back into the fold."

When Liam finally did speak again, his voice was almost hoarse. "Not . . . that they would let you out of your deal? Let you go?"

He took my silence as the *no* it was.

"Did you even think to ask?" he whispered, the first traces of anger slipping back in. "You're going back, just like that—like those agents aren't dead set on killing other kids?"

"I have to finish this," I said.

"Yeah, and who's going to protect you?" he shot back. "You're just going to give them the intel and hope for the best, *hope* that they won't go back on their promises or kill you because they feel like it? I just want to know *why*. *Why* give it to them when there's a chance we can use the intel to help ourselves? If what Cole says is true and they did find a cause, then don't we deserve to have it? Make decisions about what to do with it?"

Liam was so earnest, so passionate when he said that, it was like he was blooming back into his old self. Even the color was returning to his face.

"It's not up for discussion," I said. "I'm sorry, but we have to be realistic. Before . . . before we thought we could make it on our own, that we didn't need any help—and look how that turned out. We need help. We can still get our way, but we can't do it by ourselves."

"And the help you pick is the League?" he demanded.

I pressed on, ignoring that and the indignant noise Vida made. "All the tribes are scattered, and we have no way to bring them together in any kind of force that would matter—and even if we did, it'd just be bait for the PSFs to come round us up. I know, I *know* that you hate this, that this isn't what you would choose, but what do you honestly expect we'd be able to do with the research? Broadcast it out all over the world? Do *you* have the tech for that? The resources? I'm trying to think about what's best for the kids in those camps—"

"No," he said coldly, "no, you're not thinking at all."

"It's done, Liam," I said. "Maybe they'll go back on their word, but I'm not willing to go back on mine. Not when the stakes are so high. If . . . I won't like it, but I'll understand if you want to split now, instead of in Colorado. This shouldn't be your problem at all."

"Colorado?" Chubs and Liam said together.

"We finally got a message from Cate," I said, holding up the Chatter. "She wants to meet in Pueblo, Colorado."

"She does?" Jude started. "But why—"

"When were you going to tell the rest of us?" Chubs cut in.

And as angry as he might have been at his friend, Liam was all too happy to back him on this. "You just expect us to dump you off there? What happened to us staying together until we get to California?"

"If she's coming to get us, it's probably because she thinks there isn't a way for us to safely cross the border into California," I lied, and hated myself for it. "She probably wants to fly in. I'm sure she'll let you hitch a ride—"

"Don't even bother finishing that sentence," Liam said.

"Okay, okay, *okay*!" Chubs shouted over us, making a hard turn to the right. "Please, for the love of *God*, can we just be quiet and okay for five freaking minutes and remember that we are actually friends who care about one another and don't want to wrap our hands around one another's necks? Because that sounds really nice right about now!"

"Somehow," Vida said after a long, uncomfortable, silent five minutes had passed, "this is worse."

Liam must have agreed, because he reached over and knuckled the radio on, humming something under his breath as he scanned through the static, the Spanish chatter, the commercials, until he finally landed on a woman's deep, even voice.

"—Children's League issued this statement about the Christmas Summit—"

"Oh no you don't," Chubs said, reaching over to turn it off. "We're not getting into this again."

"No!" all three of us protested from the backseat. Jude practically mashed his face against the metal grate between him and the radio dial, and the instant Alban's voice came pouring out of the speakers, Vida was right there with him.

"That's—" Jude began in an excited voice.

"We do not believe that the peace Gray is trying to prescribe is in anyone's interest but his own. If this false meeting of the minds is to take place, it will ruin the good work that common American citizens have done to rebuild the lives he shattered. We will not sit idly by while the truth is buried under heaps of his lies. The time to act is now, and we will."

That was a nice little speech. Courtesy, I'm sure, of Frog Lips. The man wrote almost every single word that Alban forced out between his smiling teeth. I didn't even need to close my eyes to see the old man's bald head bent over his handwritten cue cards, the lights from the cameras giving his tissue-thin skin a blue glow.

"—when asked for a comment, the press secretary replied, 'Every word out of a terrorist's mouth is designed to sharpen the fear and uncertainty that still exists today. John Alban is speaking out now because he's afraid Americans will no longer tolerate his violent acts and unpatriotic behavior when peace and order are restored.'"

"He's not *scared*," Vida hissed. "They're the ones who should be terrified."

Jude shushed her, waving his hands. "Can you turn it up?"

"I have Bob Newport, senior political adviser to Senator Joanne Freedmont of Oregon, on the line to discuss how the Federal Coalition will be approaching the Unity Summit—Bob, are you there?"

The line crackled with static, and for several seconds, only the low hum of the SUV's wheels against the highway filled my ears.

"Hi, yes—Mary? Sorry about that. Our signal strength in California hasn't—" His voice cut off, only to switch back in, sounding louder than before. *"For the last few months."*

"The cell towers and satellites in California haven't been all that reliable lately," I explained to the boys in the front seat. "Alban thinks Gray is tampering with them."

"Bob, before we lose you, can you tell us about the FC's plans to approach this meeting? Can you give us a preview of the

talking points Senator Freedmont and the others are hoping to bring to the table?"

"Sure. I can't go into great detail"—the line wavered again but then bounced back—*"definitely will be discussing the recognition of the Federal Coalition as a national party, and of course, we'll be pushing for a series of elections next spring."*

Mary the newscaster let out a light laugh. *"And how do you think the president will respond to your requests he cut his third term short?"*

Bob had a fake laugh of his own. *"We'll have to see. The draft, of course, will also be a major discussion. We'd like to hear if the president has any plans in place to phase it out, specifically the Psi Special Forces program, which, I know, has been a major point of contention across the country—"*

At that, all five of us shifted toward the glowing green radio display. Jude clutched at my arm. "Do you think . . . ?" he whispered.

"Will you also be discussing the rehabilitation programs?" Mary smelled the slightest hint of blood, and now she had her nose to the ground, looking to follow the trail. *"Recently there's been a lack of information released about the status of the programs and the children who were entered into them. For instance, the government is no longer issuing letters updating registered parents on their child's progress. Do you think this is a sign the program is about to undergo some kind of transformation?"*

"They actually sent letters?" I asked. This was the first I'd heard of it.

"At the very beginning—just a short, *your kid is making good progress, not causing problems* printout," Liam said. "Everyone got the same one."

"Right now our focus is on discussing what plans we'd like to see President Gray enact to stimulate the economy and reopen talks with our former international partners."

"But back to the issue of the Psi—" Mary's voice was starting to waver now, crackling with an unnatural metallic whine.

"Pull over," Vida said, "otherwise we'll lose the signal!"

"—will you ask him to come clean about what research programs are in place and whether or not they've made any progress analyzing the source of IAAN? I know, as a mother of an infant, I'm particularly interested in finding out whether or not my son, who already goes in for weekly tests and monitoring sessions, will have to be taken in to a specialized program per the IAAN Registry's instructions. Surely enough politicians on both sides are in a similar enough position to sympathize with the thousands of parents who have been left without answers—sometimes for years. I think I speak for everyone when I say that this is unacceptable."

"That's right," Jude said, "you get him, Mary. Don't let him change the subject!"

"I believe the FC would like to modify . . . the program—" Static again. It couldn't begin to disguise how uncomfortable Bob sounded on this subject. *"We would like to continue to have five-year-olds monitored for a year's time in one of the facilities, but if they show no . . . dangerous side effects of IAAN, we would like to see them sent home, rather than automatically graduated to one of these rehabilitation camps—"*

The line went silent with a harsh *click*. The newscaster was repeating his name, *"Bob? Bob? Bob?"* over and over again, like she could somehow draw his voice back through the dead air.

TWENTY-SIX

THE SIGNS HAD BEEN PAINFULLY HONEST IN CALLING that part of the country NO MAN'S LAND. It would have felt like a bigger relief when we finally passed out of Oklahoma's panhandle and into Kansas if we could actually tell the two apart. For hours, it was nothing but once-green tall grass beaten down by ice and snow. Small towns that had had the life and people slowly strangled from them. Rusting cars and bikes left along the highway. Open, empty sky.

I had seen desert in Southern California, but this . . . this stretch seemed endless and achingly open; even the sky seemed to bow lower to meet the highway. We stopped only twice, both times to search the abandoned cars lining the road for gas. There were functioning stations along the way, but at nearly twenty dollars for a gallon, it somehow didn't seem all that pressing for us to fill our tank the legal way.

For the most part, traffic came in slow drizzles. The lone highway patrol car blew past us, in an awful hurry to get wherever it was going. Still, Chubs drove the entire first five hours with his hands clenched on the wheel. The next time we stopped for a bathroom break, Vida stole the driver's seat and locked the door, forcing him into the front passenger seat and Liam into the back, next to me.

We left the flat plains, heading toward mountains blanketed by darkness. That was the only warning we had that we were coming up on Colorado. It would be hours more before we actually hit Pueblo, but the knots in my stomach didn't seem to care. Ahead, lines of lights gave shape to distant cities that only grew larger and brighter as we descended into the valley. I was too anxious to sleep like Jude and Vida. I kept one hand clenched around the Chatter and flash drive in my coat pocket, trying to keep my thoughts focused on what was ahead, visualizing all of the different scenarios and how we would play them through.

Vida and I would scope out the location; if it was one person, Jarvin or one of the other agents, we could take him easily. She would attack him in her way, and I would overwhelm him in mine. If a group of armed agents was there waiting for us, we'd make a clean getaway without being detected. This would work. *This will work,* I told myself. The only real question was, what would we do if it were no longer safe to bring the flash drive back to HQ? If Cole or Cate were gone. Dead.

Liam's eyes were closed, and his breathing was easier than it had been in days. Now and then, a lone passing truck's headlights would fill the window he leaned against, lighting his golden blond hair. And in those few precious seconds, I couldn't see the cuts or bruises on his face. Not even the dark circles under his eyes.

The Beatles song drifting from the radio gave way to a softly strumming Fleetwood Mac, which faded, finally, into the cheerful opening riffs of the Beach Boys's "Wouldn't It Be Nice."

I don't know that, until that moment, I really understood that this was the end. That in a matter of miles, hours, I would leave that car and shut the door behind me one last time. It had been hard enough to let go before, and now . . . *this*. Maybe that was my real punishment for the things I'd done—being trapped in a world where I had to leave them again and again and again until there wasn't enough left of my heart for it to break.

I wasn't embarrassed or ashamed to cry then. Better to get it out while the others were asleep and Vida was concentrating on the dark road. I let myself, just this once, sink deeper into the pain. I let myself wonder why this had happened to me—to all of us—until I was sure the shape of the flash drive would be cut into my palm.

At least now, hopefully, we'd know who . . . what . . . was responsible. I'd have something to blame for the mess that was my life, other than myself.

And that song, it wasn't ending. It kept on playing, that stupid, upbeat swing of voices and plucked strings, the promise of a future that would never be mine.

The touch was so hesitant at first, I thought for sure that he was still asleep, shifting in dreams. Liam's hand came down next to mine on the seat, his fingers inching over one at a time, hooking over mine in a way that was as tender as it was shy. I bit my lip, letting his warm, rough skin engulf mine.

His eyes were still shut and stayed that way, even as I saw him struggle to swallow. There was nothing to say now. Our linked hands rose as he guided them to rest against his chest, and they stayed there, through the song, the mountains, the cities. Until the end.

Pueblo—HOME OF HEROES! or STEEL CITY OF THE WEST, depending on which sign you believed—was close to abandoned, but not quite empty enough to ease my mind as we drove past a line of flickering streetlights and empty car dealerships. It looked like much of what we'd seen so far, with mountains circling from all sides, rising up from otherwise flat, dry landscape. I had always pictured the state to be one giant mountain, I guess, covered in a thick skin of snow-dusted evergreens and ski slopes. There was snow, all right, capping the distant Rockies, but here in the daylight, there were no trees to provide cover, no blooming flowers to lend some beauty. Life in a place like this felt unnatural.

Vida parked the SUV across the street from the address "Cate" had sent us, letting the car roll to an anticlimactic stop.

"Are you sure this is right?" Chubs asked, glancing down at the tablet again. He had a point. Meeting at a deserted Dairy Queen did seem strange—it seemed in line with what I had seen of Cole's sense of humor, I guess, but the randomness of it all made me doubt myself.

"I don't see anyone in there," Chubs said for the tenth time. "I don't know . . . maybe we should circle around it again?"

"Grannie, chill—you're giving *me* an ulcer," Vida said, shifting the car into park. "She's probably waiting in one of those cars."

"Yeah," Liam said, "but which one?"

Most were smaller sedans in a variety of colors and shapes. The one thing they had in common, aside from the beating their paint had taken from the sun, was that every inch of them seemed to be coated with dust. The roofs, the windows, the hoods. The only exception was a white SUV—the wheels and lower half of the car were caked with grime, but the rest of it was otherwise clean. It hadn't been there long.

"She said to meet her inside," I said, unbuckling my seat belt. "We'll start there."

"Wait," Chubs began, a note of panic underlying his tone. "Can't we just . . . wait a few more minutes?"

"We can't keep her waiting," Jude said. "She's probably worried sick."

I met Vida's gaze in the rearview mirror. "Why don't you stay here and pack a bag of supplies," I suggested, keeping my voice casual. "Vida and I will get the full picture from her. We'll see what her plans are and if it's safe for you guys to travel with us."

"Okay," Jude said, "I'll meet you in there in a second!"

"Take your time," I said, stepping over his long legs. "Think about what we're going to need."

"But Cate will probably have everything we need," he protested. "And anyway, I want to see her. It feels like it's been forever."

Vida took her cue from me and unbuckled her seat belt.

I shut the door behind me, careful not to look at Liam's face as I walked around the back of the car to meet Vida. There was a faint *click* as she checked the magazine of the gun in her hand.

"We don't go inside unless we confirm we're not going to walk into a wall of guns, *capisce?* In and out only long enough for you to do brain voodoo and see if the others are all right," she said. "How long until Judith gets whiny and impatient and comes after us?"

"Ten minutes, max." Maybe twelve if Liam distracted him.

We kept to the street's shadows, weaving in and out of the cars. I hadn't felt nervous until that very moment, when I thought I caught a flicker of light and movement in one of the restaurant's windows. But Vida was gripping my arm, dragging me around the enormous garbage Dumpsters and their rotting, forgotten innards. The back door was propped open with a small rock. Vida wasted only one second to look at me, then ducked into the Dairy Queen's dark kitchen. The door slipped shut behind us, and I turned the lock as quietly as I could.

Vida's reflection flashed in the stainless steel refrigerator on the other side of the room, and I turned to see her crouching, moving along the silver fryers and empty shelves. I met her at the door leading out to the service counter and dining room.

Switching the safety off my gun, I ducked low, moving along the front counter and the empty spaces where the ice-cream machines should have been. No—despite the lights, the faintly sweet smell still clinging to the air, this wasn't an operating restaurant.

And the only soul alive in that dining room aside from us wasn't Cate.

He was sitting in the one white plastic booth not in the line of sight of the large glass windows, idly flipping through an old ratty paperback of a book called *The Collected Works of Friedrich Nietzsche*. He wore khakis, and a gray sweater over a white button-down shirt with the sleeves of both neatly rolled up. The dark hair was slightly longer than I remembered; it fell into his eyes every time he leaned forward to turn the page. And still, the strangest part of this picture of Clancy Gray wasn't the fact that he was here, in the desert, in a Dairy Queen under a faded sign advertising some kind of new waffle cone—it was the fact he was relaxed enough he had propped his feet up on the other side of the booth.

He knew I was there—he must have—but Clancy didn't move as I came up behind him and pressed the barrel to the back of his head.

"Can you at least wait until I finish this chapter?" he asked, his voice as pleasant as ever. I actually felt my stomach heave just that tiny bit. I felt something else, too—the all too familiar trickling at the back of my mind.

"Put down the gun, Ruby," Clancy said, shutting the cover.

A part of me wanted to laugh. He was honestly trying this? I let the invisible fingers of his mind brush up against mine for one single, solitary second before I threw down the razor-edged wall between them. This time, Clancy did move—he jerked forward, hissing in pain as he turned toward me.

"Nice try," I said, keeping both my voice and hand steady. "You have thirty seconds to tell me what the hell you're doing here and how you accessed our Chatter before I do what I should have done months ago."

"You clearly don't know how to bargain," he admonished. "There's nothing in it for me. I die if I tell you, and I die if I don't. How is that supposed to be motivating?"

Clancy gave me his best politician's son's smile, and I felt the long-simmering anger inside of me boil over. I wanted to see him afraid before I ended his life. I wanted him to be as scared and helpless as the rest of us had been that night.

Stop, I thought. *Calm down. You can't do this again. Control yourself.*

"Because there's a third, worse option," I said.

"What? Turning me over to the PSFs?"

"No," I said. "Making you forget who you are. What you can do. Ripping every memory out of your head."

The corner of Clancy's mouth twitched up. "I've missed your idle threats. I've missed *you*, really. Not that I haven't been keeping up with your activities. It's been fascinating to watch these past few months."

"Oh, I'm sure," I said, my grip on the gun tightening.

He leaned back against the seat. "I keep track of all of my good friends. Olivia, Stewart, Charles, Mike, Hayes. You, especially."

"Wow. You really know how to flatter a girl."

"You have to tell me, though—why did you and Stewart split up? I read the report on the League's servers. You both were taken in, but there was no mention of why he was let go."

I said nothing. Clancy laced his fingers together on the table, a knowing smile stretching over his handsome face.

"Look at you, making the impossible choice," he said. "That's what that Minder of yours said about you in your file, you know. That was her justification for naming you as Leader of your sad little team. *Ruby is fiercely protective and possesses the strong will and resilience needed to make impossible choices.* I liked that. Very poetic."

He slid out of the booth, lifting both hands in the classic pose of surrender. It was about as genuine as his smile.

"Ruby." His voice was soft, and his hands lowered, angling themselves like he was about to step into an embrace. "Please. I am so happy to see you again—"

"Stay right where you are," I warned, raising the gun again.

"You're not going to shoot me," Clancy continued, his voice taking on that silky quality it always did when he was trying to influence someone. It made my skin crawl, my hands slick. I hated him—I hated him for everything he had done, but, more than that, I hated him for being right.

My expression must have given me away, because he lunged toward me, his fingers straining toward my gun.

The shot was all lightning and thunder; the bullet ripped through the air, catching him across the arm, and the explosion of it followed a second later. Clancy howled in pain, dropping onto his knees. His left hand clutched the place where the bullet had clipped his right forearm.

I could hear Jude banging on the back door of the kitchen, his muffled yells, but it was Vida who came into view. She rose up from behind the counter, the gun in her hands aimed directly at his head.

"She told you to stay where you are," Vida said coldly as she came to stand behind me. "Next time it'll be your nuts."

I realized the danger two seconds too late, when Clancy lifted his head.

"Stop—!"

Vida made a noise like a small gasp, her face scrunching with the force of Clancy's intrusion. She shuddered, fighting it—I could see it in her eyes just before they went glassy under his mind's touch. Her arm shook as she lifted the gun again, this time pointing it at me.

"Put down your gun and listen to me," Clancy ordered. He had hauled himself back up so he was sitting on the edge of the booth, glancing at the line of blood darkening his formerly pristine shirt. I didn't budge, fighting every urge in my body to shoot him dead on the spot and just be done with it. Vida was shaking behind me; I felt the barrel of the gun tremble as it came to rest against my skull. Her cheeks were wet, but I didn't look long enough to see if it was sweat or tears.

It surprised me how very little fear I had in that moment outside of what was happening to Vida. If Clancy had gone out of his way to do this—to come here, to hack into our Chatter link, to degrade himself by waiting in a Dairy Queen of all places—then he had done it for a purpose. He couldn't talk to me if I were dead.

"Ah," he said softly, like I'd spoken my thoughts aloud.

Clancy shifted his eyes back to Vida. The gun pulled away, coming to rest against the side of Vida's temple.

"You wouldn't," I whispered.

"Are you really going to test me?" He only raised his brows and swept his hand out to the other side of the booth. Inviting me to sit. I stayed on my feet but switched the safety back on my gun and slid it into the back of my pants.

I can break the connection, I thought, letting my mind reach out for hers. But it was like a sheet of steel had melded around Vida's thoughts—no matter how hard I threw myself against it, I was knocked back. Shut down.

"You've improved a great deal," Clancy said. "But do you honestly think you could break my hold before I could have her fire?"

No, I thought, hoping my eyes would be enough to convey to Vida how sorry I was, that I hadn't given up yet.

"How long have you been monitoring our Chatter's link?" I asked, turning back to him.

"Take a guess, and then another, at when I actually started answering in Catherine Conner's place." He began drumming his fingers against the table, and Vida's hand steadied, finger tightening on the trigger. I clenched my fists but took a seat across from him, not bothering to hide the revulsion on my face. "She's very worried about all of you.

To her credit, she figured out I wasn't you faster than you figured out I wasn't her. And, even better, she sent you to Nashville. I'm guessing you ran into that little poser while you were there. Did you take care of him?"

It took me a moment to realize he was talking about Knox.

"It must have *killed* you," I said, "to know a lowly little *Blue* was parading around with the identity you built. Did you know he had one of your Reds?"

"I heard murmurs about it." Clancy gave a dismissive wave of his hand. "I knew the Red was damaged, otherwise I would have gone and gotten him myself. He would have been incredibly useful to have around, but I don't have the time to sit around and retrain that kid, to strip all of the mental conditioning and build it back up."

"They destroyed him—*you* destroyed him," I said. "By just suggesting the program to your father. That boy was . . . he was like an animal."

"And what was the other option for them?" Clancy asked. "Would it have been better to let my father's people murder all of them the way they did the Oranges? *Is it better to out-monster the monster or to be quietly devoured?*" He fingered the edges of his old paperback. "A good question from Nietzsche. I know my answer. Do you know yours?"

I didn't know who Nietzsche was, and I didn't particularly care, but I wasn't about to let him derail the conversation.

"Tell me why you're here," I said. "Is it about the Reds again? Or are you finally bored with screwing people over? I bet it gets pretty lonely with only your ego for company."

Clancy actually laughed. "I'll be the first to admit my East River plan was childish. It completely lacked the sophistication it needed to be successful. I got ahead of myself, testing the waters before they were warm enough. No, I'm here now because I wanted to see you."

Every joint in my body seemed to seize in the grip of cold dread.

His attack came at me like a knife in the dark; the strange, disconcerting feeling at the back of my skull was the only warning. But I was quick, too. It was just like what Instructor Johnson said—sometimes the only time an opponent has his guard down is when he's mid-swing. So I went for it; I knew what I was doing now. I blocked his assault with one of my own, driving straight into the deep reaches of his mind.

Images and sensations flittered by, bursting like white hot flashes, changing every moment I seemed to get a grip on one. I focused on the one that kept coming up—a woman's face framed by blond hair—and seized it, pulling it up to the front of his thoughts.

The scene slid down around me, shaky and discolored at first but growing stronger the longer I held it. With every breath a new detail would appear. The dark room wavered in my mind before a ring of stainless steel tables appeared. Just as quickly, those tables filled with glowing machines and intricate microscopes.

The woman was no longer a face but a whole person, and standing in the middle of it all. Though her face was calm, her hands were up in front of her in a pacifying way that made me think she was trying to calm someone down or defend herself.

The woman tripped on something behind her as she backed away, sending her stumbling to the ground. The glass scattered on the tile around her flared as it caught the light of a nearby fire. I leaned down over her, noticing the small spray of blood on the woman's white lab coat, and her lips forming the words, *Clancy, no, please Clancy—*

I wasn't sure how the two of us ended up on the ground, crawling away from each other with weak, shaking limbs. I heard Jude shouting my name from outside again, thundering his fists against the back door. I pressed a hand to my chest, like that would be enough to slow my heart's galloping pace. Clancy couldn't stop shaking his head—in disbelief, maybe, or to clear it. For a long, terrible moment, we did nothing but stare at each other.

"I'm assuming that's Stewart out there, banging to be let in like the dog he is?" he asked finally.

"It's not," I said, clenching my jaw. "He's gone. They left us here."

Clancy's eyes flicked over to Vida again, and I heard a whimper.

"I'm telling you the truth!" I said. "Do you think I'd willingly let him get tangled up in this mess? He's gone. *Gone.*"

He stared at me, his eyes tracing the lines of my face with faint amusement and more than a little annoyance.

The restaurant's side glass door shattered, blown out by some force I didn't see. Clancy's full attention whipped from me to Vida, anger flashing in his dark eyes. It didn't even occur to me to wonder who was breaking in—my body was way ahead of my brain. I dove for Vida's legs, knocking her to the ground and wrestling the gun out of her hand before Clancy could do anything.

I rolled onto my back, aiming both guns at him from the floor. Vida was cursing, raging in confusion as she came up from Clancy's fog, but my eyes were fixed on Clancy—and his were fixed on the boys who came charging in with such force that they slid across the piles of shattered glass. *No!* I thought. *No, not here!*

"He's gone," Clancy muttered, his voice high in a weak imitation of mine. "Gone."

Liam's gaze traveled from where I was on the ground to where Clancy still sat in the booth, rolling his eyes to high heaven in exasperation. Then Liam was moving, coming at him with a mask of pure, unflinching fury stretched tight over his features. I saw his decision there, read it in the way his fist was coming up for blood. So did Clancy.

"Don't—!" I shouted. Liam jerked to a stop, every muscle in his body seizing up, as Clancy sunk deep into his mind. I watched him slump to the ground with no way of catching himself.

I scrambled onto my feet as the president's son looked down on Liam, crossing his arms over his chest. The blood from his wound dripped down onto Liam's leather coat. Liam's face changed from a wince, to a grimace, to a red mess of agony, and I knew it was different than before; Clancy's cool smile as he looked down on him was so much more terrifying than it had been at East River.

"Stop it!" I said, forcing myself between them. I pushed Clancy back, one gun tucked up under his chin. "Let him go—*Clancy*!"

I'm not sure why he backed off then, releasing his grip. I let my eyes tell him everything I was willing to do to him. And Clancy, he'd come to realize, just as I had, that I wouldn't kill him to protect myself, but I would to save the people I cared about. And if he couldn't invade my mind anymore, then he had no way of controlling me outside of them. The anger darkened his eyes as he stepped back, jaw clenched.

I forced him into the booth, making sure he heard the safety switching off. My hands shook, not with fear but from the sudden spike in my pulse. The power I felt watching him shrink back, without even a word between us, was intoxicating. I would do it—if he tried to compel any of my friends again, I'd kill him, and the last thing he'd see was the smile on my face. We needed to get out of there. While we still had the flash drive and the upper hand.

I saw the thought flash behind Clancy's eyes, the way his whole body seemed to relax as he figured out the exact right thing to say to keep himself alive. "If you shoot me now, you'll never know what'll happen to your friends back in California. Not before they die, too."

TWENTY-SEVEN

IT WAS JUDE WHO FOUND HIS VOICE FIRST, WEAK as it was. I watched his hand fly up, pressing the compass against his chest. "What are you talking about?"

I drew the barrel of the gun closer to Clancy's face. "Answer him."

In that moment it became just as clear to me as it was to Clancy that he had never been in a situation like this before—one he couldn't wriggle out of, let alone control. Reluctance and frustration burned an ugly expression on his face. "I have a source in the League who says that they're going forward with their plans to blow those kids to hell. You kill me, and you have no idea about when or how it happens."

I shook my head, but inwardly, my stomach clenched. "Who's the source? You could have pulled those plans off a computer network for all we know."

The smirk on his face was enough to make me want to

pull the trigger. He drew the name out, twisting the vowels. "Our mutual acquaintance. Nico."

"No!" Jude cried. "No! Roo, he's lying—"

"Nico and I go way back," Clancy interrupted, glancing over to where Liam was struggling back onto his feet, coughing.

"Do you ever tell the truth?" I asked. "You would never have had access to Nico. He was in Leda's testing program until the League got him out, and he hasn't left HQ since."

Clancy looked at me like he couldn't quite believe I hadn't put it all together by now. "Ruby. *Think*. Where was he *before* that? Or do you all honestly not know?"

"I know I'm going to shred the skin off your face and turn it into hair ribbons," Vida snarled from the floor, still visibly struggling to get her legs under her. She sneered at him, pulling her fury around her like armor.

"That's the spirit," Chubs murmured, waiting for her to finally accept his help up—which, of course, she did not.

"What?" Jude was saying, coming up behind me. "What's he talking about?"

I felt sick—faint enough that I almost sat down again. "Nico was in Thurmond? While you were there?"

"Annnnnd she gets it. Finally." Clancy gave me a little round of applause. "We were scalpel buddies. They liked to compare our brains—to study kids at the opposite ends of the color spectrum. They even brought us in on the same day, way back when."

My mind was racing, trying to figure out how I couldn't have known that until now, if Nico had ever offered up a hint of it. But I couldn't remember if *I* had ever told him I was in Thurmond. Had Cate?

"Are you saying your old man had them experiment on you?" Liam's voice was rough as he came to stand behind me.

Clancy tapped his fingers against the table. He had no proof. His father had consented only if the researchers didn't leave scars. "After I walked out of that camp, I did wonder what happened to the others—I figured that they must have moved the experimentations to another location once they started expanding the camp to bring in kids like our friend Ruby. It took me some time to find they'd been brought to Leda Corp's Philadelphia lab."

My stomach turned over. I tried to say something, anything, but the picture of Nico—small, scared Nico—strapped down to one of the Infirmary's beds was too much for my mind to take. I couldn't process anything else.

"Even before East River," Clancy said, folding his hands on the table in front of him, "I realized the only kids who would ever truly understand what I was trying to do were those who had been there with me. I thought they could be useful. But by the time I traced them to Leda Corp, Nicolas was the only survivor whose brain hadn't been completely destroyed."

"And all you had to do was wait until the League broke him out to make him *useful*," I said, disgusted. "Were you planning on convincing him to break away and meet you at East River before that plan imploded?"

"I didn't wait for anyone. Who do you think slipped the intel to the League about what they were doing in that lab?

Who do you think suggested a way for them to get the kids out? I had to be patient, of course, and wait until they had him back in California before contacting him. And no—it was never the plan to bring him to East River, Ruby. He was more useful to me there, collecting every piece of intel about the League I asked for."

"No," Jude said, dragging his hands back through his hair. "No, he wouldn't . . ."

"You've all misjudged him. Underestimated him. No one has ever suspected him, no matter how much digging I had him do." Clancy's eyes were on the gun as he continued. "He's the one who told me that the League is moving forward with strapping the bombs to those kids. That's why he hacked the Chatter link for me. So we could meet. So I could do him this favor."

"He told you about the flash drive," I said. "That's really why you're here, right?"

His eyebrows rose, lips parting just that tiny bit. The eager glint was back in his eyes. "Flash drive? And what would be on this flash drive? Something I'd like?"

"You—" The word choked off. Clancy was looking at us all, like he was trying to pick which mind to invade. Which one would give him easiest access to the truth. I forced his attention back to me with the gun.

"He said you were looking for Stewart because he was in danger. My role was only to get you here, to tell you about what happened. But there's something else involved?"

"Talk," I said, "tell me everything and maybe—*maybe*—you live."

Clancy sighed, his reluctance deflating his excitement about the potential gold he'd stumbled across. "Two days ago several agents revolted, killing Alban and seizing control of the organization. Everyone who stood against them was either locked up or killed." He glanced at Liam, a smile tucked in the corner of his lips.

Cole. Cate. All of the instructors. Even Alban's weathered face, his yellowing smile, flashed through my mind.

Once the initial shock wore off, Liam began shaking—I put my hand on his arm to steady him. But it was Vida I should have been worried about. She threw her fist in the direction of Clancy's smug face. Chubs barely caught her around the waist, and the strength it took to wheel her back around sent them both crumpling to the floor. She was howling—actually howling—as she struggled and kicked him, trying to untangle herself from his wiry arms.

Liam had met the news about his brother with shock and Vida had been swallowed up by her own fiery anger. But Jude . . . he was crumbling into the kind of deep grief that was marked only by silent tears.

"What's their plan?" I demanded. "The specifics."

"They're moving them out of LA by six tomorrow morning." Shock sent me back a step, and the space between us flooded with a palpable terror. I felt it licking at my skin, leaving behind a sheen of icy perspiration. *So soon.* I tried to calculate the drive in my mind, find the extra hours in the day we'd need to make it there in time. "The other kids have no idea what's going on, according to Nico. It seems that your beloved Cate was only able to warn him before they took her, too."

And somehow—somehow that was the worst part, the hardest thing to hear.

"Took her where?" Vida demanded. "Tell me, you god-damn bastard, or I'll rip your—"

"Why six tomorrow?" Chubs asked, still struggling to pin Vida's arms.

"Because it's Christmas Day," Clancy said, like it was the most obvious thing in the world. "The pathetic attempt my father is launching at a peace summit? Why wouldn't they want to steal some of that spotlight? Undermine everything the Federal Coalition might be forced to agree to?"

No, no, no, no, I begged, like that could somehow change the situation. Like that tiny prayer could destroy the dread crawling through every part of me.

"Good luck getting back," Clancy said, malice dripping from every word. "Do you know how long it took me to find a plane and a source of gas to get out here? Days. Almost a full week of looking, and then another day to find a pilot. Even if you could drive the distance in six hours, you'd still have to make it through the blockades my father and the Federal Coalition set up on each side of the California border without getting picked up. That's going to go down smoothly, huh? Knowing that you could have saved those kids, if only you'd had just a few more hours."

I was so sure my hatred of Clancy had a natural end and that I'd hit it one day—a point I could reach not when I forgave him but when I accepted what had happened and moved on. But it didn't work that way; I saw it now. The feeling was like smoke, changing its scent and shape with the months and years that passed. I would never be rid of it. It would only grow, and grow, and grow until one day it finally smothered me.

I didn't give the others the chance to give their opinions. I didn't want any of them to talk me out of it, not when there were twenty other kids in California about to be sent off to their deaths and we had no time. No time. My eyes slid over to Jude, slumped against the wall, his fingers gripping the compass, his face such a perfect portrait of grief I had to fight to keep from mirroring it.

Instead, I let the anger flood through me again. I whipped the gun across Clancy's face and caught him by the collar of the shirt. *This is the only way,* I told myself as I hauled him onto his feet. His nose was bleeding, and he looked like he couldn't quite believe it.

"Let's go," I hissed. "You're buying us the hours we need."

"Is someone going to notice this is missing?"

I glanced back at Chubs as we scaled the stairs into the small charter jet. "Probably."

A part of me had wanted to laugh—really, truly laugh—when Clancy had finally admitted there was an airport in the city and that it was how he had come in to meet us. From the look of it, the airport had been converted to cater exclusively to private planes, though there was a single large cargo plane taxiing out onto one of the runways. I'd felt a small jolt of panic at the sight, thinking our ride was about to take off without us.

But, no, of course not. Why would Clancy travel like a commoner when he could manipulate and compel anyone into giving him anything?

The jet was ridiculously beautiful. At the sight of the plush carpet and enormous beige leather seats, I did sigh, just that little bit. Each side of the private jet was lined with bright oval windows and warm, cozy lights. The paneling along the back wall and sides of the aircraft was that glossy, expensive-looking faux wood. From what I could see, there was a fully stocked drink station between the two bathrooms in the back, past the eight enormous, plush leather seats.

"Who'd you steal this from?" I asked as I shoved Clancy inside, my gun digging into the small of his back.

"Does it matter?" Clancy grunted, dropping into the nearest seat. He held up his bound hands, nodding to the plastic zip tie Chubs had been oh so happy to supply. "Can you cut this off now?"

"Is he okay to fly?" I asked, jerking my thumb in the pilot's direction. Most people could barely remember their own name when I was in their heads, let alone operate delicate machinery.

Clancy folded his arms over his chest. "Every time he looks at us, he sees six adults on a business trip, all of whom have paid him handsomely for his services in arranging the flight details. You're welcome."

Liam caught my eye as he followed the others in. "When do we get to dump him?"

It was the first time he'd spoken to me since we'd left the restaurant. I hadn't even been able to look him in the eye before now, afraid of the disappointment I knew would be there. Liam would have fought me on this if I had let him, just like I would have fought for him and Chubs to stay in Colorado, far away from the upcoming fight.

But I think we both knew they were losing battles.

"Mid-flight?" Chubs asked, his voice brimming with hope. "Over a desert?"

Vida slid into the seat to the right of mine before Liam could. "We're not dumping him yet, are we, boo?"

She knew exactly what I was thinking. This was what the League had taught us to do when we located a valuable asset: you brought him in, bled him for intel, and then traded him for something better. I shook my head, trying not to smile at the alarm that flashed in his dark eyes. "No, we're not."

The look he gave me in return made my skin feel tight around my bones. But what could he do? Nothing that I couldn't do right back to him five times over.

I could tell Chubs wanted to ask exactly what we meant by that, but the pilot's voice interrupted, telling us he had finished his final checks and was ready for takeoff.

I didn't relax my grip on the gun until we were up in the air, sailing high above the jagged peaks of the Rockies. For all the grumbling he'd done about how much more likely it was for this kind of jet to crash than a normal passenger plane, Chubs passed out in his seat five minutes after the plane was in the air. I glanced over my shoulder, watching as he began to slowly drift too far to the right, only to startle awake for an instant and catch himself. The others had laid their seats out flat or curled up on them, using the blankets we'd found in one of the storage compartments.

Clancy unbuckled his seat belt, pushing onto his feet.

"Going somewhere?" I asked.

"To use the bathroom in the back," he snapped. "Why, do you need to come in and watch?"

No, but I followed him to the back regardless, shooting him a meaningful look as he slammed the door and locked it.

I leaned back against the shelves of drinks and service ware in the back. My eyes drifted from Liam to Vida to Chubs and then, finally, to Jude sitting nearby. He'd been so quiet up until then, I'd just assumed he'd fallen asleep like the others.

"Hi," I whispered.

He had been staring out the window to the unending stretch of land below, and he stayed that way, even when I touched his shoulder. Jude, who hated silence, whose past slithered up to him like a shadow along glass, did not say a single word.

I sat down on his chair's armrest, glancing across the way to make sure both Liam and Chubs were still asleep. I had known Worried Jude and Terrified Jude and Ecstatic Jude, but never this shade of him.

"Talk to me," I said.

Jude burst into tears.

"Hey!" I said, taking his shoulder. "I know it doesn't feel this way, but it'll be okay."

It took several minutes of coaxing for him to settle down and sit up. His skin went blotchy, and his nose refused to stop running. He swiped it against the arm of his jacket.

"I should have been there. With them. I could have . . . I could have helped them somehow—Cate and Alban. They needed me, and I wasn't there."

"And thank God for that," I said. "Otherwise you'd be trapped there with all of the others." *Or dead*. It was too horrible to even consider.

I put an arm around him, and whatever invisible string had been holding him up promptly snapped. He leaned into my shoulder, still crying.

"Oh my God," he muttered, "this is so not cool. It's just . . . I'm really scared Cate's dead, too. All of them. It's like Blake all over again, and I'm just as responsible. Would any of this have even happened if I hadn't been so stupid? If Rob and Jarvin hadn't caught us listening that day?"

I blew out the breath I didn't realize I had been holding and rubbed his arm. "None of this is your fault," I told him. "None of it. You aren't responsible for what other people do, good or bad. Everyone is just making the choices they think will help them get by."

He nodded, swiping at his eyes with the back of his hand. For a long while, the only sound between us was the moaning of engines and Chubs's rhythmic snores.

"But I could have made a difference," Jude whispered. "I could have fought. I—"

"No," I interrupted. "I'm sorry. I get where you're coming from, and they're all good thoughts, but I just don't think it's worth it. It's not worth it to weigh what you could have done or should have done when there's no way of changing it. And it's not worth risking your life over. Nothing is more important or valuable than your life. Got it?"

He nodded but was quiet again. A little more settled, I thought, than before.

"It's just not fair," Jude said. "None of this is fair."

"Life *isn't* fair," I said. "It's taken me a while to get that. It's always going to disappoint you in some way or another. You'll make plans, and it'll push you in another direction. You will love people, and they'll be taken away no matter how hard you fight to keep them. You'll try for something and won't get it. You don't have to find meaning in it; you don't have to try to change things. You just have to accept the things that are out of your hands and try to take care of yourself. That's your job."

He nodded. I waited until he had taken a deep breath and seemed a little more composed before I stood and ruffled his unruly hair. I was sure he'd groan or bat my hand away; instead, he caught it with his own.

"Ruby . . ." His face was drawn. Not sad exactly, just . . . tired, I thought. "If you can't change anything, then what's the point of it?"

I wrapped my fingers around his and gave his hand a steady squeeze. "I don't know. But when I figure that out, you'll be the first to know."

TWENTY-EIGHT

I NEVER THOUGHT I'D BE SO HAPPY TO SEE CALIFORNIA'S uneven, fractured mess of a freeway system as we headed toward the glowing high-rises of downtown Los Angeles. The ride was bumpy as all get-out, and the familiar stench of gasoline was working its magic through the car vents, smothering even the unnerving new-car smell clinging to the leather seats. It didn't matter much to any of us, though.

There had been a large black SUV waiting for us on the runway when we disembarked at LAX. I cut Clancy's hands free so he could take the car key offered by a man in a dress suit and black sunglasses, but he was back at the wrong end of my gun before he could think of trying to get away. After it just being the five of us for so long, I felt Jude flinch at the look the man passed over him.

"We need to talk about a plan," I said once we were in the car, miles away from the airport. It was just past seven in the evening. If things had been normal at HQ, the first of two night classes would just be starting. Then it would be two hours to mandatory lights-out and another hour before the agents had to retreat to their quarters. It would be safer and easier to try to round up the kids from a single location—the sleeping rooms on the second level—but there were cameras in every corner.

Not to mention success depended on three very big ifs. *If* we got that far. *If* we found the entrance. *If* we didn't get caught sneaking in.

"And that's only if they are running the usual schedule," I added. "Did Nico say anything about it? *Hey*—" I gripped the already torn collar of Clancy's shirt. "I'm asking you a question."

Clancy grit his teeth. "He hasn't responded to my last few messages. I'm assuming they took the Chatters away to keep rumors from spreading."

"They'd be running the usual schedule," Vida said with certainty from the driver's seat. "They wouldn't want any of the kids to know that Alban was out. That'd cause a massive amount of panic, right? They wouldn't tell any of them the actual objective."

"How are they going to rig the explosions *without* the kids figuring it out?" Liam asked. "It seems like a vest of the stuff would be a pretty big clue."

"That's the easy part," Clancy said. "You break them up into small groups of two or three, sew the explosives into the lining of a coat, and set it up with a remote detonator. All you have to do is wait to give the kids the jackets until the very end."

He said it casually, without a hint of disgust—like some part of him actually admired the plan.

"That means prep time at HQ will be minimal. If they're moving the kids out at six or so, wakeup will be at five. . . ." I shifted to look at Vida in the driver's seat. "Does it make more sense to go in at three or four?"

"Four," she said.

"Four?" Clancy repeated, like it was the stupidest thing he'd ever heard. "Sure, if you want to give yourself a better chance of being caught."

"Mandatory rolling blackouts," I explained to the others, ignoring him. "California has been trying to conserve energy that way. They happen every night in our area between three and five. The security system and cameras are the only things hooked up to the backup generator, but it'll at least be dark in the hallways as we're moving through them."

"Once we're in, I can go take care of the agents in the monitor room," Vida said. "We won't even have to shut the system off. How long do you think it'll take to get in and out through this entrance of yours?"

"I don't know; I've never walked it. I've only seen them bring people in and out."

"Where does it lead?" Jude asked. "And how come I don't know about it?"

I looked down at my hands, trying to keep my voice light. "It's where they brought traitors and key assets for questioning. And then . . . took them out."

"Holy shit, they did have you torture people," Vida said,

looking both intrigued and impressed. So did Clancy. "Where is it?"

"I didn't torture them," I protested weakly, "just . . . questioned them. Aggressively."

Liam kept his gaze focused on something outside of his window, but I felt him tense to the point of snapping beside me.

"It's the locked door on the third level, isn't it?" Jude asked. "The one just past the computer room?"

"Alban told me once it leads out to an entrance near the Seventh Street Bridge over the Los Angeles River," I said. "If they're holding any of the agents or hiding the evidence of what they've done, it'll be in that room."

"Okay, well, bypassing the fact that the League has a secret torture dungeon," Liam said, "are we sure they won't have blocked the path in and out?"

"Why do you all keep saying 'we'?" Clancy asked. "I hope you don't think I'm coming down in that shithole with you."

"Too bad for you, you're the only one who doesn't get a choice about it," I said. "You want to see what's happening at the League? You want to chat with your friend Nico again? You got it. Front-row seat."

He must have suspected it would come to this all along, but he didn't look afraid. Maybe after everything, he still wasn't convinced that I was willing to serve him up on a platter to the League to let them do with him what they would. Maybe he already knew that I would trade him to Jarvin and the others if it meant getting the other kids away. If there was so much as a crack in this plan, he'd find a way to slip through it.

Which meant I would have to watch him that much closer, staying three steps ahead of him instead of just one.

"What does happen if we can't get them out undetected?" Chubs asked.

"Then they're going to have to do what they were trained to," I said, "and fight back."

The Los Angeles River was a forty-eight-mile stretch of concrete that had always served as more of a punch line than an actual river. At one point in its long life, it probably had been a real waterway—but humanity had swept in and constrained its flow to a single concrete channel that wound its way around the outskirts of the city, lined on either side by railroad tracks.

Cate had pointed it out once when we'd left on an Op, telling me that they used to film car chases down there for movies that I'd never heard of. Now, though, if you were to walk its length, which was usually as parched as the ground had been in Pueblo, you'd be hard-pressed to find anything other than the electric colors of graffiti tags and wandering homeless folks trying to find a place to settle for the night. If it did happen to rain, which was rare in Southern California, all sorts of things washed out of the storm drains and into the open river: shopping carts, trash bags, deflated basketballs, stuffed animals, the occasional dead body. . . .

"I'm not seeing anything," Chubs muttered, holding the flashlight higher so I could scan the bridge's support pillars again. "Are you sure—"

“Here!” Vida called over to us from across the channel. Liam waved his flashlight once, so we’d see them. The streetlights were off, and without the light pollution that usually came from the city, we were both struggling to see anything beyond a few feet in front of us and to not be spotted by anyone else.

I took Liam’s arm and guided him down the slope of the embankment, then up again to the other side, to the place where the arch of the bridge’s underbelly met the ground. I kept my flashlight aimed at Clancy’s back, making sure he walked the entire way in front of me.

Jude, I thought, counting them off with my eyes, *Liam, Vida, Chubs.*

“I think this is it.” Vida stepped back, keeping her own flashlight aimed at the huge, swirling patterns of graffiti. There was a blue star at the center of it, but it was the way the paint looked that gave the hidden door away—it was thicker here, to the point that it looked sticky to the touch. I felt for a disguised handle before throwing my shoulder against it. The panel of cement swung inward, scraping the loose rubble on the other side. Vida, Liam, and I leaned in, shining our flashlights down the metal staircase.

I reached over and hauled Clancy to the front. “You first.”

If it were possible, this tunnel was somehow even cruder than the tunnel we usually took in and out of HQ. It was also about ten times longer and filthier.

Clancy stumbled in front of me, barely catching himself with a quiet curse. The walls, which had started out wide enough for us to walk three across, narrowed until we were forced into a single-file line. Liam was at my back, the damp, rancid air wheezing in and out of his lungs in a way that was starting to worry me.

I slowed a step, letting him catch up and nudge me forward again. "I'm okay," he promised. "Keep going."

In the distant dark, I could hear the rush of some kind of water, though the sludge we were shuffling through had clearly been there long enough to start to rot and solidify.

How many prisoners had they brought in this way, I wondered, and how many bodies had they hauled out? I tried not to shudder or turn my light down to see if the water was as red as my mind had made it out to be. I tried to stop myself from picturing the way Jarvin and the others would have dragged Alban out—Cate out, Cole out, their lifeless eyes open, gazing at the string of small flickering lights hanging overhead.

"After this, we're all bathing in bleach," Chubs informed us. "And burning these clothes. I keep trying to figure out why it smells so much like sulfur, but I think I've decided to leave that one alone for now."

"That's probably for the best," Clancy said. His face was bone white as he turned in to my flashlight's beam, which made his already dark brows and eyes look like they'd been stained with soot. "How many of these tunnels did the League make?"

"A few," I said. "Why? Planning your escape already?"

He snorted.

"Time?" I called back.

"Three fifty-three," Vida answered. "Can you see the end?"

No. I felt the first cold drip of panic down my spine. No, I couldn't. We'd been walking for close to a half hour, and it felt like we hadn't covered any ground at all. It was the same cement walls, the same sloshing of our footsteps—every once in a while, one of our flashlight beams would catch a rat as it scampered against the wall or darted into some black crack in the ground. The tunnel seemed to draw us into its darkness like a deep breath. The walls shrank around our heads and shoulders again, forcing me to bend at the waist.

How much longer could it be? Another half hour? An hour? Were we really going to have less than that to find the kids and get them back out again?

"We're almost there," Liam whispered, taking my arm and aiming the flashlight toward the far end of the tunnel, where the path began to slope upward, out of the sludge.

Where there was a large metal door.

"Is that it?"

I nodded, relief and adrenaline pulsing through me as I whirled back toward the others. "Okay," I called softly. "This is it. Vida, start the clock. Fifteen minutes in and out. Everyone remember what you're doing?"

Jude squeezed past us to get to the electronic lock that flashed on as he approached.

I scanned the nearby ceiling and walls, looking for any sort of camera, only half surprised when I didn't find one.

Interesting. Alban had either been dedicated to keeping the interrogation block a protected, classified secret from anyone other than senior staff and advisers, or he had been worried about the thought of someone getting visual evidence of the people he was trafficking in and out. Both, probably.

Good. One less thing to worry about.

I had just clicked the flashlight off when I felt a warm hand close around my arm. I turned right into Liam's waiting arms.

The kiss was over before it ever really started. A bruising, single touch filled with enough urgency, enough frustration and *wanting* to send my blood rushing. I was still trying to catch my breath when he pulled back, his hands on my face, his lips close enough to mine for me to feel him pant, too.

Then he was stepping back, away, letting distance flood in between us again. His voice was low, rough. "Give 'em hell, darlin'."

"And for the love of *God*, bitch, don't get stabbed this time!" Vida added.

I would have smiled if I hadn't heard Clancy's faint laughter at my right. "Any sign of trouble from you is the only excuse I need to use this," I warned him, pressing the gun to the curve of his skull. "The only excuse I need to leave your body down here to be eaten by the rats."

"Got it," Clancy said in his low, velvety tones. "And if I'm good, do I get a kiss, too?"

I shoved Clancy forward, keeping a grip on the collar of his shirt.

"Okay, I'm ready," Jude said as he put his hand against the lock pad to fry it. "Lead on, Leader."

The air down in the interrogation block was no fresher or cleaner than the tunnel had been. The familiar stench of human vomit and filth twisted my gut as I stepped through the doorway and down the short flight of stairs. I had my flashlight in one hand and the gun in my other, both aimed at the door on the other end of the hallway of metal doors with their observation windows. I swept the beam of pale light around the space, and, finding it clear, signaled for the others to come through.

"Right behind you," Vida called, her heavy footsteps matching my pace. Somewhere behind us in the dark, the others were working their way down the doors, looking for prisoners—for Cole.

At the door, I crouched, releasing my grip on Clancy's shirt and motioning for Jude to get behind me. Whether I actually drew it up from deep in my memory or it found it naturally, my training with the League had me propping the door open, scanning the hall with my gun in front of me before I so much as thought about stepping through.

My pulse pounded in my ears, jumping, jumping, jumping with my nerves as I stepped out into the hallway and pulled Jude after me.

Vida split with us as we came around the hallway's curve and took the first set of stairs. *One level*, I thought. *Fifth door on the right. She has the hard job here, not you. You have one level to go up; she has two to get to the surveillance room. One level, fifth door on the right.*

There was a loud clatter to my left. I skidded to a stop, Jude crashing into my back. My heart was in my throat when I turned back to where Clancy stood a short distance ahead, fading into the dim light. I jogged to catch up to him, waving him forward.

We kept to the curve, heading around to the other staircase. Without the gentle hum of static in the computer room, it felt like the first I'd ever stepped foot in this place. Which was why, I guess, it was appropriate that the first unfriendly face we saw after we climbed the stairs and opened the door to the next level was one I didn't recognize at all.

There were dozens of agents at the League's headquarters in Georgia, even more at the one in Kansas. I should have known Jarvin and the others would bring in every sympathetic soul they could to help take Alban out.

I could smell the alcohol on him, the spice of whatever he had eaten for dinner that night. He must have been headed up to the agent quarters on the first level, but the sight of us was clearly enough to make him forget as much. His shaggy blond hair fell into his eyes as he jumped at our sudden appearance. The lazy, stupid smile on his face dropped to a scowl.

"What the hell are you doing out of bed?" he demanded, reaching for me. I was faster, whipping the butt of the gun across his face and yanking him back into the stairwell. Jude caught the door before it slammed shut, peeking out through a crack to watch the hall.

Slipping into a drunk mind was like sliding a spoon through pudding. The only challenge was trying to find what I was looking for in the tangle of thoughts, all of which seemed to wash into one another.

"Roo!" Jude whispered. "Let's go!"

If the man's memory was right, there were other agents on this floor, most of them in the infirmary, but one, for sure, stationed between the doors of the two sleeping rooms.

I dragged the agent off to the side of the stairs, narrowly avoiding where Clancy stood silently waiting. I tucked the man into a corner and relieved him of the knife he was carrying in his back pocket.

"Stay behind me," I told Jude, my eyes on the way Clancy seemed to be fading in and out of the shadows. "The whole time."

The power was still out, and the hallway was little more than a dark curtain we were trying to fight our way through. They used glow-in-the-dark tape along the edges of the floor and around the different door handles and lock pads, but the combined light was less than a fraction of what it would have been if I could have turned my flashlight on.

I counted the door handles as we moved. *One, two, three . . .*

This is actually going to work.

. . . four, five.

Please let this work.

The agent posted outside of the sleeping rooms—Agent Clarkson—wasn't a stranger. She was tall, lanky, with dark features and a fondness for knife fighting that had gone uncontested for years. She'd been fighting so hard to be made a senior agent, her confidence had warped into desperation, and then, from there, a frustration that she could only ever take out on the ones below her: us. She was the opposite of Cate in so many ways that hadn't mattered before now.

"Andrea," I called softly. "Andrea?"

"Chelle?" she said. "It's already time? I thought wake-up was at five?"

There was a flutter of movement about seven feet ahead, on my left. I couldn't meet her eyes to trap her that way, but the moment I caught the whiff of detergent and the subtle shift of warm breath that stirred the air in front of me, I lashed an arm out, catching her across the chest.

Her gun clattered loudly against the floor, but her body was soft and silent as I pushed the image of her sitting and sinking into a deep sleep. She slumped against me, and I eased her down onto the floor.

Jude bolted past me, heading for the boys' door. I took the handle of the girls' door, the same I'd opened for months without a second thought, and stepped inside, pulling the door shut silently behind Clancy. I flicked on my flashlight.

"Up—" I started to say, shining it into the nearest bunk.

The room wasn't large. It only needed to house twelve girls, though there'd always been an extra bunk bed crowding the right wall, on the off chance the League ever picked up another kid. The bunk Vida and I shared, in the back right corner, had been neatly made, the sheets stretched tightly over the mattress with Vida's military-like precision. All of them were— Almost like . . .

Like there was no one left to sleep here.

Too late.

"Don't say it," I warned Clancy. "Not one damn word."

He stared ahead at the empty bunks, a cold expression on his face, but he stayed silent.

My knees buckled slightly, mirroring the feeling of my heart as it dropped like a stone through my chest. *Too late*.

Those girls, all of them—they were—they were—

I pressed the heels of my palms against my forehead. Slamming them there, over and over, as a silent scream rippled up my throat. *Oh my God. All of them.*

Too late.

I ripped the door back open, letting Clancy slip out ahead of me as we moved to the boys' room. Jude wouldn't know—wouldn't think to be silent— He'd wake up the entire base—

Where the girls' room had been cold and dark, this one was filled with the light of flashlight lanterns and the natural body heat of twenty kids, all awake, fully dressed, and crammed together on the bunk beds.

My eyes flew around each of their faces before they settled on the small pile of weapons gathered at Jude's and Nico's feet in the center of the room.

"No, no, *no*!" Nico cried. "What are you *doing* here?"

"I told you: we came for you," Jude said. "What the heck is going on?"

"I thought you knew about their plans," I said, "about the bombs and camps? You didn't think we'd come to get you out after *your friend* told us what happened here?"

Clancy only had that same unreadable expression on his face as he surveyed the room.

"Of course I knew!" Nico let out a low moan. "We've been communicating on the Chatters this whole time. You were supposed to stay away! I told him to tell you not to come back until it was safe! Until *tomorrow*!"

"What the hell?" I said, whirling toward Clancy. "What game are you playing?"

The faces around me looked just as confused as I felt. "Who are you talking to?" Jude asked, glancing around.

"Him!" I snapped, exasperated. I tried to grab Clancy before he slipped back out the door. "Who else?"

"Roo . . ." Jude began, his eyes wide, "there's no one there."

"Clancy's—"

"Clancy?" Nico said. "He's here? He came?"

"He's right *here*," I said, grabbing for his arm. My fingers passed right through it, drifting through cold air. The sight of him wavered, flickered.

Faded into nothing.

He's . . . My mind was gripped with panic. I couldn't finish the thought.

"I didn't see him get away," Jude said. "Did Vida take him to disable the cameras . . . ? Roo?"

"The cameras are already down! We hacked into the program hours ago!" Nico said.

"We have to stay here," one of the other kids added. "They told us to get into one room and stay until it was all over. You're too early."

"Until what's over?" Jude was asking. I barely heard him over the roar of blood in my ears. "What's happening at six?"

Nico let his head fall back for a second, taking a deep, frustrated breath.

"That's when Cate and the others are coming to get us."

TWENTY-NINE

IT WAS A TRICK.

"Okay . . ." I said, trying to catch one of the thoughts flying through my head long enough to put it into words. "Okay . . . we just . . ."

He was there. In the tunnel, he was there. He came in with us. If he was going to get away, why didn't he do it before? Clancy could influence more than one person. He could have tricked all of us by never getting off the plane in the first place. But he had. I had dragged him down the steps myself, felt his pulse jump when I pushed him toward the ladder down into the tunnel. Why not escape then? It had been just as dark outside. . . .

"What should we do?" Jude was asking.

Because he needed me to get him in here. Before Cate and the others came back.

"You have to stay here where it's safe," Nico rambled. "If you go back out there—"

I let him play me again.

"Ruby—*Roo!*" Jude grabbed my shoulder, turning me back toward him, forcing me to break my gaze with a crack on the far wall. His hair and eyes were both wild, his freckles overlapping points on a map I'd only recently learned to read. He was anxious, but he wasn't afraid. This was a good Jude to have.

"Go down and get Chubs and Liam and bring them up here," I said, "but come back if you think, even for a *second*, that you might get caught. Understand?"

He nodded eagerly.

"Vida will be here in a few minutes," I told the others. And probably in a holy terror of a mood when she realized I'd sent her up to disable the cameras for no reason. "Once the four of them are back, move the bunks and barricade the doors. No one else comes in."

"What about you?" Nico asked.

"I have to go take care of *your friend*," I said, hoping my voice was enough to convey how deep Nico's betrayal had buried us in this mess.

"I should go with you. . . ." Nico whispered. "He's here? Really?"

I'd seen that look a hundred times, a thousand, at East River—the wide-eyed adoration of someone who either had no idea there were scales under Clancy's skin or someone unhinged enough to just not care. I thought of Olivia and the way she had all but clawed at her own throat when she said his name. I'd been nursing my anger toward Nico from the moment Clancy told us he'd been slipping him intel all this time, letting it grow into thoughts like, *I'll never forgive him*. But looking at him now, I forgot it in an instant. Heartache just tore it away, and what was left was the true realization of how damaged the kid in front of me was. His paranoia, his nervous fidgeting, his silent moods. Of course Clancy was his hero. He had saved him from a hell too terrible for nightmares.

"Did he ask you any questions about HQ recently?" I asked. "About particular files or people . . . ?"

By the way Nico's mouth seemed to twist, it was looking more and more likely that his loyalty to Clancy was going to win out over his alarm that Clancy had flat-out lied and brought us here despite the warning he'd given him.

"He gave me a list of words and people to look for," Nico said. "There were a lot of them. . . . One of them pinged in the system a few weeks ago. An agent called Professor."

I tensed. "Professor? You're sure?"

"The agent was doing some kind of research at our Georgia base—it just suddenly popped up on the classified server a few weeks ago. I think he knew who it was because he wanted the base's location."

What had the adviser said when he came into Alban's office all of those weeks back? Something about a situation in Georgia with Professor—and a project called Snowfall.

"What about stuff here at HQ?"

"He asked about the different tunnels and the blackouts. . . ." Nico said slowly.

"What else?" I pressed. I was aware of the ticking clock, even if he wasn't. "What about the blackouts?"

"He wanted to know if they shut off things like the lock pads or retinal locks—"

I turned on my heel, throwing Jude off me as I opened the door and bolted out into the hallway. Spots flashed in front of my eyes as they struggled to adjust again. I counted off the door handles as I ran. I kept to the outside curve, one eye always on the dark infirmary windows to my right. They'd drawn all the curtains. Not even the machine lights were bleeding through.

In fact, the only light on the entire second level seemed to be the flashlight Clancy clenched between his teeth as he riffled through the filing cabinets inside of Alban's office.

All of the lock pads and retinal locks *were* on the backup power generator, and normally they would have been enough to keep even Clancy out, had they actually still been attached to the door. Someone had taken something—a crowbar, an ax, a small explosive—and blown them off that way.

I slid forward, nudging the door open farther as I slid my gun out of the waistband of my jeans.

Clancy made a small, triumphant noise as he ripped a bulging red folder free from where it had been trapped among a hundred others. He wasted no time flipping through the pages as he turned back around to Alban's desk. Someone had flipped it onto its side as he or she ransacked the place. He used one of its wide, flat legs to lay the folder out and free up his hand to hold the flashlight. The look on his face was so painfully eager I felt a twinge of apprehension.

"Found what you were looking for?"

Clancy's head shot up at the same moment his hand slid the folder back, off the desk, into a metal trash can. For a moment, anger fought with exasperation on his face, but Clancy settled on a devastating smile as he stared down the barrel of the gun.

"I did, but . . . don't you have more important things to worry about?" His voice had taken on the quality of smoke. "Other people more important than me?"

He inclined his head toward the other end of Alban's office, and even before I turned, the metallic scent of warm, sticky blood was everywhere. Just past my initial line of sight, I saw the two of them on the floor. Chubs had crumpled, curling in on himself the way a leaf would just before it fell from the tree in autumn. Liam was slumped over him, his face the color of ice. And he was looking at me, watching with unblinking eyes that had faded from a pale blue to a dull gray. His arm had been thrown out over Chubs, like he had tried to shield him, and now those same hands that had held my face so gently between them . . . they were in the pool of dark liquid gliding along the concrete floor.

The gun slipped out of my hand.

Clancy skirted around Alban's desk, watching me with that same faint smile. He dropped what looked like a lighter into the trash can.

Not real. I forced the words through my mind. *Not them.* I forced myself to look again. Really look, no matter how horrifying the image was. Chubs's glasses were gold instead of silver. Liam's hair was longer than it was now—Clancy clearly hadn't made as close of a study of the way his hair curled at the ends as I had.

It was a painfully close, near-flawless imitation. But it wasn't them.

I let Clancy come up beside me and allowed him three seconds of thinking he'd be able to slip by me, distracted as I was by my own grief. He was murmuring something in low, husky tones. He was close enough now for me to feel his warm breath on my cheek—which meant he was also close enough for me to punch him in the throat.

I threw my mind at him in the same blow, drawing it down like a knife and shredding the image of Chubs and Liam he'd pushed there. Clancy stumbled out into the hallway, clutching his head, gasping for breath. The image of the woman in the white lab coat filtered through our connection again, but I forced myself to push it away for now. There was a line of smoke rising from the trash can; I tipped it over, scattering the burning pages onto the ground, stamping out the flames under my boot. If he wanted these pages gone, I wanted to see them.

"Dammit." He was panting when I met him again in the hallway, heaving in a deep breath, falling to his knees. There was some thin, fraying line of connection between our minds. I seized it before it could snap completely, flooding his brain with the illusion of heat. I couldn't see him in the dark, but I could hear him frantically slapping at his arms and legs—at the limbs his mind was telling him were burning down to the bone.

Then, his hands slowed to a stop.

"You . . ." Clancy began, "you really want to play this game?"

There was a kiss of cold metal against the back of my neck—so suddenly that I had already convinced myself it was another one of his mind games. But when you lose a sense like sight, it's true what they say: the rest of them are sharpened to ruthless efficiency. I felt the warm breath, heard the squeak of additional boots, smelled his sweat. Agents—they'd found us.

Clancy twisted away to run; I didn't see it happen, only heard the sickening crack as something hard connected with his head and sent him crumpling to the ground.

And there was Jarvin's voice in the dark saying, "I knew you'd be back." There were his hands, as one closed over the back of my neck and roughly shoved me down to my knees. The barrel slid down to the sweet spot where my skull met my spine. "Rob said all we'd have to do is wait."

In their fatigues, he and the other League agent behind him were a shade lighter than the air around them.

The safety switched off.

"You don't want to do this," I warned, feeling the invisible hands inside of my mind unfurl. I felt anxious but not afraid. Controlled calm.

"No," Jarvin agreed. "I'd rather do this."

There was a faint *click*—the only warning before the White Noise flooded the hallway and drowned me alive.

It was possible to forget that kind of agony after all.

There was a time in my life, a few months into my stay at Thurmond, that they had turned the White Noise on nearly every day. Back when there were Reds to control and Oranges to punish, a single wrong look would have a PSF radioing in to the Control Tower. It was a given part of my life; maybe I had just grown so used to it, the actual impact dulled over time.

But it had been months, and the onslaught of pain twisted my stomach to the point of sickness. I collapsed onto the floor, close enough to Clancy that I could see the cut across his forehead seeping blood. There were thoughts in my head; there was a voice that said, *You can take Jarvin; you can take him; you can ruin him* . . . but even that was silenced as the White Noise rose and fell over us like a wave, crushing down on my chest.

And it was amazing—everything we could do, the kind of power we could have over others—it all meant nothing. It all came to nothing.

At Thurmond, we would have heard two warning blares, and a heartbeat later, the noise would explode from the camp's loudspeakers. It wasn't something that could be easily described—it was shrieking static, cranked up, sharpened to drill through the thickest part of your skull. It passed through us like an electrical current, making our muscles jump and twitch and sing with pain until the only thing left to do was to try to drive your head into the ground to escape it. If I were lucky, I wouldn't pass out.

I wasn't so lucky. I felt myself fade, drift back into the darkness of the hallway. I couldn't move my arms out from where they were pinned under my chest. My legs had turned to air. Finally, seeing that I couldn't so much as lift my head,

Jarvin switched it off. I drifted from one moment to the next, my ears ringing. The blackness of the hall pulled me in, pushing my head under its murky surface.

When I came to again, someone had a grip on my arm. I could hear Jarvin talking to the others around him, only because he was shouting now. "Get the damn lights on! I don't care what you have to do—switch them on, dammit! Something's going on. Can someone just give me a *damn light*?"

It was a warm Southern voice that answered him. "Sure, brother. I got you covered."

There was a snap, just one, and the tiniest flame appeared in the dark, illuminating Cole Stewart's furious face.

I thought, at first, he'd struck a match, but the fire at his fingertips bloomed, swallowing his hand, devouring the arm he sent flying toward Jarvin's face. There was screaming, so much screaming, as the fires around us grew, catching the soldiers behind him and engulfing them in a wave of heat that sent them running down the hall, stumbling over one another until they finally collapsed. The smell of burned skin made my stomach convulse. I couldn't escape it.

"Holy shit, you're—!" one of the agents began to say.

One of us, my mind finished, shutting down at the sight of the fire between Cole's fingers again, the way he threw a ball of it at the agent who had spoken. How he stoked it, letting it rip over the screaming man's body until I could only see the dark silhouette trapped in the flames dancing over his skin.

Red.

No—no, he was—Cole was too old, he wasn't—

"Hey—*hey*!" The fire was gone now, but Cole's hands were still hot to the touch as he tried to haul me to my feet. My legs still weren't there. He tried lightly slapping my face. "Shit . . . kid, come on. You can do this; I know you can."

"You . . ." I tried to say. "You just . . ."

He let out the breath he'd been holding, relieved. Cole lifted me over his shoulder, smacking the back of my thighs in irritation. "Dammit, Gem, making me worry like that. I heard the Calm Control from down the hall, but I had to wait until he turned it off. I couldn't get close. I'm sorry; I'm so sorry."

He kicked the door open to Alban's office, dropping me to the ground behind the desk, rearranging my limbs so I was at least sitting up, and un-holstered one of his handguns to press into my limp fingers.

Then, he gripped my face between his palms. "You can't tell, you hear me? No one else can know, not even Liam, especially not Lee—okay? Nod your head."

Jesus—Liam didn't know? No one else knew about this?

"You, me, Cate, and Alban," Cole said, as if reading my thoughts. "That's it. And we're now a party of three. You tell, and it's over for me."

I nodded.

". . . other one . . ." I said weakly, tilting my head toward the hall.

Cole grunted. "I don't do the damsel-in-distress thing with dudes."

I shot him what I hoped was a glare and not a cross-eyed look. He sighed and stood, squaring his shoulders in the way

Liam always did when he was set on something. Cole disappeared for a second, ducking back out to grab Clancy. I doubted he even looked at Clancy's face before he dumped him next to me.

"The Greens sent us the message you were here, so we decided to start the party early," he explained. "Couldn't wait one more day to see this handsome mug, could you?"

I coughed, trying to clear whatever was lodged in my throat.

"If you know what's good for you, you'll stay in here," he snapped. "Leave this room before we give the all-clear, and I'll skin your ass!"

When he turned for the door, it was like his confidence and control clicked back into place. His movements were smooth, assured.

I don't know how much time passed before the sound of the firefight reached us—five minutes, ten, maybe even fifteen. Feeling was returning to my limbs in hot rushes of pins and needles, but I preferred the pain to limp uselessness. When I could, I pushed myself onto my knees and began to shove Alban's old desk against the door. I knew it wouldn't provide much cover or pose much of a challenge to anyone hell-bent on getting in, but it felt better than doing nothing. And, if I were being honest, it was a visual block for me, too. A reminder that I needed to wait and let Cole and the others clean out Jarvin's infestation before I went to find the others.

They're all right; they're all right; you're all right . . . I crawled back over to the filing cabinets, drawing my legs up to my chest and wrapping my arms around them, trying to cage in the feelings that felt too big to keep inside.

They are okay.

Clancy shifted beside me, a stray lock of dark hair falling into his eyes. As much time as we had spent together at East River, I'd never seen him sleep before—he would never, I realized, ever let someone else be around him while he was so vulnerable.

My eyes drifted over to the trash can and the papers I'd spilled out of it. I crawled over to them on my hands and knees, scooping up the flashlight Clancy had dropped. There was so much shouting happening outside of that dark room that I couldn't understand what any one voice was saying.

I took a deep breath as the shooting eased off and the doors to the staircase slammed open and shut repeatedly. *They are okay; you are okay.*

I aimed the flashlight away from the door, down at the scorched pages I'd gathered into my lap. A quarter of the pages or so were unreadable—sizeable holes had burned through the photographs and pages. Aside from the smears of soot and smoke stains from the top sheets, the bottom of the stack was in much better shape. Most were charts and graphs, all in that same strange scientific language that would have tripped up even Chubs. These were medicines—medical terms. They had the same sort of complicated names as the list of medicines Chubs had given me in Nashville. Every now and then my eyes would catch a few stray words of plain English.

Subject A is free of symptoms following the procedure and routine . . .
Showing signs of passive behavior . . .
Conclusive results are pending . . .

But at the top of them all, printed in bold black text, were two words I did recognize: **Project Snowfall.**

I only stopped flipping through the pages when I reached the photographs. The one that showed the woman's face.

It was one of the unexpected drawbacks to living almost half of your life locked away in a camp with no access to any kind of media. You got the feeling that every face you encountered on TV or in the papers was somehow familiar, but the name would slide away from you before you could grasp it. I felt it now, staring at the familiar blond woman.

The shot itself was strange—she was glancing over her shoulder but not into the camera itself. There was an unmarked brick building behind her that seemed oddly run down in comparison to the neat, classic navy dress suit she was wearing. The look on her face wasn't afraid so much as nervous, and I wondered, for a second, if she rightfully thought someone was tailing her. The next photo was smaller, torn in a way that made me think Alban had started to rip it up, only to change his mind. In this one, she sat between the former leader of the League and a much younger President Gray.

The connection stole my breath.

Clancy, no, please, Clancy—

"Holy shit," I whispered. The woman I'd seen in his mind . . . this was . . .

The First Lady of the United States.

I reached for the other scattered pages, gathering them back up in a pile. Out of their proper order, the documents and reports didn't make much sense, but there were diagrams of brains with tiny, neat *X*s marked over them.

I skimmed through the newspaper articles describing charity work Lillian Gray had done across the country; someone had highlighted different key phrases about her family ("a sister in Westchester, New York," "parents retired to their farm in Virginia," "a brother, recently deceased") and her different school degrees, including the PhD she'd earned in neurology from Harvard. She'd also given a "touching" eulogy at the vice president's funeral, "flanked by the smoking wreckage of the Capitol," and had refused to comment on the president's reluctance to immediately replace him.

The last article I found was focused on her disappearance from public life shortly after the attack on Washington, DC. In it, the president was quoted as saying, "My wife's protection and security is my number one concern," with no other details given.

And that was her legend. Not the dozens of award ceremonies she'd attended, not her groundbreaking research in systems neuroscience, or any of the parties she'd hosted on her husband's behalf. Not her treasured only son. According to the *Time* article Alban had slipped into the folder, there were rumors that she'd been killed or abducted by a hostile country shortly after the outbreak of IAAN. It became especially alarming when Clancy went out on the road alone on his father's behalf to praise the camp rehabilitation program, showing himself to be its first successful subject.

It had been nearly ten years, and she had yet to show her face publicly.

But here she was in this folder, her face, her research . . . her handwritten notes. I clenched my hands into fists and released them several times, trying to force them to stop shaking.

There were three notes mixed into the mess of documents, each only a few lines long. There were no envelopes, but the sheets were still sticky with whatever they had been sealed with. Someone must have passed this to him by hand, then, rather than risk sending it digitally. Alban's clear cursive had filled in the dates at the top, likely for his own recordkeeping. The first, from five years before, read:

No matter what's become of us, I need to get out of his reach if I'm going to save him. If you help me disappear, I'll help you in return. Please, John.

The next, two years later:

Enclosed are the most recent findings of our work; I'm feeling incredibly optimistic this will all be over soon. Tell me you've found him.

And the final, from only two months before:

I'm not going to sit around waiting for your approval—that was never our deal. I'm leaking the location onto the server tonight. If he doesn't come looking for me, then I'll find him myself.

Clancy was still out cold, his head lolled to the side. I watched the steady rise and fall of his chest, something sharp twisting low in my gut.

"You sad son of a bitch," I whispered.

This was why he'd come here. This was the task he couldn't entrust to anyone other than himself.

I combed through the pages again, trying to decipher exactly what she'd been working toward. A part of me had suspected it had something to do with us when I saw the diagrams, but why would she be secretly running her own experiments about the cause of IAAN at the same time Leda Corp was? There was that mention she made in her first note of needing to get out of "his reach"—was it possible she thought her husband would tamper with the results of what Leda Corp would find and that the misinformation would jeopardize Clancy's life?

But then . . . why would he want to destroy this? I flipped back to the pages of charts and graphs, and there, at the bottom of each page, were the initials L.G. I combed through the pages again, making sure I was looking at each and every one. Why had he wanted to destroy this? To protect his mother's whereabouts? To destroy proof that she was somehow providing information to Alban about her research?

None of this made sense to me. Her final note said she was leaking "the location"—her location?—onto a server. That was in line with Nico's earlier explanation that the word

Professor, one that Clancy had asked him to watch for, came up on the server. But she only leaked it when she was ready. Only after Project Snowfall was complete.

She didn't want him to know what she was working on, I realized. But why go find him? Why let him find her, when it was obvious that he was the one she truly needed to be protected from?

THIRTY

THE LIGHTS AND MACHINES AROUND ALBAN'S OFFICE came back on in an explosion of noise and static, and I was up and off the ground before the radio scanner clicked on, blasting the room with a rousing choral rendition of "O Come, All Ye Faithful." I drew my hand up in a weak attempt to block the glare as I stumbled toward the corner of the office. My eyes were watering and I couldn't see any of the radio dials, so I settled for slapping and turning them all until the sound finally dropped to a bearable level. After the White Noise, even a faint scratch against the door would have sounded like thunder. For a long, terrible minute, I forced myself to stay still and readjust to the world of light—just as long as it took Clancy to let out a low moan and start to shake his head.

And for me to realize my window for being able to control him was slamming shut.

The fighting outside had faded into a lone spray of bullets firing one floor up. It was a risk to assume that they'd already cleared this level of rogue agents, but reason had overridden my fear. Most of the agents would have been on the first level, in their quarters, asleep when Cole and the others had entered the building, with a few, like Jarvin, on patrol.

I would be fast. If the hallway was clear, I could go down to find the others after taking care of this. Make sure Liam and Chubs were tucked away with Jude and Vida in the safety of the barricaded sleeping room. I just couldn't leave him in here, not with the locks already busted.

I circled my arms around Clancy's chest from behind, trying to get a good grip on him and tearing off one of his coat's gold buttons in the process.

"You are . . ." I gasped, feeling the stitches in my back pull, "officially the biggest pain in my ass. . . ."

I had to drop him to shove the desk out of the way again. I took one more step out, taking a deep breath to steady myself against the sight of Jarvin's and the other agents' bodies—but the hallway was empty. As I dragged him out into it, I had a thought, a brief one, of pulling him into the infirmary, but I could see figures moving in there behind the curtains and I wasn't sure I was willing to take the bet it was someone from Cole's team. There were any number of doors along the hall, most of them leading into rooms I had never been allowed to see. But there was only one closet that was open, and the rack of guns in there had been picked clean—leaving enough room for a human body to be shoved in.

I had just angled Clancy into the tight space when I heard my name shouted for the whole damn base to hear.

I whipped around, searching for the source. Cate was suddenly there, rushing out of the infirmary, pulling the rifle strap off her shoulder. She ripped the black ski mask off her head and let it fall behind her. I was in her arms, in her warmth, before I had the sense to brace myself for the impact. A relief I didn't expect passed down through me as I leaned into her.

"What are you doing?" she asked.

And I was honestly still so shocked at her appearance, I actually told her the truth. "Locking Clancy Gray in a closet."

She pulled back sharply, looking down at the prone form at our feet. And Cate, for the first time in her life, didn't ask me if I wanted to talk about how I was feeling. I didn't need to explain why we couldn't leave him in the infirmary or in one of the rooms where he might escape. She knew what he was and what he was worth.

"Okay. I'll go get the keys."

"Cate," I said, catching her arm. "Is it over?"

She smiled. "It was over ten minutes ago."

"Really?" My voice was small in my own ears. I felt five years old, the way I had after getting lost in a mall and suddenly finding my dad's hand again after frantically searching for him. I knew it was stupid to cry, but exhaustion had brought me to the breaking point, and the sudden, unexpected release of fear and pain pushed me past it.

Cate stepped toward me, taking my face between her hands. It was like staring into a full moon rising as it cut through night. "I knew you could do this."

I squeezed my eyes shut and a white tent bloomed behind my lids. There was Mason, taking his last breath. The smell of a stiff leather muzzle. Rob screaming, screaming, screaming . . . I wanted to tell her everything, to unload it on her and let her share the crushing weight of it. She had offered to so many times, and every single instance I'd shot her down, thrown it back in her face. Even now, I felt that same reluctance wrap around my chest, trying to protect the weak, beating muscle there.

"It was horrible," I whispered.

She smoothed a stray tear away from my cheek. "And you were stronger."

I shook my head. "I wasn't . . . I was . . ."

How could I put it in a way she'd understand?

"That's not what Jude and Vida told me."

I opened my eyes, searching her face for any sign of a lie. "Are they okay?"

"They're fine," she promised. "Worried about you. I can take you up to them, but first, I think we need to take care of our little problem." She nodded toward Clancy. "All right?"

"Yeah," I said, taking a deep, shuddering breath. "All right."

Cole and Cate's team had moved the kids into the atrium and shut the doors, blocking the steady flow of bodies that were being lifted out of the residence hall and brought down to the infirmary. They were the agents that overthrew Alban, all of them. A part of me thought it was ridiculous they were trying to keep us from seeing it. Another part of me felt grateful.

I took a breath, shaking the tension out of my shoulders, then reached for the door.

They'd pushed most of the tables to the outer edges of the room, leaving the center of the room open for cots. Some of the kids and agents were being treated by the medical staff for bumps and scrapes. It seemed insane that they were ignoring the fully stocked infirmary in favor of hauling gauze and antiseptic up here—until I remembered that same infirmary was currently functioning as a makeshift morgue.

"Are all of them dead?" I asked quietly. In addition to the twenty-odd League kids huddled at the center of the room, eating whatever it was they'd dug out of the kitchen store for breakfast, there were something like forty agents ringing the perimeter of the room in clusters of black. But these were the faces that I had expected to see: agents who were in charge of Psi teams, instructors, the ones who looked at us with sad, longing eyes when they thought we weren't looking.

"The ones who wouldn't stand down," Cate said carefully.

So—all of them?

"I know it must have felt like they were all against you, but there were a number of agents who were blindsided by Alban's assassination and only stayed because it was too late to get out without retribution from Jarvin. They didn't put up a fight when we swept the sleeping quarters and were free to leave if they didn't want a part of this."

My eyes didn't stop scanning the room until they'd found them all. Chubs and Liam stood in front of one of the televisions, their backs to me as they watched news coverage of some kind of white domed building. Jude and Vida were near them, crouched on the floor in front of Nico, who looked like he was making a real effort to curl up into a ball and disappear forever.

Cate followed my gaze. "We'll talk about *that* later."

"Talk about what?" came the drawl behind us. I felt a heavy arm drop over my shoulder. "Could it be about little old *moi*?"

I tried to tug myself free, but he held me there, ruffling my already disastrous hair. I couldn't keep myself from flinching when I smelled the smoke on him. *Red.*

Psi.

Impossible.

It just . . . I rubbed the back of my hand against my forehead. He was so together, when Mason had been crumbling from the inside out. And it wasn't that Cole wasn't intimidating—he was, in a way that disarmed you and left you flustered. It was that every other Red I had come across at Thurmond acted like an animal that had been caged by his own skin. They refused to meet anyone's eyes, walking around with these vacant looks, listening to a voice in their mind, I think, that the rest of us couldn't hear. Every once in a while, they'd come back to themselves, a hunger darkening their faces. You'd catch them staring at another kid, these little, twisted smiles tucked into the corner of their mouths, and you knew—*knew*—what would come next.

But Cole not only had kept himself in check, he'd flourished.

Red.

The two of them shared a look over my head. "He mentioned that you've been . . . trusted. With a very important secret."

I didn't say anything, not because I couldn't think of a response but because I couldn't pick one out of the thousands of questions billowing through my mind. Finally, I turned to him and settled on, "How long have *you* known?"

"Since I was twelve," he said. "Late bloomer compared to the rest of you. Scared me shitless. Mom and Harry always thought I was sneaking in matches or lighters—burning things to *act out*. It's not the kind of thing you talk about if you don't want to get bused to some god-awful camp, you know?"

"Why not tell Lee?" I asked. "Why keep it from him?"

Cole's eyes narrowed. "I have my reasons, none of which is your business. You gave me your word you wouldn't—"

"I won't," I said, hating him for it. Another thing to keep from him. Another lie. "I just . . . How is this even possible? You're too old. Are there . . . more like you?"

No wonder Alban had valued him—a Psi who could move among the adults, never detected, just because he missed the supposed age cutoff.

Cate glanced around, making sure there were no prying ears nearby. "Far, far, far fewer. A few hundred age outliers. But it's not the time to talk about it. We have bigger concerns right now."

"Speaking of which." Cole lowered his voice as he leaned down. "You couldn't have mentioned Damsel-in-Distress Number Two was the president's kid?"

"Let's see how many words you can get out after having your brain scrambled."

"Fair." He glanced at Cate. "Is he going to be a problem?"

"He's in closet B-two," she said, raising her brows in what looked to me like a challenge.

"Okay, okay," he said. "This first, that . . . later. There weren't any guns left in there, right?"

I don't know who looked more irritated at the suggestion, Cate or me.

Cole was still smirking when he asked, "You bring back the big prize along with my jerk-ass little brother?"

I patted my pockets, feeling for the small plastic rectangle. I held it out to them, suddenly eager for someone other than me to carry its weight for a few minutes. Cole glanced at Cate. "All yours. You're still heading out soon, right?"

"In a minute. I need to tell my kids where I'm going."

"Because they won't know what to do with themselves without Mommy fussing over them every two seconds?"

At that, I really did wrench myself away from him, feeling my temper spike dangerously. Cole held up his hands and backed away a step. "Take a joke, Gem. Smile. Today's a good day, remember? Solid win."

"Where are you going?" I asked Cate.

"Out with a few agents to try to find some kind of transportation for all of us."

"But . . ."

"I'll be back in a few hours, I promise. I think you know that . . . it probably wouldn't be right to stay here after this."

"Where are we going?" I asked. "Kansas? Or Georgia?"

"Roo!"

It was impressive we'd been able to stand there for that long before Jude's radar started to ping. He was up and on his feet, pushing through the agents standing between us, nearly tripping over a group of kids who were clearly just trying to sit and eat and not burst into tears. Out of the corner of my eye, I saw Chubs and Liam turn around, but just as quickly they were gone, and the only thing in my world was Jude as he threw his long arms around me.

"You scared the crap out of me!" he said. I hugged him back. My one-kid welcoming committee.

"I was worried about you, too," I said. "Did anything happen?"

He shook his head, curls flying. "Did you find him?"

"I told you she was fine." Vida put a hand on his shoulder and tried to peel him off by force. "Judith. Unclench."

Cate laughed, patting his back. "Come on, I have to tell you two and Nico something."

That was enough for Jude to ease up just a bit. "He still won't talk. I can't get him to say a word. He, like, shut down."

I gave a faint wave as she led him and Vida back over to Nico.

"Ah." Cole muttered. I felt him stiffen, adjusting his posture from a casual slump to one that was solid. Collected. Even his face seemed to harden. He kicked off where he had been leaning against the wall and pushed past me without another word. He threw a single warning glance over his shoulder.

That was less than what he gave Liam—and even less than what Liam gave *him*—as they brushed past each other and continued in opposite directions. I met Chubs's look dead-on, and the expression there was enough to tell me there'd be a story later.

Alive, alive, alive, alive, my heart sang. I let the poisonous memory of what Clancy had shown me bleed out until there was nothing but the buzzing brightness in my chest. It took my breath away. *Alive*. The dirt on their faces was nothing. The cut that had reopened on Liam's chin was nothing. The crack in one of Chubs's lenses was nothing.

They were everything.

The two of them stood in front of me, arms crossed over their chests, wearing identical disapproving looks.

"Are you guys okay?" I asked, since they clearly weren't about to say anything.

"Are *you*?" Liam shot back. "What were you thinking, going after him like that?"

I bristled at his tone. "I was thinking that he let himself be dragged here for a reason, and I was right." I reached into my pocket, fishing out one of the photos from the folded stash of documents. Chubs eyed the stained paper I held out with a measure of distaste.

"That blood wasn't in your body at one point, was it?"

I pressed it against his chest, forcing him to take it. "I tracked him to Alban's office. That's what he was after."

Liam leaned over to look. They didn't have the same mental block I did, apparently. Recognition lit up their eyes. Chubs's jaw actually dropped.

"He's looking for her," I said. "The photos were in a file with what I think is research she was conducting. I don't know if he thought she was here or he knew Alban might have some kind of clue, but—"

Cole climbed up onto the table at the center of the room, clapping his hands twice. He cupped his hands around his mouth. "Can I get your attention?"

There was a formality to his tone that sounded unnatural. The Cole of sly smiles and infuriating teasing had apparently retired for the morning. Agent Stewart had no time for him.

"All right. I'll make this quick." The agents and kids in the room were shifting, flowing around the cots and tables so they were standing in front of him. "What happened here . . . it's done. You did your part beautifully. And while I wish I could say they wouldn't have gone through with their plan in the end, I think we all know that'd be a damn lie."

Liam shifted, leaning back against the wall in the exact pose his brother had assumed a few minutes before. He kept his eyes focused on me, clearly waiting for something.

"Look, I'm not one for pretty speeches. I'm not going to lie, because you've been lied to all of your goddamn lives, and it's got to stop. Here's what you need to know." He cleared his throat. "When Alban started this whole thing, he only ever wanted to expose the truth about IAAN and for Gray to own up about the camps. More than anything, he wanted this country to go back to what it was before—the place he was proud of and was happy to serve. The Children's League was his dream, even if it turned to shit in the end. He wanted that life again. But I say we can't go back."

I turned more fully toward him, stepping around Chubs to get a better look. The other kids watched, riveted. Why wouldn't they be? It was the same as all of those times I'd heard Liam speak about freeing the camps; the passion behind their words undercut all the doubt they claimed to have about their ability to express themselves. They let themselves burn when so many of us were afraid to be warmed by the fire.

He's one of us, I thought. The others had no idea, and they still felt that this was right. That he was supposed to be taking charge.

Liam scoffed, rolling his eyes. Chubs and I glanced at each other, and I wondered if he could feel the wave after wave of disappointment Liam was sending our way, too.

"It's forward or nowhere for us now. We—all the folks who came back—are leaving this place, and this name, behind. I don't know what we'll be yet or if we'll take another name, but I know what we're going to do. We're going to figure out what the hell happened to cause IAAN, expose anyone responsible, and get those poor damn kids out of those cesspools of misery. We are *leaving*; we're going up to the ranch—there are agents reopening it right now. We want you to come. We want you to want to fight. We want *you.*"

Cate stood from where she'd been sitting with the others and gave me a wave as she exited through the door on the other side of the room. Vida, Jude, and Nico didn't look up as she left. They were nodding, letting Cole's promises sweep them up in the heady rush of possibility. I felt it fluttering inside me, too. There were no advisers feeding him lines, no locked filing cabinets, no dark hallways. This was honest. Real.

"What's the ranch?" Chubs whispered.

"It's the League's old temporary headquarters near Sacramento," I said. "They shuttered it when they finished this one."

"We want you," Cole repeated, his eyes sliding our way. "But it's your choice."

I met his gaze dead-on, trying not to roll my eyes as he winked. He knew he had me.

And so did Liam.

He shoved away from the wall, but he let me catch him by the jacket as he passed. His shoulders shook with each deep, ragged breath he drew in. After days of regaining his strength and coloring, Liam was back to looking a step away from collapsing. His skin was ashy and his eyes burning as he stared at me.

"Tell me you're leaving with us today," Liam whispered. "Chubs and me. I know you're too smart to buy all that bullshit. I *know* you."

He saw the answer in my face. His hands captured my wrists and pushed them away.

Just before Liam reached the door, he turned back and said, his voice hoarse, "Then I have nothing left to say to you."

Cole disappeared after his speech, muttering something about "going to check on it," without giving another word of explanation to what or who "it" was. I had half the mind to follow him and make sure *it* wasn't Clancy Gray, but I'm not sure I could have stood up from the table if I had tried. The five of us—Jude, Vida, Chubs, Nico, and I—had claimed one of the circular tables near a TV, mostly, I think, to stay out of the way of the agents who were trying to "retire" the building and strip anything and everything they might need from it.

An hour had passed. More than enough time for Jude to ask, "Is Cate back yet?" and me to start worrying about Liam. It felt like the longer I sat there, though, the heavier my limbs became, until I was mimicking Nico across the table and resting my head on my arms, easing that weight off my shoulders.

"She said it'd take a while," Vida said, checking the time on her old Chatter again. "There're seventy of us. That's a lot of wheels to round up."

"We're coming to you live from the Texas State Capitol building, where President Gray and representatives from the Federal Coalition will start the Unity Summit in less than fifteen minutes now—"

Jude reached over to turn the volume up. He'd been the picture of calm all morning; there hadn't been so much as a whimper of how hungry or tired he was. Of our sad group, he was the only one who was actually paying attention to the screen. Nico had retreated so far in on himself, he was basically comatose. Chubs kept glancing between the watch on his wrist and the door.

The news coverage of the Christmas Day peace summit had started fifteen minutes before at nine o'clock Texas time.

There were mostly crowd shots, and of that only a very small section. When the cameraman had accidentally panned over a group of protesters and their signs, all of which were being kept as far from the building as possible, the feed had been cut.

Cole slid into the space between Jude and me, nearly knocking the kid off the bench. "Hey, Gem, need to borrow you for a sec."

I turned and buried my face deeper into my arms. "Can it wait?"

"*It* is awake and very angry, and I would appreciate some guidance on how to approach, seeing as you are the only one who might be able to tell me if he's trying to melt my brain."

"People know what he really is?" Chubs asked, surprised. "You told them?"

"Alban already knew," Cole said. "He saw Clancy influencing one of his Secret Service agents during one of his press tour stops after he got out of camp."

I sat up at that.

If Alban already knew what Clancy was and what he could do, Lillian Gray's first note could be taken a whole different way. *I need to get out of his reach if I'm going to save him.* Lillian might have realized, even before President Gray had, that her son was using his abilities to influence the people around him.

The timeline was coming together for me, finally. Alban would have seen Clancy do this just before he left to join the League—he removed himself from, as Lillian called it, Clancy's "reach." If she had tried asking her husband or any one of his advisers for help disappearing, Clancy would have had access to that information. It really had been a plan of desperation.

"Then why the hell didn't he do anything with that?" came Liam's voice behind us. The lines in his face deepened with his frown. "That could have blown the whole camp charade apart."

Cole rolled his eyes. "And he was going to prove it how? The kid was a ghost. We tried to put feelers out to see if he'd come willingly, but he never bit."

"Because he doesn't need you," Nico said, his voice hoarse. "He doesn't need any of us. He takes care of himself."

I opened my mouth to explain my theory, but Liam cut me off.

"Shouldn't you be helping the others clean the place out?" he asked pointedly. He stared at the place where Cole's hand was on my shoulder.

It was insane to see them standing side by side like this, wearing almost identical expressions of anger on almost identical faces.

"Feel free to leave any time, Lee," Cole said, dismissing him with a wave. "No one's keeping you here. I told you how to find Mom and Harry, so go on. Run back and hide. I wish I could be there when you explain to them how you almost managed to fuck over an entire group of kids because you're too idiotic to pay attention to what you're doing and where you're going. After you tell them about what happened when you tried to break out of your camp, of course."

I heard Vida swear under her breath, slamming a hand down on Chubs's arm to keep him from trying to jump in. There was no one there to check me.

"Stop it!" I said. "Listen to yourself—"

"You—" A flush of red swept up Liam's neck, and he was visibly struggling to keep his face in check. "You have *no* idea . . ."

"Oh, don't cry about it," Cole said, standing. "Haven't you already embarrassed me enough? Just . . . go. Jesus, just *go* already if you want out so damn bad. Stop wasting my time!"

"Guys—" Jude's voice went high, cracking on the word. "Guys!"

"Please," I tried again. "Just—"

Jude leaned over the table and grabbed my arm, turning me back in the direction of the television. "Shut up and *look*!"

President Gray had exited his car and was looking around at the crowds, lifting his hand in a well-practiced wave. His hair was grayer than I remembered it being even a few months ago. Heavier bags rimmed his dark eyes. But it was still Clancy's face, a glimpse of what he'd look like in thirty or forty years, and for that alone I wanted to look away.

"What's—" Vida began, just as the camera panned to a small hooded figure shoving his way past the pretty blond broadcaster, leaping over the police boundaries.

The president was slowly making his way up the pristine white steps of the Capitol, his hand outstretched toward the governor. Behind him, both the American and Texas state flags were swaying with the breeze. He didn't seem to notice something was wrong until the men in suits beside him pulled their guns, and the governor's face went white as bone.

The police officers that lined the steps were thrown to each side, shoved through the air with such force that they smashed through the lines of cameramen and photographers. He hadn't needed to touch them, only slash his arms out in front of him, like he was throwing open a heavy curtain.

"Christ!" Liam said behind me. "That's a kid!"

He was slight, all lean muscles and tan skin, like a runner who'd spent his summer out on a high school track. His hair was long, tied back with a small elastic to keep it out of his face; it gave him a clear view as he swung the small gun up from his sweatshirt's pockets and calmly fired two shots into the president's chest.

The TVs, each tuned to a different station, erupted at the exact same moment, catching the scene from every angle.

"Oh my God, oh my—" the newscaster was moaning. She'd dropped to the ground; all we could see was the back of her head as she watched the police and Secret Service pile on top of the kid, burying him under a sea of uniforms and coats. The crowd behind her was screaming; the camera shook as it swung around to capture their escape from the scene. Every look of terror. Every look of disgust. All turned now from the president himself to the kid who'd just killed him.

"Did you do this?" Liam snarled, swinging back toward his brother. "Did you order that kid to do that?"

"He's not one of us," Vida said. "I've never seen that piece of shit in my life!"

Cole spun on his heel, diving headlong into the stunned silence in the atrium. No one was moving aside for him, and

I had no idea where he was going. Vida grabbed the remote and turned the volume up.

"Ladies—ladies and gentlemen—please—" The broadcaster was still on the ground, trying to protect herself from the stampede of bystanders fleeing the scene. The picture cut away to the horrified faces of the anchors back in the studio, but they were there for only an instant before the screen clicked to black and bold words appeared there.

EMERGENCY ALERT SYSTEM

THE UNITED STATES GOVERNMENT HAS ISSUED AN EMERGENCY ACTION NOTIFICATION

DO NOT TURN OFF YOUR TV AT THIS TIME

IMPORTANT INFORMATION WILL FOLLOW

But the message stayed on the screens, and the only thing that did follow was the low wailing tones of the emergency alert system, the same ones we'd all heard a thousand times as they'd run the tests on televisions and radios.

There was a muffled *bang* that came from somewhere above us, almost inaudible under the sound of panicked voices in the atrium and the blaring television screens—two of them, three, four, all firing off in rapid succession like the crackling Fourth of July fireworks we used to watch at home from my backyard. They were too far away to be truly frightening. For a moment I wondered if they *were* fireworks. Were people really crass enough to already be celebrating President Gray's apparent demise?

It all washed away with the overpowering sound of rushing water—no, more like static. A ferocious wave of noise, cracking, snapping, hissing like a rolling hurricane.

And then it all cut out with a low, mechanical whine—the kind an animal might make as it took its last breath. The lights, the TVs, the air-conditioning, everything switched off, throwing us back into the same impenetrable darkness we'd just left.

If Jude hadn't still been gripping my arm, I would never have been able to catch him as he swayed toward the ground.

"Whoa," I began.

Vida was instantly at our side, helping me lower him back into a seat.

"It . . . Something just happened . . ." The agents around us were snapping on glow sticks, illuminating the room in that small way. I could see his hands clenched in his hair—the expression on his face was dazed, drunk almost. "Something bad."

"What do you mean?" I asked, letting Chubs in closer to look.

His eyes were still slightly unfocused. "It was a big . . . a big burst. Like a flare, and then it was gone. Everything is so quiet . . . nothing's talking anymore."

I scanned the room, searching for the team of Yellows. They were in the exact same dazed state, limp and unresponsive to the other kids' efforts to get them on their feet. I could see their faces in the faint, dying light of the glow sticks.

"What the hell?" I heard Chubs say. "Another rolling blackout?"

I shushed him, trying to listen as an agent quickly ran down the situation for Cole as they made their way back over to us. "Backup generator is still up and running, no cell or radio connections available. The cameras on the streets have shut off. Bennett is trying to get them restarted—"

"Don't bother," Cole said calmly. "They're most likely fried."

Fried? But that would mean . . .

It was too much of a coincidence for the power to have gone out at that moment. But what Cole was suggesting wasn't that someone had tampered with Los Angeles's power grid—he thought someone had disabled every single piece of electronic equipment throughout the city.

"You think it was some kind of electromagnetic pulse?" another agent pressed.

"I think we better get our asses moving before we find out." Cole cupped his hands around his mouth, shouting over the panicked whispering. "All right, I know you've drilled this. Take what you can carry from this room and go straight for the hole. Nothing else. Keep to your lines. Mandatory evac starts *now*!"

Vida gathered Jude to her side, leaving me to haul Nico up from his seat.

"It could just be another blackout," an agent protested. "It can't have been in response to the assassination. Our best bet is to go down to level three and ride it out."

"If this is an attack," another one put in, "then the safest place for us to stay is here!"

"The safest place for us is out of this—"

There were three loud knocks, like someone was standing directly above us, politely asking to be let inside. I don't know why I did it, or what I even thought the noise was, but I tackled Nico to the ground and, a moment later, felt Vida do the same with Jude beside me.

"Cover!" someone screamed, but the word disappeared in the white-hot flash of light.

Then the world rained down fire over our heads.

THIRTY-ONE

I DIDN'T FEEL THE PAIN RIGHT AWAY, ONLY THE heavy pressure against my spine.

I woke in total darkness with Nico shouting my name, gripping my shoulders. There was a single blessed moment where my brain was in tatters, and it couldn't connect what I was seeing, and smelling, and feeling with the reality of what had just happened. Everything was filtered through darkness.

"*No!* I have to find her first—"

"Dammit, Liam, *move*!" Cole roared. "Go with the others!"

"They're here," I heard Vida say. "Help me with this—"

The weight pinning me on top of Nico lifted, and smoky, dust-stained air flooded into my lungs. I coughed, my hand sliding across the floor until I found what felt like a glow stick.

It wasn't. It was someone's finger, and it wasn't attached to his body.

I was hauled up and onto my feet, held there until my knees solidified. "Everyone—" I started to say.

"Bunker busters," Vida said. "We gotta go."

"Jude—"

"I'm here," he said. "I can't see you, but I'm here—"

"Everyone's here; we're all okay," Chubs cut in. "Tell us where to go."

"Down—" I coughed, clearing the thick dust coating my tongue and throat. My eyes were adjusting now, and I was realizing that the dull orange glow surrounding us wasn't from the glow sticks but from the fires caused by the explosions. Everything else rushed at me with the force of a bullet to the head: wires were hanging down from the partially collapsed roof, along with pieces of the roof itself. And the sound of distant thunder—it was still there, louder now, firing off on a driving beat.

They're bombing the city. It didn't matter who "they" were, not then. I wiped at the slick rush of warmth running down my jaw, glancing over to make sure Nico was okay. He and Jude were huddled together, their arms wrapped around each other.

I turned on my heel, counting them off as I went. Chubs stood, watching the dark shapes of kids and agents limping out of the west exit of the room. Liam was trying to get back to us, shoving at Cole, who was trying to force him to line up behind the others. And Vida—she was staring at the still bodies strewn across the floor, some half buried where the ceiling had actually caved in. The whole room smelled like scorched meat and smoke. Sneakers and boots were scattered, thrown off bloodied, unmoving feet.

"We can't leave them," Jude cried, starting to reach toward Sarah, one of the Blue girls. Sarah stared back up at him, her chest caved in by the scaffolding that had fallen on her. "We— It's not right; we can't leave them down here! *Please!*"

"We have to," I said. "Come on."

We'd run evacuation drills a total of two times since I'd been with the League, both using a different exit to leave HQ. One was out through the elevator and tunnel, the way we would have normally come in. The other was an enormous stairwell that twisted and curved its way up to the surface, a short distance away from the factory that was supposed to serve as our shield. Neither of them was an option now. I could see that just by looking at Cole's face.

"Move, move, move," he was telling us, shoving each kid and agent through the door. "Down to level three; we're going out the way you came in. Follow Agent Kalb!"

I tried to count the heads as they passed, but it was too dark and the smoke was too thick. The whole structure shook, throwing me forward toward Liam, who was waiting for us at the door.

"Are you okay?" he asked in a rush of breath. "He grabbed me; I didn't want to go—"

Cole took him by the collar and hauled him out into the hallway before us. It was clear they'd been aiming for the dead center of the building. We stumbled after, a line of us, trying to navigate through the concrete, flaming rubble, and the hissing, spitting steam pipes that had burst. Still, it was some small miracle it hadn't been damaged the way the atrium had.

The stairwell down to level two was clogged with more smoke and steam. My shirt was drenched through with sweat. I started to strip my jacket off, automatically feeling for the flash drive that wasn't there.

Cate, I thought. *Where's Cate? What's happening to Cate?*

I was thrown forward into Liam's back with the next impact. One of the kids up ahead of us screamed, but all I could hear was Jude behind me, whispering, "Oh, God, oh my God," over and over again. I don't know what he was picturing in his head, but if it was anything like my image of being crushed under ten tons of cement and dirt, I was surprised he could even function at all, let alone keep moving forward.

The line slowed as we rounded down to the second level, clogging with some problem we couldn't see. I slipped around Liam and grabbed Cole's arm to get his attention.

"What about the people in the infirmary?"

"If they couldn't get up and walk themselves out, we're not doing it for them," Cole said with a note of finality.

"What about Clancy?" I asked, though a part of me already knew the answer. "Did they let him out?"

"There was no time to clear the floor," Cole said.

I glanced back over my shoulder, wishing I could see Liam's face in the dark. I felt him instead, hands on my waist, gently pushing me forward. Then his voice was in my ear saying, "What would he do if it were you? Me?"

It didn't make it any easier to swallow the bile in my throat. It was one thing to bring a person in as a prisoner, and another to sentence him to what was very likely death.

"Are you fucking *kidding me*?" Vida snarled as she and

Chubs gripped a panicking Nico and kept him going. I could see Jude's pale face behind them, looking on in horror.

"I'll get him," Nico said. "I can get him!"

"No!" Jude cried. "We have to stay together!"

The aftershock of the next explosion tossed us all to our knees. I smacked my head against the wall, spots bursting in front of my eyes. I hauled myself up and then we were all running down the steps, through the dark hall, jumping down into the interrogation block. Sections of the wall to my right were already partly collapsed.

"Stay right behind me," Cole said, glancing back at us. "Come on, we need to be at the front."

He was able to edge his way up through the line, but everyone was bottlenecking as they reached the door to the tunnel. I could only imagine what the response would have been if the six of us tried to cut to the front of the line and follow him.

We were finally close enough to see what the problem was. On the other side of the door, each kid and agent had to carefully climb over the pipes and cement that had been shaken free from the tunnel's ceiling.

My blood was beating hard inside of my head, but my limbs felt hollow with panic as we waited, and waited, and waited for it to be our turn. Liam was bouncing on the balls of his feet, like he was gearing up to bolt forward at any moment.

Once we were at the door, I stopped and stepped aside to let the others go in front of me, but Liam was having none of it. He all but lifted me up and over the debris, then climbed over himself, his body the wall that kept me from turning back.

I heard Vida curse behind me and Chubs's labored grunt. The tunnel felt hot and humid with so many bodies crammed into it. The blasts from above had collapsed sections of it, slowing our progress again and turning what had been a simple path into an obstacle course.

I felt the thundering vibrations before the sound of the crashes actually reached my ears. It was a series of four low bangs, each louder and worse than the next. Vida shouted something up to us I couldn't hear over the vicious wave of noise that followed. My stomach, my heart, everything inside of me seemed to drop, like the tunnel had given out under me. The seconds passed at half their speed, giving me just enough time to turn away from the explosion that blew out through the door we'd just come through.

We threw ourselves to the ground as a blast of gray dust and chunks of cement and glass came shooting out of the doorway. The tunnel shook so hard, I was convinced it would cave in. The kids, the agents, everyone was shouting now, but I heard Cole's voice amplified over everyone's: "Move, move, move!"

But I couldn't. I was only able to push myself up onto my knees, drag myself up using the wall. I could hear Vida and Chubs talking, complaining about the dark, how they couldn't see each other.

"That was HQ," I whispered. "Did it collapse?"

"I think so," Liam said.

"The tunnel back in is totally blocked off now," Chubs called up, coughing. The kids in front of us passed the news up through the line of people ahead of them. We heard the shock and tear-stained responses all the way from the back of the herd.

Those agents . . . the kids . . . their bodies that we had to leave behind, whose families would never know what happened to them, who didn't get a chance to escape, who might have still been clinging to life when—

The sob stuck in my throat, and I couldn't cough it free. I wasn't crying, but my body was shaking violently, hard enough that Liam wrapped his arms around me from behind. I felt his heart racing against my back, his face as he buried it against my neck.

He was solid and here; all of us, alive. *Alive, alive, alive.* We had made it out. But still, I couldn't stop seeing it, the way the ceiling must have caved, the falling glass, the floor that suddenly wasn't there, the darkness sweeping down.

Focus, I commanded myself. *There are still kids behind you. You're still not out of this. Don't let it take you, too. Liam, Chubs, Vida, and Jude. Liam, Chubs, Vida, and Jude.*

"Just breathe, just breathe," Liam said, his own voice shaking.

The steady pattern of it, the rise and fall of his chest beside me, was steadying enough that my grip on his side relaxed. He pressed his lips against my forehead, more out of relief than anything else, I thought.

"We're okay," I said. "We're okay. Just keep going."

My mind caught the words and carried them forward in the dark. *Just keep going.* The longer we walked, the harder it became to tell the difference between my fear, my anger, and my guilt. They were a swollen mass in my chest, a rising sore. Someone ahead of us was either laughing or sobbing; the noise was so unhinged, I couldn't tell the difference.

The biggest fear, the one that kept my heart firmly lodged at the base of my throat and my knees sliding forward, forward, forward as the cement gripped at my shoulders, was knowing that, at any point, the whole thing could come down on top of us.

Breathe.

It should have been comforting to feel Liam pressing close behind me. We finally reached a section of the tunnel that was whole and where we could stand at our full height. It felt better to be moving that way, like it was a sign we were almost through. But it was still so impossibly dark. No matter how many times I tried to look back, I couldn't see anything past the vague shape of Liam's face.

Keep going— Head down, arms in, only going forward, forward, forward as fast as I could move my feet. I lost track of time. Five minutes passed, ten minutes, maybe. Fifteen. The mildew smell changed to an all-out rancid stink as the drains constricted again. I kept my hands out on either side of me, letting them glide along the slick, dripping cement. Liam let out a strangled grunt as he cracked his head against the sloping ceiling, and a second later, I had to duck.

The standing water was thick and reeked of rotting things and mold. I heard someone start to retch, and it was like it always was—once one person started, everyone else's stomach was heaving, too.

I clawed blindly at my face, trying to clear the hair that stuck in clumps to my cheeks and neck. It snuck up on me, the suffocating—the thick, sticky air seemed to vanish, the tunnels constricted, and I couldn't see a thing, not one damn thing.

We are not going to die down here. We were not just going to disappear.

I tried to stay focused on the rhythmic, slow shuffle of skin against concrete and the way the water seemed to recede with the ceilings. How was it possible that the tunnel felt so different heading out than it had coming in? I felt it widen again, dipping down; it might have been my eyes adjusting to the dark, but I could have sworn it was getting lighter.

I *wasn't* imagining it. The change had been gradual at first, a hint of a glow, but it was bright enough now that I could see Liam's surprised face as it turned down to meet mine. The tunnel filled with sounds of relief. I stood on my toes, trying to see over the heads in front of me. The smallest pinprick of light was staring us down the long tunnel, and it grew just that tiny bit larger with each step. A sudden burst of energy kicked my legs up, moving them faster, and faster, and faster until I could see the ladder, the figures climbing up out of the crippling dark and into the light.

For a long time, there was nothing beyond the smoke.

It hung around us in a curtain of graying brown, warmed only by the setting sun. The debris that had been blasted in the bombing still hadn't settled. It floated down through the open door, a fine, crushed cement that swirled as we stirred it. My arms shook the entire climb up the ladder. Cole was waiting for us at the entrance to the tunnel, gripping my arm and hauling me out before turning back to get Liam.

"Goddammit, you stupid kid!" he cried, shaking him. His voice was hoarse, and he seemed to choke on each word. "You scared the shit out of me! When I say stay behind me, I mean *stay behind*. Why didn't you just leave when I told you to? Why can't you just *listen* to *me*!"

He wrapped his arms around his shoulders, and Liam, in all of his relief and exhaustion, let him. I couldn't understand what they were saying to each other as they stood in front of the door, but Vida's "Some of us are still trying to get out, assholes!" shattered the moment.

Another agent guided us down the embankment of the Los Angeles River, to the spot where the others were huddled beneath the center of the bridge overhead. I pulled my shirt up over my nose and mouth to avoid breathing it in, but the chalky taste was already in my throat. I had already swallowed the day's poison down, letting it mix with the smoke and bile.

The sights of Los Angeles and the warehouse district were too much for any of us to take. No one was willing to turn around and face the wreckage in the distance. We knew, all of us, that the city had been attacked, but to actually see the burning skyscrapers on the horizon, watch the black smoke funnel out and up and into the clear blue sky, was sickening.

Liam and I sat down a small ways from the other kids, who were crying and hugging one another. It was enough for me that he was sitting next to me, that his shoulder was pressed against mine. I watched them, the tears streaming down their faces, and I wished I could have let myself break down, too—to clear out the twisting mass of terror still churning inside me.

But out here, my exhaustion numbed me. The sight of the everyday objects scattered nearby in the river quieted the thoughts racing through my head. The dust-covered cars in inches, the ground in feet. It gave way under us like playground sand. We were miles from downtown, but we were finding papers, an office chair, sunglasses, briefcases, and shoes that had been dropped and forgotten or blown out from nearby demolished buildings. The airstrike had left One Wilshire, the old skyscraper that housed the Federal Coalition, a burning black husk. I had seen it, just for a second, belching out rolling streams of smoke, turning entire city blocks dark.

And all Liam could say, over and over, was *"Damn."*

I took a deep, steadying breath. Out of the corner of my eye, I saw Jude standing out from under the bridge, his eyes closed, his face turned up to the patch of sun that had broken through the smoke. I couldn't bring myself to stand, but I pretended I was there, too. Tilting my head back, letting the warmth dry the sticky, wet clumps of my hair. Letting it burn away the taste of fear on my tongue. Pretending we were somewhere far away from here.

Liam stood as Chubs and Vida came toward us, their dark skin plastered with silvery dust. He hooked an arm around his friend's neck, guiding him over to where I was waiting.

"We heard Cole talking to some of the other agents who got out of the tunnel first. They said every car and every phone they found was dead. Cole thinks it really was some kind of electromagnetic pulse. We just couldn't tell because we were so far underground."

That was one of the reasons Alban had insisted on building it so deep into the earth, for protection from that kind of thing. If Cole was right and they had set off an EMP, everything fell into place the way Alban had assured us it would. The detonation knocked out the power station supplying electricity to HQ, but the backup generator had kicked in, at least for a time.

I couldn't believe Gray—or whoever was in charge—had gone this far—had fried every vehicle, computer, and TV, ensuring he'd be helpless. Defenseless.

"We can't make contact with Cate," Vida said.

"She's all right," I told her, hoping I didn't sound as hopeless as I felt. *The flash drive. Cate still has the flash drive.* And if something had happened to Cate, then . . .

"The city . . . ?"

"Swarming with soldiers, apparently," Chubs said. "It's not good."

"Full-on invasion," Vida said, dropping next to me. She pointed to where Nico was standing at the door leading down to the tunnel. He was staring down it, as if waiting for one last person to come through.

I rubbed my face with my hands, trying to clear away the image of Clancy Gray trapped down in the dark. *That's where he belongs,* came the savage voice in my mind. He was the only reason we had come here in the first place—he'd lied and risked every one of our lives, and for what? So he could work out some kind of demented mommy issue?

I didn't want to think of the dead, so I focused on the living. I kept my thoughts on the people beside me, the rare kindness life had shown in getting us out just before the whole structure collapsed. It didn't feel real to me yet, but these kids were. Liam, his head bent toward his best friend, whispering, "We'll stay with them until we figure out how to get out of the city." Chubs nodding, visibly struggling not to cry. Vida lying back, her hands on her stomach, feeling its rise and fall with each deep breath she took.

And Jude—

I turned to my right, glancing around the circles of kids. And—there he was. The dark head of curls I was looking for was walking away, chattering excitedly with some other kid. Where the hell did he think he was going? He tilted his head back toward us, and was—

Not Jude.

Why did I think that? This kid, he looked nothing like him—he was one of the Greens, a good head shorter than him. Why did I think that was him? I had taken one quick glance at his hair, and it was like my mind had defaulted on memory.

Why would I ever think that?

Every muscle in my body, every joint, every ligament hardened to stone. I was shaking again with the effort to move, to spin around one last time. I tried to call out for him, but the sound came out like a gasp. I brought a hand up to the base of my throat, pressing hard to dislodge whatever nightmare I had just swallowed.

"Ruby?" Chubs said. "What's wrong?"

"What?" Liam said, turning toward me. "What is it?"

"Where . . ." I began. "Where's Jude?"

The boys shared a look, then turned to survey the kids themselves.

"Jude!" Vida called, looking around. "Judith! This isn't funny!"

I didn't see his face in the kids sitting around us, and the agents were making sure that no one left the cover of the bridge now. Faces were starting to turn toward us, including Cole's.

"He came down, right?" I asked, my voice high with panic. "He was with you guys at the back, wasn't he?"

Oh my God.

Vida's brows drew sharply together. Some dark thought flickered over her face.

"Vida!" I grabbed the front of her sweatshirt. "When was the last time you talked to him? When was the last time you saw him?"

"I don't know!" she cried, pushing me off her. "I don't, okay? It was so dark—"

I started at a run, pushing past Vida to get to the tunnel's opening at the top of the embankment. Nico looked up at me, and I finally understood that he was waiting for Jude, not for Clancy.

"Ruby . . ." he began. "Where is he?"

"Stop," Cole said, catching my elbow. I struggled against him, trying to twist away. Jude was down there. He was down there. And the last place I would ever leave Jude was alone in the dark.

"You were at the back, weren't you?" he continued. "I sent one of the agents down to make sure we didn't leave anyone behind. They said the whole structure must have caved in—"

"Shut up!" Liam said. He pulled me away from Cole. "Chubs and I will go, okay? I'm sure he just got separated from the group."

"No way in *hell* I'm letting you back in there," Cole said. "I will knock your ass out if you take one step closer to it."

Liam ignored him.

"He could have twisted his ankle maybe or slipped and hit his head," Chubs added, but he looked sick. "Maybe he's just caught in the debris . . ."

"No!" I snarled. "He's my—"

"Ruby, I know, okay?" Liam said. "But you and Cole and the others need to figure out how to get us out of here, and fast. Let us do this for you at least."

"It's on me," I said. "*I'm* Leader."

"You're not my leader," he said softly. "Remember? It'll be faster if Chubs and I go. We'll be back before you even know we're gone. You and the others have to figure out how to get us out of here."

I shook my head.

"Ruby, let them go," Vida said, taking my arm. "Come on."

Cole let out a sharp, angry grunt, shoving a glow stick against his brother's chest. "You have an hour, no more. Then we're leaving without you."

Liam glanced at Chubs, tilting his head toward the waiting door.

THIRTY-TWO

THEY DID NOT COME BACK IN AN HOUR, OR EVEN two.

I tried to guess how long it had taken us to get through the tunnels the first time—it had only been, what, a half hour? Longer? At the time, it had only felt like forever.

Vida and I sat on either side of the opening, backs flush against the wall. She had her arms folded across her chest, her legs stretched out. Every few minutes her fingers pressed hard into either arm, and she began anxiously shaking her foot.

Cole and the others were arguing about splitting the group up for the third time. Most of the kids had crashed, no matter how hard they fought it. They curled up in the shade or leaned against one another's backs. Every so often, a breeze would carry Jude's whispered name up to us, spoken in the same breath as the kids who had been killed in the initial blast.

Eight of them, gone in an instant. Almost half our group.

I caught the sound of the footsteps first and pushed myself off the ground. Vida stayed exactly as she was, keeping whatever thought was skipping through her head to herself. I squinted into the darkness to find the source of the movement. I could count them by their dim, shadowed shapes as they moved up the ladder. *One—two—*

Two.

Two.

Liam was out first, stretching a hand toward me without a single word of explanation. I let him guide me back down the embankment, into the sunlight and away from the others. I looked over my shoulder just the once to see Chubs crouch down next to Vida.

"I know," I heard her say, her voice gravelly. "Don't bother."

Liam brought my attention back to him, clearly struggling to tame his own emotions. So they hadn't found him. Now I could try. I knew Jude better than they did—there must have been miles and miles of tunnels under the city, and I'd have an easier time guessing—

He turned my hand up and pressed something smooth into it. His eyes were such a fair blue, the irises the color of a new morning sky. When they drifted down, mine followed their path. Down his torn shirt, across the stained skin of his wrists, to the bent, twisted remains of a small silver compass.

And it was so strange how swift the numbness was to settle. How it smothered every word, every thought, until I forgot I needed to keep breathing. I felt my lips part at the same moment my chest seemed to collapse in on itself.

"No." My fingers clenched around it, hiding it from sight, denying it was there. The glass face had completely shattered, the red needle was gone, and the force of whatever had crushed it had folded it almost in half. *No.* It was just that one word, but it was enough to spark a blaze of furious denial. *"No!"*

"We traced the path back," Liam said, holding onto my hand like an anchor. "All the way back to the entry point. As far as we could get with the debris . . . and . . ."

"Don't," I begged. *Don't tell me this.*

"I don't—" His voice choked off. "I don't know what happened. I almost didn't see him at all, but there was . . . I could see his shoe. We found him, but there wasn't anything we . . . Chubs couldn't do anything. He was already gone and we couldn't get him out. He was at the back; the explosion must have just caught him—"

I threw the compass at him, and when that didn't rock him, when that didn't hurt him, I threw my fist after it, pounding against his shoulder. He caught it with his other hand and pinned both of mine to his chest.

He's lying. It wasn't possible. I had seen him outside, looking up at the sky. I had heard him, seen him, *felt* him.

I felt myself rock forward, the instant before my knees went. Liam had a good enough grip on me to prevent me pitching forward, but he was exhausted, too, and it was amazing he was able to keep us upright at all.

"We have to go get him," I said. "We can't just . . . He can't stay down there; he doesn't like the dark; he can't handle silence; he shouldn't have to be alone—"

"Ruby," Liam said gently. "There's not going to be anything to get. And I think you know that." I recoiled violently, trying to push back against him, against the reality. But that burst of energy was as quick to pass as it had been to come. The tears were hot on my cheeks; they mixed with the dirt, rolling over my lips, dripping off my chin. His hands came up to either side of my face, wiping them away, even as I felt his own drip against my hair.

"I c-cant," I said, "I can't—"

For the first time, I wondered if the reason he hadn't wanted me to go wasn't because he thought they wouldn't find Jude but because he thought they would.

"He was alone," I cried. "He didn't have anyone with him—he must have been so scared. I told him we would stay together."

My mind was fixed on Jude's face, the way his ears stuck out from the sides of his head like they'd been mismatched with the rest of his body. What was the last thing I said to him? Stay close? Keep going? And what had he said back? All I could remember was his pale face in the faint light of Cole's yellow glow stick.

Follow Leader. He had followed me out and I had led him to this. I had done this to him.

"Lee!" Chubs called, and again, louder, when neither of us moved. There was a plane flying low overhead, dropping a cloud of something that looked like red gas. Liam raised his arms, covering our heads as the wind blew it toward us and dropped thousands of fluttering sheets of paper.

The kids and agents left the safe cover of the bridge to try to catch one. I snatched a stray sheet as it winged past us. Liam leaned over my shoulder and I held it up for us to read it together.

Centered at the top of the page were the presidential seal, an American flag, and the insignia for the Department of Defense.

Following the assassination attempt by the disturbed Psi youth, President Gray was taken to an area hospital where doctors examined him. As he was wearing a Kevlar vest during the attack, he sustained only abdominal bruising and two fractured ribs. Once he was discharged from their care, he released the following statement:

"Today we received confirmation on two disturbing intelligence reports I had prayed were only hearsay. First, that the Federal Coalition and its supporters are in the pocket of the terrorist organization, the Children's League, and, together, they have established a program that conditions your children—the same ones they have stolen away from the life-saving rehabilitation camps—to be soldiers. To fight and kill with a ferocity that is as inhuman as the abilities they possess. Seeing no other alternative, I immediately launched an airstrike against the seat of these organizations, Los Angeles.

"These were targeted attacks, designed to minimize the damage to civilians. Do not mourn the loss of these reprehensible human beings. There have been times, in the course of human history, that fire has been needed to burn out an insidious infection. These are such times. This is the only way for us to build our nation again, stronger than before."

"He forgot the *God Bless America* part," Liam muttered, crumpling the paper.

A gunshot fired behind us. I wheeled around, gripping Liam's arm to force him behind me. The agents had formed a circle around something—someone—on the other embankment. The men and women who were armed had their weapons out. Aimed.

"Are you *kidding* me?" Liam breathed out behind me. Vida practically screamed in rage, running toward the cluster of agents faster than any of us could catch her.

Some of them knew to move out of the way as the Blue girl tore through their circle, but only Cole was dumb enough to try to keep her from tearing out Clancy Gray's throat.

"How?" she howled as we wedged ourselves through the kids and agents, pushing our way to the front. *"How?"*

Clancy was filthy—covered in sewage and dust and blood that caked around his swollen nose and eyes. But even from where they'd pushed him onto his hands and knees, he managed to look smug. Defiant.

For the first time, I noticed the door open behind him. It was directly across from the exit we had taken, on the opposite embankment, hidden in the blind spot in one of the pillars, under a layer of bright graffiti.

Clancy let out a low, humorless laugh. "Through the drain in the boys' showers." His dark eyes met mine. "After I had to smash my way out of the closet."

"Was that how you were planning to get out?" I demanded. "After you got what you needed from Alban's office?"

Clancy shrugged, unbothered by the guns pointed in his face. "Didn't know about that exit, did you?"

"Jesus," one of the agents said. "This is . . . this is really the president's kid?"

Clancy is alive, I thought, turning in to Liam's side, *and Jude is not.* He tucked his arm around my neck, drawing me in closer. It didn't make sense—it wasn't possible.

"He's our ticket out," another said suddenly. "We trade him for safe passage! Come on, Stewart—uniforms are swarming the city, and we have no transport or way to contact the ranch. What other card do we have to play?"

"Well, it's not exactly going to be a cakewalk dropping him off with our new neighbors, either. He's an Orange; he'll find a way out of it." Cole glanced at Clancy, ignoring the shocked noises from the others. "So maybe it's better to end him now and send the body back. That'd be quite the message to dear ol' Dad. We'll find another way out of the city."

There was a murmur of agreement from a few of the others.

"You're not getting out of this city," Clancy said. "My father's not reactionary. That's not his game. He'll have accounted for every possible exit strategy. Trust me, this has been in the works for months, maybe even years. When he got tired of waiting for an excuse to justify the attack, he created one."

That was almost too ridiculous to believe. "You think your father arranged a hit on himself?"

"It's what I would have done. I'm assuming he survived?"

Liam's hold on me tightened until it was almost unbearable. I was shaking again, only this time it was anger blazing through me. Vida and Chubs both glanced over my way, like they were waiting for me to contradict him. I don't know what terrified me more: that he wasn't wrong or that this was the old Clancy, the one who knew he could always get his way.

"You guys believed me when I said we were starting over, didn't you?" Cole was addressing the kids and agents who were still sitting beneath the bridge, looking torn and petrified. "Well, this is it. We make our own road. But he's not coming with us."

"Think of the intel we could get out of him!" another agent cried, throwing her hands up in the air. "We can sedate him—"

"Try it," Clancy dared. "See how it ends for you."

"Yeah, you're right," Cole said, rolling his eyes. "We probably should just kill you."

"Go ahead, then." Clancy's teeth were stained with blood as he smiled. "Finish it. I finished what I came to do. And you all—" He turned toward the huddled masses of kids around him, his eyes focusing on Nico. The boy trembled under the intensity of his gaze. "You all can thank me when you can still fight back. I saved us. *I* saved us."

"What the hell are you talking about?" Cole was losing his patience. He glanced back at me, but I couldn't look away from Clancy Gray. Not when I felt the first trickle of realization working its way through the grief still clouding my mind.

That morning, a whole city had been destroyed, and countless lives with it. There would be so many people who would never return home to their loved ones that night, though those mothers, father, daughters, sons, wives, husbands would pass through the afternoon and midnight hours, waiting, hoping. The smoke would seep into the concrete that lined every inch of this place, permanently bruising an already beaten city. In ten years, twenty years, it would still be too terrible to speak of what happened—a morning that a thousand other blinding, brilliant mornings would never ease from memory. But somehow, when Clancy spoke again, it was his words that changed everything.

"The *cure* for IAAN," he spat. "The one my mother developed, the one Alban kept hidden from you, waiting for the right opportunity to trade it to my father to benefit himself." Clancy swiped at the blood draining from his nose, laughing in that same humorless way. "The one that would have taken our abilities away and left us *helpless*. I burned it to ash, and my father buried it without realizing. Now her memory of it is gone, and no one will ever have the research—no one will take away what's ours."

A cure. That single word was chiming like a bell in my ears, ringing again and again. My mind couldn't grasp it, couldn't recognize it. I'd spent so many years conditioning myself to accept that it was impossible, forcing myself to let go of thinking there was a world beyond the camp's electrified fence, that the word no longer existed in my vocabulary.

I felt myself start to turn, looking to Jude for his reaction—but Jude wasn't here. I had left him behind. I had let him fall back into the darkness. And it was like seeing Liam and Chubs climbing out of the tunnel alone all over again. It stole the breath from my chest.

One of the younger kids began to cry loudly behind me, asking in a panicked, confused voice, "What? What is he . . . what is he talking about?"

Oh, I thought. *Oh my God.*

I had been wrong—so wrong. The first lady hadn't been studying what caused the disease. She had invested her life in figuring out how to end it.

I felt myself step toward him, away from the others. Chubs was visibly shaking, about to collapse under the weight of what could have been. I caught Liam's eye, but his expression was so open, so raw with pain and longing that I had to turn away. I knew what he was imagining. In my mind, we were standing on that beach, too, with the crystal clear skies overhead and our beautiful, whole families around us.

A cure.

Alban had been right when he said Lillian Gray had never been blinded by her love for her son. She knew Clancy would never willingly give up his abilities, and that she'd never find him. No. He needed to come to her, to be lured by the satisfaction of tracking her down after being shut out and denied access to her for so long. He had to be the first one to receive the treatment, because if he heard so much as a whisper of the possibility of it, he'd disappear forever. It made me wonder if that was the reason Alban had sat on the secret for as long as he did—if that was part of the deal.

Clancy first. Then, he could present it to the world. He could be the nation's hero.

I studied Clancy's face as I crouched down to his level. His gaze flickered toward my hand as I slid it into my coat pocket.

Behind all of his venomous words was the sting of true betrayal, an ache that ran so deep, his whole body seemed to throb with it. His mother, his *own mother* had set up the trap. And he had done what in return? Burned down her lab, attacked her, scrambled her mind, and used the situation at HQ to his advantage to finish what he'd started in Georgia.

That's how he knew she sent the results to Alban, I thought, slowly smoothing the papers out over my knee. I had his full attention now. *He must have seen it in her mind.*

Clancy loved the idea his father had inadvertently buried the one thing that could potentially fix his country and salvage his legacy. But the true irony here was that if Clancy hadn't come looking to destroy his mother's research, we never would have found it in time. It would have been left behind like everything else as we escaped.

He'd come here to close that door, but instead he had left it wide open for me to walk through.

There is a cure. The insanity of that thought made me feel like the hand on Jude's compass spinning, and spinning, and spinning, searching for its true north.

He deserved this. I blinked back the prick of tears and let my anger rise to swallow the anguish for now. I let it propel me forward. Because Jude deserved to live to see this moment—he should have been here, now, next to me, suddenly seeing that everything was alive with the possibility of change.

I held up the rumpled, smoke-stained papers directly in front of Clancy, high enough for the ring of Psi and agents around us to see them, too. And I don't know what was more powerful and gratifying to me—the look of terror that swept across his face, or the exhilaration of knowing I finally had my future back in my own hands.

"You mean this research?"

ACKNOWLEDGMENTS

RIGHT OFF THE BAT, I NEED TO SHOWER SOME LOVE on the fantastic team at Disney-Hyperion for the incredible amount of hard work and enthusiasm that they've put into this series. Thanks especially go to my editor, Emily Meehan, Laura Schreiber, Stephanie Lurie, publicist extraordinaire Lizzy Mason, Dina Sherman, LaToya Maitland, Andrew Sansone, Lloyd Ellman, Elke Villa, and Marci Senders.

None of this would have been possible without my fearless agent, Merrilee Heifetz. It's not an exaggeration to say that I couldn't be in better hands, and I'm grateful every day that I have you in my corner.

Much gratitude to Anna Jarzab and Erin Bowman who read early, terrifyingly messy drafts of this story and gave me incredible, thoughtful feedback that made this story so much better than I ever imagined it could be. Thanks also to Sarah J. Maas, not only for her many reads and critiques, but the overwhelming amount of love and support she sent my way during an incredibly difficult year.

Much love to Tyler Infinger and Catherine Wallace—the friendship and care they've shown me over the years has meant more to me than words can express.

To fall back on a cliché, I *really* hit the jackpot with my colleagues and friends at RHCB, especially Adrienne Waintraub, Tracy Lerner, and Lisa Nadel. I really could not admire each and every one of them more.

And, finally, all the love in my heart goes to my family for their bravery, resilience, and strength this past year. Just when I think they can't be more amazing, they go and prove me wrong.

NEVER FADE